AN EVOLUTION OF MINDS

By: K.R. Jensen

Thanks for a great Thanksgiving!

Thanks for your friendship!

For M.S

and

M

"No man ever steps into the same river twice, for it is not the same river and he is not the same man."

- Heraclitus

"I came not to bring peace, but a sword . . . To cast fire upon the world."

- Jesus Christ

K.R. JENSEN

1

It was only a matter of time before somebody died.

Doctor Jonas Moorea knew he was playing with fire from the day of the first surgery. The end goal was so alluring, he put his reservations aside—and now a life was lost. Jonas sat on a cold floor, feeling slightly nauseous, with a vague recollection of how he came to be where he was. The lights flickered on and off in rhythmic waves that rose and fell in luminance, making it seem as though the room was pulsing. Jonas picked himself up off the floor and felt a sharp pain in his chest. In the strobing white lights of the narrow lab space, he lifted up his shirt, finding a concentric circular bruise fanning out from the skin above his sternum. Moorea winced as he touched the blackish-blue skin. He faced a large window, separating him from a clean room designed for surgery. In the translucent glass, Moorea caught his own reflection. There was a soft glow to his fair skin and an almost unsettling look of intensity that fell from his dark eyes. Through the surgery window, a colleague lie motionless on the operating room floor, in a pool of crimson. *Poor bastard,* Moorea thought.

The ever overconfident neurosurgeon, Sangupta Rami, had seen his last sunset over the New England hills, and the man's departure was not peaceful. Minutes earlier, Moorea watched as Rami grasped frantically at a hot stream of red, as it flowed from his neck. Now the man's hands were covered in blood, resting in the shadow of his crumpled body.

Moorea moved through the narrow lab space he was in, passed through a prep area, and entered the operating room. Rami was splayed out on the ground, and still held a look of surprise—his dark eyes were open and slack-jawed mouth ajar.

Moorea knelt down, and wrestled a small object out of Rami's moist surgery scrubs; it was an electronic device about the size of a cell phone, with an LCD screen and two ports—one circular and one rectangular. The only other feature of the device was a nickel-sized button with the word TRANSMIT written above it. Moorea pocketed the small instrument. He knew he had to get Rami's body cleaned up and off the premises. Moorea was three stories underground, beneath New Life, a state-of-the-art fertility clinic. For the past four years, Moorea, Rami, and a third associate, Salison Sinsway, had been working in the depths of New Life on a highly secretive project aimed at testing the limits of the human body and mind.

Salison, the mastermind behind the project, was quite a specimen, and his oddity extended light-years beyond his name. At age fifty, the man was well known for his pioneering work with the world's largest and most powerful particle accelerator—the Large Hadron Collider— and many said he was a shoe-in to win the Nobel Prize for his seminary work characterizing various elements of the Standard Model of particle physics.

So Moorea was quite surprised, when five years ago, Salison approached him on a Boston side street and asked to buy him a drink. Moorea was immediately struck with Salison's presence. The man was tall and muscular with dark-bronze skin. When he spoke, in an unfamiliar accent, he strung his slow syllables together in a calm, fluid way that sounded strangely pleasant and rhythmic.

For the better part of four hours, Salison spoke on a plan he called 'Metamorphosis'—in time, he told several enigmatic stories regarding humanities most powerful prophets—Jesus Christ and Buddha—and initiated a dialogue that made it clear he had an intimate understanding of the latest neuroscience techniques.

Despite Rami's death, Moorea did not regret meeting Salison—he was beginning to believe in the extraordinary capacity of the human body and mind that Salison spoke of.

But now there was the mess of Rami's death to deal with…

It took only a matter of minutes for Moorea to clean and wrap Dr. Rami's wound—he removed Rami's blood-soaked clothing and covered him in a turquoise lab gown. Moorea swung the body over his shoulder and exited the operating room. His pace was quick, but something he saw out of the corner of his eye caused him to slow in his tracks— Salison's lab computer.

Salison had been secretive and withdrawn for the past few months; and his lab computer was always securely locked when not in use. The device now displayed his desktop icons.

Moorea set Rami down and took a seat at Salison's unlocked computer. Moorea tried multiple times to hack it; but had no luck. Salison must have left it unlocked in his recent haste.

On Salison's computer were dozens of folders with journal articles, experimental results, and analyses. Moorea started with the most recent folders and began working his way backwards. The most recent documents on Salison's computer dealt not with their joint project at New Life, but with something else altogether.

Moorea's pulse rose and small beads of sweat formed on his upper lip and brow as he scanned through the experimental results and research strategies on Salison's computer. Time melted away and was scarcely felt, until the pull of the present beckoned Moorea's subconscious. He glanced at his watch and cursed. He spent nearly forty minutes scanning through the data on Salison's computer. He did not have long before the janitor would be in.

Moorea produced a small USB flash drive and quickly transferred a few folders he found relevant on Salison's computer to the portable drive. Before getting up to leave, Moorea double clicked Salison's Internet browser. Sure enough, the man's personal email was open. The inbox displayed about two-dozen emails. Only one had been read. The email consisted of a single sentence: In eighteen hours, you're in.

With his hazel eyes burning focus, Moorea stepped away from Salison's console and picked up Dr. Rami. He again positioned the man over his shoulder and took the elevator from the basement to ground level.

Outside, the air was cool. A large sliver of a moon, glowing amber-red, fell towards the tree line while the staccato flash of firefly light fought through the surrounding fog. Aside from Moorea's Audi and Dr. Rami's Buick, the parking lot was empty. Moorea was thankful for that, as he plopped the body of Dr. Rami in his backseat.

In a few minutes, Moorea was about a mile up the road from New Life, pulling over to the shoulder. He grabbed Rami's body from the backseat and approached the railing of a bridge that ran over a swift, muddy river. Rami's limp body was soon falling over the bridge, into the dark water below. A splash could be heard as the wind picked up and the trees began to quiver.

The body of Dr. Rami bobbed and weaved in the current, before it began to sink. Moorea knew Rami's body would soon be found, but that did not worry him. He had no official ties to New Life and had the feeling he would not be coming back. What did worry Moorea was what he found on Salison's computer. The documents hinted there may be a dark and trying time for mankind approaching.

In the distance, there was a rolling of thunder.

A storm is coming, Moorea thought, as he turned from the railing of the bridge and began his flight into the night.

2

Twenty-six hours earlier:

The rain fell in torrents.

Thick sheets of water were illuminated briefly during free-fall by a young man's headlights, as his SUV careened down a slender road. As Adam Riley drove—a bit too fast for the current conditions—a flash of lightning sparked a dark horizon to the east. Adam watched as the lightning broke apart into fractures and radiated across the sky, tearing apart the darkness as it went. Adam listened for the sound of thunder, but it never came; there was only the pounding rain.

To Adam's dismay, the rain began to fall harder as he pulled into his parking space. Adam jumped out of his Jeep, covered his head with an old *Science* journal, and ran towards his apartment complex—in six quick strides he was out of the rain, climbing up two flights of stairs, to his studio. A key barely grazed the surface of a tattered lock as it was thrust inward and turned to the sound of a small metallic *clink*.

Adam eased his door open with his knuckle and went inside, paying no attention to the squeak of his wet sneakers on his wooden floor. Small beads of rainwater swam over his clothes—some of them bled together before succumbing to gravity, falling like glass bombs, scattering across the floor on impact.

Adam went on, oblivious to the chaos below, as he maneuvered his way towards the kitchen. He did not bother to hit the light switch. A small red light pulsed out of his living room—it was his answering machine, letting him know there was a message.

There was a flicker of curiosity in Adam, as he kicked off his wet shoes in the general direction of his kitchen rug and walked over to the dusty machine, pressing play. He was surprised that someone had tried to get a hold of him using the landline. There was a short beep then the message began playing,

"I pray you found the song," a man's rhythmic voice said. "I fear the time is nigh."

A few moments after the words were spoken, a second beep sounded off indicating the message was over. Adam recognized the man's voice immediately—it was Dr. Salison Sinsway.

Salison was a brilliant particle physicist and the strangest person Adam knew. Three years ago, Salison, a giant of a man, took leave from his job at CERN to research among all things, cell biology—more specifically, a recently discovered family of proteins called resonance proteins.

Resonance proteins were discovered in the inner ear of bats and would change their structure, switching between active or inactive states, when subjected to certain frequencies of sound. In a short period of time, Salison set up a lab at Boston College and recruited Adam to work in his lab. Since then, the pair published two Nature papers and a half dozen others regarding the properties of resonance proteins.

Adam was not terribly surprised a man so well-versed in particle physics would have such an advanced understanding of the properties of protein folding and acoustics; but it was a bit eerie how quickly Salison was able to identify, isolate, and engineer, new forms of resonance proteins.

After graduating six months ago, Adam stayed in Salison's lab for some time, before accepting a position in the acoustic pharmacology department at Boston Memorial, which studied among other things, selective drug delivery via sound.

So Adam split his time between Salison's lab and his own at the hospital.

For the past year Salison had been a ghost in his own lab, and only communicated with Adam via email. Salison had been hounding Adam to finish up work on what the two of them referred to as *'the song'*. *The song* was an artificially created sound—a string of pings, whistles, bass notes, and other acoustic components, strung together to create a single flowing 'melody'. Adam was creating the melody so he could manipulate genetically engineered resonance proteins. In fact, Adam was finally ready to test if his sequence of strung together sounds could restructure resonance proteins in living tissue. He was going to perform the experiments on the morrow.

Adam reached into his pocket and grabbed his cell, holding it out to illuminate the small caller ID display that was built into his house phone. 'Private' was all the display read.

Adam figured he would send Salison an email once he completed his experiments and had something to report. Salison was perpetually asking for experimental data; but this time, Adam knew Salison's nagging was for good reason. If Adam's next experiment worked, it would be the first to demonstrate that sound could be used to treat disorder, through the action of resonance proteins. It could be the start of a new branch of medicine.

It was late, Adam was tired, and it finally began to sound as if the storm was growing as weary as he was. Adam's eyelids became heavy as they fell over his eyes. Adam soon collapsed onto his queen-size bed.

...*the time is nigh*... Adam thought, as his mind drifted into the night.

Adam found himself in complete and total darkness. But there were sounds—hushed voices, weaving their way between the rustlings of footsteps. Adam strained his ears to listen but words could not be made out. The young man was not sure where he was. The damp air and the way his footsteps echoed in the darkness, made him think he was underground. Adam could tell from sound alone that there were other people in the room, and they all seemed to be moving slowly forward. Was he searching for something? How did he get here? Adam was not sure, but he began to follow the sounds of the moving crowd as the whispers among them intensified.

Footsteps in the room seemed to quicken as Adam's mind wrestled with the enigmatic nature of the dark place. Adam saw a glow ahead that split through the darkness; a dim horizontal line of pinkish-purple light peeking out from under what Adam assumed was a doorway atop a flight of stairs.

Up the stairs and through the door Adam went. On higher ground, there was no house nor any other structure to be seen—it was just him and the open land.

Night had fallen and the air was chilly. A large violet star beat above as if it were a living heart fed by blood. The orb outshined all the rest in the sky, raining down a sea of electric purple pulses as it pleaded with the darkness. Adam stood in awe of the quivering ball of gas as it spun livid violet light onto a vast mountain range in the distance, with their peaks raised in reverence. Then, in an instant the star went supernova. Adam felt the air around him begin to vibrate. A flood of hot colors radiated outward from the epicenter of the star, forming a brilliant butterfly pattern in the sky as a shock wave cut through the air, knocking Adam to his knees. He tried to keep his eyes to the heavens, but the light became blinding. Adam felt it burning his skin as the vibrations in the air intensified. The waves of sound and light lifted him into the air. The young man felt himself flying, as if he were a comet on fire. He felt himself burning, until there was only darkness.

The ringing of Adam's alarm clock struck at his senses. He awoke with a start, maneuvering his arms out of his covers as quickly as he could to subdue the loud alarm. The vision of the massive supernova lingered for a moment in Adam's mind as he tiredly rose from bed. He smiled, recollecting his stellar dream, as he jumped into the shower.

It was not long before Adam was dressed and ready for work. He needed to be at Boston Memorial by eight a.m.. As he checked the time, he realized he was cutting it close, as usual. He grabbed his keys off his countertop and headed toward the door; as he did, his kitchen radio changed tracks. Waves of air pressure born of the radio's speakers came to splash against Adam's tympanic membranes causing flows of electricity to travel from his inner ear to his cortex, where the sounds were processed into his flowing image of the world. The patterns of electrical impulses gave rise to other patterns—iterations upon iterations bouncing around in his brain until they played just the right sequence and he began to *remember*.

In his mind's eye, he saw himself lying on his back, eyes wet with bliss on a soft sky-blue sofa, while the same chords rang through the small living room he was in. Pink-pastel light streamed through the windows as the sun went down on a perfect day. One of Adam's closest friends, a young man now departed, sat next to him, humming along with the song.

The last time Adam heard the melody was in this moment. Now, Adam knew; the waves of sound and emotion that were flowing in him that day were functioning to give him a benchmark in time—something his mind could hold on to so that everything he felt in that moment, he could feel again—so that a part of him could go back to that hallowed home where a sweet sonata played—a place he would never truly be again, where he felt anything was possible.

AN EVOLUTION OF MINDS

The fine hairs on the back of Adam's neck stood on end, rising in a wave down his shoulders to his hands as a slight shudder radiated through him. He laughed aloud. *Time Travel*, he thought, as he opened the door to leave. *What a wonderfully absurd idea.*

3

Three hours and thirty-three minutes into his workday, Adam Riley found himself in his laboratory. He was about to test a question that had been resonating in him: Could the delivery of sound to the body and the subsequent activation of resonance proteins treat symptoms of debilitating disorder?

Night and day Adam had been working towards this end: testing and refining the tools Salison created. The pair were able to attach resonance proteins to neurotransmitters in order to render the neurotransmitters inactive. Neurotransmitters were signaling molecules, used by billions of neurons in the brain to pass messages to other neurons. By attaching resonance proteins to neurotransmitters, they were able to block a neurotransmitter's ability to bind and activate it's receptors. Only until the resonance protein's structure was changed with sound, would the neurotransmitter be released and able to bind its receptor, in order to signal onto nearby neurons.

Adam did experiments in cultured neurons, then live brain slices, showing that resonance proteins could bind and inactivate neurotransmitters as well as other pharmacological drugs. He was also able to alter neural activity by applying engineered sound trains to live brain tissue that contained resonance protein-bound neurotransmitters. But problems arose when trying to deliver sound trains into deep brain tissues, in live animals. Sounds were significantly distorted by the skin, skull, and brain tissues, on the way to their destination. This meant that resonance proteins could *not* be coaxed into changing their shape and detaching from their neurotransmitters when inside the body. Adam hoped the latest iteration of his song would be more stable, penetrate deeper into neural tissues *and* cause a greater conformational shift in the resonance protein, so it would be more likely to separate from its neurotransmitter.

Using sound as a therapeutic agent was not a new concept. Ultrasound had been used for over a decade to facilitate drug delivery by activating chemotherapeutic drugs in tumor tissues, or by activating anti-clotting agents within blood clots. Ultrasound was even being used to aid in healing flesh wounds and bone fractures.

Adam's work was quite different though; if today's experiment was a success, it would be the first to demonstrate that a new type of sound therapy could be used to treat illness—one that used specially engineered trains of both audible and inaudible frequencies of sound to target resonance proteins.

To perform his experiments, Adam obtained rats genetically engineered to carry a mutation in a gene that was altered in dystonia-parkinsonism, a disorder characterized by a co-contraction of opposing muscle groups. The genetically modified rats, just as human patients, had attacks of dystonia that could be triggered by stress. By applying foot-shocks to the rats, Adam could stress the animals to such an extent that a bout of dystonia would be triggered—manifesting in twisted and contorted limbs and an inability to walk.

A white rat explored a plastic tub that sat on a lab bench next to Adam. The floor of the tub was made of a metal grid allowing for electricity to be delivered. By applying electricity to the grid, a small foot-shock could be given to the rat enclosed within.

The rat within the tub wore a cloth collar that contained six ultra-small, yet powerful speakers arranged in a hexagonal, grid-like pattern. The speakers were positioned above the rat's cerebellum, a region of the brain involved with dystonia and movement. Adam pressed a button and pulses of electricity were sent into the tub. In less than a minute the animal within was in a full bout of dystonia. Its limbs were twisting and writhing and it could not walk or stand. Adam reached towards an audio switch on his computer.

Here goes, he thought.

Adam hit the switch and his engineered sound train was delivered to the speakers in the collar. A string of woven together pings, whistles, bass notes, and other artificial sounds swam to the rats cerebellum. After ten seconds there was no effect. The animal remained in its distorted posture. Adam made a note of this in his lab journal and then waited. For a full minute the animal remained dystonic. Adam only delivered a ten-second loop of resonance protein-activating sound. He increased the stimulus and delivered a minute long train of sound. Still nothing. Adam hoped the song would travel to the cerebellum and function to free the neurotransmitter GABA from the resonance proteins that bound it. GABA would then bind inhibitory GABA receptors and work to silence over-active cerebellar neurons that contributed to the twisting and writhing movements. But the sounds were having no effect on the animal's dystonia.

Adam anticipated this and attended to his lab computer. He was altering the frequencies and patterns of sounds in the sound train, compensating for the distortion of sound waves as they traveled through various layers of body tissues before reaching neurons deep in the cerebellum. This particular resonance protein could only be re-structured by a narrow range of sound patterns. The distortion of sound waves as they traveled through various tissues of the body was hampering the capacity of the sound train to alter the resonance proteins. Perhaps a new iteration would work better. When the pattern of sound was reconfigured, Adam removed the dystonic rat from the tub and took off the speaker-containing collar. There was a knock at the door that Adam paid little mind. He grabbed a fresh rat and fastened the collar around its neck. There was another knock and a moment later a young blond technician quietly opened the door and poked his head in. Once he saw Adam he stepped inside. As if the blond intruder could tell Adam's mind was elsewhere, he quietly closed the door and leaned against the wall.

Adam triggered the electric current that ran through the tub and the rat began to exhibit severe postural dystonia. With his eyes on the ailing animal, Adam triggered the train of resonance protein-activating sound. There was no effect, at first. But after a dozen seconds, the animal's dystonic limbs began to relax. Adam's cobalt eyes shined as he watched the disorder dissipate. The dystonia was gone! The animal shook himself off and began walking fluidly around with no abnormalities to his gait. Adam's sound train had reached the deep nervous tissues of the cerebellum, where the sound waves collided with resonance proteins, causing them change their shape and detach from their neurotransmitters. The GABA neurotransmitters, once free, were then able to bind their receptors within over-active neurons, in order to *correct* their aberrant activity—this was enough to cure the rat's dystonic symptoms.

Adam laughed aloud, richly. He was grinning ear to ear. He turned his attention to the young blond technician for the first time.

"That is fucking right my friend!" Adam said, as if the tech grasped the gravity of what had just happened. The kid looked bewildered, yet managed a smile.

"Sorry to bother you, Dr. Riley," he said, as Adam began writing in his lab notebook. "You know Dr. Sinsway from BU right?"

"Yes." Adam said. His focus was back on the rat in the tub, which was still moving around easily and freely. "Why, what's up?"

"Dr. Sinsway arrived in the ER a while ago. I heard he was seizing pretty bad. I'm not sure how he is now. I just thought you would want to know." The tech smiled sympathetically and left.

Adam set down his lab notebook. The ER was on ground level, seven floors down. Adam may have just made a breakthrough, but now he was worried for his friend, the man who made Adam's present experiment possible.

In a few moments, Adam had the functionally cured rat back in its cage. He grabbed his keys from off the countertop, hit the lights and headed towards the door.

4

In the waiting room of Boston Memorial, Adam Riley sat staring at the floor beneath his feet.

Adam tried to see his friend and mentor, Dr. Salison Sinsway, but the receptionist would not allow it. She did, however, tell Adam that Salison crashed his car into a ditch and en route to the hospital, began seizing violently. Adam tried to get more information from the receptionist, but she insisted that was all she knew. She took Adam's name and told him to have a seat.

Adam did not like hearing his friend was having seizures. It made him think Salison sustained a serious head injury during his accident. Or perhaps a seizure had caused the accident? It was troubling news and now all Adam could do was wait. As he sat in the lobby, he pondered Salison.

Salison was the strangest, most brilliant man Adam knew. With glowing tan skin, he stood at just over seven feet tall, and spoke in a strange flowing accent. It was curious how no one at Boston University, or even CERN, knew where the man was originally from. It was hard to narrow it down because of Salison's worldliness. Adam had personally heard Salison speaking at least nine languages. Once, at a conference, Adam saw Salison switch between speaking Navajo, Arabic, and Hindi, in the course of an hour. On one occasion, Adam asked Salison about his origins. With a smile, Salison had simply said he came from across a great sea, from a place of balance.

Unsatisfied with Salison's cryptic answer, Adam did some digging. Yet all he found were things he already knew—Salison received his doctorate from MIT in the mid-1980s in the lab of the Nobel Prize winning astrophysicist William Fowler. Salison made a name for himself as a brilliant nuclear physicist and he contributed significantly to the understanding of neutrinos and their oscillations; work for which it was thought he was going to win the Nobel Prize.

It was around this time his daughter Silloway was born. Soon after her birth, Salison accepted a position at CERN. When Salison's daughter started college, Salison opened his acoustic biology lab at BU, and then split his focus between the Large Hadron Collider (near the border of France and Switzerland), and his lab (in Massachusetts).

Adam could not find any information on Salison before his doctorate in the 1980s though.

As Adam sat in the waiting room of Boston Memorial, recollecting Salison, a silver-haired doctor caught his eye and began walking towards him. The man looked stern and collected; his eyes narrowed beneath his golden spectacles.

"Adam Riley?" he asked.

"That's me," Adam said, rising to his feet.

The doctor looked Adam up and down, almost as if he were sizing him up.

"I'm Dr. Halloway. Salison's physician..", the man began, "Salison is awake, and he is asking to speak with you."

The request puzzled Adam.

How did Salison know he was here? And why would he be asking for one of his lab members? Adam nodded his head though, in agreement, as he followed Dr. Halloway towards where he assumed Salison's room was.

"How did you know Salison was here?" the doctor asked, as the two of them walked down the hallway. Adam explained he worked in the building and a lab technician told him the news. Halloway seemed unfazed by Adam's answer.

"Salison came in about an hour ago." he said. "His car crashed into a ditch. It was a low speed collision from what we gather. There was little damage to his Lexus, yet the airbag deployed. When paramedics arrived, Salison was unconscious. En route to the hospital, he began seizing violently. We administered anticonvulsants and he came to, not long ago. He's severely concussed, he's still a little out of it, and he's also refusing to take any medication." Halloway finished with a question. "Does Salison have a history of epilepsy?"

"Not that I know of." Adam replied,

"And has Salison been traveling anywhere tropical, lately?" Halloway asked.

"Salison frequently travels overseas to collect biological specimens. And yes, some of the places he goes are in the tropics." Adam responded. "Why?"

"His skin." Halloway replied, with no elaboration. Then, he added, "We still don't know what set off the seizures. We think a seizure may have been the cause of his crash. Right now, we have more questions than answers about the man's condition."

After guiding Adam through a few corridors, the doctor stopped and glanced down at his watch in an impatient manner. "I have a lot to do here," he said. "Salison's room is around the corner. I'll be back to check on him. He's scheduled for brain imaging within the hour."

Without another word, the silver-haired doctor turned and walked briskly away.

Adam picked up his pace as he approached Salison's room, excited to see his friend; but just as he approached the door, it opened from the other side and a dark-haired man exited. Adam immediately recognized the man as Dr. Jonas Moorea, a neuroscientist that had—on occasion—dropped by the lab to talk to Salison. Adam was, only once, briefly introduced to the man.

The young doctor was dressed casually, in a pair of faded jeans and a white T-shirt. He looked as if he were pondering something, intensely, as he exited the room, and initially turned to go in the opposite direction. As Moorea swept out the doorway, his gaze fell on Adam. There was a look on Dr. Moorea's face that Adam could not quite place, as he tossed something small and shiny in Adam's direction. Adam instinctively caught the object, as Dr. Moorea turned and briskly walked off in the opposite direction, without a word.

Adam glanced down to his left hand, as his right reached towards the handle of Salison's door.

Moorea threw him a crimson-feathered metal dart.

Well, what the hell? Adam thought. He rolled the dart around in his hand and noticed a clear chamber, within the dart, that had a small amount of translucent liquid clinging to the side. Adam's curiosity regarding the dart did not last long, for he was soon inside Salison's room.

Salison was lying in bed, wrapped in an ivory bed sheet. The man's violet eyes were pleading. Adam knew immediately that something was wrong. There was sweat dripping down Salison's brow and a look of cautious realization and perhaps even desperation on his face. His breaths were quick and, as he spoke, his voice strained.

"The song," Salison said. "The sequence of the song and the surrounding sounds?" he asked.

Adam was confused—the feathered dart, Salison's strange nature—both hints that there was something very wrong. Yet Salison was speaking on the experiment Adam had just performed upstairs. Salison wanted to know if Adam figured out how to manipulate genetically modified resonance proteins in tissue, with his engineered train of sound.

"Yes," Adam said. "Just now. I figured it out. I still need to do more experiments though, to—"

Salison cut him off. "Get the sounds to I, or Silloway pray." the man said.

"Sure," Adam responded. "Salison, what's wrong?"

In the next instant, Salison's eyes widened and his back arched as he inhaled sharply. Then, Salison began seizing.

His whole body was radiating in tremors. The force of the oscillating giant was something Adam had not experienced before, the whole room was vibrating, and light seemed to dance around Salison as he seized. Adam tried to protect Salison's head, by placing a pillow under it. He tried to raise the guard rails of the bed but Salison's long heavy frame was shaking all over the smaller bed, keeping the rails from being raised. Adam had to do his best to keep the shaking man from falling onto the floor. When Adam touched Salison, as he resonated with a high frequency, he had the odd sensation that his own hands were wet; yet the sensation was overcome by the tremendous velocity Salison was generating. Adam felt his own body vibrating, down to his bones.

For what felt like ages, Adam fought against the rising and falling of Salison's body; to keep him on the bed and a pillow under his head. Then, incredibly, through clenched teeth, Salison spoke.

"Take flight for Jonas. Save Silloway, son."

Salison's eyes rolled back after he spoke the words. Adam felt as if he were ringing like a bell, as he struggled to keep Salison from falling onto the floor. And something was playing with Adam's senses. He heard sounds, behind himself, that sounded elongated and contorted. Then, Salison's body jerked, and Adam heard Dr. Halloway yell for him to move. Halloway pushed Adam out of the way, as a nurse brushed past. The nurse was soon struggling to inject Salison with a syringe of liquid, which she prepared in mere moments. Adam kept his eyes trained on Salison, as violent tremors radiated through him.

As Adam watched, he thought of what Salison said.

Salison said to follow Jonas. He also mentioned his daughter Silloway as well, making it sound as if she were in danger.

Adam felt as if he had to stay with Salison though. How could he leave his friend like this? Adam was not sure he could, yet the look in Salison's eyes had been undeniable. There was not much else he could do here anyway.

For a split second, Adam stood frozen in place, his mind reeling. Then, he turned and took off towards the door.

Adam walked briskly through the hospital. As he recounted the urgency in Salison's voice, he increased his pace to a jog, traveling through pale blue corridors, towards the nearest exit.

How long had it been since Dr. Moorea left? Fifteen, twenty seconds?

Adam was not sure. The doctor could not have gotten far though. Adam picked up his pace to a sprint, as he pushed past a doctor and a group of nurses. Adam shortened his route to the parking lot by choosing an alternate exit from the hospital. He put his weight into a collapsing metal bar within a manual door, and shoved it open, making his way into the sunlight. The temperature had risen since he arrived this morning. A newborn heat hung in the air.

Searching the parking lot, Adam felt his body begin to perspire. The sun was beating down, reflecting off rows of cars, causing the space to shimmer every time Adam changed his location. Adam glanced towards the exit of the hospital and saw a silver Audi A4 leaving; Adam noticed the profile of the driver—a young man with short black hair and light skin—it was Jonas Moorea.

Adam ran to his Jeep, reaching his vehicle in no time. Soon, he was pulling out of his parking space. Adam saw where Moorea's silver car had turned from the parking lot. His hands glided over his leather steering wheel as he followed suit. Moorea's car turned onto Armitage Avenue and stopped at a red traffic light. Adam tried to keep his head down as he too pulled up to the traffic light. Moorea's vehicle was about a hundred feet in front of him.

Adam wondered what all this could be about, as he left his friend, Dr. Salison Sinsway, behind.

5

Nearly 10,000 miles away, in Port Kembla, Australia, the sun was setting. From out her window, Kalanidhi Kalidasa had a good view of the marina. Her sepia skin shined softly in the day's last light as she admired a sailboat swaying rhythmically in the harbor. Growing up on the Bay of Bengal, Kalanidhi learned to sail at an early age; dodging booms and tying bowlines as long as she could remember. Her parents owned, and taught her how to sail on, a much slower and less maneuverable vessel than the one outside her window. Aboard it, she became quite accustomed to the sea.

Kalanidhi was envious of the young man who was securing the cruiser to the dock. Feeling the wind on her face and the salty spray of the ocean as it lapped against the hull would be a welcome recess from the stuffiness and long hours at the hospital. Kalanidhi forked at the Caesar salad on her desk as she watched the young man tie the lines of the ship to the cleats of the dock. The man's movements were strong and fluid in the failing light.

Kalanidhi finished her salad and tossed it in the wastebasket, turning her attention back to her computer screen. She had been working on a case report that had to be finished by end of the evening. Kalanidhi worked at Port Kembla Base Hospital, which was well known for specializing in the treatment of infectious disease. Dr. Kalidasa, as head of the infectious disease ward, was well aware that a dozen people—mostly children—in the last three weeks, had been infected with an especially virulent and drug-resistant form of *Escherichia coli* (E. coli). She was working on a report that summarized the latest case.

The New South Wales health organization was tightly monitoring the E. coli outbreak, which was traced back to a petting zoo located near Sydney, about forty minutes to the north. So far, there had been no fatalities, although a toddler and an old man had been hospitalized for over a week.

In her report, Kalanidhi determined it was the same strain of E. coli that afflicted the thirteen-year-old boy as the others. Kalanidhi was about to send the report, when a knock at her door stole her attention.

"Yes?" she answered.

One of her students, a young blond Australian man with a prominent overbite, walked through an open doorway, into Kalanidhi's office.

"Sorry to disturb you doctor," he said, "but we need you on the floor."

In a few minutes, Kalanidhi was in the intensive care unit, observing a young boy.

My god, Kalanidhi thought, as she examined the child.

When the eleven-year-old boy arrived this morning, he presented with muscle aches, chills, vomiting, and fluid accumulation in the lungs. The boy's parents, at first, thought he had the flu; but when he began wheezing and nearly passed out, they brought him to Port Kembla. Upon the presentation of jaundice—a yellowing of the eyes—which was indication of liver failure, Kalanidhi diagnosed the child with the Hantavirus.

Hanta was a rare pathogen that was carried by rodents and passed to humans by contact with contaminated animal urine or feces. Prognosis for those with Hanta was grim but the kid was strong. And with oxygen, riboflavin, and a steady IV of nutrients, it almost appeared as if his condition was improving. But that was a few hours ago. Now, his affliction looked like something else entirely. The boy had developed large boils around his groin, botches of dark purple coloration on his arms and legs, and his blood pressure was falling fast. The kid moaned with pain as Kalanidhi felt his appendages and the skin around his boils.

As Kalanidhi examined the boy, her student arrived; he had taken a detour on the way to the ICU.

"We got the lab results," he said. "His blood tested positive for the Hantavirus."

"Run the test again," Kalanidhi said softly. "This can't be Hanta. This is something much worse."

6

Oceans away, back in the United States, Adam Riley felt the heat, and reached down to turn on his air conditioning. He glanced over three cars in front of his own. The silver Audi carrying Dr. Jonas Moorea turned left onto Vintage Street. Dr. Moorea was heading out of Boston.

"My God." Adam said aloud, as he drove, recollecting Salison's seizure.

Adam was worried about the man he left behind; but if there was anything threatening Silloway, he knew he made the right choice: to follow Moorea.

Salison's daughter, Silloway, was twenty-three, and had attended Boston College with Adam. She was curious, and beautiful, with the same haunting violet eyes as her father.

It was rumored that a geneticist at Boston University had become obsessed with the Sinsways, due to their violet eyes, and on numerous occasions, asked both Salison and Silloway if he could have a sample of their DNA, in order to sequence their genomes and determine their genetic background.

The geneticist, Dr. Jean Hebert, was only one of many people that were curious about Salison's origins. Numerous students and faculty were intrigued by Salison, and speculated on where he could be from. Salison however, had always laughed off any request for a DNA sample.

Through teaching biology courses at Boston College, Adam had come to know Salison's daughter, Silloway. Adam knew that she too had denied Dr. Hebert's genotyping request. So Salison's origin was still a mystery, and so was at least half of Silloway's.

As Adam drove on the expressway, pondering the Sinsways, he saw in his mind's eye a supernova whose epicenter fanned out in the sky, burning away the surrounding darkness. Adam was, for the moment, unsure of why the violet vision found him, as he watched Moorea's vehicle slow ahead.

The neuroscientist put on his blinker, switched lanes, and appeared to be approaching an exit. The stellar scene in Adam's mind vanished as he took note of Moorea's actions and decelerated. There was old tan pickup truck and a new blue Toyota directly between him and Moorea, along with a few other cars that were running nearly parallel to them. Adam was nine seconds behind Moorea, as he watched the man take the New Haven exit on the right. Unfortunately, Moorea's car was the only one to do so. Moorea's car briefly went out of sight, following a winding exit ramp.

Taking the exit, Adam once again spotted Moorea's vehicle. After about twenty minutes of driving through city and suburb, the man finally pulled into a neighborhood. It did not take Adam long to realize he was in a fairly nice area. There were large healthy lawns, elegant homes, and imaginative architecture, spaced out between a fairly thick forest that blanketed the land on either side. When Moorea pulled into the neighborhood, his vehicle disappeared out of sight. Now, every time Adam passed a driveway, he would slow and scan for Moorea's Audi.

Adam was beginning to get nervous. The tree cover was so thick in some areas that he could not see to the end of the driveway in order to ascertain if Moorea had taken the path. Soon, the trees began to thin out and the elevation became steadier, and in about a mile, Adam saw what he was searching for—Moorea's silver Audi, sitting next to a SUV, on a weathered brick drive. The vehicles sat in front of a mid-sized cottage. Adam kept driving, and followed an iron gate that encompassed the property. He followed the gate and the slight curve of the road, as Moorea's dwelling disappeared behind him. The road sloped downward until the gate surrounding the property broke away, to follow a perpendicular road. When Adam was out of sight, from both Moorea's house and the drive, he pulled his Jeep over in front of a collage of maples, concealing his vehicle from the neighboring property.

Salison told him to follow Moorea, and he had. But what now?

Adam thought about calling the police—although he had no proof that Moorea had Silloway, just a few words from a seizing, nearly incoherent man. Adam mulled the thought over in his mind as he grabbed his cell phone from his pocket. He looked down at the phone and laughed softly, shaking his head. His cell phone was dead and he did not have a portable charger. He dropped his phone onto his passenger seat.

Only one thing to do. Adam opened his door and jumped out of his vehicle. He felt a cool rush of autumn air as he did. Adam jogged across the street, toward the cast-iron gate that surrounded Moorea's property. The gate separated Adam from a shroud of trees apart of Moorea's land. The neuroscientist's house was not visible though, since the land rose up to block the view.

Adam studied the iron gate as he approached. It looked to be over six feet tall. The tops of the vertical beams were squared off and flattened at the top. Adam did not quite know why he was here, or if he was making the right decision to trespass on Moorea's property, but neither of those things perturbed him as he quickened his pace and leaped into the air. At the height of his jump, his hands grasped the top of the towering beams of the gate and he swung his body upward with the gained leverage of the poles, catapulting himself over, lightly rolling as he impacted the soft earth on the other side.

7

A few dozen miles to the east, back at Boston Memorial, the emergency room physician, Dr. Halloway, was at a loss. He stood beside a now sedated Salison Sinsway. Salison looked peaceful enough, with his eyes closed and an oxygen mask covering his mouth. But there was indeed something very wrong with him. His vitals had been falling ever since his last seizure had subsided. His heart rate was slowing, his blood pressure was dropping, his breathing had nearly all but ceased, and nurses were constantly replacing bags of vasopressors the man's body required to stabilize his blood pressure and return blood flow to vital organs.

Halloway knew that Salison's failing health was due to whatever was inside the crimson-feathered darts found in Salison's room. Six darts in all were recovered; and Halloway had observed a single, post-car crash wound on the side of Salison's abdomen. After finding the darts, Halloway called the police. Nearby officers were placed outside of the room, and a detective was now on his way to the hospital.

Halloway knew it would take time to analyze the contents of the feathered darts; and it would be awhile before he knew how to best treat the famous physicist. It was frustrating. Halloway could only wait and keep Salison under close observation.

As Halloway examined Salison's IV, he noticed something strange. There were thin lines of pigment, running down Salison's arm. The lines were razor thin and barely visible against the man's tanned skin. As Halloway's eyes focused, he saw the lines traveling up towards Salison's shoulder and down to his hands, breaking apart near his wrist, branching out and terminating at the ends of his fingers. Halloway turned Salison's arm over. There was another line that traveled down Salison's arm and spread apart at the digits. Halloway could tell that the lines of pigment and their secondary branches followed the major divisions of the ulnar, radial, and median nerves, down to the fingertips.

What in the world? the doctor thought. The scarring looked as though it could be from laser surgery or an incredibly sharp scalpel.

Halloway, with his eyes and hands, followed the lines up Salison's arm and shoulder before they branched out, terminating a few centimeters away from the man's spinal cord. Halloway found two parallel lines of odd scarring, running down Salison's back as well, along his vertebral column. Halloway set Salison down, circled the bed, and examined his other arm. There was the same razor-thin scarring here, too. Halloway approached Salison's legs. Again, the scarring—miniscule lines running down the man's appendages—lines that branched apart to follow the major divisions of the man's nerves. The doctor could not imagine how the lines had gotten there, or what type of elaborate procedure would result in such scarring.

As Halloway examined Salison's leg, a loud beeping sounded off through the room. Salison's heart had stopped beating. Halloway went for the defibrillator paddles, just as a nurse rushed into the room. The nurse opened Salison's gown above the chest and applied a thin film of a clear, jelly-like liquid. Halloway applied the paddles, and sent a charge of electricity towards Salison's heart, in hopes of jump-starting it back to life. On the monitor of the electrocardiogram (ECG), there was only a single voltage deflection, caused by the defibrillator.

"Again," Halloway said. After delivering another charge, there was a single weak heartbeat; and then, a straight, linear, line.

Halloway waited a moment and administered the defibrillator again. He held his breath, as he stared at the ECG; there was a stimulus artifact and then a flat line. Halloway tried one more time, with a look of desperation in his eyes—he saw nothing but a brief spike on the ECG.

Salison's heart had stopped beating. He was dead.

"He's gone.." Dr. Halloway whispered, as his eyes met those of his nurse.

Halloway turned his gaze to the clock and made a note of the time, as the nurse pulled an ivory sheet over Salison's lifeless body. Halloway then turned and left the great man, Salison Sinsway, in a shroud of white.

8

Adam Riley stood on Dr. Jonas Moorea's lawn, as a warm breeze swam in from the east, causing long blades of grass to dance around his feet.

A small fire burned in Adam's cobalt eyes, as he took in the land of which he was a part—the earth rose steadily upward. It looked as though the periphery of Moorea's land were a thin forest. There were tall healthy trees dotting the landscape, spaced well apart to accommodate the spread of their uppermost appendages.

Adam followed the land uphill in a brisk jog, ascending to a group of towering conifers. At the apex of the land, the trees thinned out; and from his vantage point, Adam saw Moorea's house. It was about fifty yards away and on the same plain of land that Adam stood. The house was two-stories high and elegant, in a more traditional way. There were beams of aged wood, which were aesthetically placed amidst the architecture, as well as cut stones laid upon each other, donning light hues of rich moss. There were no shades at the windows of the second-story balcony and from where he stood, Adam had a partial view of an upper-story room.

Adam immediately recognized Moorea, standing upright, his arms flexed in front of himself, while his hands grasped, what Adam assumed was, a table ledge below. He was shaking his head, eyes bleeding emotion, as they stayed fixed on an object that was not a part of Adam's view. It was time to leave the sparse tree line behind and get closer to the house, so he could see more of this situation unfolding upstairs. Adam sprinted forward, towards the house, losing sight of Moorea and the second floor as he did so. Adam tried to approach the house from the corner, to elude the view from the smaller first-floor windows. Adam noticed a pair of cellar doors, embedded in the ground, off to his left. The wooden doors looked strong, yet, at the same time, as if age had taken its toll on them. A dull gray chain and padlock secured two iron handles together, that were attached to the two cellar doors.

Adam sprinted past, and quickly found himself at the base of the stairs, which led to the second-story patio. Adam found himself smiling, as he slowly climbed the planked staircase—he was energized by the mystery of the moment and the unknowns in his future's path. His smile quickly dissipated though, as he heard a man's voice rise sharply, sounding on edge. Adam peered above the last step. His glance shot past a sickly looking potted plant, into the living quarters beyond large glass panes. The view Adam now had, although on the opposite side of his initial reconnaissance, was solely of Moorea; though now the view was of her back. Adam was trying to figure out the best way of moving forward, to see who Moorea was engaged with, when he heard a woman's voice cry out.

Adam recognized the voice. He rose, in an instant, on hearing the sound. The young man forgot how quick he was, as he made his way through the unlocked door, into the house. It was all a blur to Adam; he did not think, he simply acted.

Inside the house, Adam glanced a surprised-looking Moorea, to his left; and as his head swiveled to his right, he saw a large muscular young man, who held Silloway strongly by the arm. They were both standing at an intersection of—what may have been—a kitchen, a living room, and a hallway (leading to a space beyond).

Silloway's eyes were wet. She looked at Adam as though he were a ghost; and Adam lost himself—for a moment—in the purple storm of her irises, as he approached the man who held her.

There was an impact upon Adam's chest as he readied himself to deliver a blow. Adam felt perturbed, as he lost focus. He tried to steady himself. He looked down and noticed a small, metal, crimson-feathered dart, protruding from his shirt, a few inches below his right clavicle. He glanced the muscular man that held Silloway; he was raising a small silver pistol with a wide barrel in Adam's direction. Adam heard Silloway's voice, as he tried to lunge forward.

Just as the muscular man appeared as if he would fire yet again, a yell from behind Adam rang out.

"Don't," Moorea said.

The second impact was not from a second dart, but from Adam's body falling onto the floor. His forehead was jolted by a coarse, wooden floorboard as he landed; it reminded Adam of high school—of the days when he used to box. There was a brief second of recollection, then darkness.

9

Chaos was in the air as Detective David Brennan pulled up to Boston Memorial Hospital. The parking lot was littered with police cars—with flashing sirens radiating through the air.

Boston Memorial had not seen excitement like this for some time; it was not every day that a world-renowned scientist was brought to his end, inside its walls.

Detective Brennan opened the door of his Camry and stepped out into the late afternoon sun. He entered the hospital through a set of double, sliding-glass doors, glancing the weary faces of a few waiting within the lounge. Brennan saw a young man in a police uniform approaching him. It was Officer Patrick Middler, a cadet who had been shadowing Brennan for some time. The kid was interested in the prospect of becoming a detective. He was well built, with dark friendly eyes, and an energetic step.

Brennan and Middler walked beside each other, approaching the crime scene. Routine chatter filled the gap between them.

"Time of death?" Brennan asked.

"2:23 p.m. Dr. Halloway, an emergency room physician, is the man that called us. He said the circumstances surrounding Dr. Salison Sinsway's death were suspect and that there were custom-made darts in the victim's room, the kind shot out of an air pistol. The crime lab took them for analysis. We're still waiting for the results."

The two men were met by curious glances as they walked through the waiting room.

Brennan's eyes acknowledged what Middler said as the two of them continued past the reception desk, towards the recovery rooms.

"Cause of death?" Brennan asked, pushing open a pair of double doors.

"Respiratory failure or cardiac failure," Middler stated. "Take your pick."

"Who do we have here from the lab?" Brennan asked.

"Ben was here earlier. He took the darts, as well as a few things from Sinsway's room, back to the lab for analysis. Ning's here now," his voice trailed off for a moment. "I think she's taking photographs." As Middler said this, he handed a folder to Brennan. "Here's what we have on Dr. Sinsway, and here's the file on a young man—Adam Riley—seen leaving the victim's room about twenty minutes before time of death."

The two of them arrived in the hallway outside of Salison's room. All entrances to this area were blocked off with yellow police tape. Unlike the rest of the wing, the area was devoid of activity. The detective turned to Officer Middler, "Put out a BOLO (Be On the Lookout) for Adam Riley. We're going to want to talk to him."

"Sure thing," Middler said.

Brennan steadied his gaze on Salison's room while Middler jogged off in the opposite direction.

Brennan was curious as to what Ning Sun would be up to. Ning was new to the crime lab. She was only twenty-five and had started as a crime lab supervisor, just one step down from being in charge of the whole crime lab. Her predecessor was nearly twice her age. Apparently, the woman held a Master's Degree in Forensic Science and a PhD in Criminology, graduating with distinction in both. Brennan figured the woman must be smart, but he was curious if she had any intuition about her; if she could put together the pieces of a crime scene. Brennan was in the academy with people who did fine on all their exams, but hadn't the slightest bit of sense about them.

As if in answer to his musings, Ning Sun exited Salison's room and quickly spotted Brennan. She smiled as she approached.

"Hello, detective," Ning said. "We have a dead male, Salison Sinsway." For a fleeting moment, she looked to be about to smile; perhaps reflecting on the odd nature of the man's name, but she continued. "Aged fifty. It looks as though he may have been poisoned. Tranquilizer-looking darts were found scattered about the room. They were sent to the lab to be analyzed."

"How many darts were found?" Brennan asked.

"There were six. One in the trash receptacle and five more around the room."

"How many with blood on them?" Brennan asked.

"Just one. And there was a wound to Dr. Sinsway's abdomen that was incurred after his car wreck. Although the wound is not entirely consistent with that of a puncture wound from a dart."

Brennan stayed silent as Ning continued.

"We have a statement from the ER physician, Dr. Halloway, who claims a young man, Adam Riley, was with Dr. Sinsway only moments before he fell into a fit of violent seizures and the kid disappeared soon after the onset of the seizures. Curiously enough, Dr. Sinsway asked specifically to see Adam once he recovered from an earlier series of violent seizures. Adam actually works upstairs as a researcher. He's twenty-three."

"Seizures?" Brennan asked. "Why was he seizing?" As he asked the question, he began to thumb through the folder that Middler had given him.

"Well…" Ning started, sounding hesitant for a brief moment. "Dr. Halloway wasn't quite sure. His best guess was that Salison had sustained some sort of head trauma during an automobile accident that landed his car in a ditch this morning. But like I said," Ning finished, "He wasn't quite sure."

Detective Brennan leaned against a pale blue wall, nodding his acknowledgement. The color in his eyes looked like fields of swaying sea grass, as his irises pulsed in the overhead light. The man rubbed his hand through the stubble on his face, eyes fixed on an intangible moment in space.

"I'm done here and heading back to the lab," Ning said. "I'll call you when we have something on the darts or the agents used in the assault."

Brennan offered the woman a smile as she left. He knew that if she found anything relevant, he would be among the first to know. Brennan's gaze shifted towards the entrance to Salison's room. The man contemplated what lay in wait within. It was something he had still not gotten used to, despite countless hours on the job. His stomach always sank in anticipation, before examining a body. The unease was pushed from his mind, as a voice rang out from down the hall.

"Hey Brennan.", It was Officer Middler, on his way over.

"The lab just called about the prints on one of the darts we found," Middler stated. "I just told Ning, the prints were Adam Riley's."

Brennan's face showed no tell of his emotion as he took in the news.

"Halloway said that the two of them were friends," Middler added, his tone indicative of this curious element.

Brennan, again focused on Salison's room, feeling inquisitive eyes upon him. As he stared, the doorway blurred, in lieu of his inner musings.

The kid's prints were on the dart, Brennan thought. *This one might not be so bad, provided we can find Adam Riley.*

10

A ringing sound echoed in the darkness.

Adam Riley found himself lying on the ground. His head was pounding, and there was a tinnitus reverberating throughout his skull. As he opened his eyes, he came to the realization that there was no light in this place; not even the hint of a single ray. Or so it seemed. Adam lay on his back. His right eye opened fully and his left was swollen almost completely shut. He reached up to touch his swollen orbital and felt a light shawl wrapped around his forehead, covering the wound. His fingers pressed up against the mesh of blood and wet fabric covering the upper left side of his face. Adam figured the bleeding was over and was thankful for that, although there was probably a nice gash above his eye.

With one eye open, Adam scanned both left and right—he could not make anything out—the room was so dark that he did not notice a difference in lighting when his eye was opened compared to when it was closed. Adam's mouth was dry and his whole body felt as if it had been thrown down a flight of stairs. Despite his discomfort, Adam tried to gather himself in the darkness.

Where am I? How did I get here? He vaguely remembered his ill-fated first steps into the cottage.

What happened? Did someone bash me in the face and throw me in a dirt closet? Well shit. This day just gets better and better. Adam laughed to himself shaking his head, trying to get a bearing on where he was. There was a wall close behind him. He pulled himself towards it and propped himself up against the barrier of earth. As he was straightening his back against the wall, he heard what sounded like a door being opened, somewhere above him—this was accompanied by a brief flash of dim yellow light which was soon swallowed up by the darkness, in tandem with the sound of a door closing swiftly. Adam became vigilant. His attention peaked, as he listened—relying solely on his auditory sense. He heard light footsteps coming nearer to him, most likely down a flight of stairs.

"Adam?", a voice asked, "Are you alright?"

It was Silloway. The woman's voice caused Adam to smile, despite his pain. From the sound of it, Silloway Sinsway was now approaching the base of the stairs, which happened to be only a few feet from where Adam was now rising to his feet.

"Ya." Adam replied, trying not to sound too flustered. The pain in his head intensified as he stood. He was about to ask Silloway how she was, when she spoke again.

"You took a tranquilizer dart in the chest and you hit your head pretty good on the floor."

Adam sighed. His head was pounding and he still felt dizzy. There were so many questions ringing in his mind, but before he could inquire, Silloway began again.

"How did you know I was here?" she asked as her hands found Adam in the darkness—her touch was brief, before she continued deeper into their dark confine.

As Silloway passed, Adam picked up on the scent of lilac and citrus.

"Adam?" Silloway asked, with a little urgency in her voice. Adam could hear the woman turning back towards him.

"I'm sorry," Adam said, "My head is still ringing. Your father told me to follow Dr. Moorea, here."

"Is he alright?" Silloway asked , "My father?"

"I don't know." Adam replied to the darkness.

Adam wanted to tell her about the seizures and the hospital; but for some reason, in this moment, the silence seemed right. As if he were trying to read Silloway's mind and there was more to be learned from her ponderings than any words he could speak. There was something enigmatic in the woman as she stood in the darkness; a deep contemplation running in the back of her mind, or perhaps it was some sort of wanting. Adam wasn't sure; but it fell from the soft breaths she drew in and expelled.

Before Adam's mind had assembled his musings, Silloway's voice rang,

"We have to get out of here," she said, "I think Jonas is gone."

The way Silloway spoke of Dr. Moorea made Adam wonder how well she knew the man; but right now, he had more pressing issues at hand. Silloway again began moving, away from Adam. The sounds of her movements echoed in the dank air.

Adam stared into the opaqueness of his surroundings, trying to subdue the pulsing pain from behind his eyes, rubbing his temple, "Where are we?", he asked.

"We're in the cellar, beneath the house," Silloway answered, still slowly moving away from Adam, her hands studying the space she was in.

Adam felt a surge of energy growing within. There were a number of things he wanted to do, such as contact the police, inquire about Salison and discover what Moorea was up to, but first things first; they needed to get out of this place.

Instead of following Silloway, Adam turned from her direction and made his way to the base of the stairs. After one or two cautious strides, the wall he was following fell back into the opening of a stairway. Adam fell forward as his foot caught the bottom step. He stabled himself and then traveled up the steep staircase.

He reached the top and put his hands out in front of himself to test the door that was separating him from the rest of the house. The door was smooth and Adam could tell from the texture that it was wood. He pushed it to test its strength; it was incredibly solid.

Damn, he thought.

There was not going to be any kicking in of this door. He put his shoulder against it and leaned forward, just to test the barricade again. The door was thick and the wood was strong. Adam searched for a handle and found a large metal one. He felt around the thick, cold iron bar to see if there was any accessible lock—there was none. The door must have been secured from the other side. He tried pounding on the door, but it was so thick that it hardly made any sound at all. If there was a way out of this dark dank basement, this was not it.

After checking if the door had any hinges on his side (which it didn't), Adam turned to walk back down the stairs. Once reaching the base of the cellar, he could hear Silloway still moving, further along the wall than where she had been when he left. As if she heard him coming closer, she spoke, "We're not getting out that way."

"I'd say so." Adam said, in the darkness.

Silloway was still facing away from Adam, but he could tell she stopped moving.

"There has to be another way out." She said.

At this, Adam had an idea.

He began to move away from Silloway and the wall—he kept both eyes closed as he walked, since he could not see anything with them open and his head felt better with his eyes relaxed anyway. Adam had his hands out in from of himself as he dragged his feet across the dry earthen floor. It was only a few paces before he ran into a rough, wooden, structure. He pushed against it and it slightly tilted off the ground. Adam could tell it was fairly lightweight. It seemed to be a shelf. Adam's hands studied the object in the darkness. He got a feel for where one of the horizontal beams of the shelf was and hit it with considerable strength, in a downward motion with a clenched fist. The wood broke at the right angle it made with the vertical stands. Adam then ripped off the other side of the horizontal shelf and with a few more well-placed strikes, was left with a pile of debris and pair of five-foot wooden boards. Adam took one of the planks and walked around the room, hitting the wooden board on the old concrete ceiling as he listened to the sounds of the collisions. It was hard to maneuver. He could tell this room was possibly a storage area, home to old furniture and things of that nature. Frequently, he would run into what he assumed were wooden chairs and the bases of sofas or ottomans.

Silloway must have figured out Adam's plan, for behind himself, he could hear her grab a piece of wood from a pile of debris and head in another direction, thrusting the wood up against the ceiling of the cellar. After a few cautious strides, Adam ran into a group of loosely arranged standing beams, which were situated against a more sturdy structure. He continued forward, tapping his timber against the ceiling. It was only a few more steps before Adam heard what he was searching for—the sound of wood hitting against wood and a slight give. Adam was directly underneath the cellar door that he had seen on the way in. Adam pressed his beam of wood against the top of the cellar door and pushed upward. As the plank of wood rose, a shard of sunlight fought its way into the dusty space. Both chained doors were rising up; the cellar became more and more illuminated, until the chain went taut. Adam tested the strength of the chain that locked cellar doors and then let them succumb to gravity. Again consumed by darkness.

He walked back to the group of wooden poles he found before and identified one as a metal-tipped shovel. He grasped the shovel in one hand and carried an ottoman in the other, as he traveled blindly back to the cellar doors. Adam stood up on the ottoman, and raised his arms over his head, holding the metal portion of the shovel. He pushed open the cellar doors and then positioned the wooden handle of the shovel between the chain that secured the handles together. The chain became taut as Adam wound it by rotating the shovel like the hand of a clock. Adam got a steady grip on the wooden rod after rotating it to the maximum and pulled downward with all his strength. The cellar doors opened, bending inward, as sunlight rushed through. Adam strained himself, hoping the shovel would not break. A loud *crack* rang out. The iron handle to one of the cellar doors busted apart from the door, yanked off by the taut chain. The dangling chain and padlock now held no more sway on the strength of the security.

Adam was hoping that the man who had shot him with the tranquilizer was not looking out on the yard, as his foot found an earthen groove in the wall and he reached up to swing one of the cellar doors open. The room was now bathed in light with dust hanging in the air. Adam could see Silloway, smiling as she approached. Adam provided for her a step with his hands. She used the wall for leverage and pulled herself upward, rolling onto the soft grass as she exited the cellar. Adam was close behind. Once out the cellar, Adam and Silloway took off running towards the setting sun, to free themselves from Moorea's land.

11

A silver Audi sped down the Boston Freeway. A man in his early thirties thought to himself as his hazel eyes shined with fire in the setting sun.

Dr. Jonas Moorea was in turmoil; even his dreams of late had been dark. Salison Sinsway had pushed him to the brink. Salison was cold, reckless, and his genius was quite outdone by his never failing need to be right about everything.

Today though, Salison paid the price for his pride. And Moorea was not worried of things coming full circle. He put his fear away. Moorea wondered how far Salison had traveled into the void.

As Moorea drove, he contemplated the possibilities and the problems, for they were numerous. Unfortunately, the answers to many of the questions that riddled Moorea's mind, may have dissipated with the last full breath that escaped from Salison's lips. Moorea knew he now had his work cut out for him.

Jonas Moorea had always been a driven man—graduating from Cal Tech with advanced degrees in both Molecular Cellular Neurobiology and Biochemistry at the age of twenty, before attending medical school at the University of California, where he received both his doctorate in Neuroscience, and his Medical Degree. Moorea had once dreamed of a Nobel Prize and immortality within an elegant equation, but his focus shifted the day he met Salison Sinsway.

"*A metamorphosis of men*" is what Salison had called it. The man claimed to know the path to true enlightenment—a way to evolve not only your spirit but your mind and body as well. Salison claimed to know the secrets of the prophets—the truth behind their ability to perform miracles.

Salison spoke much on the lives of both Jesus and Buddha. Salison reasoned that an extremely rare biological phenomenon, generated by an incredibly rare genetic potential and a lifetime of training and facilitating environmental factors, gave rise to men that could interact with the fabric of space and time in a different way, allowing them to have command over nature, to change the biology of others, to manipulate matter, and to move through space-time with a heightened speed and focus.

Salison spoke on the Buddha's ability to translocate, or appear in two places at once and on the ability of Jesus to calm the seas or wither trees at will. He spoke of the prophets' power over human biology: used to heal the sick or raise the dead. Salison went on to describe Jesus's ability to multiply matter, as he did at Bethsaida, and his ability to turn water into wine, as he did at Cana. Salison said that the miraculous abilities of the prophets were side effects of their enlightenment and that he had a plan to harness their powers for himself—a plan to induce enlightenment—in order to become something akin to a god.

Jonas had listened as Salison laid out his proposal. And although it had at first seemed fanciful, the man's science was sound. Salison, however, needed access to equipment and materials that Boston College could not supply. Furthermore, Salison was not as well-versed in the more intricate techniques of neurobiology and physiology as Moorea was.

So Salison had asked for Jonas's help; and although Salison offered no money for compensation, Jonas agreed to assist Salison with his project. Salison had enticed Jonas with the promise of something more than material, something that he claimed only a few men have ever found. Jonas could still remember the man's words.

"Never have you felt it," Salison said, with an alluring tone in his voice. "You probably never will," he added. "But it exists, I assure you."

Jonas's soul filled with fire as he thought of Salison's words.

Years ago, the two of them began searching for something, something within themselves. Moorea had the feeling that he was beginning to glimpse the thing that they were searching for and that Salison may well have found it. It was in the man's movement, his rhythm; it bled from his shining violet eyes and even resonated from the hum of his voice.

Moorea shook his head as he drove, wondering if he would ever experience the world as Salison did. His hand made its way to the base of his neck, and he massaged the rough skin.

As the doctor calmed his mind, a vibrating sensation stole his attention. It was his cell phone. He grabbed the secure cell and answered the call, speaking only one word into the phone.

"Yes?" he said, quickly.

His eyes glanced out the window, to the hills rolling off into the distance, rising and falling in the approaching twilight.

"He's arrived." a dull voice said.

"And you know what to do?" Moorea asked.

The man on the other end of the line sighed. There was a brief moment of silence before he spoke. His voice sounded as if he were trying to reason.

"It's the middle of the day." the man said.

Moorea felt a rage bubbling to the surface. "I don't care how you do it; but I need it done and I need it done soon." He said.

The man on the other end of the line gathered himself as if he had expected this.

"We're ready."

"Good. You know where I'm headed."

Moorea ended the call without another word and slipped his phone back into his pocket. What he was about to attempt was damn near impossible; but Salison was hiding numerous things from him. The man was doing his own private research, had attained a level of being that eluded Moorea, and worst of all, had unlocked a secret to something that could be Moorea's salvation.

If he only had more lives to live, Moorea's measures would not have been so cold; but as it was, this was his only chance. Salison was his only chance: to get the information he needed to survive and further the evolution of his body and mind. Brilliance can only get you so far. Moorea's genes had encoded for him only so much potential. And he needed more.

Dr. Moorea reached for a cold bottled water and opened it in a quick motion, as he glanced down at his watch.

Almost there, he thought.

He allowed himself a small smile, as he realized that he had just lost track of time while thinking.

He knew it would not be the last time it happened.

12

The sun was low in the sky, nearly blinding Adam, as he and Silloway ran across Jonas Moorea's property, having just escaped from the neuroscientist's cellar. Adam looked behind himself, towards the house, as he made large strides over Moorea's lawn. There was no one in sight—no movement within the first-floor windows at least. Adam was thankful for that. Silloway and Adam wove their way between trees and shrubs as the land sloped upward. The pair were quickly to the periphery of the property. Their feet lightly padded on fallen autumn leaves and small twigs, with sounds of defeated foliage radiating through the crisp air.

Moorea's cold cast-iron gate came into view, as the two approached a group of towering trees. Adam brushed his hand along the rough surface of one of the aged conifers. His eyes followed the rise of the majestic trees, as they fought toward a tangerine sky, blotched with pastels of warm colors, pouring out just before the twilight.

Soon, Adam and Silloway came to a halt next to the rising beams of the perimeter gate. The moment Adam glanced Silloway's face in the failing light, he recalled why he had always enjoyed teaching her classes—her eyes like churning violet seas from a thousand feet.

Adam knelt down to form a stirrup for Silloway's foot, by intertwining his fingers. His hands showed a few dark patches of dirt and small beads of sweat, which collapsed under tension as Silloway placed her foot onto his palms. With Adam's help, Silloway rose, took ahold of the top horizontal beam of the gate and then swung herself over it. Adam was surprised at the young woman's athleticism. She landed gracefully on the moist New England ground on the other side and ran across the road towards the Jeep.

Adam grabbed the keys from out his jeans and unlocked the doors with a press of a button, as he looked back, towards the house—still no one coming. He took a few steps back so that he could gain some speed and then sprinted towards the gate. Soon he was in flight, catapulting himself over the top of the towering iron beams. Adam rolled his body as he impacted the ground on the other side to absorb the force of impact. He rose and quickly sprinted to his vehicle. Inside his Jeep he found Silloway sitting next to him, already buckled up, looking slightly anxious.

Adam's breaths slowly began to drift to their natural rhythm as he maneuvered his way out of the neighborhood, going as fast as he could without careening into a ditch. He lightly massaged his chest through his weathered T-shirt and noticed his right hand was bleeding. He figured he probably injured it dismantling Moorea's old shelf.

There was in Adam's mind now, a cascade of questions; each one somehow tied to the next and all without an answer. "Silloway," he said, glancing over to her, "what's going on?"

The young woman looked thoughtful, yet worried; and her reply left much to be desired.

"It may be beyond me." She said, softly.

Adam waited for more of a response from the woman, but it never came. He let out a sound of frustration, his eyes back on the road.

"Well let's start with this." Adam said, "How did you find yourself on Moorea's property?"

"Moorea abducted me from work yesterday and I've been trapped with him since." Silloway answered.

Adam waited for more and Silloway continued,

"He wants something desperately from my father and he was using me for leverage."

"What does he want?" Adam asked.

"I can't say for certain. Jonas made it sound as if it had to do with a secret project he and my father are working on together."

"What kind of project?" Adam asked.

Silloway stayed silent before shaking her head, "I don't know."

Adam pondered Silloway's words. He had the feeling she knew volumes more than she was letting on, but her current disposition was far from receptive. So he did not feel like pressing her for information, not yet anyway. What he really wanted to do was get to a police station, drink some water, inquire about Salison's condition, and report Moorea, for whatever the hell he was up to. He looked over at Silloway and figured that she too must want these things. She remained silent as she stared out the window to the world passing her by.

Adam saw streaks and blotches of autumn colors as they faded into the failing light. There were countless issues dancing around in his mind, but they fell into the background. Adam hoped that in time, the answers would become clear, but for now, a small part of him were merely content that he and Silloway were out of Moorea's cellar.

13

Detective David Brennan sat at his desk back at the station. In his hand was a heavy silver coin from antiquity, its curves and contours smoothed out from millennia of trade and travel, shining with patina. Brennan rolled the coin over his knuckles. Rhythmically. In his mind's eye, he examined his day.

At Boston Memorial, Brennan had an interesting conversation with Dr. Phillip Halloway, the emergency room physician that treated Salison Sinsway. Halloway told Brennan that Salison had radiating scars that ran in fine lines throughout his body. The doctor had spoken of the scars as if he were hypnotized by their nature, saying that it looked as if an incredibly delicate and complex microsurgery had been performed on Salison. Brennan was not sure what this could mean, yet the doctor had spoken of the scars as if he were deeply interested in them. Halloway also said that there was another aspect of Salison's skin that was odd, but once the words had escaped his mouth, the man decided not to elaborate.

Brennan may have paid this comment little mind; but when he examined Salison's body, at the hospital, he had seen for himself, that even in death, Salison appeared to be *glowing*. The man looked healthy, shining some sort of youth even in his demise.

For these, and numerous other reasons, Brennan was anticipating the autopsy findings.

He was now working on his case report; writing it, reading it, and going over the events in his own mind.

***

After spending time at the hospital, gathering information from staff doctors and nurses, Brennan drove to Boston College. The place was resonating with news of Salison's passing, and the sorrow was spreading. The man was well-liked by both students and faculty alike.

At BC, Brennan questioned the present staff, on among other things, the nature of Dr. Sinsway's work there.

Brennan learned that a few years ago, Salison took leave from his post at the Large Hadron Collider to set up a lab at BC. Salison's lab focused on the isolation, characterization and genetic manipulation of resonance proteins. Brennan was told that although Salison was not the one who discovered the proteins, he had published a dozen papers that characterized different isoforms of the protein and described methods for selectively manipulating them with sound. Salison was also using genetic engineering to alter resonance proteins and attach them to specific regions of DNA and other molecules, like neurotransmitters, allowing him to directly influence gene expression or brain activity with sound.

The scientists at the lab assured Brennan that this was groundbreaking work, which had many relevant applications in the treatment of disease and disorder. Among other things, the researchers said resonance proteins could potentially be used for gene therapy or local drug delivery via sound.

Brennan was no biochemist, but Salison's science sounded intriguing. Despite the importance of Dr. Sinsway's work, the general consensus at BC was that Salison was a ghost in his lab.

For the past year, few people actually saw him come or go from the college. Brennan was told that the only member of the lab that routinely spoke directly with Salison was the most senior member of the lab, who curiously enough, was Dr. Adam Riley.

Riley had begun working on his doctorate at the same time Salison set up his lab at Boston College. Riley, apparently a bright kid, had finished his doctorate in three years and had gone on to start his own small lab at Boston Memorial. Despite working at the hospital, Riley frequently still visited the college, to advise and consult with Sinsway lab members regarding the nature of the experiments they should be doing.

Brennan was surprised to learn that Salison's reclusiveness was not a terrible problem, as he, and Adam Riley, were still managing to oversee a solid group of researchers, who were turning out good scientific papers bearing the Sinsway name.

Brennan also learned that Salison had been doing quite a bit of traveling over the past few years. Many of his flights were to Geneva, Switzerland; presumably, to consult with physicists at the Large Hadron Collider. Salison had also been to many other places, such as Japan, India, Malta, Indonesia, and Australia. Brennan was told that this was, in part, to collect and study bats from all over the world, so that Salison could isolate new forms of resonance proteins, which were found in the animal's inner ear.

Brennan had a hard time reconciling the fact that Salison was a brilliant particle physicist *and* a man that was at the forefront of a new field of structural biology and pharmacology. He shook his head. A genius, who few had seen in the past year, shows up with thin radiating scars along his entire body, glowing, and seizing in an unbelievable way.

A tap at Brennan's office door interrupted his musings. The door opened before Brennan could say anything and in walked Officer Middler, carrying a brown manila folder in his hands. He acknowledged the detective with a nod as he took a seat in the leather chair in front of the detective's desk.

"So what do you think?" Middler asked, making himself comfortable.

Brennan smiled at the officer's blunt question.

"Sinsway was murdered," Brennan said. "The lab ran the analysis on the liquid contents of the darts that were found around Sinsway's room. A significant percentage of it was a chemical, tetrodotoxin. Samples of Sinsway's blood also showed traces of tetrodotoxin."

Middler put on a face that indicated his pondering, before he leaned forward.

"Tetrodotoxin...that's the stuff in, ah...puffer fish, right?"

Brennan nodded his head, as he reached for his coffee mug. He took a small sip and grimaced before retorting, "That's what they told me. A little bit can paralyze the muscles of your body, including your diaphragm, which means you'll stop breathing. Ning also identified trace amounts of drugs that target the heart and could cause it to stop beating. Either way, if you shoot a dart containing that stuff into somebody, you're doing it for one reason."

Middler nodded, in agreement. He leaned forward in his seat and reached to the back of his neck, softly massaging the area, before straightening out.

"So why did the shooter need six darts to hit Dr. Sinsway once?" Middler asked.

"That's what I'm wondering," Brennan said. "Perhaps Sinsway is more agile than we think."

Middler laughed.

"To dodge five shots in a fifteen by fifteen foot room? Maybe the shooter was blind?"

Brennan shook his head. "And apparently, there was no obvious dart wound on Salison. Dr. Halloway said that the one post-car crash wound he found on the man had the appearance of a line, a linear abrasion—about three centimeters in length—the width of a dart needle, but noncircular and inconsistent with a puncture wound from a dart tip."

"Maybe Sinsway was shot, then rolled over, tearing the wound open?" Middler said.

Brennan nodded his head. "Perhaps."

Only a moment of silence was allowed, for ponderings, then Middler continued.

"I went to the Boston Zoo, where the daughter works, in the entomology lab. She left on break today and never came back. Her car is still in the parking lot. They've been calling her cell. No answer."

The news caused Brennan's attention to rise.

"A black and white is on the way over to the daughter's apartment now; it's a few miles outside of town,"

Middler spoke with his face down. He now leaned over and forward in his chair, still rubbing his neck.

Brennan sighed. "Is something wrong?"

"Oh," Middler started. "I was at the gym last night. There's something about my back."

As if he could feel Brennan's eyes rolling above him, the young man straightened up, exhaled and grinned, as his gaze—once again—fell to Brennan.

"Riley's our main suspect?" Middler asked, in a rhetorical chord.

"Find the daughter and find Adam Riley." Brennan answered.

Middler reached down towards a manila folder that was resting between his ankles. He grabbed the folder and placed it on the wooden surface of Brennan's desk.

"These are Sinsway's personal effects."

Brennan opened the folder as Middler continued, "A set of car keys, a cell phone, and a security card. I identified the logo on the card—the jet-black serpent—as the emblem for Sidewinder Securities. They handle security for large firms, mostly medical facilities, making sure employees all have badges, key cards, and in some cases, pass codes to gain access to select facilities. They also work in surveillance."

As if he felt Brennan's pending inquiry, he continued, "Neither Boston Memorial nor the University use Sidewinder Securities."

"Thanks," Brennan said, as Middler got up to leave. Middler knew Brennan liked to think in solace and there were plenty of things he could be doing.

Brennan smiled a farewell to the young cadet and briefly examined the contents of the manila folder. Then, he shifted his attention away from the Sinsway case. On his computer monitor, he opened a different case file; his mind always worked like this. He perpetually had more than one case open; and had to juggle the pieces of all the crimes at once, working to separate the strands of storylines that wove themselves together between his subconscious and his waking hours.

This had been a busy month. Along with the murder of Salison Sinsway, there was a gang shooting in which three males were killed, and a young woman was just stabbed to death in what looked like an attempted robbery.

A ringing began to emanate from Brennan's slacks, stealing his attention. He fished out his cell. It was Officer James Robbins, who worked the switchboard.

"Hello, Detective Brennan," the officer began. "We have yet to locate Silloway Sinsway. She was not at her apartment, but the place was torn apart. Probable ten twenty-five."

Breaking and entering, Brennan thought.

"Signs of a struggle?" he asked.

"It was almost as if somebody was looking for something," James said. "Mattresses split open. Books torn off the wall. That sort of thing. No blood or sign of the daughter."

Brennan stood and grabbed his keys from the drawer of his desk.

"You have the address?" he asked, as he headed towards the door. A beeping on his phone let him know that there was another call coming in. It was Ning from the crime lab. He ignored it, for the moment, as the switchboard operator gave him the address of Silloway Sinsway's place. Brennan was going to examine the scene. It sounded as if the dead man's daughter may be in danger, or worse. Brennan hung up the phone and slipped it back into his pocket.

Soon, he was pulling out of his parking spot. It wasn't until he was on the freeway that he remembered Ning had tried to call him. He dug out his cell phone and called the CSI, as he wove between mid-day traffic. Ning answered her phone, "Brennan?"

"Ya, it's me."

"You're not going to believe this," she began, as Brennan drove.

Brennan's jaw dropped as he listened to Ning. He wasn't sure if he heard her right, but he did not interrupt her. He kept listening and slowly began to apply the brakes. It was not long before he hung up with Ning and his phone was back in his pocket. Brennan pulled onto the shoulder and stared out the window, shaking his head in the slightest degree. He could scarcely believe what he had just heard.

Then, Brennan pulled back onto the road and accelerated through a sharp U-turn, heading now in the opposite direction, towards the Boston morgue.

14

The sun had fallen in the west and the last of its rays softly illuminated the land, as Adam and Silloway continued their flight from Jonas Moorea's cellar. Adam filled Silloway in on her father's car crash, his subsequent hospitalization and Moorea's actions at the hospital. The two were now heading to Boston Memorial, to check on Salison's condition and call the police from there. Adam glanced Silloway's reflection as he drove, she was peering through the glass at the horizon as if she were pondering some deep notion. Behind Silloway, Adam saw the rolling hills of the countryside. A vast forest rose and fell as if on a serpent's winding back, as it swam off into the distance.

Adam had more than a few questions for Silloway; but for now, he let her rest and take in the world. His curiosity regarding their predicament had dwindled slightly; yet he was still anxious and worried about his friend. As Adam drove he softly rubbed his chest.

"Damn tranquilizer dart," he said, fingers massaging the rough skin.

A small smile formed on Silloway's face as she gazed through the window. Adam realized he was running low on fuel and it was not long before he spotted a small gas station and pulled in. After pumping gas, he picked up a portable cell phone charger from the station store. Once back on the road, it was only a few more minutes of driving before the pair approached a small town outside of Boston.

Seeing all the restaurants made Adam realize how hungry he was. He and Silloway decided to stop at a restaurant and pick up something to go, and eat as they drove back to the hospital.

Adam approached an island of concrete that looked to be the home of a small strip mall—there was a grocery store, a Chinese restaurant, a GAP, and what looked to be a mom-and-pop diner. Adam pulled into a parking spot in front of the restaurant. Silloway said she wasn't too picky and that Adam could get two of whatever he was ordering. The young woman unbuckled her seatbelt, yet looked as if she wanted to stay put. Adam jumped out of his Jeep and approached the small diner.

Inside, there were booths along the windows and a café bar, which separated the booths and a narrow walkway from the kitchen. As Adam entered, a chime rang out from the door. He caught the scent of burgers and fries as his stomach growled. There was a family of four chatting to his left in one of the booths and a few people sipping coffees at the bar; the place was not very busy though. Adam noticed a pair of police officers, sitting in the booth farthest from him, alongside the window, near the register. Both officers were middle-aged and overweight. Adam approached the officers and glanced a menu that was situated above the bar. As he did, he made out the sound of a police radio cutting through the clinking porcelain and friendly conversation. A woman's voice echoed through the radio. She sounded dull and unexcited.

"...male, five foot nine, one hundred and seventy pounds. License plate jay-nine-seven four-three-five-seven..."

Adam slowed as the woman's voice trailed off. He played the numbers back in his mind. Had he heard that right? The numbers she read off...those were the numbers on his license plate.

As Adam strained to listen, a child cried out behind him, and he had the feeling he missed part of the woman's transmission. Adam's sympathetic nervous system kicked into gear, his pores opened, his temperature elevated and, as his mind raced, he began to sweat. Adam moved slightly to his left, to stay out of view of the officer facing him. He was now halfway between the cash register and the booth where the two police officers were sitting. He kept walking towards them, slowly, straining his ears to listen. The woman's voice continued. "...regarding a probable one-eight-seven."

A cascade of neurons fired in mere microseconds within Adam Riley, as he realized what the woman had just said. Adam had learned a few police codes while playing video games with a friend of his that was a police officer. Among others, Adam knew the police code for *Homicide*. It was 187.

There was nothing else from the radio. Adam pretended to look over the menu, making sure to position his body away from the officers. His energy rose. Was he wanted for murder? He went back to the moment right before he saw Salison. He saw Moorea exit Salison's room. Then, Moorea had thrown him the crimson-feathered dart. The chaos of Dr. Sinsway's seizure had pushed the memory from his mind, but now he saw it with clarity. Adam had caught the dart Moorea threw at him, then he simply tossed the dart in the garbage, realizing there was something wrong with Salison.

"Shit," Adam said aloud, softly. *Had anyone else seen Dr. Moorea there? Was there a nurse in the hall that saw? Could Salison be dead, and if so, how?*

Adam recalled seeing the man lying in bed, his eyes shining in desperation. Then, the violent seizure. *Moorea had no trouble with kidnapping, could he have harmed Salison?*

Adam's prints were all over that damn feathered dart, which had God-knows-what inside of it. Adam tried to remember if Moorea wore gloves, but he could not recall. As his mind raced, he turned around, glancing out the large window that separated the diner from the parking lot. He saw Silloway. She was nearly straight across from him, about thirty yards or so away. Her curious gaze was lit softly from one of the light posts in the parking lot as she sat in Adam's passenger seat. A panic rose in Adam's chest. He flashed back to the two nights he spent in jail after getting into a brawl outside of a bar. Any hardened criminal knew that two nights in jail was nothing. Adam decided then though, that such an environment would drive him mad. Adam recollected news articles about men who were wrongly convicted of crimes they did not commit and hence put away for years, even lifetimes. He thought of the sway of prosecutors and the way they weave their words to incriminate any in their path, regardless of true guilt. Adam ran a hand through his damp hair as he tried to calm himself.

The young man's thoughts were interrupted, as he heard the crackle of the radio.

"Attention all units: Suspect and vehicle spotted, corner of Elm and route thirty-four. Location: Sandy's Diner…"

As Adam heard the words he felt a surge of adrenaline. He quickly turned towards the door. As he did, he glanced at the two police officers. The pair, for a moment, looked as if they had awoken from a dream.

"Don't move kid!" one of them shouted, as he went for his Taser and began to rise. Adam had already made up his mind. He was not going back to jail—he was not going to let these men take him in and decide his fate.

The officer closest to Adam lunged at him, as it was Adam had a look about him he was not sticking around. Adam moved quickly, avoiding the brunt of the officer's tackle as he was pushed backwards into the stools of the bar behind him. Before Adam even knew it happened, he landed a devastating blow on the lunging officer's chin. The officer's jaw twisted up and to the left, as Adam's fist followed through. The man was mid-sized, looking to be about twenty years Adam's senior—his soft body was heavy as it hit the floor.

The other officer went for his stun gun and was now in the process of pointing it at Adam. He pulled the trigger. Adam quickly maneuvered his body out of the way—in a split second—as the electrodes went flying past him into an employee behind the counter who was not quick enough to react to the developing situation. The officer looked surprised as the woman behind the counter hit the floor, shaking. He dropped his stun gun and reached for his Glock.

Adam stepped over the fallen officer that he had knocked out, in a heartbeat, as he shoved the larger officer that was going for his gun as hard as he could. Adam used both of his palms to hit the officer with a concentrated blow to the chest. Adam had his feet planted firmly on the ground as he connected. The officer fell backwards, towards the window. He crashed through it as chaos erupted within the small diner. In that moment, there was a flurry of color about the place. Shades of black and blue shimmered in the dusk as glass, looking to be shards of opaque obsidian, flew through the air. The pieces glimmered in the shallow light, as time itself seemed to slow for Adam, as he watched the officer tumble through space. Before the last shard of glass hit the ground, Adam jumped through the fractured window. He ran towards his SUV, as one officer lay with eyes closed within the restaurant and another tried to rise to his feet on the sparkling sidewalk. Adam saw a stunned look on Silloway's face as he ran in her direction. As he did, a white car across the street turned on its sirens. It must have been the squad car that radioed him in. It wouldn't be long before the police car would be in the lot.

Adam jumped inside his Jeep. Silloway looked at him with a stunned expression.

"Buckle up." Adam told her. He had the car started in seconds.

"What the hell happened!?" Silloway asked him, her voice strained and elevated.

Adam looked over at her, and quickly glanced down. The woman's face showed disbelief; she had not made a move towards her belt.

"Alright." Adam said. "Then hang on."

15

The Boston Morgue lie six miles away from Adam Riley and Silloway—there, two stories underground, sat a shining, metal, autopsy table. Detective David Brennan felt a slight unease growl in his stomach as he caught sight of the thing. Brennan sensed an aura surrounding the cold assemblage of steel; as if it were still hanging on to a bit of all those observed upon its smooth surface. The aging detective pushed the unsettling thought from his mind, as he walked into the autopsy room.

Just over an hour ago, Salison Sinsway's body was atop the autopsy table. Now, the body was gone. To where, Brennan did not have the faintest idea. It seemed a fair trade was made though; for forty minutes earlier, a lab technician was found lying on the morgue floor—unconscious—with a small hole through his white lab coat that penetrated a few inches into his skin.

"Someone stole Salison's body." Brennan stated, almost in disbelief. "How could this happen, in the middle of the day?"

His gaze turned to the young woman that entered the room behind him. She blew a strand of jet black hair from in front of her face.

"We don't have too many people in the morgue. It's not like it's a bank, David." Ning Sun gave Brennan a sideways glance before she continued. "It looks as though the attendant on duty, the man in charge of placing bodies in cold storage, was one of the two people hit." Her eyes glanced the wall, where silver-handled embedded squares indicated the drawers that stored cadavers within.

"The man said that someone approached, aimed a wide-barreled gun at him and fired. He then felt an impact on his chest and after that, he doesn't remember anything. The receptionist, who is usually in charge of making sure people sign in to identify remains or deliver corpses, said the same thing. She also had a small wound in her chest.

Both have a hazy memory regarding the incident, yet both were able to identify the assailant as a white male, midsized and muscular. He wore a short-sleeve shirt and had on a black ski mask, covering his face. Judging by the diameter of their wounds, I'd say it's certainly possible that the same type of dart gun was used as the one in Salison's murder, perhaps just filled with a different compound."

At this, Brennan simply nodded.

"Sinsway weighed about what? Two hundred and forty pounds?" he asked.

"Yes, about that much." Ning replied. She grabbed a camera that was sitting on a lab bench. She had responded to Brennan, but she had the feeling that the man did not need a response, as if he were merely thinking aloud. Ning figured Brennan was wondering if the man that fired the dart gun could have taken Salison out of the morgue by himself. From the man's description, she figured it was possible.

Ning continued. "We're working on analyzing a sample of their blood now, to determine whatever agents were used to knock the two of them out."

"Fingerprints?" Brennan asked.

"We've lifted a couple. I haven't heard back from Ben yet."

"Witnesses?"

"Not even in the parking lot."

Ning glanced at Brennan as she finished. The man held a stoic demeanor. His attention flew past her, into the crime scene beyond. For a moment, it looked as if the man's attention was brought back to the encompassing world; as if he might say something. Ning waited, but instead, Brennan reached to his slacks pocket and pulled out a vibrating cell. Ning smiled and turned away.

Brennan opened his phone, holding it up to his ear.

"Brennan." he said into the receiver. He did not hear a reply, as he brushed off the front of his polo shirt. Brennan took the phone from his ear and examined it.

"The reception down here isn't great. You'll have to go up to ground level." Ning said.

Brennan nodded to indicate his leave and it was only a moment before he found himself outside. He looked to the west, noticing the sun had already fallen; although the very last of its pastel rays still blanketed the land.

AN EVOLUTION OF MINDS

Brennan took out his cell and dialed the number that tried to reach him earlier. It was the operator from the precinct. As the phone began to ring in his hand, he wondered if the Sinsway situation could get any more peculiar.

16

Adam Riley put his SUV in reverse and slammed the petal to the floor, just as the squad car across the street from him began pulling into the lot. The sirens of the squad car were on and the officer behind the wheel held a livid demeanor, as if Adam was about to be in a hell of a lot of trouble.

In reverse, Adam steered towards the nearest exit, which was on the opposite side of the lot from where he entered. Unfortunately, this was where the squad car that radioed him in was turning into the lot. Adam had no choice but to go this way though—the alternate route was blocked by cars. There was no way he could have gone forward.

Adam accelerated at considerable speed with his vehicle aimed directly at the approaching squad car. He slammed the back of his Jeep into the front of the police car—the sound of metal crunching and tires squealing filled the air, along with Silloway's screaming voice. Adam kept his foot pressed firmly on the gas as he pushed the squad car out into the street. He glanced left, back towards the diner. His eyes were there long enough to see that the officer he put through the window was running to his car.

The sound of the forceful collision radiated through the air, as Adam's vehicle crushed into the police car behind him. The cruiser was partially mangled, lying perpendicular to the back of his Jeep. He heard Silloway yelling his name as he punched his vehicle into drive and tore off down the street, leaving a mutilated squad car in the middle of the road behind him.

Adam could tell from how his vehicle was handling that the damage to his own truck was merely superficial. At least he hoped that was the case. There were a number of other secondary accidents—cars strewn across the pavement, others honking as Adam sped away. He accelerated as he crossed the median to get on the right side of the road, glancing behind himself quickly, to make sure there were no police cars following.

"I'm never going back to jail," he managed to say, as he increased his speed, all the while maneuvering between slower traffic.

"What's wrong with you, Adam?" Silloway yelled as Adam glanced back to see if anyone was following. Still no one. But that did not mean they were not closing in, for Adam heard the sirens, cutting in between Silloway's elevated voice. Adam could not make out the woman's words though; he was solely focused on driving as fast as he possibly could, without careening into approaching vehicles. He felt adrenaline coursing through his body. He had felt this before—a total rush. The sounds of surrounding cars began to blur as his speed rapidly increased.

Adam was beginning to think he may have overreacted; but then again, he was wanted. And for what? There could only be one thing. Adam's mind was torn between his internal thoughts and the external world, a world that was now racing by at what was approaching 80 mph. There was no turning back now, Adam had to get off the freeway, lay low, and find out what the hell was going on.

Was everyone right about me? he thought. *Am I really this reckless? No, there is something going on here, beneath the surface. Something sinister happened to Salison after I left the hospital. The police radio made it sound as if I'm a suspect.*

Up ahead, Adam saw a turnoff. He glanced back, to make sure that there were no officers in sight and slowed a little as he did, to take the turn. His tires squealed while he and Silloway were pulled downward from the inertia of the veering maneuver. Adam had a feeling that if he did not get off the main road, he would be wearing an orange jumpsuit to bed. Adam looked over at Silloway, The woman did not look as upset as Adam would have thought, but she was saying something about his "goddamn ADD."

Adam felt as if he needed to try and explain himself,

"Silloway, someone's been killed. And I'm a suspect."

Adam, rolled his hands over his leather steering wheel, taking yet another turn, leading him further westward, away from the city.

Silloway stayed silent. Adam felt something change in her. She was thinking about the same things he was: Moorea, the crimson-feathered dart, Salison's seizures, and now someone was dead...

"I'm sorry I flipped out." Adam said. "When I heard I was wanted, I just—"

"Adam, please," Silloway said, cutting him off. "Give me a moment to think."

At this, Adam stayed silent.

Silloway was taking deep calculated breaths, looking out her window, to a tree line basked in dusk. She seemed to lose herself in her ponderings. Then, she took her gaze from the forest and grabbed Adam's phone, which had been charging in his center console—she quickly moved her slender fingers along the screen and when she was finished, rolled down her window and simply tossed the phone out the window.

"Hey! What the hell?" Adam inquired, as he slowed his Jeep.

"Keep driving," Silloway said, softly. "How long do you think it would take the police to find us if you have your cell with you?"

Adam was pulling over to the shoulder. To Silloway's question, he merely shook his head. He could see from Silloway's reflection, that her eyes were wet; yet there was strength in them. Adam pulled back onto the road and continued driving.

"You know," Silloway said, "I could have probably cleared you of any suspicion. Moorea *did* abduct me from work, and you *are* the one who freed me from him."

At this, Adam simply shook his head. A part of him wanted to try and explain his actions, but he stayed silent. Maybe Silloway was right.

"We'll have to find a payphone or borrow someone's cell, so we can figure out what happened to my father," Silloway said.

Adam glanced over at Silloway when she mentioned her father. The woman looked in sync with the coming night—through her reflection, Adam saw the moon was high in the heavens, looking to be a sharp sliver of light—the points of the perfect crescent appeared to be angled upwards as if the celestial body could pierce the foot of an immortal if ever he walked the sky. Adam took in the satellite, feeling Silloway's sadness, yet he did not allow the feeling to take ahold of him (not yet anyway); he did not want to believe that his friend and mentor could be gone.

"Why would Moorea want to hurt your father?" Adam asked.

Silloway seemed to contemplate for a few moments; she wiped her eyes and replied, without taking here gaze from window, "The lust for something more, can make men dangerous."

Adam waited for more, but there was nothing else.

"Silloway," Adam said, with a hint of empathy in his voice, "I don't really know what that means."

But there was nothing else from the woman. After watching the forest outside pass her by, she spoke up again, softly.

"We're on our own now."

Her words caused confusion in Adam and again he felt like the woman knew more about their present situation than she was letting on. The Sinsways certainly loved turning everything into a puzzle.

Before Adam had a chance to inquire, Silloway began again.

"My father, he may be gone."

Adam felt for the young woman and he knew she was probably right; Salison's death would seem to explain both law enforcement's and Moorea's actions. Adam felt a sense of sadness creeping up on him, but he choked the feeling back; he was thinking on how to say he was sorry about Salison, as Silloway spoke up again:

"Adam," Silloway asked. "What did my father speak to you about at the hospital?"

"He told me to come get you," Adam said, as he slowed to take another turn near a weathered, wooden-planked barn, covered in moss and vines. "And he asked me about the project I'm working on in lab."

"What did he ask in regards to your project?" Silloway asked. Adam could feel the sadness in her dissipating, in lieu of something else.

"He wanted an engineered sound train that I've been working on for the past year. Basically, it's an artificial song that I use to activate genetically modified resonance proteins in living tissue. He's been hounding me about it. Interesting, he would bring it up when he's at the hospital, seizing…" Adam looked over to Silloway.

Silloway seemed to contemplate before speaking,

"Adam, I need that sound byte."

Adam could scarcely believe his ears. "Your father, you know he could be…" He let his voice trail off, not wanting to say the words. "And you're worried about my experiments?"

"Do you think he would have mentioned it, with what could have been his dying breath, if it wasn't important?" Silloway countered.

"Well, it's back at Boston Memorial." Adam said, "So we sure can't get it now."

"We have to, Adam." Silloway said.

Adam laughed softly, "I'm a wanted man, Silloway. Why is it so important you need it tonight?"

"Adam, you know that sound train is a key component of a system that may revolutionize how we treat certain types of diseases and disorders. Progress toward that goal should not be slowed for the loss of one man."

"That may be true." Adam said. "But it's also B.S. I think you know more about our situation than you're letting on."

"That sound byte was promised to someone." Silloway said. "A collaborator, who is working on a deadline and needs it as soon as possible."

Adam pondered Silloway's response. Salison often collaborated with other scientists. Sometimes, Adam didn't even know the collaborations were taking place, until the studies were near complete. Silloway put her hand on Adam's forearm and looked him in the eyes. There was still a hint of heartbreak in her, yet her touch was warm and intimate.

"Please, Adam. I know somewhere nearby we can switch vehicles. No one will know we went back to Boston. Adam recalled the desperate look in Salison's eyes as he asked Adam to deliver the sound byte to him, or to Silloway.

"I can't believe this.", he said to himself. He drove for a mile or so in silence, before speaking up. "Alright. Where are we going?"

"Just keep heading west for a while. We're going to Newton." Silloway replied.

Adam, frustrated, drove in silence, pondering not only Silloway but Salison's fate as well. In some time, he came to a crossroads and took a turn. The two of them were now heading south, towards Newton.

17

Detective David Brennan left the Boston morgue with fresh knowledge that Adam Riley and Silloway Sinsway were together and on the run. It wasn't long after leaving he arrived at Silloway's place in Brighton, Massachusetts. The young woman's apartment looked as though a hurricane passed through. Whoever broke in was looking for something that apparently could have been hidden just about anywhere. The assailant ripped apart the bindings of books, emptied pillows, and tore open electronics. Food containers were emptied and tubs of ice cream thawed, presumably, to make sure nothing was hidden within.

Brennan wondered what object was so sought after, the nature of the circumstances that brought Adam and Silloway together, and how these things played into Salison's murder, as he drove back to the police station. En route, Brennan got a call from dispatch, letting him know there was just a shooting near Harrishof Street, in Dorchester, with at least two casualties reported.

"Possible gang activity," was what dispatch had said. "Possible" was a laugh. Certain parts of the city were overrun with gang activity. During prohibition, the Boston gangs consisted of Irish rum-runners and money launderers. Today, they consisted of drug traffickers, thieves, and violent criminals. And nearly all of them had access to firearms. The police found dozens of guns hidden around Boston—stashed in common areas and shared by gang members—in an abandoned dresser, inside a rusty grill, or even under rocks. There were guns hidden in every neighborhood and plenty of thugs in the vicinity that knew just where to find them.

Brennan had personally started a task force to search for guns. Many had been found, but each month the shootings and the body counts continued to rise.

When Brennan pulled up to the crime scene, he saw that there was a crowd of people forming. He parked his car next to a weathered street lamp, just as it flickered on, illuminating a four-story apartment complex and a dirty street corner, both already bathed in flashes of red and blue. Brennan headed to the epicenter of the crime scene and noticed something out of the corner of his eye. He jogged up a narrow flight of concrete stairs and leaned over a rusted steel railing. Beneath a second-story window, there was a hole in the brick wall, looking to be about a half inch in diameter. Brennan took out a small bundle of cloth from the inside of his jacket pocket. Nestled within were various instruments. Brennan took out a long narrow pair of metal tweezers, using them to fish out a fairly thick, crumpled, metal projectile from the hole in the wall. He leaned back from over the railing and produced a small plastic bag from his jacket.

.44 special, Brennan thought, dropping the bullet in the bag. *This one's not going to be pretty.*

Nearly two hours later, Brennan pulled into the station parking lot. His stomach growled as he entered the police station. He was only back for a few minutes before a young officer named Carol Cooney approached and began speaking with an Irish accent.

"There's someone here to see you detective. He says he has information relevant to the Sinsway case." She motioned to a middle-aged man sitting behind a thick pane of glass separating the officer's pen from a civilian area.

"Is Middler here?" Brennan asked. Carol upturned her palms.

"If you see him, tell him I'm looking for him," Brennan said.

He checked his cell phone and motioned to a young officer that manned the barrier between the station and the waiting room. The officer pressed a button. With a buzz, a thick door popped ajar. Brennan walked through and introduced himself to the man that had been waiting for him, who identified himself as Dr. Jean Hebert, a geneticist that taught classes at Boston University and had a lab in Cambridge. The scientist had a thin beard and a small, strong frame.

"Walk with me," Brennan said to the doctor, heading towards the door.

"What do you know about the Sinsway case?" Brennan asked. Then, after noting the abruptness of his words, he added, "I don't have much time tonight."

"I can image," Hebert said. "I've worked with Salison for the past three years. Can I ask you what you know of the man's origins?" His eyelids fluttered as he spoke.

Brennan smiled as he pushed through a set of glass double doors, into the cool night beyond.

"Doctor, I'm the one that's supposed to be asking the questions."

"You may have heard he is Turkish," Hebert said. "I can promise you, the man is not Turkish. He exhibits a number of physical characteristics that are in stark contrast to anyone of Anatolian descent."

Brennan noted an odd nature about Hebert. When he spoke, his fingers rubbed together so that you heard the sound of his digits in motion beneath his words. It looked something like a nervous tick, but the man spoke with confidence.

"And why is this so important?" Brennan asked.

"At some point, you are going to want to know who Salison really was," Hebert replied. "His true lineage and place of birth."

Brennan picked up his pace as he grabbed some crumpled cash from his pocket, while approaching a food truck that was often parked at the corner, outside of the police station.

"You want anything?" Brennan asked. "This place has great gyros."

The geneticist picked up his pace and did not divert his focus, continuing:

"I've been told that Salison may have died as a consequence of a massive seizure. If I could sequence his DNA, I could ascertain if there were any genetic factors that could have contributed to his epileptic episodes. I could also tell you his real genetic background."

"Can you prove Dr. Sinsway is not who he said he was?" Brennan asked.

"Not without a small sample of his DNA," Hebert answered. "The sequencing of a genome and the deciphering of the genetic code, is no trifle of a thing. I'm offering my services."

Brennan grabbed a bottled water from the truck's cooler and cracked it open, downing nearly the entire thing.

"Doctor," Brennan said. "I have to say, I'm quite curious as to why you're so curious. About Sinsway, that is."

Hebert did not sound bashful as he answered, "Detective, there was something very different about Salison Sinsway. The man was a true genius, having mastered at least a dozen languages and making significant contributions in the fields of physics, biology, and acoustics. Are there genes for intelligence? For our capacity for language? For creativity? Looking into Salison's genome may help answer these questions. I'm also familiar with nearly every physical trait, and variation of that trait, that has been observed in our species. Never," Hebert said, with emphasis, "Never, have I seen anyone with eyes as violet as Sinsway's. And I want to understand the genetics responsible for such a trait."

"And this is your last chance to get a sample of his DNA." Brennan finished.

"I think we can help each other." Hebert said, nodding his head rhythmically. "Here is my cell phone number."

With a smile, Hebert handed Brennan a torn out page from a small notepad. Brennan pocketed the piece of paper, just as the vendor, a large Greek man, handed him a paper bag smelling of french fries and cooked lamb. Brennan thanked the vendor and began walking back to the station. "Thank you, doctor. I'll keep it in mind." He said, handing Hebert his card. "If you come up with hard evidence proving Dr. Sinsway's past is a façade, I'd be curious to see it."

With that, Brennan jogged back up to the station.

Hebert zipped up his hoodie and walked west towards Jamaica Plain. He wondered if Brennan would take the bait. The truth was, Hebert already had proof that Salison was not who he said he was, but he still wanted a sample of Salison's DNA. He needed it. Hebert did not tell the detective what he knew about the Sinsways, because he obtained his information in an unlawful fashion.

What he learned about the pair had been mind-blowing though. And it confirmed his suspicions—that the Sinsways were unique in the world, and that there was something truly mysterious hiding behind their violet eyes.

18

Doctor Jean Hebert spent a good portion of his life gliding on the ice with the Arctic wind in his face and his shadow sliding in the moonlight. When he moved to San Francisco, to study genetics, he began to miss the pickup games, the fights, and the physical exertion. To release his excess energy, he picked up surfing and spent long days at the lab.

The head of his lab was Juliet Magnusson, a woman who had contributed greatly to the understanding of the genetics of eye color. It was believed that at least sixteen genes could influence eye color, turning them blue, brown, gray, green, hazel, amber and, in rare cases, red or violet.

Every pair of violet eyes that Hebert had seen though, were in patients suffering from albinism, a condition resulting from the lack of the pigment melanin. The condition caused the skin of those affected to be ashen white and caused their eyes to be red, and in extremely rare cases, violet.

But Salison's and Silloway's eyes were different; neither of them were albinos and the intensity and brilliance of the color in their eyes was like nothing Hebert had ever seen.

More than their eyes though, Salison had a tall, strong, sinewy frame and skin that glowed bronze. And he showed youth in his years; for although it was believed the man was fifty, he looked at least fifteen years younger. He also had an odd flowing accent that no one could place.

Hebert needed to understand Salison's odd nature and he knew the answers were in the man's genome. On more than one occasion, Hebert asked Salison if he could get a sample of his DNA; but Salison merely laughed at the request, and Silloway, when asked, had politely declined as well.

To satisfy his curiosity, Hebert came up with a plan to steal a sample of Salison's DNA—by collecting saliva from a discarded coffee cup, plucking a strand of the man's hair, or stealing a discarded tissue during cold season. The problem was, just as Hebert hatched the plan to steal Salison's DNA, Salison disappeared. Hebert had only seen the physicist a handful of times in the past three years. And in the past six months, Hebert had not seen Salison at all. It was tough to connect with him because his lab was on the other side of campus. Not only that; Salison rarely came to the university.

With Salison nowhere to be found, Hebert turned his attention to the next best thing—the man's daughter, Silloway.

Hebert frequently jogged to Boston College and once he found out that Silloway worked at Franklin Park Zoo, he changed his running route to take him right past Franklin Park.

Three weeks prior, Hebert had seen Silloway, hopping out of her MINI Cooper on a side street, very near the zoo. He made a mental note of this and henceforth scanned for the woman's car as he ran through the area.

Two weeks ago, Hebert was jogging by the zoo and again saw Silloway's MINI with the front windows cracked open. Hebert had approached the vehicle and pretended to catch his breath. After making sure that no one was in the vicinity, he quickly reached into the window and placed a miniscule piece of fabric on her headrest. It was the same color of the seat and barely visible.

The piece of fabric that Hebert adhered to Silloway's seat had an outer surface like Velcro—it would trap a few of the woman's hairs and when she exited the vehicle, it would pluck them from her head. The square of fabric was tiny and it was probable that the woman would not even register her hair being removed. By pulling her hair out, Hebert greatly increased the chances that the shaft of the hair would be connected to the hair root. The hair root was what Hebert was after. It would contain Silloway's nuclear DNA, a great portion of which would have been inherited from her father, Salison Sinsway.

Two days after Hebert had placed the small piece of fabric on Silloway's seat, he spotted the woman's MINI again. He cautiously approached the vehicle and to his delight saw there were three strands of jet-black hair caught in the trap. With a grin, the geneticist removed the miniscule square of fabric and placed the hairs in a small plastic bag.

Over the course of the next week, Hebert's lab extracted the nuclear and mitochondrial DNA from the hairs and then sequenced the DNA that was obtained. At first, Hebert was not quite sure he could believe what he had found; but he ran the sequencing multiple times. The placement of genes on chromosomes—the chromosome structure—and variants of many genes were as Hebert had never seen before; there were uncharacterized mutations in a vast number of genetic sequences.

Many mutated genes were involved with neurological conditions such as dyslexia, schizophrenia, and autism. Others were involved with cellular respiration, cell metabolism, pigmentation, aging, and—as Hebert had suspected—eye color. There were also changes in noncoding regions of DNA as well, in regulatory regions that functioned to enhance or silence the activity of other genes.

Hebert could not make any sense of it.

And Hebert had a good idea who Silloway had inherited her abnormal DNA from. Humans have two copies of each gene and in Silloway's case, only one copy was abnormal. By analyzing the mitochondrial DNA, which is strictly maternal, Hebert determined that Silloway's mother's DNA was more or less 'normal' and that the woman was of South American/Amazonian descent. Interestingly, Silloway's mother's DNA was of an extremely rare haplotype.

Hebert reasoned that Silloway's mother may have been from a remote, genetically isolated 'lost' tribe, so to speak (there were, at the time, estimated to be at least ninety on the planet, which had no contact with the outside world). It was enigmatic, but the mother's DNA lacked any mutations such as those found in Silloway's nuclear DNA. Hebert therefore reasoned Silloway received her 'normal' copy of each gene from her mother. Which meant that Salison's DNA must have been out of this world. For despite her mother's DNA, Silloway, genetically speaking, was like no other person on the planet.

To put things in perspective, humans diverged from Neanderthals around 500,000 years ago, and there is about a 99.7 percent sequence homology between the genomes of humans and Neanderthals. Incredibly, there was only a 99.4 percent homology between Silloway's genome and the rest of the population's. This meant that technically, the woman was not quite human.

Hebert expected the genetics governing eye color in the Sinsways to be unique, but had not expected to find something as groundbreaking as this. Hebert told no one about Silloway's DNA; and he was not going to, until he knew more about how such a thing could have come to pass. And as for Hebert's goal of determining Salison's origins, that was turning out to be much harder than anticipated. Silloway had genetic markers in her genome that indicated Amazonian ancestry, most likely passed on by her mother; but Silloway's DNA also contained markers from many other genetically diverse populations as well. Not only did Silloway's DNA contain distinct Asian, European, and African markers, there were also markers that indicated Navajo, Inuit, Polynesian, and even Tibetan ancestry as well, just to name a few.

Every rationale Hebert had come with up to explain Silloway's incredible genotype had been more implausible than the last. Hebert briefly entertained the idea that Salison could be the product of a selective breeding or eugenics program; but if that were the case, it would have to have been going on for at least tens of millennia, for there to be as much genetic variation as Hebert was seeing.

Hebert wondered if Salison could have been exposed to a powerful mutagen, but he ruled that out because there was no way Salison could accumulate so many random changes in his DNA without developing a hundred different types of cancers. The changes to Salison's DNA must have been organized in some way.

Another theory that Hebert had, was that Salison was descended from an ancient tribe, a group of people that had somehow managed to incorporate DNA from many diverse populations into their genome; then lived in isolation for thousands of years, all the while undergoing an unprecedented amount of genetic mutations.

But Hebert could not think of anything that could come close to fully explaining Silloway's fantastic genotype, it did not make any sense.

Hebert knew that Salison's genome was a major piece of the puzzle. With it, he would be closer to understanding the mystery that was Salison Sinsway. Hebert walked home alone, reflecting on the father-daughter pair. He had never seen anything like them before. Events stemming from his next phone call though, would change that.

Hebert walked past Mission High, where the football team was having late-night drills. The sound of pads colliding and teenage voices filled the air as the boys scrimmaged beneath the stadium lights. A soft buzz emanated from Hebert's slacks. The geneticist grabbed his phone.

"Hello,"

"Hello, Jean?" a woman's voice asked. "It's Karen. Karen Klein."

"Well hello, Karen. It's been awhile."

"Yes, it certainly has." Karen said. "I'm at Cornell now, working in the archaeology department. I've been following your academic endeavors since we went to school together and I think you could really help us better understand a friend of mine, someone who's been giving our team quite a few headaches."

"Oh, ya?" Hebert asked. "And who might this friend of yours be?"

"We call him Saatçi," Karen said. "And he's been frozen in snow and ice for the past 500 years."

19

Dr. Jonas Moorea closed the door of his silver Audi and inhaled deeply, turning his gaze upward. Memories of his days and deeds seemed to melt away as his eyes took in the sky. The knots in Moorea's chest slowly dissipated and his breaths began swimming in softer and slower waves. A calm began to find the man as he stood in the darkness.

Jonas Moorea knew this moment was different. The realization rang in him as he caught sight of the rising moon. The distant satellite caused a pool of emotion to stir in Moorea, for he now—more than ever—felt connected to the world, or perhaps to the space beyond.

The feeling was new to Moorea. Or perhaps it was just long forgotten. But in this moment, the air felt crisper; the night seemed to breathe around him as if it too were conscious. And although the earth was bathed in darkness, Moorea felt as if he were intimately sensing more of his surroundings. He felt *deeper* and as if this moment were somehow more *real* than any others.

It was an incredible feeling and Moorea knew it was yet another effect of Salison's project.

For Jonas's help, Salison promised power in return. Power that only a select few in human history have ever come to possess. In various ways, Salison had delivered.

Moorea knew it was all backwards, working so hard to achieve this heightened state of mind and being, only to suppress the feeling in lieu of seemingly more pressing issues at hand. His mind wrestled with the past as well as the future, as he tried to find his place in the present.

Moorea looked around the small back lot where he parked.

AN EVOLUTION OF MINDS

Aside from his Audi, there was a shiny black Cadillac Escalade and a crème white Buick in the lot, indicators he was last to arrive.

The tranquil feeling that found Moorea slowly dissipated as he walked towards the building. He tried to remember who he was in the car as he spoke to his new colleagues on the phone. That was who he needed to be now.

Moorea was soon underground, within the facility, walking into what looked to be a typical chemistry lab. The black surfaces of the lab benches gleamed in the overhead lights. The room was open and home to a plethora of scientific equipment—glassware shimmered about.

Moorea approached a doorway at the far end of the lab. He pressed his hand on a small stainless steel button next to the door and it silently slid open, revealing a space beyond. The room Moorea walked into was the same width as his lab, yet it was narrower. The far wall was a few yards away and dominated by a large glass window that spanned nearly the whole length of the room. Moorea caught sight of his reflection in the glass as his eyes focused on the space beyond: an operating room.

Dr. Moorea heard his heart beating in his chest as he thought on his intentions. The sound of movement caused him to avert his attention. To his left, past lab computers, steel cabinets, and row of refrigerators, was an older Indian man. It was a neurosurgeon named Sangupta Rami, a man who was working with both Salison and Moorea on the enlightenment project. This was the night of Rami's murder and the last night the neurosurgeon would ever see the blood-red sliver of a moon, shining in the sky above. Rami was dressed in slacks and a white medical jacket, sitting on a lab stool. The man looked almost as a disapproving father would as he shot Moorea a cold look from beneath his silver spectacles. Moorea nodded solemnly to the man, his attention averted only a moment before his eyes fell back to the large window that dominated the far wall—the operating room was well-lit by a series of lamps which hung from the ceiling. On the center table lie a large, muscular man looking lifeless, wearing nothing but a towel around his waist. Although the man's chest appeared to be immobile, there was an oxygen mask securely covering his mouth. Wires ran from the man's fingers to a monitor that sat on a steel table next to his bedside. The monitor screen displayed a traveling linear line.

Moorea knew that there were answers to be found within the man before him. Not only in his mind, but in the tissues themselves. The doctor approached a group of silver sinks, situated directly in front of the large window. He kept his eyes trained on the man behind the glass as he washed his hands.

Yes, Moorea thought, as the warm water flowed over his hands.

It is time for Salison Sinsway to give up some of his secrets.

20

Adam did not like the way Silloway's 'friend' looked at her, as the man agreed to let Silloway borrow his Camry. Yet Adam was grateful for the camouflage as he drove back into the city. Night had fallen and Adam was fairly sure he could sneak into his lab unnoticed, in order to grab his laptop, which had the sound byte Salison and Silloway wanted on it. Adam parked a few blocks away from the hospital, in a nearby neighborhood.

"They always return to the scene of the crime." Adam said, shaking his head as he jumped out of his Jeep. There was a tint of humor in his voice. He shut the door without another word and Silloway stayed put. Adam took off in a light jog towards Boston Memorial. He decided not to pass through the main entrance that was typically used by researchers. The security guards there all knew him, as did just about anyone else that would be coming or going. He did not want to risk being seen, just in case his picture had been released in conjunction with Salison's assault and his evasion of the local police.

There was another entrance though, one that was used by the general public and was connected directly to the main hospital. There was much more traffic here, with people coming and going constantly—and security was lax.

Outside the entrance, Adam waited until a woman and her elderly mother were making their way inside. The security guard on duty—a Middle Eastern man—did not raise his head from his cell phone as Adam walked into the hospital, taking what was apparently a needless precaution—partially shielding his body from the security guard, behind the couple entering the hospital in front of him.

Past the guard, Adam quickly changed his trajectory and picked up his pace, heading for the elevators that would take him up to his lab. To

Adam's satisfaction, the elevator he entered was empty and he did not see anyone in the corridors that led to his lab.

Once inside, Adam quickly grabbed his laptop, sent a few e-mails, and, without being noticed, was back with Silloway.

"I got it," he said. "And I sent the file."

Adam was referring to sending his artificial sound train, in the form of a .wav file, to an e-mail address that Silloway had given him and to Salison's university e-mail address as well.

"Thanks, Adam." Silloway said, with a smile.

"So where are we going?" Adam asked, setting his laptop on the backseat of the Camry.

"We're going to Green Harbor." Silloway said.

"We're going to your father's place?" Adam asked.

Silloway hesitated.

"Well…sort of…"

There was nothing else from the woman; and although Adam was curious about their destination, he did not press her. He figured he would find out in due time. Before too long, Adam saw the intersection of country road 17. He took a left turn and the two of them headed south, towards Green Harbor and Salison's cabin.

In a little over an hour and a half, Adam and Silloway were walking through the woods, navigating only by the shards of starlight that managed to cut through the trees above. Twigs crackled underfoot as the two pressed on through the night.

Adam decided to park on the neighboring property, off-road, away from Salison's driveway and cabin. He had driven through the brush until he was satisfied that his vehicle would not be sighted by anyone out under the stars. Now, he and Silloway trudged through a dense forest, in the direction of the small lake behind Salison's cabin. Silloway had told him that her father had a secure room in the middle of his property, near the lake; and it was there that they were heading.

After a few minutes of walking, the forest began to thin out.

Adam saw the placid surface of a lake in the distance. The water swayed rhythmically in the darkness, with starlight dancing about the surface. Tall grassy reeds and brush covered the muddy ground, separating Adam and Silloway from the water. Adam figured that Salison's cabin, as well as his small dock and fishing shed, were on the other side of the lake. On a couple of occasions, he had joined both

Silloway and Salison there, along with other lab members, to have barbeques, beer, and fish on the lake.

For about a hundred yards, Adam and Silloway walked through the brush, with the hum of insects and croaks of frogs accompanying their gait.

"There." Adam said.

It took Silloway a few moments to see what Adam was pointing at; but then she saw it—the silhouette of her father's old fishing shed.

Silloway and Adam picked up their pace, as they jogged around the lake, in the direction of the shed. Adam saw the wooden dock that jutted out from the earth, ten or twenty yards away from the shed.

Adam and Silloway slowed, a short distance away from the starlit wooden structure.

"This is where it is, huh? I would have never thought." Adam said.

Silloway did not look over as they passed in front of the wooden dock.

"I don't think many people would," she answered. "That's why it's here."

Silloway pushed open the wooden door of the old fishing shed and peered inside. A creak could be heard as the door approached a ninety degree angle. Adam thought Salison would be insane to hide anything valuable in the small wooden shed behind his house—a rickety old shack without even a lock on the door. Adam did not even think there was electricity, until he remembered that there was a refrigerator in here for beer.

Adam followed Silloway into the shed. She approached the far end of the structure, moving deeper into the darkness. The silhouette of her body turned to face a shelf in the middle of the room that divided it in half. The woman was midway between him and the far wall of the wooden shed. Adam heard rusty metal brushing along the coarse surface of the shelf, as Silloway moved in the darkness. Adam tried to recollect what was there. He could not remember. Although the color red shot into his mind. A flurry of firing neurons lit the way unto his recollection. It was an old steel tackle box, the red paint so defeated, it had nearly all but vanished from the metal.

Silloway grabbed the box and held it gently in her palms, before bending down and setting it on the rough wooden floor. Then she rose and appeared to be examining the space where the old tackle box had been.

"Silloway?" Adam asked quizzically. "Are we going fishing?"

The young woman remained silent. Then, a small light appeared, beneath her hand. Adam approached. He saw Silloway's bronze skin bathed in the weak electric-blue hue of a small illuminated number pad. She had flipped up a wooden panel embedded in the shelf's surface, to uncover a small secret space. Silloway pressed a series of soft buttons nestled within the panel.

A hidden number pad? In a run-down shed of all places?

Adam smiled. He had an idea where this was heading.

"We have to move." Silloway said as she passed him and walked towards the door.

Adam followed Silloway to the entrance of the shed and turned to face the darkness they left behind. A moment passed.

"Sillow—" Adam started, sounding inquisitive.

He did not get the woman's name past his lips before he heard a noise from the back of the shed. He watched as a neon blue light appeared in the darkness. The light started out as a long straight thin line, running parallel to the far wall of the shed, in between the middle shelf and the one against the wall to his right. The line of blue light began to extend along the floor. The width stayed the same, as the depth widened while approaching Adam and Silloway. It took Adam a moment to realize what he was seeing—the floor was sliding open to reveal a space below, a space that was lit so softly that anyone outside could have easily missed it. The floor opened just wide enough to reveal a row of narrow stairs, leading downward.

Silloway looked back at Adam with a small smile on her face, then turned and briskly made her way down the stairs, beneath the shed. She left Adam in the blue darkness.

"Well then." he whispered, as he went on to follow her.

21

Adam and Silloway walked stealthily down into Salison's hideaway. As Adam descended into the earth, he noticed the floor was made of a strong material that did not sound like metal or wood as his feet padded on it. The ceiling was lit by two strands of blue optic fiber, encased in what appeared to be clear plastic. A glow of midnight blue barely lit the back of Silloway's shoulders as she walked down in front of Adam. There were two long flights of stairs to be followed, until the steps leveled out and became the floor of a narrow passage.

The hallway that Adam found himself in was quite long. About thirty yards away was a door at the end of the passage. Silloway and Adam traversed the area. Silloway approached the door, and it began to slide open as if it somehow knew she was coming, anticipating her movement. Adam followed Silloway into her father's secret bunker, surprised at how thick the door was as it retracted into the wall. The room was quite large. There was a pair of red leather sofas and wooden floors stretching back thirty-plus yards away.

Along the wall, to the right, there were ornate, crimson, hanging tapestries with elaborate flower designs on them. They looked aged, and quite beautiful. Up ahead, the space turned to the left, giving the room an L-shaped appearance.

Silloway approached an elegant wooden desk that sat at the perpendicular of the room. The desk looked to be covered with various papers and journals. Silloway gave the desk a quick once-over, before she moved out of sight, into the opposite leg of the room.

It was almost as if she were searching for something.

"Silloway?" Adam asked.

He glanced around. There were stone Buddhist statues on the floor and various species of bonsai trees, sitting on small terraces that jutted out from the wall. The room had a spiritual feel to it. There was no answer from Silloway but once Adam was at the perpendicular of the room, he saw her kneeling down, leaning forward, peering into what looked to be a small refrigerator. Adam walked closer to Silloway and noticed a peculiar structure to his right. There was a smooth wooden arch built into the wall. It was ornate and beautifully crafted, taller than a doorway and a few feet wider. The arch did not lead to any open space though; beneath it was a panel of what appeared to be thick glass. An odd feeling rose in Adam. He felt almost as if he needed to catch his breath, staring at the oddity before him. He placed his hand against the smooth surface of the murky glass; it was cold to the touch.

Adam tried to peer through it, but only a cloudy opaque darkness could be seen, as well as a few shards of light dancing in the glass. The material did not feel entirely like glass though, there was some strange nature to it that Adam could not quite place. Movement caused Adam's focus to shift. It was Silloway, rising to her feet. The small fridge she was peering into was now closed. Her eyes found Adam's as she approached him. She was already shaking her head. Adam looked like he was about to inquire about the structure.

Silloway spoke first.

"All I know of that," she began, "is that my father calls it 'The Library.'"

Silloway put her hand up against the glass, perhaps pondering its nature as well. She looked tired.

"Adam," the woman said. "I'm going to go outside for a while. Tomorrow we can get a prepaid phone and I can call and see what happened to my father."

When she spoke of her father, her tone indicated she was already convinced of his fate.

Adam stayed silent. He did not want her going anywhere alone. He did not want to lose track of her. But he too, liked to be alone when his mind was tormented. It helped him work things out.

"You can pull out the sofa," Silloway said. "And there are blankets in the closet."

"I'll start going over some of your father's papers," Adam said. "Maybe they can shed some light on what this is all about."

As he said this, he motioned to the ornate wooden desk that was covered in articles and journals.

"Sounds great," Silloway said. "I shouldn't be too long."

With that, she turned to leave, moving toward the entryway door. Adam walked along with her. The woman paused for a moment.

"Thank you for coming to get me today.", she said.

"No problem." Adam replied, with a smile.

Silloway turned and exited through the sliding door.

Adam watched her walk away, wishing he had thought of something better to say.

"A secret room." he spoke to himself, almost in disbelief. He sat down on one of the crimson leather couches, resting his elbows on his knees. Too many questions were running through his mind. And Adam was disappointed; he managed to learn nearly nothing from Silloway about his present situation. The woman offered him only a few vague lines, which Adam interpreted as being either wisdom or a great skill at dodging questions.

He knew the woman was clearly dealing with her own issues though and he had not yet felt as if Silloway's disposition had been receptive enough for him to question her. Adam knew that eventually he was going to have to press her for answers as to what was going on though. Even if Silloway only knew little about what was happening, she surely knew more than him.

Adam figured he would work on sorting this all out in the morning. He rose to his feet and approached Salison's desk, lightly massaging his still swollen eye. The desk was skillfully crafted, with elegant curves and spiral designs worked seamlessly into its strong form. It looked smooth to the touch, shining in the light. There were numerous journals and articles covering the tabletop. Close to Adam, there were stacks of scientific research articles, while across the desk, loose stacks—of what appeared to be mosaics of packets and individual pages—slanted slightly to and fro as they rose.

Adam grabbed a journal near him and thumbed through it. Reading the abstract, he could tell that it was a research paper dealing with the properties of neurons, specifically the speed at which signals can travel through the nervous system. There were equations scribbled across diagrams depicting cables and circuits. The diagrams were analogous to axons, the transmitting highways of nerves.

Adam knew that Salison was interested in many things—Physics, Acoustics, Cell Biology, and Neuroscience—as was apparent by not only the documents on the desk, but Salison's association with Dr. Moorea, who was himself a prominent neuroscientist.

Adam set the article down. He saw a few more near him, one dealing with the properties of stem cells and another having to do with an experimental way to combat uncontrolled cellular division and growth. Adam was curious about the contents on the desk, but he felt restless.

He looked over the desk briefly and then caught sight of the knee-high ivory refrigerator that Silloway had been looking in earlier. He saw fridges like this in labs—used for storing cell cultures, tissues, or various solutions, among other things. This model had separate compartments which could be set at different temperatures, depending on what materials were stored.

He walked over to the unit and noticed that there was a keypad smoothly built into its outer surface. Adam tried to open the door. The fridge was locked. He thought it odd Salison had a locked lab fridge in this room. But then again *it was a secret room, beneath a shack*. He supposed there was no normal. Walking back to Salison's desk, Adam passed a fairly large closet and peeked inside. There were shelves, donning backpacks, blankets, bottled water, and various other items.

Adam was, of course, curious about this place, this room and the things in it. But he was exhausted and he knew that what he really needed was rest. It had been a long day and he was ready for it to be over. He grabbed a blanket and a bottled water from the closet and walked to the entranceway. He located a small plastic knob which he assumed would adjust the lights; and sure enough, as he turned the knob counter-clockwise, the lighting dimmed. Soon, the room was bathed in an even dimmer yellow glow. Adam pulled out the futon into its open position and rolled his body onto it, lying on his back. The rafters above were elegantly crafted, smooth, and evenly spaced. It was an aesthetic element that worked to calm Adam's mind. The many questions which were swimming in him slowly dissipated as his body began to relax.

There were nights when Adam's dreams, despite their abstract nature, would do well to calm his spirit. He hoped that tonight one would find him, for he had a growing feeling that the coming days would somehow change his life.

Adam was no clairvoyant, but if he had any idea of what this visceral feeling in him truly meant, he would not have been able to fall asleep so easily.

AN EVOLUTION OF MINDS

***

Outside, the air was chilly and the sky was clear. Starlight cut through the heavens, to weakly illuminate a small wooden pier. Silloway delicately used her toes to pull off her shoes and socks, leaving them lying at the base of the dock as she walked barefoot on the coarse wooden planks, glancing the rhythmic sway of the water beneath her. On reaching the end, she sat down, resting the palms of her hands on the rough surface of the aged wood. Her legs dangled off the side of the dock as she reclined on the weathered planks. Lying on her back, she closed her eyes and let her mind drift. Her thoughts fell fast, to a different time, a time when the air was warmer and she felt more at home.

Silloway awoke with a start. Not quite sure if she had dozed off—if she had been remembering, or if she had been dreaming. Her first view was of a vast panorama of stars. Within her now, a story resonated. Her father told it to her years ago, saying he first heard the story himself, in another world.

With her eyes on the sky, Silloway pondered her path, recounting her father's tale of balance.

22

Day 2

An electric hum rose steadily from behind a pair of large stainless steel doors, indicating an approaching vessel. The sound gradually increased in its frequency before it ceased and a pair of large elevator doors slowly slid open. A once quiet hallway was filled with laughter, along with the sound of uncoordinated footsteps on a burgundy carpet. Three attractive young women exited an elevator on the arm of a well-dressed, well-groomed, very intoxicated man.

Ataxic strides brought the group to a closed oak door donning the number 6452. The quad stood in place while the young man shuffled through his slacks, locating a magnetic keycard, which he swiped through a silver lock nestled on the door. With a click, the door was opened. The man entered first, turning his head as he did, glancing his company. The women were dressed sparingly, with perspiration shining on their bare skin, as the lights went from off, to a dim shade of gold.

There was a distinct aroma of tequila about the group, which played with the man's senses, as he stumbled his way past a large mounted flat screen television and a black leather half-moon sofa, moving towards the balcony. He seemed to forget about the young women who accompanied him this evening, who approached the large sofa dominating the spacious living room. The man passed a small bar which separated the kitchen from the rest of the penthouse and grabbed a bottle off of it. He heard the chime of another, nearly empty, liquor bottle being set on his opaque marble table. A voice behind him inquired on the location of a restroom. He paid it no mind as he opened a thick glass door separating him from the black night beyond. The young man inhaled deeply once he was subsumed by open air. He felt a small weight from his chest lift. From this great height, the vast New York City skyline reached into the distance. The man tried to gather himself; but the alcohol in his system was wreaking havoc on his mind. His synapses were uncoordinated and out of sync. He rested his arms on the stainless steel ledge as he closed his eyes and exhaled. His thoughts were lost in chaos as he tried to focus. A shiver emanated from his body as a brisk wind rose up. The man looked back into his suite. All he could see was the reflection of his tall body and his light skin, bathed in the dark of night.

Thomas Bishop took a step back and smiled. Rows of flawless teeth reflected in the glass. Bishop was often consumed by the grasp of pleasurable things; filled with joyous feelings which overcame the soft voices that nagged at him frequently—those notions in the back of his mind hinting there was a deeper plain to be reached than the one found with enough money and market. Thomas raised a glass bottle he was holding to his lips. The rush of liquor within his system felt like a flow of flames warming his viscera.

Why am I outside? he thought. *Why am I outside when the women are inside?*

The young man had forgotten why he came out to his balcony in the first place—perhaps to smoke—but as he checked his pockets, he found that he had nothing to smoke. He ran a hand through the soft curls that fell over his forehead and walked back inside. He stumbled to his love seat, passing a glistening black piano. Although Thomas did not know how to play the instrument, the shining keys and polished wood did well to accentuate the room's refined form.

Thomas was grinning as he brought his attention back to the three gorgeous women who had almost forgotten he was there.

"How's everyone doing?" he asked as he approached, maneuvering his way between the women, before falling onto the sofa. The two guests to his left inquired about turning on some music and obtaining more alcohol, as Thomas turned his attention to the blonde opposite him, who was sitting on the floor.

The woman batted her lively emerald eyes. Her silver hoop earrings glimmered in the faint light. She leaned over and used a credit card to cut up a fine white powder on a large mirror sitting on the black marble coffee table. Small pieces of the substance she was cutting, leapt up into the air, while the finer grains adhered to the surface of the plastic card, as she raised it up and down very fast, increasing the surface area of the powder.

Thomas Bishop could barely see straight, but he could see well enough the white lines on the table before him. He thought about how much he loved life, as he got down on both knees and approached the large mirror lying on his jet black table. This was the best that life had to offer; for some time, this was his heaven.

Some hours later, Thomas Bishop lay awake—and alone—in his king-size bed, with his satin sheets barely covering his naked body. He had almost managed to fall asleep about an hour ago, but his mind was still amped from the night before. One thing was for sure; he felt like death. He rolled onto his back, as he felt something begin to vibrate. It took him a moment to realize that it was his cell phone. He moved around in his bed, until he located his pants; he then tried each pocket, until his hand grasped his small silver phone. Thomas looked at the display screen.

Moorea, he thought.

He let the phone ring a few more times, all the while trying to sober up as much as he could. The young man felt a growing fatigue as of late, but he knew that a lifestyle such as his left little room for rest. He took a few deep breaths and tried to gather himself before accepting Moorea's call. Once he opened his phone, he began speaking immediately, sounding more annoyed than hung over.

"Did you figure this thing out or what?"

There was a calm breath from the other end of the line.

"We've got some problems," Moorea started, solemnly.

As Moorea explained the current situation, Thomas Bishop felt himself growing more and more upset. It was not long before he interrupted Moorea.

"Listen, you two promised me something. I have given you everything you asked for, and in return, you have begun to fulfill your part of the bargain."

He let his words sink in, listening to Moorea breathe on the other end of the line. He had a feeling the man was not used to being spoken to like this.

"We both know," Thomas continued, "that Salison is keeping something from us. I know that you are a scientist and I know this sort of work takes time. But for fuck's sake, if Salison could figure it out, why the hell can't you? Aren't you the damn neuroscientist? If you can't get the information from him, get it from his daughter. We know where she is. And didn't Salison say she was the key to all of this?"

"Salison did say something like that." Moorea replied, "but we had him filled with a cocktail of chemicals."

"And wasn't sodium pentothal one of them?" Bishop asked.

"Using truth serum is not some magical way to find answers. We both know Salison has a strong mind."

At this, Bishop stayed silent, thinking things over. Then he responded.

"I think we should keep going." he said.

"I agree."

Thomas thought he heard hesitation in Moorea's voice; but the man continued.

"I'll call you when everything is ready." Moorea said, with a finality to his voice.

Thomas Bishop left Moorea with no parting sentiment, ending the phone call with the press of a button. He slowly maneuvered his body over his sheets. He swung his legs over the side of his bed and sat up on his mattress. His left hand lightly massaged his right forearm as he pondered his predicament. He would continue on with Salison's metamorphosis project—Bishop had begun to taste the enigmatic thing that Salison promised him—a heightened state of mind and being. It had only come to Bishop in brief bouts though, unpredictable shards of moments—small pieces of what he knew could be a grand mural; a vast plain of consciousness yet to be attained. Bishop now, thanks to Salison, knew enlightenment was real.

Looking down on his naked body, Bishop could barely make out the thin radiating lines that ran like vast highways across his thighs and arms, running longitudinally down the length of his extremities, terminating at his fingertips and toes. He stared at the rays of pigment, and wondered what power truly was, and if he would ever truly possess it.

23

In Adam Riley's mind, a world was being born. Adam saw himself in an underground subway station, with glass ceilings and glass walls that resonated with a tremendous force, generated by a storm above. Through the translucent station, Adam saw tornadoes above, sweeping over the land outside. The twisters caught light from the setting sun, causing them to glow like fiery swirling sidewinders, cutting through the twilight. A melody echoed throughout the station, fighting through the howling wind. The notes of the melody trembled; Adam knew the song was an answer to a question that had been burning in him. The song sounded as if it were falling away—yet, at times, as if it were coming together, as if he could grasp the delicate rhythm.

Adam needed only a few more moments in this hallowed place, for he could almost make out the entirety of the song. Adam strained his focus, but he could not hear the entire sequence. The secrets that laid in wait within, began falling away from him as he slowly awoke.

Adam's eyes opened and a sense of disorder lingered in him as if his world were a broken pattern. He sighed, slightly wincing, as a dull pain radiated from his still swollen eye.

There were still visions in his mind, of unidentifiable forms and sounds bleeding together, of a grand design which he knew he had failed to grasp. Thoughts of his intangible pursuit vanished though, as he saw a woman as she slept. Silloway was only a few feet away, wrapped in indigo, curled up, facing away from him. Adam saw her body slowly rise and fall with each breath she drew in and expelled.

Adam drifted further from his dreams. He was now awake and there was much to do in this awakened place.

Adam quietly turned from Silloway, maneuvering himself from under his blanket to an upright position. Sitting with his legs over the side of the futon and his bare feet resting on the wooden floor. His heart sank as he recounted the events of the previous day.

Adam was worried for his friend and mentor, Salison Sinsway. There were many questions brewing in Adam regarding the previous day, but one thing was for certain.

Jonas Moorea was up to something sinister—the man kidnapped Silloway and assaulted Salison, and as a result, Adam may now be a murder suspect. Adam knew he had to clear his name. He figured Silloway could help him with that, but he was not going to take any chances. If he was wanted for murder—Adam hated the thought of Salison being dead—he was going to make damn sure that he understood the truth behind Salison's demise, before handing himself over to the police.

The evidence thus far, indicated Adam was with Salison only moments before a fit of—what turned out to be—lethal seizures; and also indicated that Adam's prints were all over the weapon that was used in the assault.

The fact that Moorea kidnapped Silloway did not mean that he was the one who assaulted Salison. Adam needed stronger evidence against Moorea, before letting himself be taken by the police. He was not going to let some court-appointed lawyer play dice with his life and his future.

So what was Jonas Moorea up to? And what was going on with Salison? Perhaps the two things were linked?

When Adam thought of Salison, he could not help but recollect the sensation he had as he approached Salison at the hospital and placed his hands on the resonating man's skin. It was like nothing Adam had ever felt before—and it reminded him of a story Salison once told him.

The story was about a group of ancient travelers who, in their time, were regarded as enlightened monks and great magicians. Through meditation, fasting and physical training, they came to possesses the ability to perform a number of mental tricks, such as one called *stopping time*—in which they would appear, to an outside observer, to move in and out of the visible spectrum, disappearing and reappearing at will.

A fan of Einstein's theory of relativity, which states that time is a relative phenomenon that can be uniquely experienced by different observers, Adam speculated that there was a bubble of space-time dilation that existed within and around the individuals in Salison's story (that was generated by their nervous system). And that within their reference of time and space, things were moving slower. Due to their training, the monks could move through their altered space-time in an extraordinary way, hiding in the void that exists between what our flickering consciousness can perceive.

Adam had not thought about it then; but now, he wondered what it would be like to be close to someone that generated such a bubble of dilated space-time around them. Perhaps, one would begin to experience the slowing of time as well and not only light would be distorted, but sounds as well…

Curiosity got the best of Adam as his eyes found Salison's desk; covered in documents and manuscripts. Perhaps hints pertaining to the nature of their situation and Salison's peculiar state, were on the wooden surface.

Adam rose and approached the desk. He saw a column of papers he failed to examine the night before. In the middle of the column, Adam noticed material that stood apart from the modern, ivory-colored papers that encompassed it. Adam fished the document out. It appeared to be an aged map, made of rough material. It felt like dried, aged, animal skin. Adam could tell the map depicted parts of the Middle East and Asia, Egypt and the Red Sea towards the west, extending eastward into Western China and Northern India. Accompanying the aged line running from west to east (that looked to originate in Israel), were scribbled passages, written in a language that Adam was not familiar with. The track of the line followed what Adam knew to be the northern regions of the Persian Gulf and the Arabian Sea, until it rose steadily into the northern most region of India, finally terminating near the Himalayas. Adam's fingers took in the peculiar feel of the object. He studied the map before setting it aside, examining another document from the pile that harbored the map. It was a drawing on aged parchment. This material was thinner and did not feel as old as the map. It was a drawing of what Adam believed to be some sort of flying device, with a biconvex body and sleek appendages flowing from the main part of the vehicle. Within the interior of the craft were schematic drawings, almost looking to be mechanical diagrams of what resembled engines and circuit boards. There was writing as well; a few lines of characters dispersed throughout the drawing. The writing was in a language foreign to Adam, perhaps Sanskrit.

He looked over the parchment fleetingly, then shuffled it to the side. Next, was another drawing, appearing to be more modern. It was a photocopy of a rough sketch. Portrayed was a flying pillar, which hung in the sky horizontally atop clouds of fire. The only writing on the page was a note at the bottom. Adam recognized the script as Salison's. It simply read: Exodus 13:21-22.

Adam was not sure what to make of the drawings. He looked through the remainder of the texts in the pile. There were passages from the Mahabharata and Ramayana, the book of Exodus and Ezekiel, the apocryphal Book of Giants, color copies of documents appearing to be Mayan and Aztec, and a couple pages of strung together syllables, which could have been Native American.

The night before, Adam viewed research articles, something he expected to see on Salison's desk. These items were culturally diverse—mysterious stories sown into humanity's most ancient works of literature. It was not lost on Adam that the religious texts contained detailed descriptions of ancient man's interaction with their gods, which often appeared as flying crafts the gods used to travel; like the chariot of fire bearing wheels within wheels seen by Ezekiel and the weapon-bearing flying vimanas depicted in India's oldest works. Adam was curious, but felt a tightness growing in his chest as well. It was too bad Salison may be gone. Adam could scarcely believe where he was or the events which had transpired. As he recollected the past day, the young man could not help but question his actions. Yet he felt as though he made the right choice to run. It was as if there was something he needed to do, an unknown task beckoning his subconscious.

Adam's eyes were drawn to a packet of paper on Salison's desk. The top page was covered with Salison's flowing script, penned in ink and looking as if it had been written some years ago.

Adam picked up the packet and examined it. After shuffling through it, Adam realized he was holding a plan—a plan to alter the human body and nervous system. Salison wrote out his plan with lengthy bullet points, which were, at times, accompanied by beautiful, flowing drawings of the human body, brain, and nerves.

Adam was not sure if this was a final plan or if Salison had just been brainstorming. There were numerous question marks within the text. Adam noticed a simple quad of words, written across the bottom of a page. It was a phrase: *Time is an Illusion.*

Adam was not only drawn in by the smooth curves and subtle beauty of the writing but the phrase itself, which caused a cascade of thoughts to bloom in him. Adam had heard the phrase before. And he knew what those words meant to the Salison. They meant that anything was possible.

Salison believed—as some physicists, biologists, and eclectics do—that time and space were merely illusions created by our mind, in hopes of making sense of the outside world. He also believed that he had identified many genes that, when mutated, could alter our perception of time and space. Some of these genes were connected with conditions such as schizophrenia, autism, dyslexia, depression, and bipolar disorder. For according to Salison, these conditions were not actually disorders, but the ingredients for a great leap in human cognitive evolution. He claimed that the evidence of this was found in the brilliance of the autistic savant, the sublime artistic talents in those with depression, and the heightened intelligence and depth of thought which is observed in many suffering from schizophrenia and attention deficient hyperactivity 'disorder'. He said dyslexics actually had a heightened ability to see patterns and it was this strengthened sense which gave rise to their difficulty reading a simple linear alphabet. He recognized that these conditions deceptively appeared as disorders in this era of evolution, but said that in time, mother nature would weed out the negative symptoms of each of these conditions while sowing together the enlightening symptoms, to create another caliber of human. Salison took it a step further. He said that if one were to have genetic mutations in these so-called disorder genes which regulate thought *and* mutations in genes which enhance overall health—such as one's strength, speed, agility, rhythm and endurance—this person would be born with the tools to experience the world a different way. He said that this hypothetical person would be able to see deeper into the space and time which encompassed them and they would be able to move differently through it.

Salison said there were a very select few in humanities vast realm that were born with this rare genetic potential and these men were the great eclectics and prophets whose names echo throughout thousands of years of world history. Salison believed there were many ingredients to enlightenment and if you understood the science behind the phenomenon, you could perhaps create such a feeling for yourself.

Adam and Salison frequently, most often between bouts of discussing experimental designs and data interpretation, would humorously debate wild scientific scenarios. Salison spoke of such things with a romantic chord in his voice, sounding different than he would during a physics lecture or lab meeting, but still with a steady conviction.

From across the room, Adam sensed movement and saw Silloway waking up.

Adam's mind raced as he watched her run a hand through her dark hair, sitting upright on the futon. She was wrapped in an indigo blanket, her shining eyes still waking, glancing in Adam's direction.

"Adam?" Her voice sounded tired as she inquired.

"Silloway," Adam said. "I think I know what your father may have been working on."

As soon as Adam's words reached Silloway, she let go of her weariness; she could have been peering off towards a distant horizon, as if there were an expanse of land and sea behind Adam. She stayed silent though as Adam continued.

"And if it's what I think, it would be something to kill for."

24

"Every great man wishes to become more."

Adam heard Salison speak the words. The man spoke of prophets and their powers. With a quixotic chord in his voice, Salison spoke of men who could manipulate matter and defy the laws of space and time. He told tales of Buddhists and saints alike, who were said to have the ability to bilocate, or appear in two places at once. He mentioned ancient ascetics, who were able to walk on liquid water, or glide across it as if it were a sheet of glass. Salison even postulated how Jesus Christ could interact with the biology of others and alter the chemistry of life itself.

The great physicist believed that if you were born with a magical genetic potential and then trained your body and mind for decades you could become what only gods of men have become.

Adam only heard Salison speak on things a handful of times, but the man's words always resonated with belief. There was wonder in the man's voice as well, as he sowed stories of this quest for a heightened state of mind and being. Beneath the surface, there was also an enigmatic element swimming in the man's spirit that Adam could never quite place. He knew now what it was.

He glanced down at Sinsway's elegant script and smiled. For it was lust. Lust for such a state of being. Salison wanted to *induce enlightenment*. It was not a matter of science fiction for him, it was a matter of becoming something else entirely: harnessing the powers of the prophets. He wanted to manipulate, multiply and transform matter, command nature, heal the sick and raise the dead. Of course that kind of power would be something to kill for. Adam recounted his own words and his smile faded.

"Adam?" Silloway asked, almost in an attempt to bring the young man's mind down to earth. "What do you think he was working on?"

The way she spoke the words made Adam unsure for a moment of his conclusion. His hesitation lasted only a second though as he recounted Salison's nature.

"You said before," Adam said, "that Moorea asked you what you knew about a certain project—a project that your father was working on. I think your father was trying to become a different caliber of man. I think he was trying to heighten his consciousness; to evolve his body and mind—so that he could interact with the fabric of space and time in a different way."

From the look in Silloway's eyes, Adam could tell the woman already knew.

"Silloway," Adam said. "What do you know of this?"

There where chords of frustration and wanting in his voice. He continued, "I mean what's going on here? Why did Moorea—"

Adam stopped short, still not wanting to say the words. After a few seconds of silence, Silloway spoke.

"Moorea believed my father was hiding something from him.", she said.

"So he was really trying to induce enlightenment?" Adam asked, with a smile on his face, despite himself. Silloway mused for a few moments.

"My father wanted to *become* something, Adam. He wanted to experience the world in a different way."

She spoke the words as if Adam knew this, and he did.

"I'm not sure how he wished to accomplish it, in terms of the science...there was always something in him though."

Her voice sounded as if she were falling into her past, or perhaps pondering something in her future.

"And Moorea?" Adam asked. "What does he want?"

"When Jonas questioned me, he made it sound as if he was not quite sure of what he was looking for. He told me it could be a list; a list of plants, animal parts and chemicals, that could alter human biology, with directions dealing with how to prepare and mix them in the right proportions. Moorea also asked if my father gave me any kind of data, such as a jump-drive or computer disk. He said it could be tissue or blood samples too. Jonas is looking for something, for anything—"

"So did your father succeed?" Adam asked. "Did he find the powers of the prophets?"

Silloway seemed hesitant. "Adam, I only saw him a handful of times in the past couple years."

Her eyes locked with Adam's for a moment, sensing he wanted more. "And I'm not sure as to what he became."

Adam could see that talk of her father was emotionally draining for Silloway. The truth of her words reflected in her eyes.

For a few breaths shared between them, the two tried to make sense of each other and the situation that subsumed them.

Silloway's voice broke the silence.

"Adam, we can't stay here." she said.

At this, Adam rose from his chair.

"I know." he said.

He, of course, wanted to hear more from Silloway about her father's science and examine the documents on Salison's desk, especially the plan he just found; but he knew the woman was right. The sun would soon be up and he did not want anyone following their tracks off road to discover their vehicle. They could be on the property of a recent murder victim, a place the authorities may soon want to visit. Moorea could also be coming to Salison's to search for whatever he was after.

"Where will we go?" Adam asked.

"Maine." Silloway said, with no elaboration, as she approached her father's closet, to gather provisions. In a few minutes, Adam and Silloway had filled a couple duffle bags with some cash and a selection of Salison's belongings. Silloway said she wanted to bring some of her father's writings, documents and collections, to a separate property that he owned, on the rocky coast of Maine, and that's where they were headed. Adam brought the bags over to the exit, as he did, Silloway disappeared into the perpendicular arm of the room. Adam was unaware of Silloway's actions, as she approached the secure lab fridge, and pressed a sequence of numbers into the small pad on the door. The door popped open and Silloway removed a cold metal cylinder from the fridge and placed it into her pack. There was a look of sadness in the woman's eyes as she wondered what her father was truly capable of, as she wondered what she, herself, were truly capable of.

Silloway placed the cylinder in her pack and approached the exit. When she saw Adam, his eyes were shining.

"Alright." he said, "Maine it is."

25

Detective David Brennan knew he had a full day ahead of himself, as he pulled up to the precinct. His body was tense as he rose from the seat of his vehicle. He tried to shake the feeling, and loosen up, as he walked to the entrance. There was a façade of brick and mortar to meet him and a thick glass double-door, donning the address: 575 Cutlass Avenue.

Before entering the building, Brennan took a few slow deep breaths, tasting the fresh morning air. The tension in his body began to dissipate. He was used to working thirteen or fourteen hour days and he did not mind. The pay was alright; but it was the mysteries in the moments he fought his way through, that kept him coming back.

The detective barely managed to get situated in his office, when there was a knock at his door. Brennan uttered a rough "Come in.", leaning back in his chair. His door opened and in walked Officer Middler. The young officer came in grinning; his steps were brisk and full of energy. He took the seat opposite Brennan.

"Can you believe that Sinsway's body was stolen from the morgue?" Middler started, as he let out a small laugh, in disbelief.

"Have you ever heard of anything like that before? And tranquilizing the coroner…"

Middler's voice trailed off as if he were waiting for Brennan to shed some light on the unique situation. When Middler realized he was not getting a response, he pressed on further.

"And Riley, throwing an officer through a window?"

Brennan nodded, seeming to recognize the oddity of the situation.

"Do you…" he began. "Do you have the doctor's phone records?"

The young officer decided not to continue his questioning and instead reached down to his lap and grabbed a few sheets of paper. The pages were light blue with names and numbers on them. He set them on the desk.

"Salison's phone records." Middler stated, "It seems Dr. Sinsway wasn't much for talking on the phone, although he seemed a pretty popular man to call. Over the past week, we have thirty incoming calls from a Thomas Bishop. The number is unlisted. We also have a couple calls from his daughter, Silloway. In the past three months, we only have six outgoing calls. Three days ago, he called Bologna, Italy, the residence of a man named Tonino Lutzo. Lutzo is a radio and magnet engineer that builds parts for, among other things, particle accelerators. Salison and Tonino talked for about a half hour.

Salison's also been calling the Italian particle physicist Fabiola Gionatti. She's a director at the European Organization of Nuclear Physics."

"So two people that he probably knew from CERN." Brennan said.

"I imagine." Middler replied. "I called both of them. I wasn't able to get through, so I left messages. Here's the kicker. Calls to Fabiola and Tonino account for only five of six of the calls. The sixth call was to Adam Riley's home phone two days ago at 8:16pm. There was no answer."

Brennan seemed to take the news in stride.

"Well, we know Salison and Adam Riley were colleagues and friends. I gathered that much at the hospital. And not only that, I was told that Salison was asking for Adam shortly after being admitted to the hospital. What about this Thomas Bishop?"

"Thomas Bishop, age twenty-five, has property all over the East Coast. When his father died, the kid was left with millions. Instead of pissing it away, he received degrees in marketing and economics from Harvard. Then, he started investing in stocks and real estate. Now, the kid's worth about a quarter of a billion."

As Officer Middler spoke, Brennan's hands ran over his keyboard. Brennan had a friend in the FBI and was allowed access to files that may or may not necessarily have been public domain or accessible through the police database. Brennan used the program to gather useful information on suspects or individuals that did not have much of a rap sheet. He was now using the program to look up this young man, Thomas Bishop. The first thing Brennan wanted to find out was just how long he and Salison had been in contact. A few keystrokes later, he found that Thomas and Salison had been exchanging phone calls for the better part of three years.

Brennan's fingers moved quickly across his keyboard as he conveyed his findings to Middler. Soon Brennan had a list of all of Thomas Bishop's acquisitions over the last five years. As Brennan scanned down the list, he found that it mostly consisted of nightclubs and other real estate properties which the young man would just turn around and sell. Then there was a place that caught Brennan's eye, New Life Industries. It did not sound like a nightclub or real estate to be flipped. Brennan clicked on a link next to the name and a website came up that shed light on the property. New Life was a state of the art fertility clinic, located a modest drive from Boston.

Brennan clicked back and looked at the date of acquisition. It was just over three years ago. It appeared as though once Thomas Bishop and Salison started talking, Bishop's focus left the realm of superficial pleasures and turned to the medical field. Bishop began buying stocks in numerous pharmaceutical companies and renovated the New Life facility with state of the art equipment.

Middler listened as Brennan narrated. It was not long before the young man chimed in.

"So where do we think Bishop's newfound love of the sciences came from?"

Brennan's hands slowed on the keyboard. He brought up a logo on his screen and angled the screen so Middler could see it.

"Look familiar?" Brennan asked.

Of course Middler recognized the image. It was the jet-black serpent depicted on the plastic card found on Salison's person.

"I checked yesterday." Brennan said. "This logo belongs to a fairly large security firm. The firm's clients are usually hospitals, blood banks, and various types of clinics."

Middler was already nodding. "New Life." he said.

"Yes." Brennan replied. "They're on the client list."

Brennan was already turning his monitor back towards himself. Brennan knew Boston Memorial used a different company to set up their security and was waiting to find a link between the logo and Salison. Now he had one. The security card was the only thing that Salison had on him at the time of his death. It was reason enough for Brennan to investigate New Life. On paper, Salison had no ties to New

Life, nor any other firm which used Sidewinder security systems. Brennan turned his eyes from the computer monitor to Middler.

"I want you to check out this fertility clinic. It's the only logical connection we have between Bishop, Salison, and the security card. Ask some questions. See what you can find out about the business. I want to know why this millionaire is involved with our murder victim. We will want to talk to Thomas Bishop, too. See if you can get ahold of him."

Middler nodded his head, in recognition.

"Did you ask Ning about the genetic stuff?" Brennan asked.

When Brennan first looked into Salison's history, he was amazed at how little was known about the man. It was believed Salison was born in Turkey, in the late 1950s. His original birth certificate had been destroyed in a fire at an orphanage in the small Turkish town of Silivri, where Salison grew up. It was unknown who Salison's biological parents were, yet his file indicated he attended a Turkish boarding school. Aside from that, there was no information on the man before the late 1980s, when, at the age of thirty, he graduated from MIT with degrees in Particle Physics, Astrophysics, and Optics. Curiously, there were no pictures of Salison before he began working at the Large Hadron Collider, in his early forties. The geneticist, Jean Hebert, piqued Brennan's interest in regards to Salison's origins, when he spoke of the man with such reverence. Brennan was not sure how knowing Salison's origins could possibly shed light on the nature of his demise; but he had, on numerous other occasions, gleaned invaluable information in the most unlikely of places.

Mostly out of curiosity, Brennan had asked Middler to inquire as to how the crime lab could go about determining Sinsway's genetic background.

"Ning said that her hands are full." Middler answered, "But she knows a couple of private firms that can sequence DNA and determine ancestry. They can do it pretty quickly and cheap, too. She's checking into how we can get clearance to send Salison's DNA over to a private firm. She may just go ahead and order the sequencing, once she figures it out."

"Sounds good." Brennan said. "I have the lab checking out Salison's laboratory. I'm going to head over to Salison's cabin in Green Harbor and see what I can find."

Brennan grabbed his track jacket, turning to Middler, he said, "Let me know what you find out at New Life and if you're able to get ahold of Bishop."

"Sure thing boss." Middler replied, as he fell into step beside the detective. Detective Brennan and Officer Middler walked down to the parking lot together. Brennan slipped into his Toyota Camry and Middler hopped into his Dodge Intrepid. As Brennan pulled out, his window lowered. Middler noticed and rolled down his window, too.

"You've got directions?" Brennan asked.

"I've got GPS on my phone. You should really join this century, Detective. It's easy. I can show you how it works."

"Sure." Brennan said. "Soon."

He put his car in drive and glanced down at his own notepad with the directions to Salison's place jotted down.

"Be careful," he said, before he drove off, leaving Middler to himself.

Middler drove with his smart phone nestled in his dash, while a woman's voice read out directions to New Life. It was going to be about an hour's drive to Worchester, Massachusetts. Middler turned on his radio and let his mind find an easy rhythm, as he pulled onto the freeway and drove westward.

26

Benjamin Grant, a tall, slender, twenty-six-year-old Minnesota native, worked for the Boston crime lab as a crime scene investigator. He enjoyed the work, although most of the crime scenes he analyzed were pretty cliché and the crimes unremarkable. The Sinsway case was different. Benjamin could not believe two morgue employees were assaulted and a body was actually stolen.

I guess there's a first time for everything, Ben thought, as he arrived at Boston College.

Detective Brennan came to Ben directly and asked him to go through Sinsway's laboratory at BU, in order to collect samples and try to figure out if the man was working on anything out of the ordinary. Perhaps it had something to do with Salison's death.

Ben learned that Dr. Sinsway rarely came to his lab, and if so, only at night. Interestingly, Salison actually had two separate labs. One was often very busy and full of researchers, working on—among other things—resonance protein purification, sequencing, and genetic engineering. Ben recently learned of another lab though, a lab that Salison opened just over two years ago. None of Salison's researchers, nor his students, knew the late doctor had another lab. The information reluctantly came from the head of the Biomedical Sciences Department.

Ben was not sure what he would find, as he jogged down two flights of stairs to the subbasement, to where Salison's second laboratory was. Ben unlocked the door to Sinsway's lab with a key he obtained from security, creaked open the door and flipped on the lights. Before doing anything else, Ben grabbed a bottle of meds from his pocket and cracked it open. He took a few pills and swallowed them with a swig from a bottled water. Ben felt as if he was coming down with a cold. It was not too bad though, nothing to keep him from work. Ben could see the lab was much simpler than he would have imagined. There was a large centrifuge to his left, looking almost like a washer with its ivory hue. There were bottles of solutions and powdered salts along shelves, buffers of varying concentrations, and an assortment of acids and bases. The lab benches were barren. Ben walked over to a lab fridge and opened it. Inside was an assortment of test tube racks and small bottles. There were also a few collections of frozen solutions, containing within—what appeared to be—small, multicolored, translucent, plastic tubes.

Ben knelt down to better see the contents of the fridge, examining the labels of marked materials. Some of the items he observed had histological importance: agents used for staining and examining cells or tissues under a microscope. There were also a few cylindrical Petri dishes, stacked one atop the another. They were unlabeled and did not seem to have any colonies growing on them, just a thin pink film, covering the bottom of the dish. There was not much else in the fridge.

Looks like a microbiologist's fridge, Ben thought. *Nothing out of the ordinary.*

He counted himself lucky the fridge was not filled even close to capacity. It was easy for him to collect anything of interest from the fridge and place it in the refrigerated sample container he brought with him. Any suspicious substances would be analyzed by the crime lab, in due time.

Ben securely packed up a few unlabeled items that he found in the first fridge, then walked across the room to a second, larger fridge. This one was also nearly bare. Inside, were a few cloning kits, containing various agents used for genetic experiments. Some were used to amplify DNA by means of importing it into a bacterial colony. There were also kits for extracting DNA from tissues and bacterial cells. Various vectors and restriction enzymes, materials used for genetic engineering, were in the fridge as well.

Ben had seen things like this before; it appeared as though Salison was a bit of a geneticist.

The young lab technician carefully documented all of the items in the fridge, collected a few of them, and added them to his sample container. Ben then examined an opaque-blue freezer. It came up to his waist and opened from the top, like a chest. Ben was not surprised to find that this container was nearly empty too. Along the side were dual compartments that appeared to house a few materials. There were small multicolored centrifuge tubes, each with a small amount of frozen material in them and quite a few sealed glass vials. The vials appeared empty and were labeled with various numbers preceded by the letter H. There were also small metallic objects that Ben could not identify. They looked like little hockey pucks. Each had a square-shaped inlay and a few curious button-like protrusions; but other than that, they were smooth to the touch. There was a stack of six. Ben put one in his sample bag. Next to the freezer was an oscillator, used for mixing solutions for extended periods of time. It was stained with precipitation, but there were no glass flasks in it. There were eight polymerase chain reaction machines, used for amplifying segments of DNA; and there were also an assortment of electrophoresis apparatuses, laying partly assembled on the overhead shelf.

Ben walked through a door that led to a separate part of the lab and was surprised to see what confronted him. There were cages of live mice on waist-high lab benches. The cages were not made of wire or metal but a clear strong material, looking to be plastic or perhaps even glass. Ben walked closer to the cages. Small white rodents scurried around within the cages as Ben ran his hand along the material. The cages were indeed made of glass. The glass cages were like none Ben had ever seen. Each of them had holes bored in them, in a circular pattern. Near the openings were glass plates which functioned to shut the venting holes, presumably, to prevent air in the cages from mixing with air in rest of the room. There was something else strange about the confines. Each of the cages had speakers mounted in the top right corner of the cage with a plug-in cord for audio on the outer surface. Ben scanned up and down the rows of cages. There seemed to be about twelve in all, taking up the whole area of a large lab bench.

Ben took in the rest of the room. There were a couple of computers, with cords running every which way; and a lab hood that could be used to work with animals in isolation, functioning to separate the animals' air flow from the rest of the room.

On the table with the computers was a speckled lab notebook. Ben grinned walking over to it. There was something next to the notebook which drew his attention as well, a cell phone. It was a cheap prepaid phone. Ben knew this was a good find. He delicately placed the cellular into an evidence bag and put it into one of his packs. He grabbed the lab notebook and scanned a few pages, hoping it was Sinsway's—a record of his experiments and results.

Almost every page in the notebook was filled with tables, numbers, and multiple axes. He recognized the letters A-L on one of the axes. He then turned around to the cages and sure enough, each of the twelve were labeled with a letter corresponding to the axis of the tables (A-L). Other than that, Ben could not make out what any of the other numbers on the axis referred to. In the body of the tables was only the same simple sign, over and over—a horizontal dash, looking like a minus sign. As Ben scanned through the pages of the journal, he noticed that some of the numbers on the axes changed, while some stayed the same and there were these minus signs that filled nearly the whole book. About three-fourths of the way through though, there appeared a couple of plus signs. This pattern continued—with a few more plus signs here and there—until finally, on one of the last pages, there was an entire column filled with plus signs that were circled.

Ben wasn't sure of what to make of it. There was no text or dates in the notebook, just tables with multiple axes. He set the notebook down and shifted his focus to the lab computer, moving the mouse as he sat down to examine it. The screen flashed on. Multiple programs were open. The one currently displayed on the monitor depicted what Ben knew to be a sound wave, just over three minutes long. It looked as though the open program could be used to engineer and manipulate sound bytes. In the lower left hand of the window, was a keystroke log. It looked as though someone, very recently, had been using the computer and manipulating the sound wave. The keystroke log indicated someone was making changes to the sound byte on this very day, from just after midnight to about 6:00 a.m., this morning.

Ben wondered who, other than Sinsway, had access to this lab. A part of him was also curious as to what this engineered audio file would sound like. Ben saw a control panel that was used to play audio files, and clicked play. Although he could tell that the file was running, he did not hear anything. Ben shrugged and rose to his feet. As he did, he noticed large, quality speakers on a shelf above the computers.

Pretty nice, he thought.

Ben knew his speakers. He had always enjoyed working with music. He had an electric guitar and keyboard at home which he played frequently.

Ben noticed another door, opposite the one he entered and started in that direction. His first step snagged a cord on the floor, which was pulled away from the output of the computer. The male and female audio connectors dislodged and sound began to emanate throughout the laboratory. It was a sweet whistling sound, rising and falling, with intermittent *pings* of harmonic notes. Ben could hear multiple layers of melodic frequencies filling the laboratory, almost like birds were singing. Bass notes rose and fell, anchoring the song in a strange rhythm. The sound was pleasant, and for a few curious moments, Ben simply reveled in it. The sound was loud though and a bit distracting.

Ben turned around to face the computer, listening to the melody that radiated through the room. Ben felt his pulse rise, feeling as if the sound was playing with his senses. In a few moments, Ben pressed pause on the audio program and the room fell into silence.

Ben laughed.

Well that was odd, he thought.

He walked into the only room he had yet to examine. There were two light microscopes, one of which could be used for fluorescent imaging. Ben also noticed another large fridge. He was met with a rush of warm air as he opened it. It was a culture fridge. There were many tubes with cultured cells within, as well as Petri dishes of various sizes.

He was glad to have brought up two sample containers with him. When he was ready to leave, both were full. The crime lab was going to have its hands full for a few days.

But that was it; that was all of Sinsway's secret lab. Only time could tell if anything found within would be useful in solving the man's murder.

27

It took Officer Middler about forty-five minutes to reach his destination.

A blue and white sign with the name *New Life* stood in front of a large, very modern-looking complex. The building was glass and silver, donning many well-placed right angles. Middler figured it was five-stories high. Its appearance gave off an air of sophistication.

The parking lot was fairly large and mostly full. Middler scanned the lot and found a vacant spot, pulling in and turning the key to his ignition. The young officer grabbed a pen and notepad from atop his passenger seat and jumped out of his car, locking it with a push of a button on his way to the clinic. As he walked, he patted his side, checking his firearm that lay hidden within a side holster above his ribs—the weapon concealed by his coat jacket.

Middler jumped over a cement curb, landing on a healthy grass lawn that led up to—what appeared to be—one of the main entrances of the facility, glimmering in the morning sunlight. Soon, he was walking down a cement walkway leading up to two rows of automatic sliding glass doors. As he walked through the second set of doors, he was able to get his first glimpse of the facility. Middler was impressed at the interior. The ceiling was a good four stories up. The main room, which he now stood in, was open to the floors above ground level. He glanced up and saw a pair of employees wearing white lab coats, walking around an elegantly engineered causeway, only a silver railing separating them from the main lobby below.

Middler approached a security guard, sitting comfortably behind a desk. The man's skin was a dark shade of sepia.

"Appointment?" the security guard asked, as he straightened up in his seat.

"Yes," Middler said. "I'm Officer Middler, here to see Marilyn Stone."

"Sign in and have a seat. It may be a few minutes."

The security guard spoke casually and Middler obliged, signing his name.

Middler had called ahead during his journey to New Life. He was pleased how easy it was for him to set up an appointment to speak with this Marilyn Stone, a senior manager of the facility.

Officer Middler approached the reception area. There was a single row of seats along either of the lateral walls. At the far wall, opposite the entrance, was a barrier of wall and glass that separated a group of medical historians from the lobby.

Middler noticed an attractive young blonde on the other side of the pane of glass, as he walked towards a row of seats. The woman was dressed in a white lab coat, talking on the phone, her crystal earrings shimmering in the light. She smiled when she caught sight of Middler.

Middler turned to inspect a row of pictures that hung at eye level along the wall. He slowly paced as he took in the still images. There were photographs of children smiling with doctors; some of the children appeared to be physically disabled, donning wheelchairs and crutches. There were also employee photographs: groups of doctors and laboratory staff smiling in short rows.

Behind Officer Middler, a sound rang out. He turned, slowly, to see a middle-aged woman pushing her way through a glass door situated between the gap in a row of seats opposite him.

The woman was short and stocky, wearing glasses, walking firmly towards the junior detective. She seemed to force a smile as she drew near.

"Hello," she said, briskly. "I'm Marylyn Stone. You're here about the car?"

At this, Middler was slightly perplexed.

"Ma'am?" he asked.

"The car that was stolen from us this morning," she added. And then, as she began to share the officer's confusion, she said, "I'm sorry. I was told you were a police officer."

Middler smiled.

"Well yes, I am."

Marylyn looked as though she was about to say something, but then hesitated for a moment. There was an awkward silence.

Finally, she said, "Let me escort you to my office."

Middler nodded his agreement as she turned and he followed behind her.

An hour later, Middler bade Marylyn farewell and thanked her for her time.

Apparently, a company car had been stolen the night before, which was the reason Marylyn thought he was there. There must have been some confusion when he called New Life. He had a feeling he had spoken to the attractive blonde when he called during his drive. It was no matter, Middler had taken down the license plate number, as well as the make and model of the stolen vehicle, before starting his intended query.

Unfortunately, Marylyn had never seen Salison Sinsway before and had no idea how the man could have come into possession of the security card that was found in his car. She assured him that they took security very seriously, for it was she—being the director of human resources—who was in charge of distributing security badges.

The woman had been forthcoming though. She had obliged Middler when he requested information on the new employees hired after the company's acquisition by Thomas Bishop. She also spoke of the changes that were made once the business was under Bishop's control, as she was very grateful for the transformation that was subsequently made.

Apparently, Bishop had kept a few things the same; for instance, the company still specialized in genetic counseling—the process of examining an individual's genome to ascertain if either that individual or their potential offspring would be at risk of a multitude of genetic disorders.

The company also dealt with in vitro fertilization—the process of artificially inseminating an egg with a sperm to create an embryo, which would ultimately be transplanted into a mother-to-be. Marylyn had made it sound as if New Life were forerunners in prenatal care.

What was interesting though, were the changes made once Bishop was in control. The young man was apparently very interested in the potential of cord blood. Cord blood was the blood that remained in the placenta and the attached umbilical cord after birth. Cord blood was of interest because it was rich with stem cells; stem cells that could be used to treat a variety of different disorders.

Marylyn had cited a story about a little girl that was born with cerebral palsy, a disorder that affects the motor fibers of the central nervous system. The child had paralysis in her left leg and was not able to walk. Using the girl's own placental stem cells that had been stored at New Life, doctors were able to give the girl nearly full use of her once paralyzed leg, by transplanting the girl's stem cells into her body—cells that ultimately became healthy neurons, functioning to correct her motor deficits. Marylyn informed Middler that New Life was also now a cord bank, which—for a fee—would store a baby's cord blood, so tissues like stem cells could be used in the future, if that child ever had need of them. New Life also stored cord blood that was donated from hospitals.

Bishop had spent millions of dollars on the facility—new equipment and new employees. Yet, Salison apparently was not one of the new doctors hired.

Middler was still partially satisfied, for he now had a few more pieces to the puzzle. As Middler drove away from the facility, he recounted the facts of the case in his mind.

He soon approached a dark river that looked to snake its way through a shallow valley. He noticed it on the way in. It was part of a scenic route, encompassed by a rich forest on either side of the road. He drove up to a small bridge that led across the flowing water.

As Middler began to cross the bridge, he saw a flurry of police cars—at least four—with their lights on, as well as an ambulance. As his attention rose, he glanced down at his watch. Whatever this was, the cop cars must have gotten here in the last hour and a half. Middler slowed his vehicle.

Police were out of their cars and Middler noticed a few were down the hill, near the banks of the river. He decelerated and pulled up behind a police car. There was an officer that seemed to be directing him to continue driving along the open lane of the narrow bridge. Instead, Middler rolled down his window and let the man know he was a police officer. The cop directing traffic seemed uninterested in the fact that Middler was also a cop, but he allowed Middler to park.

Officer Middler exited his vehicle. His shoes fell on small pebbles and gravel that lined the roadside. Middler moved to where he believed the crime scene was located, approaching a group of officers.

"I'm Officer Middler." he said as he approached, showing his badge.

One of the officers squinted in the sunlight and checked out the identification. He smiled.

"Boston, huh? You're a little ways from home, Officer Middler."

Middler returned the man's smile, feeling slightly relieved.

"Yes, I was just at the clinic, investigating an open case. What's going on here?"

The young officer ran his hand through his short blond hair, for a moment, looking around.

"A couple of kids, fishing here about an hour ago, said they saw a body in the river."

The officer must have noticed a rise in Middler's interest because he continued.

"We dragged him out about thirty minutes ago. His wallet's gone. There's a single wound to the neck."

As the man finished, Middler heard a commotion coming from further down the embankment, closer to the river. He saw two officers lifting a body up onto a stretcher. Officer Middler offered a thank you to the young man and lightly jogged over to where the body was. As he did, the other officers seemed to take notice.

"Hey." one of them yelled. "This is a crime scene. What the hell is this guy doing here?"

This is more like it, Middler thought, as he told them he was with the Boston PD, not even reaching for his badge this time.

"Boston?" one of the officers asked. He was overweight and wearing dark glasses, puffing out his chest as he spoke, "And what are you doing here, son?"

Middler paid the man little mind, trying to get close enough to the stretcher to make out the appearance of the deceased. Moving closer to the action, he could tell he was making the other officers nervous. He heard one ask again to see some identification. Now, Middler was close enough to see the body—an Indian male, average build and in his mid-fifties is what Middler guessed. The dead man had short black hair, along with a receding hairline, weighing about 220 lbs., with a height of 5'9" or 5'10" —he wore a lab gown that appeared to, at one time, be a shade of turquoise. Middler took in the man's blank outward stare, as his lifeless eyes gazed upward, to the trees above.

As Middler peered at the man, he realized he had seen him before. He was trying to place where, when an officer began to approach him, saying something in a harsh tone. Middler again paid no attention, He was trying to figure out how he knew the departed.

One could almost see the neurons firing beneath Middler's dark-brown eyes as he figured it out. Yes, the young officer knew where he saw this man; it was in the photos at the clinic. Middler's memory was of a smiling man, wearing a white lab coat and golden spectacles, standing in front of a group of individuals, all of whom also wore white lab coats.

The dead man was from New Life.

Middler simply smiled at the approaching officer and turned away. He didn't think there was any more information that could be gathered here, anyway. None that could not be collected via a phone call to the local precinct. Middler heard someone yelling at him as he picked up his pace and began to jog to his car, already thinking of how Brennan would take the news of another murder. Middler had the feeling this was no random event.

He hopped into his Intrepid, taking his cell off his dash. He saw one of the officers, who was unhappy about his intrusion, talking to the young officer that spoke to Middler earlier. Middler did not care to stick around. He pulled off the rough shoulder of the road and drove across the bridge, with his cell phone ringing in hand.

In a couple rings, Brennan picked up. Officer Middler was instantly curious. Brennan sounded as if he was out of breath. Middler inquired about Brennan's condition, but Brennan insisted that Middler speak first. Middler filled Brennan in on the situation at New Life, saving the most interesting news for last. Brennan stayed silent as he listened to Middler and the detective did not have an immediate response to the news. It took Brennan a few moments to speak—he merely said that he found something interesting and would meet Middler later in the day to discuss. Brennan then said something, almost to himself, before hanging up. Middler was not sure of what words the detective spoke, as he slipped his cell back into his pocket.

It sounded almost as if Brennan had said, "Bullets in Battle Creeks."

28

Hours earlier, Detective David Brennan started his trip to Green Harbor, in hopes of visiting Dr. Salison Sinsway's cabin.

As the detective drove, he pondered—among other things—Silloway Sinsway. The young woman was missing. Her place had been torn apart and curiously enough, it was believed that she may now be in the company of Adam Riley. It was evident that she and Adam Riley knew each other. They had attended Boston College at the same time, and Adam taught two of her courses. Silloway, now twenty-two, worked as an entomologist at the Boston Zoo. The woman had a spotless record and received top marks in school. She was smart, just like her father. Brennan had learned this morning that Silloway, once found, would receive a life insurance payment of nearly half a million dollars. It seemed Salison's demise ensured this woman would receive a hell of a lot of money. If that was not motive, Brennan didn't know what was. Perhaps Silloway and Adam Riley had come up with a scheme to murder Salison for the money. Brennan had worked cases where people were killed for far less than five hundred thousand dollars. Brennan's cell phone vibrated in his jacket pocket as his train of thought derailed. He answered his phone and was greeted by a young woman's voice, sounding a bit timid. It was Ning from the lab.

"David, hello. How goes the hunting?"

Brennan smiled. "It's going."

There was only a split second of silence before Ning began speaking again, with purpose.

"Interesting news. The cell phone we found in Salison's vehicle, it may not have been his only one. Ben found a second cell in Salison's lab today. I haven't been able to determine if it actually belongs to Dr. Sinsway or not, since the number is unlisted. It's a cheap prepaid phone. The phone has only two contacts—there are outgoing and incoming calls from a Christopher Banks and a Dr. Denise Robbins."

For a moment, Ning sounded as if she were maneuvering a few items within her grasp. Then, she began again.

"Christopher Banks went to MIT for electronic engineering and computer science. Dr. Robbins works for the Museum of Natural History in New York. She's an expert on more than a few ancient languages.

"I haven't been able to get ahold of either of them. The calls to and from Dr. Robbins ended over a year ago, but there was contact with Christopher Banks in the last week. The young man graduated from MIT four years ago and now works for Orion Communications, the satellite radio company. He's twenty-six, has a clean record and lives with his mother in Rockland—not too far from here."

Brennan thought the case was starting to feel a bit like Masterpiece Theater.

Ning continued, "Two years ago, Christopher Banks deposited the lump sum of sixty-three thousand dollars into his savings account; soon after, his student loans were paid off. Any guess where the money came from?"

Brennan sounded slightly unsure as he answered, yet he knew he was correct as he spoke the name, "Salison?"

"That's what it looks like." Ning said.

Examining bank statements was a fairly simple task, being that the department had access to financial records and any transactions over a certain amount were flagged and easily identified.

Brennan figured it may be worth speaking with Christopher Banks and it took him only a few moments to jot down directions to the young man's residence in Rockland. He could stop there on the way back from Green Harbor.

At some point, he would work on getting ahold of this Dr. Robbins as well.

After giving Brennan directions to Rockland, Ning uttered a short good-bye and got off the phone. As Brennan drove in silence, he thought of how much he enjoyed the landscape. His eyes followed the hills rolling into the distance and time, for a while, seemed to pass with little feeling.

It was not long before Brennan approached Salison's cottage. Trees and strong earth dominated the view as Brennan drove down Salison's long winding driveway. The detective pulled up next to Salison's large barn-style garage. Brennan already knew the contents of this structure—a beautiful sailing vessel, some forty feet long and also, a few cabinets of tools. Slightly puzzling was an odd burn and imprints upon the floor, in open space, which made it look as though something large had once been positioned over the burn. Other than that the barn was pretty much barren. Brennan glanced at the large metal construction, exiting his vehicle and walking in the direction of Salison's cabin, located some forty yards away along a weathered stone path. Brennan noticed something out of the corner of his eye as he walked towards Salison's residence. It was nothing more than a few bent blades of grass and a small amount of displaced dirt, but it caused Brennan's curiosity to rise.

Before Brennan's father passed, the man made sure Brennan knew how to take care of himself. This meant years of the scouts, the outdoors, and living off the land. The man also taught Brennan how to track in the wilderness. Brennan knew he was now looking at fresh tracks. Someone was just here and they headed out into the woods.

Brennan followed the nearly invisible trail with his eyes. There was not much to go by; but as he trekked deeper into the forest, he saw small signs which he read like guideposts—a bit of scattered earth here, disturbed foliage a few yards along, blades of grass bending upward at obtuse angles to the ground further ahead, and plenty of fresh footprints from a large, heavy man.

Brennan's interest rose as he continued deeper into the forest, for he knew he was following someone who had reason to visit Salison's cottage and then take off into the woods. Brennan had no idea where this person was heading though. Salison's property was huge. He did, however, know he was traveling further away from the main cabin.

Soon the landscape became rockier and at some points, elevated quite steeply. After hiking for a few minutes, Brennan saw the forest thinning out ahead and he saw what he believed to be open sky. This made sense. The detective figured he was now at a modest elevation above sea level. Brennan quickened his pace as he approached a cliff face.

Once on the crest of the land, Brennan had an encompassing view of a valley below. Fifty or so yards down, the cliff face met the floor of the valley. However, the fall was not the thing that held Brennan's attention. The man peered at a large structure that lay in the valley, looking to be about a five or six minute jog through the woods, from the base of the cliff. The structure appeared to be a semi-cylinder, lying on its side, shimmering in the midday sun. The building itself was curious-looking; as if it did not belong in the middle of the encompassing wilderness of Salison's property.

Brennan saw a winding drive next to the structure, which ran off into the distant valley. Atop the driveway was a station wagon. Brennan walked closer to the cliff's edge. He saw the door of the horizontal semi-silo swing close. In an instant, Brennan had surveyed his surroundings; he knew the person he was following had just entered the complex that lay at the valley's floor.

Directly below Brennan, the land sloped steeply downward for thirty or so yards. There were patches of earth, several boulders and a few small trees and shrubs. A descent into this region looked manageable. However, after this traversable region, the cliff face became nearly vertical and dropped off to the valley below.

Brennan had done some rock climbing in his youth; but that had been years ago, when his body was of a different form. The detective contemplated his next move. The station wagon was too far away to make out the license plate. He may have been satisfied leaving with just that bit of information; but alas, Brennan had not thought to bring his binoculars. There appeared to be no alternate route down to the valley floor and Brennan figured this person may be gone by the time he reached the bottom, if he were able to successfully search for and find an easier descent.

If it were another case, Brennan probably would not have risked harm upon himself. But there was something about this one, something that caused a true wonder to rise in him. Brennan made up his mind. He was going to descend the cliff, in an attempt to catch the person he tracked across the Sinsway property.

Perhaps this would be a break in the case.

Shards of olive light swam in the man's irises as he surveyed his descent.

Brennan moved across the rugged terrain, making his way slowly down the precipice. He immediately lost his footing, but quickly regained it, proceeding down with a heightened focus. There were small trees and patches of brush in this area, but few were strong enough to support the man's weight. Brennan decided to lower his center of gravity. Soon, he was on his back, in a near sitting position, using his feet and palms to maneuver. It was not long before his palms were covered in earth and he approached the steepest part of the cliff face.

AN EVOLUTION OF MINDS

Brennan began to perspire and looking downward, knew the hardest part was yet to come. The foliage had disappeared from the rocky ground and in a few yards, the cliff face became completely vertical. It dropped off about twenty-five or so yards, down to the forest floor below. For an experienced and conditioned climber, this decent would not be such an arduous task, but Brennan was not an experienced climber. His pulse began to rise.

The man tried to identify future footholds and climbing notches as he surveyed the drop-off, then his gaze—for a moment—turned to the surrounding forest. The mysterious structure was not visible from this lower vantage point. The person he was following could now be gone. The thought caused Brennan to hasten his actions. He turned to face the cliff and resumed his descent. Brennan was careful as he climbed down and his confidence slowly rose as he found himself finding sufficient footholds and structures of stone to adhere to.

It was only a few meters though, before Brennan's confidence slowly dissolved. The man was losing energy. Not so much in his core or his limbs, but in his fingers. They strained to hold his weight against the pull of the planet. Looking down, Brennan knew he had quite a ways to go before he reached ground level. Alarm rose in the man as he realized he may not have the strength to make the rest of the climb down.

Brennan desperately searched for his next foothold as the pain in his fingers increased.

The fatigue in Brennan's digits was growing by the second and soon the man did not have the ability to move, either up or down. Clinging to the cliff face, he only had the energy to stay put.

And then, the energy was gone.

As Brennan fell to the earth, there was no romantic feeling of weightlessness; there was only panic. It lasted longer than Brennan would have imagined and then, an impact.

29

Detective David Brennan did not lose consciousness after his fall over the cliff face.

He remembered seeing the stone surface of the earth pass him as he fell. Then, he was consumed by the coarse embrace of the forest. Twigs and branches bent and broke as his body impacted the foliage at the base of the cliff.

Detective Brennan lay on the earth, covered in dirt, brush and small abrasions. He did not feel too bad though, considering the fall he just made. Looking up, the man figured he fell the equivalent distance as from a second-story roof.

He was rattled, but it did not feel as if he had any broken bones.

It did not take Brennan long to remember the purpose of his descent. There was someone he was following, someone who had disappeared into a mysterious structure nestled within the Sinsway valley. Brennan slowly rose to his feet, feeling a dull pain in his side as he did. He inhaled briskly, looking up, examining the damage he did to the surrounding forest as he fell. His hand found its way under his shirt, to his rib cage, as he turned and jogged in the direction of the facility.

In a few minutes, Brennan could tell that the forest was thinning out. Through the trees, he could see the horizontal half-cylinder. He swore as he approached, for the station wagon—and thus the person he was following—was gone.

As he approached the building, he could tell it was made of nearly translucent panes of glass; it almost looked as though some regions of the building, yards off in the distance, harbored panes of glass darker than the ones nearest him.

As Brennan approached the structure a vibration emanated from his slacks pocket. He was surprised he had reception in the valley. He saw it was Officer Middler and answered. Brennan lightly paced outside the structure listening to what his young colleague had to say. When the conversation was over, the detective muttered something soft to himself and hung up, shaking his head as he did. He now had a pretty good idea where the station wagon had come from, which only made him more irritated that the person got away.

Brennan walked up the concrete stairway to the entrance of the facility, sighing as he noticed a number pad embedded into the strong façade of the structure. He approached the door and gave it a pull, despite the indication of an electronic lock. To Brennan's surprise, the door opened easily.

What Brennan saw, as he got his first glimpse of the interior, caused him to smile. He could not help it. Salison had outdone himself here.

Brennan tried to imagine what the unidentified person could have wanted within this wild world, and why Salison would create a place as fantastically equipped as this. He entered the facility, and noticed an odd feel to the moist, warm air. The lab would have to make it down here. The place ignited in Brennan more questions; and as he walked forward, he had to wonder, how deep this rabbit hole was going to get.

30

Just before the dawn of the day, at a time when the sun had not yet risen and Arcturus could still be seen shining through the morning mist that blanketed the land, Adam and Silloway left Sinsway's hideaway. They trekked around the lake and through the woods, back to Silloway's friend's Camry. When the pair reached the car, their shoes were wet from the morning's dew and covered in torn grass. Their clothes were home to burrs, and their breaths heavy in their chests from the uphill climb.

During the drive to Maine, Adam managed to ask Silloway a few questions in regards to their situation. He gathered Silloway did indeed believe, as incredible as it may have sounded, that her father was trying to induce enlightenment. She also seemed to be quite sure that Moorea was searching for something, something he believed her father had hidden from him, something which had to do with the enlightenment project.

But that seemed to be where Silloway's knowledge of their predicament ended. She claimed not to know the scientific methods her father and Moorea were using to induce enlightenment. She also said she was not sure if the project was even successful.

There were other questions brewing in Adam though, questions which held more relevance to his present dilemma. It was possible he was wanted for a man's murder—Adam knew he had to find a way to clear his name.

Adam and Silloway decided to call Boston Memorial from a payphone (to inquire on Salison's condition), but not until they left Boston behind by a fair distance. The decision tainted the air with an unsettling curiosity, regarding Salison's possible/probable demise.

As if to clear the air of the feeling, Silloway spoke up, not turning to Adam, but keeping her eyes out the window. The rising sun caused the bellies of shallow stratus clouds to glow red-hot in the sky—the fortresses of ice and ember reflected in the North Atlantic as waves of pastels, swimming toward the horizon.

"Earlier, you mentioned inducing enlightenment." Silloway said "What do you know of it? And how to you tie it to Jesus and Buddha?"

Adam was glad Silloway was talking.

"As I'm sure you know", he said, lowering his visor, protecting his eyes from the rising sun, "your father believed in the combined teachings of both Jesus and Buddha. That we should have love in our heart and be good to others. However, a saint could have this love in their mind, or in their heart, so to speak, and still be lacking in the realm your father was greatly interested in—the realm of movement and the manipulation of matter. The enlightenment of both Jesus and Buddha was associated with their ability to move through and interact with the physical and biological world in an extraordinary way."

The morning sun churned in Adam's eyes as he took a turn near a large brick silo, reaching lonesomely toward the sky.

"Do you know why Jesus and Buddha both secluded themselves in the wilderness, for decades—learning from holy men, fasting, training and purging their bodies? It's because their religion was about more than just believing in something greater, it was a physical phenomenon. These men were trying to connect their mind *and* body to a higher plane. In regards to Jesus and Buddha, there are a lot of similarities between their lives and how they achieved enlightenment. Both their mothers were said to have dreams which indicated their sons would be world-changers. Mary dreamt of the angel Gabriel and the Buddha's mother dreamt of a white elephant descending a golden stairway from the heavens. Both Jesus and Buddha were said to perform miracles as children and then to have spent years in the wilderness—fasting, praying, meditating and studying from learned men so that they could achieve enlightenment. Also, when they reached their potential, it is said they could interact with the world in a way that seemed to defy the laws of space and time and the laws of biology as well—Jesus was said to be able to walk on water, heal the sick and raise the dead; while Buddha could manipulate fire and water, walk upon the air and the sea and even appear and disappear in an instant.

These men did not only show the world love, there was something special about the way they moved through the world and the way they connected with their surroundings."

Adam said this, he recounting Salison's grace and flow of movement and the way he resonated at the hospital. In the reflected glass, Adam saw Silloway's eyes showed recollection as well.

"Your father believed that these prophets were born with a rare and fantastic genetic potential, then trained harder than our most talented athletes, in an attempt to evolve their minds and bodies in a way humanity has scarcely seen before. Their heightened senses and spirit allowed them to perceive and interact differently with the fabric of the cosmos. For instance, your father believed these men were *fast*. And agile as well. The Buddha was said to be able to bi-locate—to move so fast he appeared to be in two places at once."

Again, Adam thought of Salison's seizure back at the hospital and the way the light danced around him...

"If the wind howls at precisely the right frequency, it has the power to bring down a bridge. What if a man or woman could bring themselves to resonate in such a way? What power over matter would they then have?"

Silloway's gaze was still fixed out the window, as the two of them passed a clearing with tall grasses and a few downed trees in the process of being disassembled. The sun, still low in the sky, rose, almost blindingly, when its rays cut through the eastern trees. It gave the earth a warm, healthy glow.

Adam decided to continue down a slightly different path, as he put on his blinker and took a right turn a few yards from a large weathered mailbox looking to be centuries old.

"The great eclectic Edgar Cayce once said that time and space are illusions. Illusions created by our mind to make sense of the outside world. Physicists and biologists alike agree on this, that time and space are illusions. But, as Cayce also said, they are illusions with a purpose. Your father believed that the prophets' training made them faster not only in body but also in mind. He believed they were able to manipulate their world at will and see through this illusion of space-time."

Adam paused for a moment.

"We've all been in the zone before, whether it be when we're playing a sport or perhaps in times of physical stress, when time itself seems to slow, or when we see things incredibly clearly. Many people have experienced this time-slowing when faced with death."

As if Adam had found his rhythm, he now spoke quickly, his interest in the subject matter in his nature,

"What if you could do that at will, but to a much greater extent? What if your mind could not only slow time down at will, but your body was trained in such a way that it could move masterfully through the altered space-time? Perhaps you may look, to an outside observer, to disappear and re-appear at will, to bi-locate, or even move through solid objects. It's a thin line between science and science fiction. Time, space, fluid movement, and fluid thought. You know," Adam said. "If I knew anyone who had the potential to become something akin to a prophet, it would be your father..."

There was no immediate response from Silloway. But in a few miles, she spoke up.

"You're right, Adam," she said. "My father was searching for what those prophets found. For what they became. He wanted to move through walls and walk on water. Or at least glide."

Adam smiled as Silloway spoke. She may have just been curious about what Adam would say about enlightenment—Adam had the feeling the woman knew her father (and what he was working on) quite well.

Silloway fell silent.

Then, she said, "You spoke of the similarities between the prophets. But you forgot to mention one.

These men, both Christ and Buddha, their journey towards enlightenment nearly complete, were both confronted with a dark force...

....an ominous force..."

At this, Adam took his eyes off the country road he traveled on and looked over at Silloway.

She could have been staring off into the distance, towards the trees and an ocean reflecting plumes of pinkish-purple clouds. There was nothing else from her.

Christ, Adam thought, as he brought down his visor, shielding his eyes from the sun, *this girl is going to be the end of me.*

31

Detective David Brennan sat at the corner of 5th and Broadway outside of a small sandwich shop. He was working on a crossword puzzle as he waited for his young associate to arrive. The detective had burned the calories today and was looking forward to a good meal.

After Brennan did a quick walk-through of the structure he found in Salison's valley, he made the hike back to his car. It took him about an hour to find a manageable trail through the woods back to Salison's residence. It seems that free-falling down a cliff had saved him quite a bit of time.

On his way back to Boston, Brennan stopped by Christopher Bank's place. He was the young computer engineer who had the good fortune of having Dr. Sinsway pay off his school loans. The kid was not home; but his mother, looking confused as to why Brennan was covered in dirt and small abrasions, told Brennan that her son would be home later that evening.

She was, of course, concerned with why a police detective was looking for her son. Brennan told her not to fret and to have Christopher call him within the next twenty-four hours. With a worried look on her face, the woman took down Detective Brennan's number.

Brennan's stomach growled as he stretched in his seat, feeling a small pain radiate from his rib cage as he did. The pain was no matter to him, the minor injury made him feel as if he had done his job well today. The man could not help but smile when he saw Officer Middler approaching.

The grinning young man carried a small notebook. He swung open a cast-iron gate and hopped onto the patio. Middler dodged a few tables in his path and slipped into the seat opposite Brennan.

"A secret garden?" Middler asked, enthusiastically.

Middler was referring to the large half-silo shaped structure, which Brennan found in the Sinsway Valley.

Brennan shook his head, "It was not quite a garden. It was more like an arboretum."

Middler nodded, understandingly, and asked,

"Did you find some catnip and roll around a bit?"

Brennan rolled his eyes. He was still donning patches of earthen hues and dirt on his clothes. Middler did not wait long before speaking again with good humor ringing from his voice.

"But seriously, what happened? You alright?"

"I'm fine. It seems I'm not quite the great climber I imagined."

"Glad you're OK, boss. So what was he growing in there?"

"Horticulture is not quite my forte, but it was incredible. Within the greenhouse, there were multiple distinct ecosystems: a rainforest, a desert climate, a tropical forest area, a swampland, even a frigid area with a single splendid tree in bloom. You'll have to see it. The man put the Boston arboretum to shame."

Brennan began with his own line of questioning.

"Tell me about New Life."

"Well, I told you about the deceased." Middler began. "His name was Dr. Sangupta Rami. A sixty-four-year-old neurosurgeon at..." Middler's voice trailed off as he flipped open his notepad lying on his lap. "A neurosurgeon at Cornell, until a few years ago. Dr. Rami was one of a few new doctors that Bishop hired when he took over New Life."

Brennan looked up at the deep blue afternoon sky, inquiring, "What did he specialize in?"

"The peripheral nervous system," Middler answered. "At New Life, he grafted stem cells into patients that needed new nerve fibers to combat certain disorders, such as Cerebral Palsy. He also worked with Schwann cells, the supporting cells that insulate nerves."

Brennan was not precisely sure why he was interested in Rami's expertise, yet he figured it was another piece of the puzzle. How it would fit, he did not yet know. His train of thought changed as he inquired, "You said he was killed by a wound to the neck?"

"Yes," Middler answered. "A small incision which looked to be quite precise."

"I imagine New Life is now a crime scene." Brennan stated. "The murder most likely took place on—or near—the premises, using a surgical blade. Then, the body was dumped."

Middler nodded his agreement. A waitress approached and set bowls of soup in front of them. Middler smiled at her, as she refilled his glass of water. Middler tasted his Soto Ayam and watched Detective Brennan. The man stared off into space.

'We need to speak to Thomas Bishop," Brennan said.

"Ya," Middler replied. "and find Adam Riley, the daughter, and the guys that stole Sinsway's body."

Brennan stayed silent. He was thinking of the New Life car that was stolen, which was probably the same car he saw at Sinsway's place, possibly driven by the man who killed this Dr. Rami.

Damn it..

Brennan wished the man had not gotten away.

The waitress came by, again; this time with sandwiches. She set the plates down in front of either officer, before smiling and disappearing.

Brennan stayed silent as he ate and Middler followed suit. Brennan pondered the profile of the person who had killed Sinsway.

The person was probably educated, judging by the cocktail of chemicals which were found in Sinsway's bloodstream. It was also a possibility that whoever killed Rami was also educated, given the location of the crime and the apparent precision of the kill strike. Perhaps both assailants were doctors, perhaps they were one and the same. Or, maybe it was Adam Riley all along, a motive yet to be uncovered. Then, there was this man with the ski mask that stole Sinsway's body. How did he fit into the equation?

More often than not, while working on a case, Brennan would encounter evidence or testimony which would point him in the direction he needed to go; and in time, he and his colleagues would put together the enough pieces of the crimes and it would eventually be solved. The Sinsway case, thus far, was different. The questions were piling up and although the evidence was abundant, it had yet to light the way towards any answers.

Middler's brown eyes were curious, as they gazed at Brennan from across the table.

Brennan knew that they both had quite a bit of work ahead. And he also knew that all he could do was follow the leads he had and perhaps, in time, the answers would begin to take shape.

32

Adam and Silloway drove north, with the sun high in the sky. Adam pondered his predicament, Salison's fate, the science of enlightenment, and how to go about gathering evidence on Moorea in order to clear his name. Somewhere along Route 94, Silloway spoke up, indicating she wanted Adam to pull over. Adam saw a gas station coming into view and could tell where the woman's thoughts were heading. He made out a weathered payphone on the station wall; *Salison* he thought.

Silloway hopped out of the car and was to the payphone in a few strides. She reached into the pockets of her jean shorts and grabbed a few coins. Adam watched her outside, a short distance away as she dropped the coins into the phone and dialed.

She spoke briefly on the phone and then appeared to be waiting for someone on the other end. Silloway looked composed, with a curious caution about her—she ran a hand through her dark hair, as she rose her eyes to the sky—in seventeen seconds she resumed talking on the phone.

Adam looked on as the woman's heart sank. Silloway looked saddened, but with some sort of calm focus radiating from hers, as she walked back to the car. Adam knew what she was about to say: that Salison was dead.

Hours later, Adam drove down a stone path that cut its way through a dense forest of trees. He was approaching his destination.

Both he and Silloway had not spoken much since learning of Salison's demise. Adam made an attempt to console the young woman; yet she, in her quiet nature, insisted she was fine. Aside from that, the only other words from her were to shed light on their destination, which Adam learned was a sizable property that her father owned along the northeastern coast of Maine.

A large stone wall came into view as they approached a dull silver gate seamlessly crafted into the wall. Adam saw the stone barrier running off through the trees for as far as his gaze could travel, in either direction. Salison certainly did appreciate his privacy. Adam pulled to a stop in front of the gate. Silloway unbuckled her seatbelt and jumped out. She reached into her pocket, approaching what looked to be a stainless steel panel embedded into the outer surface of the wall. She inserted a key into the panel and turned the key, exposing a small number pad. Silloway typed in a code and the gate began to retract, sliding in behind the thick stone wall. Silloway hopped back inside the car.

Adam traveled through the open gate. Then, he and Silloway drove through the forest, before the trees thinned out and the coast came into view. Adam saw the ocean. He tasted the salt in the air and smiled. A few sailboats dotted the sea, before the water bled into the horizon. Salison's house soon came into view. The abode was modest compared to the breadth of land it sat upon. The residence appeared to be one-story—with the exception of the center third of the dwelling, which rose to two stories and donned a balcony open to the outside. The house, as well as the large windows, looked aged. Faded ivory, earth, and stone reflected in Adam's windows as he pulled up.

Hours later, after a walk along the beach and a brisk review of some more of Salison's documents, Adam lay upon a large pullout sofa in the basement of Salison's abode. Silloway had split company with Adam soon after their arrival—she said she wanted her solace, and considering her father's fate, Adam could not blame her. There was plenty of space out here anyway, to get lost, and clear your head. She indicated that she would be back in the evening, but Adam had yet to see her.

In the room Adam was now in, there was a fireplace which had a medieval look to it—an aged brick frame to a portrait of chaos—flickering light fought as flames over fuel as shards of once strong hickory succumbed to the heat. There were patterns born from the smoke and ember which the world would never see again. For Adam, it was hypnotizing. He lay on his side and watched as the flickering light cast dancing shadows around the den.

In his mind, images of the ancient world played: pillars of flames floating in the desert sky as in the book of Exodus and of aerial battles between flying spheres, crosses and cylinders under a burning sun as depicted in the 1561 Nuremberg broadsheet. Adam thought of lost cities buried in the sea and in the sand and of the secrets kept within them. For a moment, he let go of these romantic thoughts regarding past civilizations, mysterious histories, and altered states of mind and body and closed his eyes, feeling the heat on his skin and a calm fall over him.

A gentle noise caused him to open his eyes. His gaze traced across the room. What he saw, caused his pulse to rise.

It was Silloway. Appearing to be delicately wrapped in silk, or perhaps it was not a fabric. Perhaps it was flows of midnight which swam softly over her skin and embraced the curves of her body. She came closer, moving slowly. Or was it his perception of time which was drawn out? Either way, her movements were smooth and seductive. Adam did not take his eyes from her. The heartbreak that found her earlier in the day, looked to have all but dissipated from her—a new energy radiated from her.

Firelight tried in vain to grasp the girl as she moved; yet all it could do was reflect in her shining violet eyes as she slid upon the sofa. She placed her hand upon Adam's chest, and felt his heart racing. Silloway knew it could be her last night with the young man and she had a curiosity in her, in regards to his nature. Silloway leaned in close to Adam's ear and whispered softly,

"What's worth saving?"

Adam moved his lips closer to hers. He felt the warmth of her body and caught the scent of spring, of rebirth and flowers in bloom, as he replied, "This."

33

Unaware of the fireworks in Maine, Dr. Jonas Moorea sat in his study, looking out on his property. Jonas held a silver knife in his hand and spun it about his palm. Flashes of metal helicoptered around his arm; then, Moorea delved the knife into a thick paper envelope addressed to him from the city of Srinagar, in Northern India. Half a dozen stamps covered the letter, some of them quite ornate and beautiful, reflecting colors of faded grass, charcoal, and hay. The contents of the letter held information that would change the flow of Moorea's path towards his future and thus had the potential to change the course of history. To understand the nature of the letter, it is necessary to understand a bit of what drives Jonas Moorea.

When Jonas was a young boy, his mother took him to mass every Sunday and had him attend Sunday school. Although the woman was not terribly religious, she saw worth in the messages of the gospels. Moorea for the most part, goofed off with his friends during his courses, yet he found himself wondering, more and more, about a particular aspect of the gospels—the miracles that were said to have been performed by Christ.

For instance, *How was Jesus able to manipulate molecules?*

It is said that with only his mind, body, and power of spirit, Jesus Christ was able to turn jars of water into perfectly proportioned mixtures of acids, proteins, sugars, minerals and phenolic compounds, producing a sublime wine at a wedding in Cana.

And, *How did Jesus multiply matter?*

Such as he did at Bethsaida, when he fed thousands of people with a handful of fish and a few loaves of bread.

AN EVOLUTION OF MINDS

How did Jesus calm the seas, raise the dead, heal the sick and wither trees at will?

Moorea's pastor had no answers for these questions, saying only that one should focus not on the man's miracles but how he lived his life. Moorea was unsatisfied with this answer. And even more so with the one given by his Sunday school teacher who, when asked the same question, suggested that perhaps the miracles had never been performed and that they were merely a legendary embellishment.

Despite his Sunday school teacher's skepticism, Moorea kept the stories of the miracles with him, as well as the questions that they raised, until his adult years when he began to look deeper into them.

In time, Moorea learned that Jesus was not the only person who was said to have performed miracles. In the Middle East, around—and before—the time of Christ, there was a sect called the Essenes. These individuals were rumored to have obtained incredible powers, such as clairvoyance and precognition, levitation and teleportation, healing of the sick by the laying-on of the hands, and bringing the dead back to life. Moorea also learned that many scholars believed that John the Baptist, the teacher of Jesus, was a member of the Essenes and most likely passed on his Essene knowledge to the well-known prophet.

Moorea found out about other groups too, such as the Kundalaini yogis in ancient India, who were believed to have mastered miraculous powers similar to those attributed to the Essenes.

And of course, there were also stories of the Buddha who was said to have performed miracles similar to Christ's. It was also said the Buddha was able to manipulate fire and water and to appear in two places at once.

Moorea was mystified by the stories he read about the enlightened. He wondered how religion could be tied to the generation of miracles. He also wondered if, perhaps, there were any of these ancient sects left in the modern world, and if they still possessed the power to perform miracles.

After Moorea received his medical degree and wrote his neuroscience-themed doctoral thesis, he took nine months off before resuming his work. In that time, Moorea traveled to the Middle East and Asia, in search of the answers to the questions that had been burning in the back of his mind since those early days in Sunday school.

In Jerusalem, he visited holy sites revered by Christians and Muslims alike; but it did not take him long to leave the beaten path. He visited the nearby Qumran, where it was said the Order of the Essenes were based from around the 8th century BC until a few hundred years after the death of Christ. At Qumran, Moorea found only an empty cave system that had been torn apart by a massive earthquake over 2,000 years ago. The great historian of antiquity, Josephus, not only mentioned the Essenes, their mysterious origins and miraculous powers, but also the earthquake that rocked the Monastery at Qumran. After the death of Josephus, the fate and the location of the Essenes became unknown.

Moorea visited local museums and universities and even taverns, inquiring if there were any modern-day descendants of the sect and where they could be found, if they did indeed exist. Again and again, Moorea came up empty-handed. It seemed as if the mysterious white-robed sect of the Essenes, had disappeared.

Continuing his search, for modern day men and women who still grasped the powers of the prophets, Moorea traveled from the Middle East into India, Pakistan, and Tibet. He spent time at Buddhist and Christian monasteries alike, and even began to learn useful fragments of local dialects.

Moorea spoke with dozens of monks, usually with the help of interpreters, in order to gain insights into the powers of the prophets.

In the village of Dharamsala, at the foothills of the Himalayan Mountains, Moorea heard of a sect of monks who were able to heal the sick and were even rumored to have psychic powers. Moorea spent three weeks in this area and the neighboring territories, searching for the group, or a good lead that he could use to track them down. But he had come up with nothing.

Moorea, distraught, had sought refuge in the city of Srinagar, in the provinces of Kashmir and Jammu in Northern India.

Srinagar, a loud and turbulent city, still had serene spots, such as the famous lush gardens—adorned with carved marble, fountains and shallow canals, with water reflecting the vast sky above and the snowy caps of the Pir Panjal Mountain Range in the distance.

In Srinagar, Moorea took in the sights and continued with his research. In time, Moorea was introduced to Professor Eric Hassnain, a short, white-haired, balding man with a warm smile. Hassnain, a scholar of international renown, was the Director of the Kashmir Research Center for Buddhist Studies and a member of the International Conference of Anthropological Research in Chicago. He was also the director of all the museums in Kashmir.

AN EVOLUTION OF MINDS

Moorea shared the story of his search for the enlightened with Hassnain and the man responded with enthusiasm. Moorea did not divulged the true purpose of his trip to his all his friends and family, for fear of ridicule; but Moorea could tell Hassnain was a like-minded individual—a man in search of the truth in history.

After speaking for some time, Hassnain leaned forward in his chair and in a hushed voice, began telling Moorea a story. Hassnain spoke of a man named Affanso Fernandez, a Portuguese missionary, who in the mid-1500s, under direction of St. Francis Xavier, traveled into Northern India. He did so with a small group of monks, in order to spread the word of God in the name of the Holy Roman Catholic Church.

Affanso and his party had been tasked with spreading the gospel to a chain of small remote villages around the Pangong Tso region (near the present day border of India and China). While traveling through the Himalayas, the party was hit by a severe storm, days away from the nearest village. Ill-prepared and without their guide (who had died) Affanso's party became divided in the storm, which lasted for days. All in Affanso's group eventually perished from the biting wind and the unforgiving snow and ice, which, at times, came at them sideways. After three days of being pounded by the wind and sleet, Affanso awoke alone, with the sun on his face, partially entrenched in a pile of ice and snow.

As Affanso lie frozen, on the brink of death, he had been rescued—by a bearded, dark-skinned man, wearing a brilliant white robe and sash.

Hassnain said that the man carried a nearly unconscious Affanso up into the mountains, into a system of caves that ran throughout the rock. Affanso had suffered a fractured leg, which he broke in a fall during the storm and numerous other injuries.

In the rock caves, the mountain-dwelling man nursed Affanso back to health.

Affanso stayed in a small chamber of the cave, perpetually lit by firelight and was for the most part immobile, laying on a thick folded cloth on the floor, with his leg in a wooden splint fashioned by his rescuer.

The man who saved Affanso was silent during the majority of the missionary's rehabilitation; but, at various times, Affanso heard the man speaking with someone else—out of his view—their voices echoing in the cave system.

Affanso had recognized the language as Aramaic; an ancient language—the language spoken by Christ. This puzzled Affanso. He was hundreds of miles farther east than he had ever heard the language spoken before. And unfortunately, the monk only knew a few Aramaic sayings, mostly those spoken by Christ himself, certainly not enough to truly understand or converse with his companion.

The mystery regarding the identity of the man that saved him began to truly blossom—when one night, Affanso heard a strange sound echoing throughout the cave. It was a rhythmic, pulsing sound, accompanied by an odd oscillating airflow that almost seemed to push and pull at him. Affanso arose in the night and with the help of a wooden crutch, slowly followed the sound in the darkness, moving blindly through the cave. In time, Affanso saw the flicker of firelight in the distance. He approached an opening that led to a large, open chamber within the cave, lit by dozens of candles.

When Affanso quietly peered into the open space, he could scarcely believe what he saw. The man who had saved him, robed as always in white, was hovering three feet above the floor, while sitting cross-legged, humming and rocking rhythmically back and forth. The missionary noticed that small pebbles on the floor, along with the airflow in and around the room, seemed to move in synchrony with the man's movement as if both the earth and air were entrained with the man as he levitated.

Affanso goes on to say that his pneumonia worsened, but one night his host came to him, laid his hands on Affanso's chest and uttered a short prayer in Aramaic. Affanso says he felt an odd sensation during this prayer in his chest and in his injured limb and after that moment, he was cured of his afflictions.

The monk, with his leg healed and his health returned to him, traveled southwest to Goa, where he rejoined the church and told his story to St. Francis Xavier. Affanso's story was written down, where it sat, nearly unnoticed, in a Portuguese library in Goa, for nearly 500 years.

Hassnain said he had examined the original manuscript written by Affanso, which was still in the Goa library in Southwest India.

Then, Hassnain continued, in the same vein, speaking of a British surveyor who, in 1887, got lost in the wilderness near Mount Kailash in Tibet and had gone missing for weeks. When the man returned to civilization, he told tales of his encounter with a mysterious sect of monks, who lived in mountain caves, spoke an unidentified language, and who were perpetually dressed in white robes. And the surveyor swore he had seen the impossible—the robed men walking on water and even disappearing from sight.

The man's story was met with widespread skepticism and even criticism. When a party of British volunteers returned to the very same caves along with the surveyor, there was no trace of the miraculous men, only hallowed rock. Most scholars believed the man made up his story in order to gain attention, for upon his return to England he had spoken extensively with the British Post, who paid the surveyor a handsome fee and published accounts of his story in the paper. In time, the validity of the tale was attacked by multiple scholars and the surveyor eventually died in obscurity. Although the man had sworn to his story till the end, most people believed the story and the surveyor were frauds.

Hassnain, however, was not so quick to dismiss the man's fantastic tale, for it bore striking similarities to that of the Portuguese monk, Affanso, who had, hundreds of years earlier, described a similar experience only a few hundred miles away. The men both painted a picture of a cave-dwelling sect of Aramaic-speaking, white-robed men that lived in the wilderness and possessed supernatural powers.

Hassnain, with no sense of folly in his voice, put forth his theory that both men had come in contact with a group of wandering Essenes, an exclusive sect that lived and operated in secrecy and still possessed the powers of the ancient prophets. Hassnain admitted that he had spent decades looking for the sect, but had thus far come up with nothing concrete. The men were ghosts.

Moorea, after conversing for some time, exchanged information with Hassnain, who wished Moorea well in his quest and promised to keep in touch.

In his study, Moorea removed the letter that had been addressed to him from Dr. Hassnain and began to read it. It was the first letter that Hassnain had sent in the last nine years.

Moorea felt his future changing as he read the letter, realizing that the answer to a question that had been burning in him (for as long as he could remember) may have been found, on the other side of the world.

34

Karen Klein popped up onto a sill of brick that encompassed the courtyard in front of Schermerhorn Hall, the home of Columbia University's archaeology department. After straightening out her baby-blue blouse, she began tracing circles in the dirt as she examined a group of pink and magenta flowers whose petals looked frail in the falling twilight.

"I don't think these Azaleas are getting enough water." she said, sounding concerned.

She turned from the plants, and set her gaze on an approaching man, softly lit by the courtyard lamps. It was her ex-husband, Charles Klein.

He ran a hand through his dark beard.

"Well, here I am," he said.

"I'm glad to see you." Karen replied, smiling—her bright eyes beaming behind, large, wide glasses. "Boy, do I have something to show you."

Three months earlier, Karen and a group of her students unearthed a naturally mummified man from Mount Shahdagh in the Caucasus Mountains. The man was originally discovered by a group of hikers along a well-traveled route to the summit, at nearly 3,000 meters above sea level. It was assumed that an earthquake exposed the body, which had been hidden under a shroud of snow and ice.

The man was well-preserved; tall, with pale white skin—rough as leather—and dressed in garments of linen and woolen cloth. Based on his attire, he appeared to be from the early Ottoman Empire, at least 400 years before the present day. But he did not look like a typical Ottoman man.

After an agreement was made with the Azerbaijan government, stating that the frozen man would one day be returned home, Karen and her team were given permission to temporarily transfer the body to their lab at Columbia, so that they could study the ice man in an environment designed to preserve his body, clothes, and belongings.

The Ottoman man—or Saatçi, as some had come to call him—had died in the fetal position. His death was, no doubt, quickened by the two arrows found lodged in his hip and abdomen. The arrows, as well as Saatçi's tissue, had been carbon dated and both indicated he most likely passed away 450 to 530 years ago.

Saatçi was found clutching a leather satchel to his breast. When the team carefully removed the satchel, they found within a folded cloth. When the cloth was unfolded, it was found to be sewn with dozens of passages of mathematics. At least a few of the passages dealt with spherical geometry, a branch of mathematics around since the time of Euclid, involving the generation of shapes and grids on a surface of a sphere. There were also advanced mathematical algorithms that appeared to be encrypted—equations that could not be deciphered without some sort of key, to give values to numerous undefined variables.

The textile was still in the process of restoration, translation and decoding; and the jury was still out on what its real meaning was.

A week prior, an article was written by the Smithsonian Institute about Saatçi. The article not only featured pictures of the naturally mummified man but also pictures of the textile as well.

The team found something else incredible on Saatçi, as they systematically removed the man's clothing and classified his belongings— something that defied logic. Karen decided not to inform the Smithsonian about the find, because, as of yet, she had no idea how to explain it. Tucked away within the folds of the man's inner garments was a device that appeared to be a small timepiece. It was about the size of a pocket watch, silver and gold in color, with thirteen dials, hands (of different sizes) and a skeleton design, allowing dozens of internal circular gears entwined within the heart of the device to be seen. There were only two timepieces from the early 16th century known to exist. The team immediately recognized that this was no ordinary timepiece though; it was out of this world. For when it was found, the hands were moving and the gears turning.

Karen immediately thought someone slipped the timepiece into Saatçi's clothing as a practical joke. The patina—or oxidative damage—on the exterior of the device, however, indicated that it was at least 500 years old. Karen knew that patina could be faked and figured the device was merely a career-ending prank for whoever played it; but that was only until the device was imaged. Detailed analysis of high-magnification photographs, x-ray and infrared images, revealed that the device utilized no known winding mechanism or power source.

The team consulted with Timothy Levine, the head of the engineering department at MIT. Levine was now splitting his time between MIT and Columbia, so that he could study the device.

The timepiece would have amazed Karen and her team if it had been found in a modern jewelry store; but it had been found on a five-hundred-year-old man, a fact that Karen could scarcely come to terms with. It made her question the authenticity of the entire find.

Maybe it was all just an elaborate hoax? But then again, what if it wasn't? The relic was certainly real... So who was this Saatçi, carrying this mysterious mathematical text and this impossible relic?

It was for these questions she decided to call in her ex-husband, Charles Klein.

Charles Klein was in his mid 50's—an archeology professor at Berkeley and well known in the field. A decade ago, he made headlines when he excavated an Incan girl from the summit of the South American volcano Llullaillaco. Charles determined the Incan girl's diet, the state of her overall health, and her ancestry. He had even isolated DNA from mycobacterium he obtained from the girl's lungs, bringing to light the fact that she suffered from tuberculosis when she died.

Karen was hoping that Charles, with his expertise, could independently determine the authenticity of the frozen mummy and help her decipher his life, his health, his identity and his origins.

Karen watched her ex-husband as he shuffled through a table full of pictures, reports and schematics of Saatçi's timepiece. Charles had been silent for thirty-two minutes now.

"So, what's turning the central sphere?" he asked, finally.

Charles was referring to something that Karen and Levine had discovered deep within the mechanical device—an ever-turning, tiny, central sphere. The team was beginning to believe that the central sphere played a role analogous to that of a mainspring and going barrel.

Mechanical watches and clocks are powered by winding, which tightens and builds up tension in a strip of coiled metal, called a mainspring. The mainspring then slowly unwinds, turning the going barrel. The rotation of the going barrel provides energy for every moving part within the machine. Just like the going barrel, the central sphere in Saatçi's timepiece was believed to supply energy for all the other moving parts within.

"Well", Karen said, "we're still not sure. "But check this out."

She fished out a black-and-white photograph from a pile of documents.

"High resolution, high magnification, electron micrographs of a small portion of the central sphere."

The picture Charles held in his hand showed a smooth yet fractured surface that was covered with triangular structures, laid out in a grid-like pattern. The miniscule triangular structures almost looked like tiny sails, covering a vast microscopic plain.

"Although the central sphere is perpetually in motion," Karen said, "its velocity is not constant. The sphere undergoes brief periods of acceleration that are unpredictable and appear to occur at random. Timothy Levine, the Nobel laureate from MIT, thinks that the sail-like structures on the sphere may be detecting subatomic particles, like neutrinos and that it is the collision of those particles with the sail that is driving the motion of the sphere."

"Neutrinos?" Charles said, in disbelief, with a smile on his face.

"There are about 100 trillion of them traveling through each of us, every second. And they've been in constant motion since the dawn of time." Karen answered, approaching a large safe nestled under one of the wooden tables.

She removed a clear plastic box from the safe and placed it on the tabletop.

Charles realized what she was doing and rose to his feet.

"Here it is." Karen said, "The impossible thing."

Charles looked in awe at the device. The timepiece was beautifully crafted. With its skeleton design, it was possible to peer into the inner workings of the mechanism. There were spinning wheels and fluidly turning dials, with dozens of jewels at the centers of the circles. It was apparent the machine was aged, although the team had done work to polish its outer surface in order to see the inner workings of the timepiece.

"Is this glass?" Charles asked.

"Yes, strengthened by an unknown synthetic polymer," Karen replied.

"Of course." Klein said, slightly shaking his head, "Who do you think could have created something like this?"

"Who indeed." Karen replied. "I think it's time you saw the genotype."

Soon, Karen had Saatçi's timepiece safely secured within its safe and led the way to her office.

Charles pondered the enigmatic device, as Karen led him down the hall; for hundreds of years, engineers had dreamt of creating a machine whose motion could continue indefinitely without an external source of energy, a so-called 'perpetual motion' machine. Due to friction and other sources of energy loss, however, the creation of such a machine had been deemed impossible.

Yet Karen and her team believed the device found on Saatçi may have been running for around 500 years.

Charles was anxious to see the Ottoman mummy, the man who had possessed the technological marvel; but before he did, Karen wanted him to take a look at the man's genome, which she said was a vital clue in determining who he really was.

"This is the condensed version," Karen said, once they reached her office. She handed him a folder.

As soon as Klein received the folder, a young man entered the office. He was grinning.

"Karen." he said, "I think...think...think we figured it out...out...out. You're going to want to see this...this...this."

The young man spoke with an echo, quickly and energetically. Karen seemed unfazed by the oddity of the syntax.

Turning to Charles, she said, "Take a look at that. I'll be back soon."

Once Charles was alone, he took a seat in the swiveling armchair, opposite Karen's desk. He opened the folder and reviewed the documents held within. He shuffled through the pages, for a few minutes.

Karen said the genetic findings were out of this world, and Charles was beginning to believe her.

The genetic analysis run on the Ottoman mummy indicated that he was unlike any other person on the planet. His mitochondrial and nuclear DNA did show some sequence homology with others in earth's population, but the homology was orders of magnitude less in Saatçi than it should be.

"Wow.." Charles whispered to himself. He thought of how to reconcile the findings.

The sound of screams broke his train of thought. He faintly heard someone yelling for help and then glass breaking.

Charles dropped the papers he was examining and exited the office, running towards the sound. He ran down the hall, passed the room that housed the Ottoman's timepiece and then turned into a neighboring corridor.

Left or Right?

Charles was not sure which way to go. Then, he heard Karen's voice. She was in a panic. In a few strides, he reached the room from where the cries stemmed.

Inside the room, Charles saw Karen on the ground, grimacing in pain, holding a cell phone to her ear. The young man who summoned her to the room was on the ground as well and appeared to be unconscious.

"I think my foot is broken," Karen said. "Is Jeremy alright?"

"What happened?" Charles asked, approaching the student on the floor.

The kid was breathing, but he was bleeding quite profusely from a head wound.

"We were attacked," Karen said. "A man threw me to the ground and hit Jeremy. He took the cloth."

Charles removed his outer dress shirt and wrapped it around the injured man's head.

There was a wooden lab bench with built-in cabinets beneath it, obstructing the line of sight between Charles and his ex-wife.

"How bad is it?" Charles asked.

He did not receive a response. He heard Karen giving their location to a dispatcher on the phone.

As Charles sat on the ground, he noticed that he was surrounded by broken glass. The humidity-controlled chamber above him, which he assumed housed Saatçi's woven cloth, was now missing the glass barrier that separated the interior of the chamber from the rest of the room.

Charles heard Karen was off the phone. "How are you doing?" he asked.

He applied pressure to the young man's wound, while cradling his head in his lap.

"I'll be alright. The police and an ambulance are on the way. How's Jeremy?"

"He's still unconscious. What was so special about that damn piece of cloth?" Charles sat on the floor, his hands wet with blood that was not his own.

Karen sounded as if she were in pain when she answered.

"We think it is a map."

"A map to what?"

"Charles," Karen answered with a laugh, despite her predicament, "If I told you what I thought, you wouldn't believe me."

35

Day 3

Ning walked into the crime lab with her hair bobbing energetically amidst her gait and her attention peaked. The woman's first order of business was to ascertain how far along work was on the Sinsway arboretum—the horizontal, half-cylinder greenhouse found in the Sinsway valley. When Ning had first seen the arboretum, she was amazed. Salison set up multiple distinct ecosystems that operated independently of each other; a dry desert climate, a tropical rainforest climate, a tropical dry forest climate, a swamp land and even a tundra.

Ning had been able to identify a few of the plants within the arboretum, but had to call in an expert for the rest, since Salison's collection was quite extensive. Ning summoned a friend of hers that worked at Harvard's Arnold Arboretum and was pleasantly surprised when he said that he was willing to make the trip to Green Harbor.

Ning's phone rang in her hand after she dialed the botanist, Kenneth Wu. For ten minutes, she talked to Dr. Wu, who apparently worked through most of the night and was already back at the arboretum. He sounded as if it were Christmas morning. The man had already identified over 300 species—of herb, shrub, cactus, flower, or tree, within the arboretum. Interestingly, he said that many of the plants found in the arboretum had known pharmacological importance. He also said that he identified over a dozen new plant species and that he still had a full day of work ahead.

Once off the phone with Dr. Wu, Ning began performing chemical analysis on the materials found in Salison's lab. In between data analysis, she familiarized herself with Salison's file. One of the things that stood out to her was how much Salison traveled over the past three years. He had been to every continent multiple times, save Antarctica. Ning was told that this was so that he could obtain diverse samples of resonance proteins—for there are many types of bats, and thus, many forms of resonance proteins. Ning figured that Salison could not only have obtained tissue samples from around the world, but also many of the diverse plants that were found in his arboretum, as well.

There was much analysis that needed to be performed, a good majority of which had to do with the Sinsway case. Unfortunately, two lab techs called in sick today, which meant Ning had a bit more work to do and was thus in and out of her office quite frequently—her contemplations all over the map.

Ning was now working on putting together a list of materials that were found in Salison's lab—there were many tissue samples of the order Chiroptera (the bat). Ning supposed that was to be expected. However, something unexpected and a bit troubling, was that the glass ampoules found in the -80 degree Celsius freezer of Salison's secret second lab, were found to contain the Hantavirus. It was troubling because Ning called Boston College and found out that Salison did not have the permits to be in possession of the Hantavirus. If Salison were still around, the man would be in quite a bit of trouble. Hanta is a dangerous virus—one that can affect both the lungs and kidney—and is potentially fatal.

In between running analysis on other things that were found in Salison's lab, Ning took a few moments to entertain a pondering she had. It was regarding the description of Salison which was given to her by his doctor at Boston Memorial. The man had said that Salison had thin radiating scars along his extremities as well as a glowing sort of tan; both of these descriptions had been confirmed by those who had come in contact with Salison's body before it disappeared.

In a few keystrokes, Ning learned Salison published a few papers—under various pen names—dealing with theories regarding human evolution. One of these papers dealt with pigmentation in *Homo sapiens* being correlated with internal energy.

His experimental results seemed to indicate that indeed, melanocytes—cells which create pigment—could be activated not only by UV light from external sources (like the sun), but also by internal energy as well, from *within* one's body: the by-product of special metabolic and neurological processes that (he claimed) were responsible for making highly pigmented individuals the world's fastest sprinters, best endurance runners, and some of the strongest and most talented athletes. He mentioned the top 10 NBA scorers and NFL rushing leaders, *all* heavily pigmented men. Ning scoffed softly, she could tell why Salison would use a pen name to publish; but the man did make a valid argument. She thought of how cancerous skin cells, dividing out of control, would produce a dark coloration—so an increase in cellular activity could indeed create changes in pigmentation. Salison's proposed mechanism was slightly different though, but the concept remained consistent: Skin cells would begin to take on a darker coloration, if they, or cells near to them, had an increased cellular energy, or metabolism—this giving rise to processes allowing individuals to move faster and with greater speed, agility, and rhythm (compared to an individual who lacks the intrinsic cellular processes that generate skin pigmentation).

Salison furthered his argument by assessing different cultures.

He spoke of baseball and its dynamics, having no requisite for stamina, endurance, sustained agility or speed, especially compared to soccer, basketball and football. And he spoke of NASCAR in the same vein, both sports conceived and initially played by, predominately unpigmented populations. He was curious as to why these 'low athletic-energy' sports would arise in less-pigmented populations, while faster-paced sports like soccer, requiring more endurance, agility, and leg-use (which requires a connection from top to bottom), would thrive in more-pigmented populations. He further proposed that skin pigment could be generated by increased nerve myelination (or insulation), which would allow for faster signals to be sent and an increase in nerve and muscle activity, especially in neurons that control body movements. He theorized these processes could generate UV radiation *internally*—a by-product of a nervous system set up, and functioning, on a higher level. This radiation would then drive melanocytes to produce pigment throughout one's life.

Salison even went on to analyze dancing, comparing dances like salsa and bachata with square dancing. He said that even a self-proclaimed 'rhythmless' individual could easily master a square dance, a type of dance conceived and practiced in purely un-pigmented populations, while that same person would have trouble with a more spontaneous and complex dance, which utilizes step patterns in threes, fives, or other numbers, further up along the Fibonacci sequence, like bachata and salsa (dances conceived and performed in pigmented populations).

Salison argued there was a 'geometry of thought and movement' and that songs or dances with two or four counts (like square dancing) were less complex than those with counts of three or five. He spoke to dozens of musicians, ranging from beginners to experts, and found that nearly all of them believed that learning songs with two or four counts were *easier* than learning songs with counts of three or five. Dancers said the same thing, in regards to step patterns in their dances.

He went on, speaking of Shakespeare's pentameter which paid homage to five, and the fact that a number of great minds, such as Nikola Tesla (the father of electricity and the inventor of the radio), were obsessed with the number three. Tesla for instance, only received his napkins in multiples of three, and had to stay in hotel rooms that were divisible by three (he lived for some time in the New Yorker Hotel, room 3327).

Salison wondered why great minds tended towards patterns involving three or five. He also speculated on why it was harder for the mind and body to 'act out' patterns of three or five, compared to two or four. His 'geometry of thought and movement' theory went beyond his pigmentation theory in a way, as Salison believed that only physical and athletic traits were linked to pigmentation, not intelligence or the ability to mentally-derive patterns. He said that one needed only their mind for intelligence and pattern forming, but a special connection from the top of their body, to the bottom, for rhythm and great athletic ability (or for the ability to *act out* mentally-derived patterns).

Ning had to laugh, for she had friends who could dance quite well, even though they lacked any amount of considerable skin pigment. Yet Salison argued that as time goes on, it would of course be harder and harder to argue his point, as a 'pure' genetic population is becoming more and more scarce, in correlation with the 'melting pot' tendency of our societies; genes, ideas, and even rhythms, are being shared among cultures and communities at a grand scale. Salison put forth the notion that the diverse sharing of genes and cultures, in time, may do away with such salient differences in skin pigmentation throughout the world (i.e. in thousands of years we may all be a shade of hazel, with rhythm and athletic energy to spare.)

As Ning finished the article, she could not help but smile. It was an interesting , albeit unusual paper.

Pigmentation, internal energy, highly unusual scarring along Salison's nerves, and a healthy glow emanating from his skin, even when life had left his body. Ning's imagination had the best of her as she pondered.

Then, a soft knock at her door interrupted her train of thought.

"Yes?" she asked.

As she did, a young man entered; she recognized the man as a security guard from the first floor.

"You're working the Sinsway case, right?" the man asked.

Ning, for a moment, contemplated asking why he would want to know; but instead, simply answered 'yes'.

The man revealed a bulky manila folder and approached her.

"Some guy just dropped this off. He said it was important that it was received by someone working the Sinsway case."

Ning's attention rose. As if the courier could sense her next question, he began again, while handing her the sealed manila folder, "I asked the man his name and he declined to give it."

Ning rose from her seat as she received the package, "What was his appearance?"

The security guard shook his head.

"White male, dark hair, I would guess about thirty. He had a athletic build, was probably about 5'9"; he was fit and dressed casually. And..."

His voice trailed off. Ning heard her cell phone vibrating from her desk drawer; she ignored it for the moment. Her dark eyes came to meet the security guard.

"And?" she asked.

"Well, he seemed quite intense."

Ning's eyes flashed a shine her mind was turning as she thanked the young man.

Ning knew that the ground floor did not have security cameras.

So who was this man and what was the purpose of his delivery?

Ning's hands studied the package. It felt as if it were full of paper documents.

She set the parcel down, as she reached into her desk drawer to examine her cell, wondering who called. She read the display. She had two missed calls and a voicemail. Both missed calls were from Detective Brennan.

She dialed her voicemail and listened to Brennan's message.

Her heart sank as the detective's message played; Benjamin Grant, the lab tech who called in sick today, was now in the Intensive Care Unit at Boston Memorial. He was in critical condition and it was only getting worse. When Brennan spoke on what Ben was afflicted with,

Ning nearly dropped her phone. A sense of vertigo played with her senses and she could vaguely sense a commotion coming from outside her office.

When the message was over, Ning slipped the phone into her pants and headed for the door. The mysterious package was all but forgotten, as Ning reached for her car keys.

Benjamin Grant's condition was getting worse by the hour. For the young man had the Bubonic Plague, yes, the Black Death. And it was like nothing the lab had ever seen before.

36

At 9:36 a.m., Benjamin Grant checked himself into Boston Memorial. He presented with chills, muscle cramps and difficulty breathing, with a frequent cough. General weakness followed, with the development of painful swollen glands, one of which—under his neck—had formed a lump and taken on a dark purple coloration.

It was Benjamin himself who suggested that the clinicians run tests for the bacterium *Yersinia Pestis*, the deadly pathogen also known as the Black Plague. When the first test came back positive, a second form of the test was already in progress, yet Benjamin's illness was manifesting itself in such a way that none of the staff doubted the first positive test result. By this time, Benjamin's symptoms worsened and curiously enough, his skin took on a light shade of blue. The doctors presumed this was from low blood oxygen levels—a symptom inconsistent with one being infected with *Yersinia Pestis*, but it did not trouble the doctors any more than the fact that the young man was presenting with a bacterium that was believed to be nearly extinct. A phone call had been made to the CDC and the hospital was on alert.

Benjamin now lay in a hospital bed, eyes closed, with an IV in his arm and a mask which supplied oxygen around his mouth. Along with fluids and oxygen, Ben was being treated with the antibiotic Streptomycin. Unfortunately, it did not seem to be helping.

Detective David Brennan was at the office when he received the news. He immediately called Ning, who, in a few minutes, called him back and was on her way to the hospital.

From what Brennan understood, there was a chance Ben might not make it. The detective quickly made a phone call to a judge, explained the situation and requested a summons of Thomas Bishop. Thus far, the young man had been unreachable and Brennan had a feeling this all had to do with the Sinsway situation.

What else could it be? The Plague, here and now?

Brennan had little to back up his hunch, but that didn't stop his attempt to get a hold of someone who could shed light on Salison in for questioning. Brennan figured any information from anyone connected to Salison would be helpful.

After Brennan set in motion events he hoped would soon have Bishop in for questioning, he followed up on what was seemingly the only other lead he had within his grasp: Christopher Banks.

The detective told Middler to collect the kid from Orion Communications and bring him in. He also told Middler not to make this experience too pleasant. He figured the more scared Banks was, the faster the extraction of information would be.

Orion Communications was located a fair distance away, but Middler was back with Banks in no time. Soon, Brennan, Middler and Banks were all in an interrogation room.

It was Brennan who began, with an audio recording running, "Tell me everything in regards to your association with Dr. Salison Sinsway."

Sitting in a wooden chair, Banks was already sweating as he pushed his spectacles up on his boyish face.

There were a few moments of silence, before the kid spoke, "What Salison and I worked on was confidential."

Christopher's tone rang with uncertainty as if he knew his response would not hold up for long.

Middler didn't waste any time retorting, the usual warmth of his voice diminished.

"You mean illegal?"

Banks stayed silent. He exhaled and closed his eyes, shaking his head slowly as he did.

Brennan saw the young man mouth one word as he sat, "*Fuck.*"

Brennan nearly allowed himself a smile, before he spoke.

"What do you know of the plague?" he asked, slowly, so he could read the reaction on Banks' face.

Brennan saw confusion in the young man as he answered, "The plague? Like in the Black Death?"

Banks let out a short strained laugh, before he continued, "Well, it wiped out half of Europe or something in the 14th century. Why?"

Banks looked quite out of his element.

Brennan continued, "Do I need to remind you that Dr. Sinsway is dead and that this is a murder investigation. You not cooperating is a felony."

Brennan looked at his notes, before he continued, "The plague, this *Yersinia Pestis*, what do you know of it?"

"I just told you what I know of it. Wait. Sinsway is dead?"

Banks certainly looked scared, and if it were for good reason, which meant he knew something, or more likely *did* something that could get him into trouble.

A few unorganized breaths escaped Bank's, before Middler spoke.

"You're obviously a smart kid. Tell us what you know. Tell us what you did for Sinsway and we'll see if we can minimize the effect this all has on your bright future."

At this, Banks rolled his eyes, yet he looked as though he was thinking it over.

Then he began speaking, tentatively, at first, "Sinsway came to me about two years ago... About the time I started working for Orion. He said he needed my help and if I were to provide it, he would pay off my student loans, in full."

Banks took a sip of water that sat on the desk in front of him, before beginning again.

"MIT was not cheap. My mother doesn't make much; and well, I knew that money could really help out—"

"What did he want?" Middler cut in, unsatisfied with Bank's casual nature.

"He wanted into the system," Banks said. Then, almost immediately as if he could feel the inquisition impeding, "Orion Communications is a satellite radio station. We have hundreds of stations and broadcast all over the world. Dr. Sinsway wanted me to hack into the system for him, so he would have access to it."

"For what purpose?" Brennan asked, taking notes.

"I swear to you," Banks began, his voice slightly strained, "I don't know."

Brennan and Middler caught each other's eyes, then Brennan spoke, "Perhaps to shut down the system or to broadcast his own signal?"

At this, Banks nodded his head, "Sure."

"So you did it?" Middler asked. "You hacked the system for Sinsway?"

"Well yes," Banks said, "for that amount of money…but it took some time."

"So, at the time of his death, Sinsway had access to all of Orion Communications? How so, a laptop? A cell phone?" Middler asked.

"Well," Banks began, "it got a little tricky.

A few weeks ago, I received word that Orion was revamping its security system, which basically would render the wormhole I created, giving Sinsway access into the system, obsolete. Almost as soon as I knew, I was contacted by Sinsway. He already knew of the security upgrade and he still wanted access."

"And again you obliged?" Middler asked.

"Well yes," Banks answered. "But this time it was harder."

"Harder how?" Middler asked.

At this, Banks almost smiled, looking at both the detective and the young cadet. For a moment, the kid seemed to gain confidence, a shine in his eyes did well to portray his worth.

"Harder." was his only answer to Brennan.

Banks took another sip of his water, before beginning again.

"But I'm not sure if I even got him in."

Before Banks had time to elaborate, there was a knock at the door; and a young woman popped her head inside, asking for Brennan.

Brennan turned to leave as he spoke to Middler, "Keep him talking."

As Brennan exited, Banks began again, understanding his role as informant.

"Like I said, I'm not sure if I made the second hack or not. If you wanted to know, you would have to find Sinsway's laptop."

"Meaning?" Middler asked.

"I was using a wireless encryption method. There was a program running on a laptop which I left with Dr. Sinsway." Banks said. "I did everything I could from my end, aside from a few keystrokes which I may have had to make, depending how the encryption went. Basically, all that was needed for Sinsway to gain access to Orion was time. Time for my program to run, find the holes in Orion's security system and exploit them."

"So Sinsway wanted a mobile device, a laptop that could hack into Orion Communication satellites?" Middler asked.

At this, Banks licked his lips.

"Well, yes, but not exactly. In the beginning, he had me create for him a transmitting pole—a custom-made, highly secure, dial-up modem—which would have to be stationary. It was from this modem and only this modem, he would be able to hack the system, using the encryption program that was running on the laptop. He wanted access to Orion, but he was very specific; he only wanted access from one set place."

"What place?" Middler asked.

"I don't know." Banks said. "I set it up in such a way that if the laptop ever decrypted the security system, it would have to be plugged into the stationary modem which I specially designed for Salison. That's the only way to gain access to Orion."

"So the laptop was running a program that would eventually give him access into Orion Communications, but it could only hack into Orion when plugged into this stationary modem? Why would he do that?" Middler asked.

Banks let out a stressed laugh.

"Did you ever meet the guy? He was out there. Who knows what the hell he was thinking. I mean, I have no idea. I did it for my family, for the money. He also had me make him two wireless mobile devices, which could connect to the stationary modem. Basically, once the program I created broke into Orion Communications, he would have access to the system, either by directly accessing the transmitting pole, or by either of the two wireless cell devices which could communicate directly with the transmitting pole."

"Where could the transmitting pole be?" Middler asked.

"Again," Banks said, shaking his head, "I don't know. It could be anywhere with a dial-up modem, I guess. I built the modem and delivered it; but I have no idea where he set it up."

Middler was trying to be thorough; although right now, he knew determining the source and nature of the plague that Ben had was first priority. He was about to ask Banks if Salison ever spoke of such things, when Brennan entered the room.

Brennan looked as serious as Middler could ever remember seeing him. Yet there was a calm emanating from the man as he approached Banks—placing his arms on the desk.

"The plague." Brennan said. "What do you know of it?"

Banks shook his head, his eyes focused on Brennan.

"Nothing." he said. A few seconds past, then, "Nothing."

He spoke the word again, not taking his eyes from Brennan.

"We'll see." Brennan said. "You're not going anywhere."

Brennan turned away, briskly and motioned for Middler to follow him. As the two men walked towards the door, Brennan caught sight of Middler's curious eyes and spoke two words, "It's spreading."

37

In New York City, the well-traveled archaeologist, Dr. Charles Klein, awoke with his heart beating fast and the morning sun bathing his hotel room in a healthy glow. After his ex-wife and her student were assaulted by the man who stole the frozen Ottoman's woven cloth, the police and an ambulance arrived at Colombia's Schermerhorn Hall, whereby the ambulance took both Karen and Charles to the hospital.

Once at the hospital they were split up. Karen went to the ER, while Charles was questioned by the police. After Charles gave the police his statement, he waited around to see his ex-wife. After getting X-rays and talking to the police, she was able to meet with him, around two in the morning. Charles learned then, that Karen had four broken bones in her right foot and it looked as though she may have to undergo surgery (before that decision was made, she was scheduled to have an MRI).

Charles also learned that the injured doctoral student, Jeremy Reynolds, had significant brain swelling and had been in and out of a coma. He had seven staples in his head, but the doctors were optimistic and thought he would be fine, eventually.

Before Karen and Charles could talk about anything else, a nurse came to take her for the MRI.

As she was wheeled away, Karen told Charles to leave and get some rest, indicating they would talk the following day.

Charles Klein showered as the sun rose higher into the sky—dried his body and his short thinning dark hair, then began to dress as his hotel phone rang. On answering, he was surprised to hear that a man was waiting for him downstairs; a man named Timothy Levine—the brilliant engineer from MIT.

Charles was soon in the elevator, on his way down to the lobby.

As Charles entered the lobby, he saw an older gray-haired man spot him and begin to rise. Judging from the image Charles looked up online, it was Timothy Levine. The engineer looked as if he had not slept.

"Dr. Klein." he said, "We have a few things to discuss. There's a diner a few blocks down. Let me buy you breakfast."

Klein agreed and soon the pair were walking north down Amsterdam, with the sounds of the city weaving between their words.

"Karen is having surgery this evening." Levine said. "They're going to put screws in her foot, to hold her subtalar joint together. They think it will help with the healing. I understand she'll be off her feet for a while."

Klein was unhappy to hear the news. Karen was an active woman—a runner and a tennis player. She wasn't going to like having to sit still.

"Who was this man that assaulted her and her student? "Klein asked. "Have they found him?"

"No, he's still at large." Levine answered. "Karen said the man that attacked her was tall, built well, with blond hair, and sunken, blue eyes. He made light work of her and Jeremy, before stealing the cloth."

Levine paused to hold the door open for Klein. Once the two were inside the diner, they took their seats and ordered. It was not long before Levine began again.

"I'm sure Karen told you that the cloth contained two parts: mathematics, dealing with spherical geometry, and encrypted algorithms, which we have yet to decipher.

Over the past weeks, our team has made great strides in understanding the text. We recently discovered that the mathematics depicted were instructions dealing the generation of a geographic coordinate system on a reference ellipsoid the exact dimensions of earth—basically, instructions on how to create a latitude and longitude system on our globe.

The text also gives us coordinates, three numbers that correspond to latitude, longitude, and elevation. We think this means that the cloth is a map and that the coordinates are giving us a starting point. We also believe that the encrypted algorithms are directions to follow once to the starting point."

Klein took a sip of his coffee.

"Directions to what?"

AN EVOLUTION OF MINDS

Levine smiled, for the first time.

"You've seen the genotype, haven't you?"

Klein nodded.

"The man Karen freed from the ice, he's not exactly human." Levine said.

"So where do you think he's from, and how do you think he came to be here?" Klein asked, sounding skeptical.

"I don't know." Levine answered. "The answer to that question most likely lies at the end of the map. You've seen the timepiece. You know what kind of technology the Ottoman possessed. It was out of this world.

I think wherever that map leads is the key to this man's origins. We still have digital images of the cloth, we have the coordinates, the starting point of the map so to speak; and we think that at that location will be an artifact, something that will give real values to the unknown variables in the encrypted equations, something that will allow them to be solved."

Levine took a sip of his coffee and forked at his omelet, seeming—for a moment—to be sizing Charles up.

"Dr. Klein," Levine said, "I want you to follow the map. I want you to find what's at the end of it; and perhaps determine who this frozen man really was and where he really came from."

Klein laughed. "You're serious?" he asked,

"Listen, Dr. Klein," Levine began, with a shine in his eyes. "We are in the unique position to shape the future. Whoever built that timepiece had access to a technology that is far greater than our own. Studying that device may lead to a technological revolution."

Levine paused, before he began again.

"Lord knows what is hidden out there. And are you not curious about who this man truly is, where he is from, and how it is possible that 500 years ago he was in possession of an object that we've yet to understand?"

Klein was indeed curious about the Ottoman mummy. And it was curiosity that drove him to study archeology—curiosity that kept him moving all those years ago, during the perilous three-day hike to the summit of the great volcano Llullaillaco.

As if Levine could feel the wheels of Klein's mind turning, he continued, "I would go, but I'm past my prime and there is plenty for me to do here. You, on the other hand, Dr. Klein, you endured the climb, the wind, and the snow, on that South American summit to free

The Incan Maiden from her icy grave. And what's more, Karen trusts you."

Klein contemplated Levine's offer. He knew the man was right about them being on the brink of a technological revolution. Klein also knew he would never get this chance again.

"You would be traveling with a young student of mine." Levine stated. "Her name is Judith Arai. She's a PhD candidate in the mathematics department, and she's quite brilliant. If you're able to assign values to the unknown variables that are depicted in the cloth, the equations will still be very difficult to solve. Judy should be able to help with that."

There were a few moments of silence. Klein finished his meal, and appeared to be mulling things over in his head.

"Will you accept my proposal then?" Levine asked.

Klein nodded, with a smile on his face, indicating he could hardly believe his predicament.

"You leave in nine hours." Levine said. "I'll be financing your trip. Anything you need, you ask me. I'll have you in touch with Judith, soon."

With that, Levine placed some cash on the table and rose to leave.

"I have a few things to take care of. We have more to discuss though. I'll see you back at Columbia. Please keep this endeavor between us."

Levine turned towards the door and began to leave, as Klein spoke up.

"Wait." he said. "Where am I going?"

"The island of Cyprus." Levine answered. "In the Mediterranean Sea."

38

Two days ago, Ning Sun could not have imagined this would be her future. Not just hers, but her city's—Boston was experiencing an epidemic of perhaps not one disease, but two.

Upon her suggestion, Benjamin Grant was undergoing treatment for the *Yersinia Pestis* bacterium *and* for the Hantavirus as well. The Hantavirus explained Ben's persistent symptom of low blood oxygen levels and also accounted for a new symptom—a failing liver.

She decided to treat Ben with the anti-Hanta drug, Riboflavin, as soon as Ben's liver began to fail. The test for the Hantavirus was less than definitive, but Ben tested positive. The virus fit his symptoms, and it was also the Hantavirus which was found in Salison's lab. If it was not for that, Ning might not have made the connection.

It didn't matter though, because none of the treatments targeting either the Hantavirus or the Plague were working. And now Ben was dying, from not one, but two sinister afflictions.

Another very troubling aspect of the situation, perhaps more so than Ben's condition, was the fact that these pathogens were spreading.

Four hospital employees, including the physician who first examined Ben, had begun exhibiting early symptoms of the bubonic plague, pneumonic plague, and Hantavirus.

There were more infected as well, such as a young man who played chess with Ben at a bookstore the prior evening, and this man's wife, too. A gas station attendant, who had a short conversation with Ben the previous night was also found and tested positive for *Y. Pestis*.

All of these individuals, as well as Ben, were now under quarantine. The new disease did not abide by the rules that should govern such things—the incubation time, the mode of transmission, it was all wrong.

Yersinia Pestis and the Hantavirus both caused illness fairly quickly; but in these cases, the time course of the disease was greatly accelerated. There were people that were showing signs of infection, even though they came in contact with Ben that very morning, not seven hours prior.

It seemed as though the pairing of these pathogens, and perhaps an unknown element in their design, functioned to make them both faster. Hantavirus usually spreads from contact with animal droppings, via inhalation of virus particles, and is one of the few viruses that can survive and thrive in open air. The odds were slim that individuals from multiple different locations would suddenly come across infected animal droppings though, especially in a place where there were basically no documented cases of virus. The nature of the Hanta infection was a complete mystery, besides the fact that Dr. Sinsway's lab had specimens on ice.

Then there was the bubonic plague. It was known it could be transmitted via a bite from an infected tick that was harboring the bacterium. Ben's body though, as well as the other's, had all been checked; and none of them were found to have a tick or tick bite on them. This was troubling, for it raised the question of how Ben contracted the disease in the first place, and it also indicated that there could be other individuals carrying the plague and infecting others out in the general population. The lab was searching for anyone else admitted to surrounding hospitals, or clinics, that had any of the symptoms observed in the patients under quarantine. Ning figured Ben could have infected all of the patients who were exhibiting plague symptoms though. For Ben was found to have the pneumonic plague, the most highly transmittable form of the pathogen. Ning also guessed, that based on his state of health, he may have been the first one to contract the disease. But Ning could not be sure; there were so many variables that did not add up.

Whatever this disease was, it had a faster incubation time, and was more resistant to treatment, than anything of its nature seen before. Amidst so many unknowns, Ning was sure of one thing—that this somehow had to do with Dr. Salison Sinsway. The man's death seemed to put all of these terrible events in motion, and it was he who was in possession of the Hantavirus.

AN EVOLUTION OF MINDS

For the time being, Ning's lab was under quarantine. Work was being done out of a couple of nearby labs who, under the circumstances, had volunteered their facilities.

Before heading across town to a collaborating lab, Ning took her lunch break.

She now sat on a park bench near a large bronze statue, donning the likeness of Paul Revere upon his horse. Ning unloaded a pile of papers from a large manila envelope—the papers that an unknown, 'intense' man dropped off at the lab.

As she began to scan through the pages, she whispered softly, "My God."

There were DNA and RNA sequences of *Yersinia Pestis* and the Hantavirus, as well as other genetic sequences and plasmids. Seeing the two pathogens together almost begged the question of whether or not this dark new disease had been engineered. It was, of course, on everyone's mind back at Boston Memorial; but no one had yet spoken the words.

Seeing the two pathogens side by side on paper was quite unsettling; there were pictures of genetic vectors and various other genetic diagrams that seemed to indicate whoever these papers belonged to, wished to manipulate both *Yersinia* and Hanta.

As Ning scanned on, she saw some proposed protein structures designated resonance proteins. After this, there were pages and pages of mathematics, looking to deal with the kinetics of chemical reactions. There were graphs depicting substrate and enzyme concentrations as well as reaction rates. Further along were pages displaying multiple axes, and what she believed to be various frequencies. Ben had found similar figures in Salison's lab...

An hour and a half later, Ning felt as if her neck was going to give, but she had made some progress. She was now convinced that whoever the documents belonged to was trying to insert the most dangerous parts of the *Yersinia Pestis* genome into a modified plasmid that also contained inserted genetic sequences of the Hantavirus.

The artificial genome also looked to code for an unspecified enzyme. It seemed as though the unknown scientist was attempting to attach resonance proteins to specific places on both the Hanta and *Y. Pestis* DNA, within a theoretical hybrid organism.

The ultimate goal, Ning began to see, was to create a pathogen that could kill like a bacterium and a virus at the same time. It was a terrible thing.

Then, Ning thought of the resonance proteins and how they tied into the equation.

In a few moments, it all seemed to make sense, and she realized she may be looking at plans for building the perfect plague.

Ning Sun stuffed the papers, as well as her heels, into her satchel and took off in a sprint towards Boston Memorial. She had one question to ask Benjamin Grant, and she hoped it wasn't too late.

39

Removed from the chaos brewing in Boston, Adam Riley felt quite calm, on the rocky northeastern coast of Maine.

He had, on this day, spoken to his only companion as of late, Silloway Sinsway, only briefly. The young woman left for town in the morning, saying she needed to sort out some of her father's affairs, that she wanted to get in touch with her lawyer; and that Adam should stay put. On returning from the city, Silloway told Adam she was going for a run—and disappeared again—there was plenty of room out here to do so.

Adam found a large sketch notebook and box of pencils in the basement, and head out to the patio. Facing east, Adam drew the ocean and the sailboats as they careened upon it. He also sketched the lighthouse, which was visible off in the distance, rising up on a pinnacle of land towards the north end of the property, overlooking a cliff face. There was turmoil and chaos in the quick strokes of graphite that ran over the paper.

Adam wondered about Silloway; letting some of his energy go in the form of dark lines and textured shadings.

It wasn't until midafternoon that Adam saw Silloway—in jeans and a Led Zeppelin T-shirt, with perspiration apparent upon her; she looked as if she was out hiking. She ran a soft hand through her opaque hair, breathing deeply as she came onto the patio, taking a seat next to Adam. For a few curious moments, she stared out on the water, looking as though she were gathering herself. The silence was almost as if she was equilibrating her energy with Adam's, before she spoke.

"Do you think we deserve all this?" she asked, sounding as if she were pondering.

"As individuals we might," she said, "on our best of days.

But what about us as a species?"

Silloway brought her gaze to Adam as she spoke.

"For thousands of years we humans have been wiping out entire species of animals. Not just hunting them till their numbers are greatly reduced, but deleting them from the planet forever. And maybe, somehow, that was in the natural order of things, when we were hunters and gatherers roaming the land. But today," Silloway said, "we're wiping out 50,000 species a year and that's just in the rainforest alone. We're not just hunting animals for food anymore. We're exterminating them for land and monetary gain. We are wiping out thousands of biodiverse plants just as fast."

Adam was not quite sure where this was coming from, but he stayed silent; and for some reason, he thought of butterflies. He knew that Silloway worked with butterflies as an entomologist at the Boston Zoo.

"And it's not just in the rainforest." Silloway continued, "It's everywhere. Every time we build a department store, or clear land for a highway, we're contributing to this process."

Silloway shook her head. It was clear this was a topic that had been brewing in her,

"It's unacceptable, Adam."

"But that's not me." Adam said. "I'm not the one who did those things."

"Of course not," Silloway answered, "but it's for you, it's for us. Whether we like it or not."

Something in Silloway's voice made Adam feel as if he should be on the defensive.

"But as individuals," he said, "what can we do? We can't stop it. This is how we all want to live. I want a home. I want roads, electric power, and a few modest material things. You must want these things, as well?"

"Adam." Silloway said, "Try not to think of yourself as a person, for a moment, but as a species. Our species. What should we be doing?"

As if Silloway sensed Adam's confusion in regards to her theme, she continued with a softer chord to her voice.

"I just want you to think about these things. I'm sorry to have brought it up out of nowhere; but it's important to me, and it was important to my father. We are out of balance."

She continued, with a different air about herself.

"I have somewhere to be today, something I have to do. I'll be back this evening."

She briskly got up to leave, turning in the opposite direction.

Adam had the feeling she was about to rush off again, without another word. But before she did, Adam got in a quick inquiry.

"Silloway?" he asked, his tone telling of his confusion.

Silloway slowed, then turned around.

"There are things that are bigger than you and me Adam." she said. "Bigger than all of us."

Then as if something had come to her, "And it's not just animals and plants we are wiping out, it's knowledge, cultures and beliefs, things past down by people other than the ones who rule. In Brazil alone, where my mother was born, colonists have destroyed over ninety indigenous tribes since the 1900s."

Silloway seemed to feel it heavy in her heart.

"It's just a shame." she finished. "We are not living like we should, nor are we learning from our mistakes. What can we do, Adam?"

With that lingering question, she turned and walked away.

Adam watched Silloway leave. When she was out of sight, he leaned back in his seat and tossed the pencil he was using into the yard, towards the beach. He sat for a few moments, thinking. It wasn't long before he rose and walked into the house. For whatever reason, Adam felt within himself an unrest, and he could have sworn he saw some beer in the fridge.

As Silloway drove away from her property, she couldn't help but ponder her father.

She knew not what made the man, she only knew a bit of what he had become. She also remembered her father's parting wishes, which he had bestowed upon her. She remembered his reasoning and calm rationale.

As Silloway drove, for the better part of half an hour, a fog came to subsume the land. Silloway could scarcely see a few yards in front of herself; yet she was able to catch sight of a large Scotch Elm tree, which she recognized as she drove. She pulled over to the side of the road. A dense mist blanketed the land. An aged iron gate came into view, running parallel to the street that she traveled on. Where there were breaks in the fog, Silloway made out simple stone slabs protruding from the earth in an orderly fashion. She knew that these stones, which ran off into the distance, lay atop the fallen.

Here, lie her mother's final resting place. And perhaps it was fate that this very day, once a year, Silloway made the journey here, to remember a woman that once was.

Silloway exited her vehicle and began walking towards the hallowed ground, breathing in deeply the moist air that surrounded her.

As she entered the cemetery, she did not notice the white station wagon, donning the name 'New Life' across the door, pull up behind her vehicle.

Silloway did not see the man behind the wheel, nor the fire in his eyes, as he fixed them upon her.

40

In the fog of Maine, Silloway Sinsway walked along a worn dirt path within the graveyard. She approached a lone birch tree, which twisted its way upward through the silver mist. A tombstone lay in the shadow of the thing, a tombstone she recognized as her mother's. The dark blue of the granite always reminded Silloway of a moonlit ocean, and tonight she saw the waves as her eyes blurred.

Silloway knelt down next to the tombstone and touched the cold surface of the stone. She wondered what her mother would think of the path that she had chosen, of the future that she planned to ignite.

Then, Silloway felt an odd sensation, as if the pull of gravity had somehow become stronger somewhere near her, somewhere off in the periphery. The young woman suddenly gained focus, as she listened to birch leaves shake above her—as she felt the dense air swim around her skin. Silloway peered off towards the west, towards the place she believed this feeling stemmed. She could only make out a few dark tombstones, as they sank into the silver fog that blanketed the land.

Silloway strained her eyes to see off into the distance. As she did, the mist began to swirl as if it were anticipating movement. Then, Silloway knew. *Someone was coming.* A form appeared in the distance. At first, it was a mere silhouette; then, it was a man. Silloway could scarcely believe her eyes.

Walking towards her was a man she believed to be dead. Walking towards her, was her father, Salison Sinsway.

41

Jonas Moorea did indeed fancy himself a modern-day Doctor Frankenstein.

Some would argue that the doctor, Frankenstein, was not the monster; yet Jonas would have disagreed.

Jonas, Salison, and Bishop, had all been using human embryonic stem cells, obtained from cord blood at New Life, to further insulate their nerves, in hopes of speeding up the signals that ran throughout their nervous system—in hopes of giving themselves a heightened sense and speed through the world.

This was one aspect of Salison's plan to induce enlightenment. He argued that the brain's ability to sense one's surroundings and to direct movement within a given frame of time and space, was limited by quite a number of things; one of which being the speed that signals travel along motor and sensory nerves—for the fastest signals are sent by the most heavily myelinated, or insulated, nerve fibers.

To insulate their nerves with stem cells, Moorea and Salison first 'persuaded' stem cells to differentiate into (or become) cells that insulate neurons. Luckily for them, a team of researchers at Cornell had found out how to do just that a few years prior. They infected cultured stem cells with engineered viruses that worked to infect the stem cells, causing them to produce proteins, called transcription factors, that would ultimately direct the stem cells to differentiate into either oligodendroglia or Schwann cells—glial cells that insulate nerves.

Using the methods of the Cornell researchers, Moorea and Salison generated cells that would insulate their nerves, born of stem cells that were taken from patients that were suitable donors. There was no shortage of potential donor matches, since the team had access to cord blood at New Life.

After multiple, extensive surgeries, Salison, Bishop, and Moorea had the insulating cells transplanted along their nerves and spinal cords, along with other molecules that would aid in their bodies' acceptance of the foreign cells (molecules such as cytokine leukemia inhibitory factor, Adenosine Triphosphate (ATP), and the cell adhesion molecule L1-CAM, which were shown by others to facilitate integration of transplanted cells into host tissue, had all been enriched in the serum surrounding the transplanted stem cells).

Salison encouraged those involved in the project to fast and restrict calories once the surgeries had begun, as he believed that the loss of fat and the toning of muscle would provide the excess room within their bodies and nervous systems to accommodate the most efficient integration of the transplanted cells. Moorea recollected stories of both Jesus and Buddha—who were both said to have fasted on towards their enlightenment—perhaps their enlightenment too, was brought about by increasing the ratio of nerve fibers and insulation to fat and muscle tissue.

In order to supply neural tissues—as well as muscles and organs—with more oxygen, the team had also been blood doping. They transfused copious amounts of red blood cells into their bodies, not only increasing their aerobic capacity, stamina, and endurance; but also supplying fuel for the mechanisms that power thought and signal transduction in the nervous system.

After only a few months, Salison's project began to generate results.

Moorea and Bishop both began to feel a heightened sense. Moorea first noticed that his reaction time had decreased dramatically. Once, at a diner, a young woman seated at a booth in front of Moorea had simultaneously knocked a cup of coffee and a glass of ice water off her table. Moorea had turned, repositioned his body, and caught both of the falling objects in a mere instant, without losing a drop from either container. And that was just the beginning.

Moorea had since realized why Salison also recommended meditation, yoga, and various forms of martial arts to further develop their newly acquired speed and focus. Moorea was not only moving faster, he had more balance; and he also felt as if he were sensing more of the world around him. Not only that, but thanks to Salison's blood doping regiment, Moorea had an incredible energy and could work out for hours without a hint of fatigue. It was amazing. Moorea felt as if he were superhuman.

And there was another effect of the procedure, which had less to do with one's physical abilities.

Moorea noticed he was getting *deeper*. It was as if his spirit was growing, or he was becoming more connected to the outside world. Some days, Moorea would burst into tears, not out of sadness or fear, or any other emotion that he could remember feeling—it was almost as if he was simply overtaken by the beauty of the moment. Whatever the new feeling was, Moorea loved it. He felt as if he was awake for the first time in his life.

A week ago though, everything changed. The dream world, which Salison created for Moorea, had in an instant come crashing down. For Moorea had found out, after suffering from increasing fatigue, that some of the cells that had been transplanted into him, had become cancerous, and that the cancer was spreading throughout his body—Moorea learned that he was dying, that he had weeks, months at best, to live.

When confronted with the news, Salison seemed to brush it off his shoulders. Although the man was nowhere to be found, he had responded to one of Moorea's e-mails, telling Moorea that he was not dying, and that it was all in his head.

Salison stayed firm in denying there was a problem, even when he was presented with Moorea's test results. And Salison did not seem to be sick at all. Not only that, but he was *more* than Moorea. He was faster. He was *deeper*. And he had demonstrated to Moorea (at New Life) that he had *truly* begun to glimpse what the prophets had found.

Moorea *knew* that Salison was hiding something from him; and he knew it was a secret dealing with life and death—he could feel it.

What was it Salison was hiding? Was it the method that allowed him to remain cancer-free? Or perhaps it was a hidden step in the enlightenment protocol that allowed him to achieve a higher state of being or consciousness? Perhaps those secrets were one-in-the-same?

Moorea was after the secrets that Salison held, and with Bishop's resources, Moorea began to search for the man. But alas, for the past three weeks, Salison's whereabouts had been unknown. He only infrequently responded to Moorea's e-mails, which could have been sent from anywhere.

So Moorea, a desperate man, had, with Bishop's help, kidnapped Silloway, in hopes she would be able to get ahold of her father, and that Salison would speak on all of the matters presented to him, knowing his daughter was in danger. Moorea had the feeling that Silloway would not go to the police after her release, as Moorea had plenty of information on her father that could get the man fired from BC or even put in jail.

They were all operating outside the law, thus there were no rules.

Yet Silloway had acted as if she did not know how to get in touch with her father after her abduction from the Boston Zoo. It was a convenience then, that the hospital had called Silloway's cell phone a few days ago, while she was in Moorea's company. Upon checking the woman's messages, Moorea learned of Salison's hospitalization.

Moorea decided then, that he needed Salison out of the hospital and immobilized, so that the man could not disappear once he was discharged. So Moorea hatched the plan of using tetrodotoxin—and a variety of other drugs that targeted the heart, lungs, and central nervous system—to slow Salison's vitals to such an extent that he appeared to be clinically dead.

The truth of the matter was, Moorea knew that delivering the cocktail of chemicals into Salison's system may very well have killed the man, but that did not worry him. He figured that it was Salison who was responsible for his own failing health and impending doom, so if Salison were to die, then so be it.

Moorea knew sedating Salison would not be easy, so he had Bishop purchase a semiautomatic, dart-shooting pistol. At the hospital, Moorea did his best to camouflage his mind so that Salison would not feel him coming. And he began firing the pistol before he had even completely made his way through the door.

Moorea watched in amazement, as Salison, lying in bed, had somehow managed to dodge the first five shots, looking almost to disappear—to move in and out of the visible spectrum in a blur—causing the air to vibrate around him and the darts to pass right through him. If Moorea had not the heightened sense, he had the feeling Salison may have disappeared altogether. One of Moorea's shots, despite Salison's resonating, still hit the mark.

With the toxins in his system, Salison could not prevent what was going to happen. His breathing eventually ceased, and his heart slowed to such an extent that even an experienced physician believed him to be dead.

Once Salison's body was at the morgue, Moorea orchestrated the theft of his body and his transport to their secret lab at New Life. Moorea was not only going to interrogate Salison in regards to his perfect health and heightened enlightenment, but he was also planning on testing Salison's blood and cerebral spinal fluid for any agents that could have contributed to his growing power.

Reviving the man had been tricky, perhaps because Salison was playing on different levels of consciousness. Moorea had fashioned Salison's IV with not only truth serum but also tranquilizers, to keep him from gaining too much physical power and to keep him from gaining too clear of thought.

Once Salison was awake, and drugged, the man indeed began to speak on things; but he evaded Moorea's questions. Salison rambled on about balance, a war that was raging (Moorea gathered it was taking place in Salison's homeland, but had no idea where that was), and a long voyage that he was planning.

On the subject of enlightenment, Salison only said that he "had become."

Moorea was not sure what to do; Salison seemed incoherent, almost as if he had gone mad.

During Salison's interrogation, Sangupta Rami had undone one of the man's wrist bindings to better reposition an IV cord running into Salison's arm. *This had been a mistake.*

Moorea was, for the moment, out of the room; but through a glass window separating him from the operating area, he saw Salison instantly regain his focus, grab a scalpel from a nearby instrument tray, and—with lightning speed—cut both his bindings and Rami's throat.

Watching Rami squirm on the floor as he bled out was a ghastly sight.

Salison rose from the operating table, calmly stepped over the writhing Dr. Rami, and walked to the door. As Salison approached, Moorea readied himself for a fight.

Moorea was not afraid. His attention heightened, as did his focus, as he trained his steady senses on the approaching man. Alas, Moorea's superior sense had been an illusion.

As Salison approached, Moorea had only seen rippling waves of colors coming at him in a flash (of Salison's bronze skin and distorted hues of his surroundings); along with a whistling sound that oscillated in its intensity, swiftly and steadily (increasing in its frequency, in less than a mere second). Moorea felt an impact on his chest; the touch had been an odd sensation, as if a somehow soft and spread out blow had come upon him, with the force of a meteor strike. Moorea flew backwards and crashed into a lab bench. He had even felt waves of pressure in the air, as Salison approached with a great acceleration and delivered his well-placed blow.

Moorea had hit his head quite hard on a lab bench (after his short flight) and soon after felt as if he were about to lose consciousness.

Moorea saw Salison though. The man was above him, accessing his computer.

While Salison's fingers danced on the keyboard, he spoke to Moorea, without looking at him.

"You are *not* dying." Salison said.

"You have to *believe*. You have to *believe* you are being healed, that you *are* healed, and you will be."

With that, Salison left, and Moorea had, for a few brief moments, lost consciousness.

Coming to and examining Salison's computer, Moorea learned that Salison was doing quite a bit of genetic engineering. He was genetically modifying the bacterium, *Yersinia Pestis*, and was also altering the DNA of the Hantavirus as well. By adding strategically placed resonance proteins to an engineered template of DNA, Salison was creating what would theoretically be an incredibly virulent and highly transmittable pathogen. Moorea was not sure why though.

Perhaps Salison was contracted by a government agency to create such a thing, or perhaps Salison had the intention of causing harm himself.

Moorea figured the chance that anyone was infected by the virus was slim; yet as a precaution, he dropped off relevant information regarding the development of the pathogen at the Boston Police station, along with instructions to give the information to someone working the Sinsway case. He knew that if Salison's hybrid was ever created and unleashed on an unsuspecting population, there could potentially be a great loss of life.

Moorea felt as if the world were crashing down on him. Cancer was killing him slowly. And there was also an odd sensation in the back of his mind; it was a feeling which he could not quite place; the feeling was dark no doubt though, and at times, would churn in his core, causing him unrest.

Salison however, in a way, had ignited a hope within Moorea when he had said that Moorea was not dying.

Moorea thought of the placebo effect. Of how *belief* alone could eradicate cancer, in a 'normal' individual. Moorea wondered if his altered state of body and mind would amplify the healing capacity of the phenomenon. Perhaps, at least for him, it was not the end.

Moorea figured that by now, the police may be on to him; but they wouldn't get their hands on him today.

Moorea was presently traveling at 38,000 feet above sea level, on a powerful jet airliner. He left Boston in the morning, traveled across the Atlantic Ocean, and caught a connecting flight in London. Judging by the expanse of water he saw out the window, Moorea guessed he was probably over the Caspian Sea, heading east, towards New Delhi, India.

From there, it was only an hour and a half flight to Srinagar, where Moorea planned on meeting an old friend, a man who had promised to point him in the direction of something Moorea had been desperately searching for—a group of men, and women, that may have been in hiding since the time of Christ (thousands of years ago) and whom may have been hiding with them, the most intimate secrets of enlightenment; a way to truly evolve to a state that was more than a mere man.

42

Pondering mysterious notions for some time can come to weigh on one's mind. On the rocky coast of Maine, Adam Riley felt a fatigue from his running thoughts and left Salison's study behind, to take in the twilight.

The young man cast steady, swiftly moving shadows upon the land, as he glided through the grass with a soccer ball amidst his gait.

Adam had only been outside for a few minutes, when he heard a car door slam shut. Adam thought it sounded as if it could be the Camry.

"Silloway?" Adam asked.

He stopped for a moment, raising his gaze to the sky. He noticed a V-formation of flying geese, as he spoke the woman's name. He juggled the soccer ball for a few times on his thigh as he waited.

In a minute or so, Silloway appeared, walking around the side of the house. As she approached, Adam noticed that there was something very strange about her nature. Her violet eyes were wet, and it looked as though she harbored an aching heart—her right hand concealed behind her back.

Silloway stopped a few yards in front of him.

"Silloway, what's wrong?" Adam asked.

Some undoubtedly deep, yet unknown emotion bled from the woman's violet eyes as she softly spoke, "Adam, have you been thinking about what I asked you?"

At this, Adam smiled. He was not sure what Silloway wanted him to say. He was tired of riddles. He simply stayed silent and shook his head. Silloway exhaled a heavy breath, and took her hand from behind her back. She was holding a dart-shooting pistol. Adam had seen this type before.

Silloway aimed the pistol at Adam. The young man's face showed his bewilderment.

Adam was about to speak, as he took a step towards Silloway, but before a single word could escape his lips, he felt an impact on his chest.

Adam could not believe what was happening. He grabbed the dart and pulled it from his chest, but he knew it was too late. He was already falling backwards, losing his balance. He glanced Silloway's face as he fell. She looked focused. Soon, Adam was on the ground, lying on his back, staring at the sky. A few clouds hung in the abyss, and birds could still be seen, as night had not yet completely fallen.

Adam heard Silloway approaching, though he felt as if he may pass out at any moment. He felt Silloway on his body. He wanted to push the woman away, or perhaps wrap his arms around her throat, but he did not have the strength. As Silloway moved, Adam used the last of his energy to lift up his head and see what she was doing. Silloway was straddling his chest, while reaching for her jacket pocket. She took out a silver cylinder and opened it, removing what Adam knew to be a one-time use shot.

It reminded Adam of the EpiPen he used to carry due to his bee allergy. So Adam knew, *this woman is going to inject me with something.*

Adam frantically tried to move, but he could not. He felt quite woozy and knew he had mere moments of consciousness left.

Silloway leaned in close as Adam's head fell upon the grass.

"My father," Silloway began, "has engineered the flood."

Her voice was soft and sweet. Adam felt a sharp pain in his neck as she continued.

"And here," she said, "is the Ark."

Adam was curious as to what had happened. He thought that the earth was quite comfortable beneath him.

Then, there was darkness.

43

In Boston, Massachusetts, Detective David Brennan felt as if there was a storm brewing in his chest. Benjamin Grant was dead. And the young man did not approach his demise in a peaceful manner. There were now six others who were on their way out, and thirteen more new cases of the sickness had been identified.

This plague, which Brennan had witnessed, was a terrible thing. Even worse, was the picture that began to develop, once Brennan started putting the pieces together.

Ning had come to him, in a near panic, and told him something that he could hardly believe. Ning told him that she suspected Salison had created a pathogen that was both a virus and a bacterium—both the Hantavirus and the Bubonic Plague…combined. Not only that, but before Ben passed, Ning had asked the young man a curious question. She asked Ben if he had experienced a sound in Salison's lab, a sound out of the ordinary.

With a solemn nod, Ben confirmed that indeed he had.

Ning told Brennan that she believed Salison had created a symbiotic organism and that this engineered organism, this bacteria-virus hybrid, would live in harmony with those it infected, until the host was subjected to a particular sound. The sound would then function to destroy strategically placed resonance proteins, which adhered to specific regions of the pathogen's DNA, and that this would function to activate the pathogen.

Ning said that these strategically placed resonance proteins on the viral-bacterial DNA, normally functioned to keep certain genes inactive. She said that destruction of these resonance proteins would set in motion a cascade of events on the cellular level that would quickly activate a variety of pathogenic genes and, ultimately, lead to the destruction of the host.

As Brennan listened to Ning speak, he was in near disbelief; yet, he managed to ask how sound could get into the body and activate a pathogen. Ning told him that the sound did not need to get within the infected body, which was the brilliance of using the Hantavirus. The Hantavirus could infect the lungs and was also one of the only viruses that could survive in the open air. So this modified Hantavirus would be surrounding anyone that was infected. It would be in the air they breathe and the spaces they traversed. The Hantavirus would thus be readily affected by sounds near to, and around, anyone infected.

Once this engineered pathogen came in contact with the right sound, Ning said that three things would happen: The Hantavirus and the Bubonic Plague would be activated, and also that an unknown, most likely engineered enzyme would begin to be produced by the virus-bacterium. The unknown enzyme would work to break down resonance proteins, thus further activating the pathogen and setting in motion a positive feedback loop that would only stop with the destruction of the host.

As Ning continued, Brennan was not sure how the situation could get worse; but as Ning spoke, Brennan realized that the situation could indeed get much, much worse.

Ning suspected that much of Boston's population could be infected with the inactivated pathogen. She said that the engineered disease was probably lying dormant in all of them, waiting to be activated by the sound that Ben had heard.

Although Brennan assured Ning he felt fine, Ning told him that many types of bacteria were living within—and on—all of us. They were called our normal flora. These microscopic organisms lived in our intestines, our stomachs, our mouths, on our skin, and just about anywhere else you could imagine. She said that they could all be infected with the bacteria-virus hybrid and not even know it, like it was a part of their normal flora.

"And this," Ning said. "This really scares me."

Ning took something from her coat pocket. It was a small, metal, hockey puck-looking object, within a clear plastic bag.

Brennan's inquisitive eyes took in the small item.

Ning told Brennan that inside the device was a small, pressurized, gas container, which could be used to dispense quite a bit of pressurized, prepared material. Although the containers they found in the Sinsway lab were empty, Ning told Brennan that if they were filled with the engineered pathogen and activated at a public place—such as a market or an airport—everyone there could be infected and not even know it. They would then carry the dormant disease with them, wherever they traveled, infecting others as well.

Christ, Brennan thought.

Ning's demeanor shown that she was thinking about the same thing he was: Salison's extensive travels.

The man had been everywhere—six of the seven continents in the past three years. If Salison had taken this virus-bacterium with him during his travels, then the whole world could be infected.

With a heavy heart, Ning told Brennan that she recently received a phone call from a doctor in Port Macquarie, Australia, who told her of at least seven patients and four doctors, perhaps even more, who had what looked to be the same disease as Ben—both the Hanta and the Bubonic Plague, combined. Five of them had already died.

When Ning asked if any of them had contact with the West, or perhaps were exposed to any peculiar sounds, the doctor seemed perplexed. Yet she answered that a young boy, who may have been the first one infected, was somewhat of a prodigy on the piccolo and frequently played other wind instruments as well.

Ning told Brennan that, at the very least, some of Australia's population could be infected with the activated and inactivated pathogen, that the pathogen may be unstable, and that perhaps it could be activated by sounds other than the one that Salison had engineered.

The homicide case had turned into something else altogether.

When Ning left, she assured Brennan that the lab was as busy as it had ever been. They were trying to figure out a method which could be used to test the general population for the inactivated pathogen. They were also trying to figure out how it was created, how it was activated, and most importantly, how it could be stopped.

A number of government agencies had now been called in. Brennan was still on the case though. And as far as the crime lab and the Boston PD was concerned, he was still running the investigation.

Brennan, for a moment, thought of Salison. Brennan knew that it may not even have been Salison who engineered the disease. Someone could have hijacked the man's labs and then used his science, his resonance proteins, to accomplish the feat.

Perhaps someone that could be involved was the mysterious character who delivered a packet of pathogen-related information to Ning...

But if it were Salison, Brennan would not be surprised; for it was he who was attempting to gain control of Orion Communications and he was the one in possession of the Hantavirus.

Ning was not gone long before Officer Middler entered Brennan's office. He did not knock, and his usual playful demeanor had dissipated. The young man's eyes bled a soft focus as he approached.

"Brennan," Middler began. "There's something you should hear. I just got off the phone with Dr. Robbins from the Museum of Natural History."

She was one of the few contacts on Salison's second phone, the one with Christopher Bank's number.

Brennan steadied his gaze upon the young man as he continued.

"She said that Salison asked her to translate a couple documents. Documents that Salison came across during his travels abroad. One of the documents was an extensive list of various plants. There were also directions on how to collect them, and mix them together, to create a potion or herbal remedy." His voice trailed off. "The other thing she translated for Salison was an ancient story."

"The story," Middler continued, "was about a holy man who had trained and studied his whole life to achieve a higher state of being."

Brennan was not sure why Middler would be interested in telling him a story at a time like this, but he stayed silent as the young officer continued.

"The man wanted to know and understand all life and he wanted the world to be at peace. He traveled the land and learned from the plants, the animals, and the insects, as he prayed and trained. One day, he came to a city which had been wiped out by a powerful illness, and he himself fell ill. But he did not die from the sickness as the others did. He recovered—he had become one with the disease. This did not pose a terrible problem, because the man lived the majority of his life in the wilderness, in solitude. In time though, the holy man heard from other wandering spiritual men, of a region, a nearby population, which was taking advantage of the earth. He heard of a people that were killing animals for sport, tearing down the forests and fields for their own growing numbers, and polluting the land. These people began to upset the balance of nature, and the holy man felt it heavy in his heart."

Middler stopped, for a moment.

"I guess this holy man, in his training, became obsessed with balance. Balance between all living things: plants, animals, the earth, and man. And since he believed himself to be an advocate of nature, he went to these territories which were abusing the land and the animals— he went to these places, and he brought death with him. City after city fell. They were wiped out by the disease the man carried within him. In the last city the man destroyed, a young boy recognized him for what he was. The dying boy asked the holy man how he could bring such darkness to the world. The man replied, that indeed, he had a darkness within him. But that he had conquered it. He said that it was not the darkness he shared with the boy's land—it was the light."

When Middler finished speaking, Brennan was staring out his window, into the night. Middler was not even sure if the man had heard him.

Then, the detective spoke.

"You and Christopher Banks are getting on a police chopper and you're heading to Maine, to Salison's property. You are going to apprehend Adam Riley and Silloway Sinsway. I have a feeling that's where they are. But more importantly, you are going to retrieve the laptop, the one which has the ability to hack Orion Communications, and the transmitting pole."

Middler nodded his head.

"Radio me when you're in the air." Brennan added.

With that, Middler turned to leave.

Brennan sat down behind his desk, bringing up the coordinates to Salison's property in Maine. A few keystrokes in, Brennan had a knock at his door. It was a young female officer.

Brennan uttered a brisk, "Come in."

The cadet held a phone that belonged to the station.

"Detective Brennan, I think you're going to want to take this call. It's Adam Riley."

44

On the eastern coast of Maine, Adam Riley awoke in the grass, lying on his back. There was a brisk chill to the salty night air. The young man had a pounding headache, and a dry mouth and throat. He felt nauseous as well. He opened his eyes and stared at the dark sky, recounting the events that led to his collapse on the earth.

Adam watched a satellite careen through space amidst a backdrop of stars. He followed the single point of light, as he pondered Silloway and her last words to him. His hand massaged his neck, where Silloway had injected him.

The skin was raised, and a bit rough, around the injection site.

Adam felt as if he could lie on the grass for some time longer, but he knew he had to rise. He slowly picked himself up from the ground. He felt dizzy, once standing. He noticed a new spot of tenderness on his chest, only a few inches from the wound left by the last tranquilizer dart. The young man sighed and cursed as he walked towards the house. He needed some water. And if he saw Silloway, he was going to tackle her before she could draw that damn tranquilizer gun, again.

Adam made up his mind before he went back inside the Sinsway residence. He was going to call the Boston PD and at least try to explain himself. They needed to know that he was not the one that killed Salison. If they knew that, there would at least be some relief to be had.

He stealthily made his way up to the door, peering in the windows as he approached. The Camry was still in the drive, which made him think that Silloway was probably still on the property. But there were no lights on within the house.

Adam quietly walked inside and checked each of the rooms. There was no one here. In the kitchen, Adam downed two glasses of water, feeling slightly better as he did. He also grabbed an apple from the fridge, feeling as though he could use the soft flesh of the fruit within his system.

Adam was soon in the study, where there was a phone—presumably connected to a landline—and a computer that had internet access. In a few keystrokes, Adam had the number for the Boston Police Department.

Once through to the department, Adam identified himself to the officer who answered and was told to hold.

Adam took a seat as he waited—his head was still pounding. It wasn't too long before a rough, "Hello." was heard on the phone.

The man on the other end of the line introduced himself as Detective David Brennan, the detective in charge of the Sinsway case.

Before Adam could begin, the detective started with his own questions.

Adam first explained where he was, and when he tried to speak about how he was not the one who killed Salison, the detective cut him off, continuing with his own questioning.

The man asked about the bubonic plague, a laptop, and a specific modem; all things Adam had no idea about. Then, the detective asked about Silloway. Adam told Brennan that the woman had shot him in the chest with a tranquilizer dart and that he had not seen her since.

At this, the detective took a couple calm breaths. Then he spoke, slowly.

"Now listen to me very carefully, Adam."

Adam listened to the detective. The man spoke of an engineered disease, of a growing death toll, and of a laptop which had the capacity to access Orion Communications and subsequently unleash hell on the earth.

Adam began to sweat as he listened. He heard his heart beating in his chest as he put it all together. Silloway's talk of balance and Salison's strange nature, it all seemed to make sense.

Salison had lost his mind as he attained enlightenment. Perhaps as his consciousness reached higher and higher levels, an evil rose within him—as it had within others seeking such things—yet the man was not strong enough to resist the sinister force. Perhaps evil had taken control of him. Perhaps Salison had brainwashed Silloway into following his lead and now the woman was going to complete his terrible plan—his plan to end the age of man.

The detective said that Orion Communications had over forty million subscribers; and if even a fraction of them carried the dormant pathogen, the disease would spread like a wildfire once it was activated by Salison's song—which Adam helped create.

As Adam listened to the detective speak, his eyes peered out of the large bay windows facing the ocean.

Adam noticed something he had not seen before. In the lighthouse, that was about a mile's hike through the woods, upwards in elevation from the house, there was a dim light that now shined in one of the windows, as the lighthouse sat perched high on a distant cliff.

Silloway, Adam thought.

Brennan said that Salison had a stationary modem, somewhere; a modem which, when paired with the encrypting laptop, would allow access to Orion Communications. If this very same person was in possession of the sound byte which activated the pathogen, they would have control over countless lives.

Adam's mind was racing; he did not hear a car door close in the drive.

Soon, Adam was off the phone with Brennan, knowing what he had to do. *He had to get to that damn laptop.*

He had a feeling Silloway was simply waiting for Bank's encryption to complete; then, she would unleash her father's flood.

Adam heard the front door close.

Could it be Silloway?

Adam looked around for a weapon. There was nothing around him; only the apple he took from the fridge. He grabbed it. He had a hell of an arm and the fruit was solid.

Adam walked to the entrance of the study, apple in hand, and looked out to the living room. There was indeed someone approaching, but it was not Silloway. It was a young man that Adam had never seen before. A young man with light skin and curly hair—he held a gun with a silencer.

For Christ's sake, Adam thought—he did not want to get shot today.

Adam figured the man was not a detective or a police officer, as there was a silencer on his gun. Also, Adam knew from the way this man moved—he was here to cause harm.

The gun-wielding young man approached the study. Soon, Adam would be in view. It did not take Adam long to make up his mind. He was *not* getting shot today. Gripping well the apple, he approached the door. The young man with the gun saw Adam, but it was too late for him to aim the gun in Adam's direction.

Adam threw the apple at the young man with all his focus and energy. The solid fruit partially exploded upon impacting the young man's skull.

It was a devastating blow. Adam felt a brief surge of pride as the man fell backward. Then, Adam heard the sound. The intruder had managed to get off a wild shot as he fell.

Adam felt the bullet, as it traveled through his body. It felt as though someone punched him in the side and released a javelin into his viscera.

When Adam saw the blood, he panicked and fell backward into the study.

Stop the bleeding, Adam thought.

Lying on the floor with pain radiating through him, Adam thought of how he had never seen such a deep red. His shirt was wet. Then, there was darkness.

45

Adam Riley lie on the floor, with his heart beating slowly in his chest. As he lost blood, his heart rate slowed and his pulse grew weaker and weaker. A 9mm lead projectile had just entered his body at nearly 1,800 miles per hour, blew through his rib cage (puncturing his lung), and then came to rest just underneath his heart having punctured his pericardium (the tissue surrounding his heart).

Adam tried to put pressure on the wound, but the blood could not be stopped. It seeped through his fingers and ran like a river over his chest, as he gasped for breath.

Adam knew he was dying. He thought of his friends and his family, of the things he would never be able to see, to do, and to say (to those he loved). He tried to move, but all he could do was stare at the ceiling.

After sixty seconds of bleeding out, Adam stopped gasping for breath—in his mind's eye, he saw a sunrise, a sunset, and fireflies dancing in the dusk against the backdrop of bonfires in his backyard.

In thirty more seconds, Adam's heart stopped beating completely.

If Adam's sensory systems had still been online, he would have registered swift strong footsteps on the hardwood floor. But Adam could not feel anything (in the traditional sense). His brain, which still harbored waves upon waves of electrical activity, had sent him to a dream world, as it fought oxygen deprivation and began shutting down.

Adam Riley was dead.

The young man's body began to cool—Adam lost his senses, and his feelings, so he did not see the dim light dancing around the room, or hear the sounds abound, as a violet-eyed, softly-glowing, tall, bronze-skin man approached and knelt down next to him. Adam did not feel the resonating hands that were softly placed on his skin, upon his wound, calling the bullet from his body. Nor did Adam experience the flows of warmth, pulling his tissues back together; he did not hear the soft words that were sung in his ear.

"I say to you, son, arise! And shed the shrouds of death!"

The sun was hot on Adam's face. He was back at home—he could hear the churn of lawn mower blades in the distance and taste the fresh-cut grass in the summer air. Adam could hear his mother's voice calling to him in the distance, as he dipped his toes into the river that ran behind his house, feeling the swiftness of the current as he checked his line, spun into his fishing rod.

Then, in an instant, Adam was whisked away. He was once again on the blood-soaked hardwood floor in Salison's study (which was now missing one fake passport, once hidden in the bottom of Salison's desk).

Adam opened his eyes and became aware of his surroundings. He was alone, and it felt like someone had drilled a hole into his side. Adam felt as if he were ringing, like a bell. His teeth were chattering, and there were tears in his eyes, as he lightly shivered.

Adam was thankful to be conscious; yet knew he was probably going into shock. Slowly, Adam propped himself up on the floor—he was, at first, afraid to look at his wound. His hand made its way to the side of his chest, and he touched the injured flesh. As his hand came in contact with the wound, there was a shot of pain.

Adam's hands were wet with blood, and he noticed a large pool of dark crimson liquid around him. His pants and shirt were wet also. He figured he must have not been out that long though, for the young man who had shot him was still unconscious, lying a few yards away.

Adam could remember the pain of being shot; but after that, everything went black.

Adam lifted his blood-soaked shirt to examine the wound, somehow finding a rising energy within himself as he did. The wound did not look as bad as Adam would have imagined. He had never seen a gunshot wound before; but it looked almost as if it were, for the most part, closed. Perhaps it was just the way the damaged tissue had arranged itself. It hurt like hell though, and Adam knew he needed to wrap the wound.

Rising to his feet, Adam went into the kitchen. He grabbed a pair of scissors and made his way into the guest bedroom. He found gauze and tape in the medicine cabinet and in a few minutes, he had securely covered his wound and thoroughly wrapped his side. The bleeding had all but ceased. And it looked as if the wound was already scabbing over. Maybe he had merely been hit by a ricochet? Or perhaps the bullet had lodged into his rib cage.

Whatever the case, it felt good to have pressure on the wound. After calling an ambulance for himself, Adam walked gingerly to the door—he knew he had to reach the lighthouse. Silloway could be up there, about to unleash her father's flood.

As Adam slowly paced to the door, he noticed that the young man who shot him was coming to. Adam kicked the man, hard in the side of the head. The moment Adam did, he knew he should not have; the pain in his side intensified, as he fell to his knees. The intruder was once again motionless.

Adam knelt down and grabbed the man's wallet from out of the back pocket of his jeans. Thomas Avery Bishop—Adam did not know him.

Adam had no way of knowing, that before Dr. Jonas Moorea left the states, Moorea had called Thomas Bishop, and left him a message; informing the young man that he had cancer, and that he had weeks, perhaps months to live. As it was, Bishop blamed Salison for his impending doom, and had quite a rage inside himself, so Bishop had come after Salison..

Adam threw the wallet to the ground and grabbed the young man's gun from the floor as he rose to his feet, reminding himself that he had to take it easy. He approached the door, and with gun and flashlight in hand, walked into the night.

In Boston, as soon as Detective Brennan was off the phone with Adam, he called the police department in Roque Bluffs, Maine and told them to send everyone they had to the Sinsway residence.

If Adam Riley was telling the truth, that he was unaware of the engineered pathogen and that Silloway Sinsway had shot him with a tranquilizer gun and then disappeared, then it was very likely that she was now in control of both the laptop, the modem, and thus the whole situation. It made her extremely dangerous.

AN EVOLUTION OF MINDS

Brennan was waiting on a call back from a higher up at Orion Communications. He was going to have to persuade them to shut down their station until this was all resolved. He was not sure of how willing the company would be though.

The detective was also in the process of getting the story out to various other parties—the mayor's office, and a few local and national news crews. It was proving difficult to issue an alert for people not to listen to their radios, but the danger was real; and with Ning's help, word was getting out.

Yet, it was not nearly enough.

Worst case scenario, if someone were to hack into Orion Communications right now and broadcast Salison's pirate signal, thousands…millions…perhaps even more would die. It was the terrible brilliance of Salison's pathogen. Had it spread like a normal disease, it could be contained—or quarantined. But since nearly everyone on the planet could already be infected with the engineered pathogen, if it were to be activated, there would be no stopping it.

So far, no uninvited signal had been broadcast on any of the thousands of satellite radio stations under Orion Communications control. Perhaps Christopher Bank's hacking program had failed; or, perhaps, with Salison dead, there was no one that would broadcast the pathogen-activating signal.

A third possibility was that someone was merely waiting for Bank's program to run to completion before they ignited all of Boston, and perhaps the world, with sickness.

A grand search was underway for Thomas Bishop, and Jonas Moorea—the young neuroscientist who was identified by Adam Riley and who matched descriptions of the man who dropped off the packet of pathogen-information to Ning.

Brennan knew, above all things, he needed that laptop and the transmitting pole.

Brennan's mind, for a moment, fell on Adam Riley. He figured the kid had no idea how many lives may now be in his hands.

46

Years and years ago, a man with purple-plum sapphire eyes that churned like the sea, and a gait wrought with rhythm, came to the coast and built a lighthouse, overlooking the bay of his land. He spent many cycles of the moon on the course igneous rock of the earth to complete the structure, which was crafted of stone, mortar, and thick panes of glass—his lighthouse now sat on an elevation, on the bedrock surrounded by sparse soil, with a grand view of the ocean. A pathway led upwards, through the rising forest, to the aged construction.

Adam Riley fought his way through the darkness, as he tried to overcome his growing fatigue. The pain in his side had become a dull ache. His hand pressed on the wound, as he hiked upwards, towards the apex of the land—the cliff face and the lighthouse. His pace was slow—had he not been injured, he would have traversed the rising earth in no time. But he found himself walking, in between brief periods where he would attempt to jog, until the pain became too much. The landscape did not allow for a comfortable run anyway; it rose steadily and, at some points, quite steeply.

Adam was glad he had the flashlight. He would have been lost without it.

He figured he had traveled nearly a mile, when he reached the top of the cliff. Here, the trees thinned out and the land became a shelf of rock. Adam followed a stone path to the house-like base of the tower. He set his flashlight on the ground as he approached, noticing a dim light within.

Adam took out Thomas Bishop's gun, as he approached the lighthouse. He was not sure if he could shoot anyone, especially

Silloway. Despite that, he held the gun so he could quickly aim and fire it, as he approached the door.

It was unlocked.

Inside the lighthouse, Adam was in near darkness. Through the main entryway, some thirty yards ahead, at the base of the rising tower, sat Silloway, bathed in firelight. She sat on the sixth step of a cast-iron staircase that wound upwards, into the night. She reminded Adam of a storm—her purple eyes the color of the sky before cyclones are born.

Adam held the gun loosely in his hand as he examined a wooden desk to his right. There was a computer monitor here; the screen was not on and the modem, beneath the table, was also off. It also appeared to be the wrong make—not the brand of the modem that Banks made for Salison. The laptop was nowhere to be seen.

"Where is it?" Adam asked, as he held his side and opened the drawers of the desks.

"Where's what?" Silloway answered, calmly.

Adam walked to the base of the lighthouse, towards Silloway. He stood a few yards away from her, pointed the gun at the sidewall, and fired a shot into the stone.

Silloway flinched.

"Where's the laptop?' Adam said. "People are dying."

"Adam," Silloway said, softly, while rising to her feet. "Are you alright?"

"Move." Adam said to the woman, firmly, as he began up the stairs.

He kept his eyes on Silloway as he passed her. There was an aura about the young woman he had never seen before. It fell from her breaths and shined in her eyes, as she watched him rise.

Adam was in pain, yet he was, at the same time, surprised at how well he felt as he traversed the stairs. He passed a window that faced the ocean. Three candles lit the sill, their light reflecting in the crystal as he continued upward. Adam's hand found its way to his side. His gunshot wound felt as if it were pulsing with warmth. All along the stairs, and at the top of the lighthouse, there was nothing to be found, save the encompassing darkness of night.

Adam traveled back down the stairs and found Silloway waiting for him at ground level, standing against the wall.

"Silloway. Are you going to do it?" Adam asked, "Are you really planning on activating this pathogen, this plague?"

Adam sat down on the stairwell, holding his side, breathing heavily.

Silloway had an odd calm about her,

"Is that a gunshot wound, Adam?"

Adam laughed.

"Oh, you care about my health, huh? Your plan is to kill me and everyone else, and you're worried about my health?"

"No Adam," Silloway said, "Not everyone, and I injected you with a cocktail that contains a synthetic compound that irreversibly binds to resonance proteins, preventing their decay; and also an advanced vaccine against Hanta and *Yersinia*."

At this, Adam's attention was piqued. So there was a way to combat the engineered pathogen...

"Do you expect that to be a consolation for me?" Adam asked.

He rose to his feet, and walked across the room, searching.

"You and your father's plan is to let world burn? And protect yourselves? You're both cowards."

Adam examined a large bookcase that sat opposite the desk, along the western wall at the base of the lighthouse.

"I haven't been injected with the cocktail, Adam, and neither has my father."

Silloway took what looked to be a cloth out of her pocket and held it out to Adam. The cloth was covered with a thin layer of insulation and nestled within was a clear glass vial, filled with liquid.

"Take it." she said. "It's yours to do with what you will."

Adam grabbed the vial, as Silloway continued.

"As for my father," she said, "this world is not his own. And he is going back home."

"Oh, I wish I had the time to ponder what the fuck that meant." Adam said, growing more frustrated, "We *have* to shut down the hard drive, Silloway. Where is it?

You're planning on killing hundreds of people. You're insane."

"Hundreds?" Silloway asked. Her voice sounded stronger than Adam could ever remember hearing it. "Think bigger, Adam. Thanks to my father, nearly all of humanity will be shaken from the earth, like water from a wet dog. And in time, man will once again live *with* the land."

Adam laughed.

"You're dreaming. People are dead. They're going to take you away."

"No, Adam," Silloway said softly in reply. "Don't you see? We are no better than the trees we clear, the sea we taint, or the countless species we push to extinction. I am preserving the grand diversity of life. I am also saving the few virgin tribes of this world; which still remain, the ones that haven't been decimated or assimilated. I am saving their beliefs, their ways of life, their cultures, and the secrets they hold. I'm saving all of them, Adam, from the disease of modern man."

"You created the disease, Silloway. You and your father."

Silloway shook her head, as she spoke back at Adam.

"My father's pathogen will fall away in time, along with a great number of this world's human population. There will, of course, be those that survive. They will band together and form tribes. They will follow the roaming of animals and the changing of seasons. Balance will be restored. Man will, once again, be just another piece of nature, not the driving force that works to tear it apart."

Adam smiled.

"That's romantic talk, Silloway. Why don't you speak plainly, and call it what it is; genocide, mass murder, pure insanity."

Adam took a few breaths to gather his energy. He straightened his posture, his gaze, and tightened his grip on the pistol.

"Shut it down, Silloway. You can't let this happen."

There were sirens approaching, in the distance.

"They're coming for me, Adam." Silloway said.

Adam's mind raced. He was thinking of balance and of nature. He knew Silloway was contemplating a terrible thing—but would the world be a better place without the billions and billions of humans scurrying to and fro, with no thought of the land and the life that was sacrificed for their trespass?

The sirens, growing louder, brought Adam's mind back to the present. The police were almost here. They would take him and Silloway away. Adam was fairly sure, that after telling the police what he knew, he could keep himself out of jail.

But what about Silloway?

She was probably already a party to murder...

Adam wondered if someone could take a life out of love though. Love for all things, not just the forms that take on their own likeness.

Regardless, Silloway had to be stopped. Perhaps, in time, maybe he could persuade the woman to fight the disease. Adam knew nothing of the so-called vaccine Silloway claimed to have injected him with. Silloway, surely, knew more about it.

Before Adam could assemble his musings, Silloway began again.

"I'm sorry," she said, "but I cannot allow them take me. There's more work for me to do."

Adam could sense an odd nature in Silloway's words, as if she were saying good-bye.

"I called you here, so you could know my thoughts." Silloway said, moving backward, towards the wall. "And," she added, "so that you could have a chance to fight this. You're a good man, Adam. I will pray for you."

Then, in an instant, she darted quickly to a dark corner within the base of the lighthouse, out of Adam's view. Adam moved toward her, quickly, as he heard a sharp scrape of metal along the base of the building's floor. There had been a door directly in front of Silloway, built into the eastern wall facing the cliff face, hidden from Adam's view.

Adam heard a sharp *clink*, as he reached the door and tugged on it. It was locked, from the outside. Adam put the full weight of his body into the door. There was no give. The barrier was solid. Adam took a step back and gathered his energy, but as he moved to kick in the door, there was loud blast from the other side that shook the whole wall and rocked a cloud of dust into the air.

The tremor looked to loosen the door. Adam moved quickly to it and kicked it off its hinges. The smell of gunpowder and metal met him, as he looked down the cliff face, to the ocean. Adam saw the door, and pieces of a platform, falling to the earth, crashing into the wet seaside rocks below. The rocks and debris were bathed by the ocean, as it violently clawed at the base of the cliff below.

Adam looked along the cliff face. In the starlight, he saw a cast-iron stairwell that was built into the vertical rock of the cliff. There were six flights of stairs to be followed downward, to the rocky beach and the ocean below. In the darkness, Adam saw Silloway, bounding down the last flight of stairs, landing on a wooden platform that was a part of a dock that led up to a boathouse, whose platforms and pylons rocked gently in the sea.

There was no way for Adam to reach the stairs. Silloway had blown the platform leading to the stair base, which was a good twenty-five feet away.

"Silloway!" Adam yelled.

His words, in the wind, blew back onto his face. He saw Silloway momentarily pause on the dock, looking up in Adam's direction. Adam could not even make out the features of her face. Then, she disappeared into the boathouse.

Adam cursed. There was no way he could reach her. She was about to be gone.

Sure enough, Adam heard the muffled sound of a gasoline engine starting up; and soon, he saw a small cruising yacht take off from the boathouse into the open water.

Adam turned from the door and jogged to the entrance of the lighthouse, moving away from Silloway, towards his future, an uncertain fate, and the soon-to-be-waiting police.

47

Day 4

The renowned archaeologist, Dr. Charles Klein, and Judith Arai, the young mathematics student from MIT, boarded a large, dual-engine Airbus A330 and took off, heading east, towards Germany (over the North Atlantic Ocean), at 7:45 p.m. Eastern Standard Time. Klein and Judith were embarking on a journey to find what was hidden at the end of the frozen 500-year old Ottoman's encrypted mathematical map—something that some believed could shed light on the man's incredible genotype, and the physics-defying mechanical timepiece that he was found with.

Charles Klein had yet to meet his partner, although he was told that she would be accompanying him on this very same flight. Klein arrived at New York's LaGuardia Airport just in time to make the last call for boarding, and he had no idea where the young woman was seated.

He figured that he would have to wait until he arrived in Germany to meet. In Munich, there was an hour and a half layover, before their next flight to Larnaca, Cyprus. The overnight trip to Munich was nine hours long and Klein had no time to grab a neck pillow at the airport—he was trying to get as comfortable as he could, as the vast, blue North Atlantic Ocean came to dominate the view outside of his cabin window.

Charles Klein would try to sleep, for at least a few hours during the transatlantic flight; but for the moment, he let his mind drift, listening to Charlie Parker wail on the saxophone, as his own fingers danced along his armrest.

AN EVOLUTION OF MINDS

Klein was pondering Saatçi. And as he did, his train of thought found another man long dead—King Xerxes I of Persia, a man who, over 2500 years ago, commanded an army of over two million men; and with it, tried to conquer the known world. A few years ago, Klein was very interested to hear that the tomb and mummified body of one of King Xerxes daughters had been unearthed and put on display at the National Museum of Pakistan.

Hundreds flocked to the museum to see the ancient woman born of the great king.

A visiting scholar, however, noticed that the inscription on the princess' tomb had used the Greek form of her name rather than the proper Persian; and once the exhibit was tainted with doubt, it was only a matter of weeks before the whole find was declared a forgery.

Klein knew of this, and many other instances, which demonstrated that there were people who would go to great lengths, and spend thousands of dollars, to create a believable forgery.

Klein wondered if Karen's Ottoman was someone's brilliant hoax, some sort of modern Piltdown Man. Klein knew that just as there were advances in every scientific field over the years, the art of forgery frequently progressed as well. But someone would have to do a hell of a lot better job at forging than those who created the Persian Princess, if they wanted to fool Karen and the rest of her team at Columbia. Klein was not sure if many people on the planet would be up to such a task.

The Ottoman was found with a variety of different objects which could be carbon dated, such as a leather backpack, a bow, a quiver, wooden arrows, a wooden compass, and tools for working flint and starting fires. He also had on his person dozens of plants, herbs, and spices in leather packets, some of which were thought to be used for trade, for curing and preparing meat, and for medicinal purposes as well.

Every time the carbon dating had come back, it indicated that the carbon-containing items had stopped incorporating a radioactive isotope of Carbon 14 into their biological makeup, around 500 to 600 years ago. Klein knew that it was possible someone had found all these genuinely-aged items separately, and then placed them with the mummy in order to boost the perception of its authenticity.

But the physics-defying watch...that could not be faked.

Dr. Levine, the brilliant engineer, assured him of that. And there was also the incredible genotype. Klein had been trying to think of a way to fake a genotype, but he had yet to come up with anything. Karen and her team from Columbia had taken tissue samples from multiple regions of the mummy, even from internal organs. Klein had sent a short e-mail to a few friends who studied genetics, and had inquired on how one could go about altering vast sequences of DNA in a uniform way, throughout a person's entire body. Klein had yet to hear back from anyone.

For the time being, Klein had to believe the impossible—that Saatçi was the real deal. In truth, he would not be on this plane, if he thought otherwise.

Klein pondered the impossible man, as he closed his eyes, cruising comfortably at 36,660 feet above sea level.

At 9:40 a.m. Central European Time, Charles Klein began gathering his luggage from the overhead compartment and, in a slow-moving, single-file line, shuffled his way to the exit of the plane. As he walked through the gate, into the terminal, he saw a young Japanese woman smiling and waving at him—she had large, lively, flying saucer eyes, that shined beneath her wide glasses.

"Dr. Klein, hello! Can you believe it?" She asked, then, "Sorry I'm Tim's student, it's just crazy don't you think?"

Klein laughed, scratching his dark beard.

"Yes, you have my agreement there. So you're what? Like a mathematical whiz kid?"

Judith laughed as she grabbed the handle of her rolling pink suitcase, falling into step beside Klein,

"I like numbers; and they like me. What about you? I read about the Incan Maiden you found atop frozen Llullaillaco.."

Judith was beaming, as the pair walked to the exit—she had an energetic hop to her step.

"Who would have thought someone frozen for hundreds of years would hold such a sway over our fate?" she asked, glancing Klein.

The archeologist smiled, Judith had a spark to her.

"Saatçi has a story to tell," Klein said, nodding, "just like the Ice Maiden. And it looks as though his, as hers, may have been a Tragedy..."

"But in his case," Judith replied, "I'd say the circumstances surrounding his life, are a bit more intriguing."

Klein laughed, "Ya, you can say that again."

In a little over five hours, at 6:27 p.m. Eastern European Time, the pair stepped into the sun, outside of the Larnaca International Airport. The smell of citrus and seaside salt filled the air—accompanied by the subtle taste of dirt that rose in clouds as cars came and went from the airport. The two hailed a cab, plopped their luggage in the trunk, and headed northwest, away from Larnaca.

Judith's honey-hued skin shined in the amber light of the setting sun, as she peered out the windows of the taxi, at the banks of a saltwater inland lake, with seagulls circling above the shore.

Klein reclined in his seat, peering out the window as well.

The pair were not able to talk much at the airport—their layover disappeared due to heavy winds over the Atlantic.

Klein took his eyes from the window, and looked over at Judith,

"Listen, I don't want to scare you, but a dangerous person may be headed to the same location we are."

Judith turned away from the wild olive trees and rocky Troodos Mountains rising up in the west.

"Someone who has no problem with seriously injuring young academics, and women, to get what he wants." Klein continued, "When we get to Denizli, I'm going to procure weapons; not firearms but something: a Taser, a stun gun, something that could help us if we run into trouble."

Judith looked as if the gravity of their situation had until this moment eluded her.

"Yes," she replied, nodding her head. "I suppose we should."

"We're going to have to tread lightly." Klein continued, "No credit cards, no cell calls. Lucky for us, your boss provided us with enough cash to purchase half the city."

Judith smiled.

"Yes, he likes to be prepared. I know he wishes he was here."

Klein shifted his weight, finding a more lighthearted nature, "Tell me about the mathematics. From what I hear, the equations are pretty complex.."

Judith glanced out her window as she answered, "Well, the mathematics involved in the generation of the geometric coordinate system, which we followed here, are not terribly complex and involve principles that have been around since at least the time of Eratosthenes of Cyrene, who composed his work Geographika at the Library of Alexandria in the 3rd century BC."

Klein felt himself warming up to Judith, as she continued.

"The encrypted equations, I dare say, are another monster. A single algorithm lies at the heart of those mathematics. And I cannot solve the algorithm without three variables, to plug into the equations. This 'lock and key' system is the most advanced of its time. Even if I'm able to glean the unknown variables from the relic, or landmark, that lies at the coordinates in the cloth; it will take some time to solve the equations. When I do, the solutions, we expect, will be directions to follow from the original coordinates, to the spot where the map ends."

"So X marks the spot?" Klein asked, with a smile, looking over to the woman, "What do you think is at the end of the map?"

His eyes caught the setting Cypriot sun.

"Treasure?"

Judith let out a soft sound of amusement and thought for a moment, turning her gaze to the countryside. She shook her head.

"No. Not treasure…" She answered,

"…Something else… You're the expert. What do you think is hidden out there?"

Klein laughed. "I'm no expert. I've never seen anything like that timepiece back at Columbia. I've never seen anything like the genotype. And Levine said the material used to sow the cloth was unique as well?"

"Yes, that's right. The mathematics are not sown with cotton, linen, silk, wool, or any other known material." There was only the slightest tell in Judith's voice, reflecting this was an incredible fact. "From what we gather, the cloth is woven with something akin to spider silk that has been strengthened by some unknown synthetic compound."

"Ya." Klein laughed. "This is all beyond me. I don't know what's out there. But I sure as hell want to find out."

Judith smiled. "Amen."

In a little over an hour, Judith and Klein arrived in the Mediterranean village of Denizli, where stone houses and pistachio trees dotted the land, and sailboats swayed in the azure bay. Judith and Klein lugged their belongings up a brick passageway, towards their hotel, with the scent of oranges in the air.

The sun had set during their drive, and the land was now bathed in darkness. The two approached a beautiful, four-story, ivory building that had large, arching balconies, and small, rounded windows dotting the façade. Lush palm trees flanked the pair, as they approached the entrance of the hotel.

The two checked in, and were soon heading up to their rooms.

Neither of them saw the slender, violet-eyed young woman outside, exiting a cab.

After fashioning a backpack around her shoulders, the young woman followed in the footsteps of Judith and Klein, upwards along the brick path, until she entered and checked herself into the same hotel.

48

It was a hot, humid, dying day in Northern India, with moisture hanging in the air—as Dr. Jonas Moorea jogged up a small flight of stairs, catching his own reflection in a placid fountain pool that encircled a grand black-marble pavilion. Moorea had been summoned to the serene Shalimar Bagh Gardens within the Indian Provinces of Jammu and Kashmir by his old friend, the scholar and curator, Dr. Eric Hassnain.

After an eighteen hour trip from Boston, via London and New Delhi, Dr. Moorea arrived in Srinagar's Shalimar Bagh in the evening, just as the falling sun hit the horizon in the east, causing waves of heat to dance in the air.

Although the origins of the Bagh could be traced to the late first century *anno Domini* (AD), the surrounding canals, horticultural arrangements, and marble structures had been raised in 1619 by the Mughal Emperor Jahangir.

The Black Pavilion, built for Jahangir's Queen Nur Jahan, was deserted. Moorea slipped off his sneakers and got a feel for the hot marble beneath him. He knelt down, Indian-style, amidst the croak of frogs and batting wings of dragon flies as they darted through the moist, organic air, flowing from the nearby Lake Dal.

Moorea focused on his breathing as his consciousness began to bloom.

He *prayed* on his journey to Asia and had come to know that Salison was right; Moorea was not dying. He *knew* it was true. There was no need to test for the cancer that had been killing him, for Moorea felt it within his limbs and his core, and he harnessed onto it with his mind, sensing its dissolution. The division of cells within Moorea's body was now completely under his control.

Why should it be any other way?

Moorea was more now, in this moment, than he had ever been before. And it was all because of Salison's project.

Like pebbles in a river against his mind's flow, Moorea sensed a heartbeat, off in the periphery. And in sixty-some seconds, he felt the reverberation of footsteps on the marble floor. Moorea rose to his feet, slipped into his sneakers, and smiled.

Dr. Eric Hassnain approached. The white-haired scholar looked aged and tired. Moorea camouflaged the realization in his eyes as Hassnain smiled, widely.

"My friend! It's been too long!"

Hassnain took Moorea by the shoulder and moved to shake his hand. When Hassnain touched Moorea, he flinched, slightly, but composed himself fluidly. As the men embraced, a curiosity came to light Hassnain's deep blue eyes, as he took Moorea in.

The two men began walking around the pavilion.

Professor Hassnain began, "I am glad you are here. You look healthy..."

"It's great to see you again. Thank you. How are you, Eric?"

"I've seen better days, heart disease is taking its toll."

Moorea frowned.

"I'm sorry to hear that."

Eric smiled.

"I feel good today, Jonas. I imagine you may be, at this point, quite curious."

"Yes. Tell me."

The humid air swam around the men, as they passed a thin canal banked by stone fountain terraces (steadily overflowing with water) and large, green, bushy chinar trees.

"Five hundred and fifty-some miles to the southeast of us," Hassnain began, "lies the remote Lungnak Valley, in the Himalayan region of Ladakh. There, three days journey on foot from the nearest village, is the Phuktal Monastery; surely a sight to behold. It is built into the cliff face, like a honeycomb, within the area's natural caves.

For the past 2,500 years, these caves and the monastery, have been used by monks and sages for meditation, study, and prayer. My daughter-in-law recently traveled there. She's a botanist, working for the Jawaharlal Nehru Botanical Garden. She was searching for, and writing an article about, a rare flower."

Moorea stayed silent as the two walked; he knew Hassnain liked to tell a good story.

"In the 1940s" Hassnain continued, "a flower that was called the most beautiful of all lilies was found atop a hill in the district of Manipur. The *Siroi lily* it was called. For the next fifty years, it was thought to exist in all the world, on only that single hill in Manipur; until it died, and was feared extinct. My daughter-in-law, Fazluna, heard from backpackers traveling through the area and natives of Ladakh that a day's journey on foot from the Phuktal Monastery, brought you to a large mound that lies within the shadow of a Himalayan cliff—there, in that grassy plain, they said, lie a beautiful, bowing lily of pink and violet."

Hassnain sat down on a stone enclosure that encircled a fountain pool. Behind him, a veil of water fell, illuminated by a swaying oil lamp that fought against the encroaching darkness. Moorea, with his attention still steadily on Hassnain, and his story, sat down next to the man.

"Two weeks ago," the aging curator continued, "Fazluna, believing that the flower described could have been the Siroi lily, traveled to Raru, and from there to Chatang, and then on to Phuktal. From Phuktal, she traveled alone further east, in search of the lily."

"Jonas," Hassnain said, as he looked around, and then leaned in. "She found the Siroi lily, atop a large mound, just where the backpackers said it would be; but not long after, she had an encounter that she cannot explain. As she made her way into a surrounding valley, she claims she heard strange noises—vibrating, rhythmic pulses that filled the air. And she was overcome with a strange sensation. She said it felt as if the pull of gravity had become somehow slightly stronger upon her—the pull coming from somewhere off in the periphery; so she curiously sought the place from which she believed this feeling and the curious pulses arose."

At this, Moorea's attention began to rise—a shine in hazel eyes portrayed the thought beneath them, as Hassnain continued.

"Over a tall ridge, in the bowl of a mountain peak, Fazluna saw a white-robed woman praying in the shade of a broad-canopied saman tree. She said the woman sat crossed-legged on the ground, and that she *saw* the air moving around the woman, almost in tandem with her breaths as she drew in and expelled them."

Hassnain seemed, for a moment, hesitant to continue. Moorea sensed that the logical region of Hassnain's brain, which had been refined over decades of research, stout observation, and scholarly endeavors, was now at odds with the centers of thought that harbored Fazluna's story.

The man continued though, as he ran a hand through a short, fading, white beard.

"As Fazluna watched the woman from a distance, she swears she saw her begin to split apart, like one woman was slowly becoming two—mirror images of each other, and that as this happened the saman tree, behind her, began to bloom out of season, until the tree was covered in flowers. Then, Fazluna said the woman disappeared altogether."

The scholar shook his head, as if he could not reconcile his own words. Yet, he must have trusted in them enough to call Moorea here, after nine years.

"That's quite a story." Moorea stated. "Do you believe it?"

"Yes," Hassnain answered. "I do."

Hassnain took a small flower from out of his shoulder bag and handed it to Moorea. The flower was made up of dozens of individual petals that appeared as threads. They were beautifully colored in a concentric circular pattern of white and magenta—the thin threads fanned out from a central disk—it was a blossom from a saman tree.

Moorea marveled at the thing. He could feel its peculiarity, as it sat lightly in his hand. He looked up at Hassnain.

"You think it was the Essenes?" he asked.

"Taking into account the woman was wearing a white robe, the surrounding caves in the cliffs, the depiction of what sounds like a bilocation, and the commanding of nature, I would guess that it's the Essenes, or their descendants."

"How well do you know the area where your daughter-in-law had the encounter?", Moorea asked.

"I could show you exactly where she was on a map. Fazluna knows her way around. We wouldn't let her embark on these trips if she didn't. But I have to tell you, Jonas, it's not going to be a trifle to get to that blooming saman tree.

From Srinagar, it's an eleven hour drive to Raru, where the road literally ends. And from there, it's a three days journey—on foot—to the Phuktal Monastery, and then another day of hiking from there, until you get to your destination, which is so remote, it can only be reached by several treacherous cliffside trails. This is not a journey for a novice."

Moorea figured he could handle the journey. He pondered his options. As if Hassnain sensed Moorea's pending inquiry, he took out a letter from his shoulder bag.

"I've written down directions to the oasis of the saman tree, should you travel via Raru. The satellite coordinates are there as well. You know if I were a younger man, I would make the trip with you."

Hassnain arose from the marble ledge that surrounded the reflecting pool.

"You probably haven't much time." Hassnain said. "There is a reason these people have stayed hidden for the past 2,000 years. I'm sure every time they get the feeling someone is on their trail, they relocate."

Moorea nodded his agreement.

"Thank you, my friend." he said, as he took the envelope. "I promise I'll be by to see you on my return from Ladakh."

Moorea began to turn from Hassnain, then he hesitated, and looked to gather himself. He softly rubbed his hands together, for a few moments, before he placed one hand on Hassnain's chest and one on his back, with his palms across from each other.

Hassnain, the aging scholar, almost looked to be about to protest, then allowed what appeared to be a cautious, curious, calm fall over him.

Moorea's eyes were closed in focus, as his hands began to vibrate, ever in the slightest degree, yet with a great frequency—Moorea began humming a sharp, simple melody. For minutes, Moorea's resonating hands were on Hassnain. The vibrations born in Moorea, manifested in Hassnain's own body and breaths. The crimson light of the setting sun danced, along with some enigmatic notion, in the sea of Hassnain's blue eyes, as Moorea removed his touch from Hassnain, and kissed his forehead. The curator looked to be catching his breath, slowly, as he felt a warm healthy glow flowing from within. Then Moorea turned, and jogged away, through the Shalimar Bagh, away from the swaying lanterns and hot marble of Queen Nur Jahan's black palace.

49

What would it take to *evolve* your mind and body to a state where you may hold sway over life and liquids—to control the seas, the storms, and the biology of others? What level of consciousness would you have to reach, so as to manipulate molecules, and interact more intimately with the fabric of space and time? Moorea, more than anything, wanted to know *God*, and he had a feeling that out there—on towards that blooming Saman, there may be those who could aid him in his quest.

Jonas Moorea knew he was beginning to glimpse enlightenment, but it did not compare to what Salison had attained, not yet anyway. His last encounter with the man at New Life had demonstrated that.

And now, Moorea was sure:

Salison Sinsway was up to something sinister.

What was happening in Boston and Australia was world news.

Moorea somehow knew it was Salison. And knowing Salison, Moorea knew it was only the beginning.

But who in this world could stop the man?—Salison could move like a phantom in the light, so fast, he would appear to drift in and out of the visible spectrum.

If anyone could stop Salison, they would need a power to rival his.

And Moorea now had an inkling that the source of Salison's heightened enlightenment may have somehow involved the Essenes…

Nearly a month ago, at a diner, Moorea and Salison had been discussing the enlightenment project—how it was affecting their speed, their senses, their consciousness, and how best to proceed. As dinner concluded, Moorea asked Salison if there was anything else that the man was doing to further his enlightenment. Moorea could not explain it, but he somehow knew that Salison was deeper and more powerful than him. Moorea felt it, and he wanted to know the nature of the depth.

Salison must have somehow known, in advance, what Moorea was going to ask, perhaps demonstrating precognitive powers or clairvoyance. For on being asked the question, Salison reached for a small binder, opened it, and then handed Moorea a delicately folded silk cloth.

There was an enigmatic smile on the man's face. Then, without a word, Salison rose up and walked away. That was the last time Moorea saw Salison, before their meeting at the hospital, three days ago.

Moorea brought the cloth that Salison gave him, and its contents to India. The items had somehow felt right in his hands as he packed for his journey. And now he knew why, and that Salison's gesture had not been hollow or devoid of meaning. For inside the cloth, was an aged, dried, beautifully preserved flower of ivory and magenta, with dozens of thread-like petals reaching out into space, taking on the form of a waxing-half moon—it was a blossom from a saman tree.

50

Thirty miles outside of Boston, Adam Riley sat at a lab bench, placing a small amount of liquid into a metal centrifuge tube. Once he did, he screwed the tube closed and stuck it into a powerful breadbasket-sized, benchtop centrifuge. Adam closed the lid, heard a click, and set the timer for ten minutes, dialing in the speed to 45,000 revolutions per minute before pressing start. A soft whirring emanated from the small device as the wheel of the centrifuge turned faster and faster.

The previous night, Adam traveled with Officer Middler from the helipad of a hospital in Roque Bluffs, Maine, to Gloucester, Massachusetts, where some members of the Boston Police Department—such as Detective Brennan—were based.

At that time, Salison's pathogen had not spread beyond Boston's city limits.

At the Gloucester Police Department, Brennan had questioned Adam, at length, about the events of the last few days, about his association with Salison Sinsway, and about the present location of Silloway and Jonas Moorea, among other things.

Adam told Brennan of the secret bunker under Salison's property and of the cottage where he picked up Silloway three days ago, that lie outside of Boston. But that was his only guess as to where Silloway and Jonas could be. Adam told Brennan that he had been shot; although incredibly, Adam seemed to be fine, needing no real medical attention. Adam had learned that a bloodied, battered bullet had even been found inside Salison's study. The forensic investigators had assumed that, somehow, the bullet had only grazed Adam. Perhaps he was only hit by a ricochet.

Adam went on to tell Brennan of the glass vial he received from Silloway, indicating Silloway told him that within the vial was an advanced vaccine against the Hantavirus and the Bubonic Plague, and curiously, also particles that may prevent the breakdown of Salison's artificially engineered resonance proteins, functioning to prevent the harmful regions of the pathogen's DNA from being exposed and activated.

Adam recounted Silloway's apocalyptic message to Brennan, confirming that she did, indeed, plan on setting the world ablaze with her father's engineered pathogen.

Brennan, seemed to believe Adam's story and with a glint in his olive eyes, he asked Adam for his help. Adam was familiar with resonance proteins, much more so than Ning and the rest of the crime lab, so Brennan asked Adam to collaborate with Ning and other scientists, so that they may try to find a way to stop the pathogen, which had already—by 8:00 p.m. this very day—taken sixty-eight lives (forty-two in Boston and twenty-six near Fort Kembla, Australia). This had all happened since Ben first contracted the disease, some forty-eight to fifty-six hours ago.

Detective Brennan had Ning meet Adam at a private lab outside of Gloucester, where the two were now working together and directing others in the crime lab, in an endeavor aimed at understanding the pathogen that Salison created, and also, the so-called 'vaccine' that Silloway had given Adam. Brennan, perhaps not the most trusting of individuals, also sent a patrolman to the private lab, to keep an eye on Adam.

The fact that Boston was experiencing an engineered epidemic was now international news. And the media was having a field day, speculating on how the virus was created, how it was transmitted, and how many people, thus far, had been killed or infected.

Adam had just learned, via the television, that there was a Japanese woman in Tokyo who had recently flown out of Boston, and that she and half a dozen of her family members were exhibiting symptoms of Salison's plague.

Similar stories were beginning to emerge from San Antonio, Texas; Punta Cana, Dominican Republic; and Novosibirsk, Russia. The pathogen was spreading fast, but the most drastic of measures were being taken to quarantine it. Citizens exhibiting symptoms had been put under quarantine, and half a dozen airports (those that received passengers from Boston) had, for the time being, all their flights grounded.

The world was now on alert, thanks to Salison Sinsway.

Adam guessed, that Salison, if he really did engineer a vaccine, had probably utilized viral vaccines; vaccines that were encoded in viral DNA. These therapeutic viruses had to first be injected into the patient, and infect the patient's genome, in order for them to become active, and protect their host against pathogens. Salison had become an expert at engineering pathogenic viruses, and plasmid DNA, so such a thing would not be terribly difficult for him.

Adam now worked to isolate the genetic material inside the vial that Silloway had given him. By multiplying, isolating (by centrifuging), and filtering the DNA that was found in the vial, Adam was beginning to see that there were indeed distinct, separate, viruses—four in all—in the cocktail that Silloway had given him.

For Adam, the next step had been to make vast clones of the viruses and suspend them, as Salison did, in growth factors that would allow them to 'survive' until injected into someone's body.

Towards this end, Adam had been using genetic cloning kits to amplify and isolate the separate forms of the viral DNA, before then infecting bacterial cultures with the isolated viruses. These bacterial cultures would ultimately be infected by the viral DNA and begin to produce a great many of the viral vaccine particles, which could then be isolated from the solution surrounding the infected bacteria.

Adam had gotten as far as infecting bacteria with the isolated viral DNA that he had obtained from Silloway's vial. It was going to take some time though, for enough viral particles to be produced that would warrant their collection from the bacterial solution.

Concurrently, Adam was also genetically engineering the viruses—he wanted multiple outlets for producing a usable vaccine, in case Salison unleashed his plague.

There was also work being done that was aimed at testing the efficiency of the vaccine that Silloway had given Adam—and that was where Ning came in.

Ning had obtained, from the Center for Disease Control, not only a handful of bright researchers to help decipher and understand Salison's pathogen, but also a dozen Rhesus monkeys to be used, under the dire circumstances, to study the pathogen that Salison had created. The CDC had quickly produced the proper clearance and protocols to allow for the lawful use of the animals in scientific studies, under their—and Ning's—supervision.

Ning Sun had taken a portion of the liquid that was in Silloway's vial and used it to study the solution's efficiency at stopping Salison's disease within a model primate system.

Towards that end, Ning had followed the direction of the only writing on the vial: '.2ml, sc.' Ning figured it meant that roughly .2 milliliters of solution was to be injected per person, subcutaneously—under the skin, if they were to gain immunity from Salison's pathogen.

Ning had injected two monkeys with Silloway's vaccine and exposed one of them to tissue ripe with viral particles cultured from the lungs of a dead plague victim. She had also exposed an unvaccinated monkey to the viral tissue as well. Ning had also exposed two monkeys (one vaccinated and one not) to the sound train that Ben had been exposed to, to determine if sound alone could really activate Salison's pathogen.

Adam was still waiting to hear back from Ning on the outcome of her experiments and had, thus far, not even had time to think of the progress that she made. Adam had his own hands full, generating and maintaining bacterial colonies, mixing media, centrifuging, washing, pelleting, re-suspending portions of DNA, and sequencing the resultant DNA that was finally isolated.

Adam had been directing about a dozen other lab members to help him with his analysis and cloning, and he was getting the feeling that they were coming closer and closer to understanding the viral vaccine that Silloway had given him.

As Adam used an automatic micropipette to transfer small volumes of cherry-colored solution, a knock at the door stole his attention.

Ning Sun walked in. She looked as if her attention were peaked; sweating and breathing hard, a focus apparent on her.

"How goes it?" she asked.

"I'm making progress." Adam said. "I think Silloway may have been telling the truth. I found four separate active viruses suspended in the solution she gave me. Two of them contain DNA sequences that code for proteins—which appear to show some inverse sequence homology with resonant protein structures."

"Inverse sequence homology?" Ning asked, sitting down.

"We know the complete structure of many resonance proteins" Adam replied, "—the position and charge of every amino acid within the protein and the three-dimensional structure of the protein as well. I sent the DNA sequences I found in the viruses to the structural biologist, Dr. Ned Williams at Emory. He designed a program that predicts three-dimensional protein structures based on the sequence of base pairs that are found in the protein-coding DNA.

Using the data I gave him, he was able to generate some theoretical protein structures for the proteins that would be created by the engineered viruses in the vaccine. Take a look at this." Adam said.

He moved from his bench, and grabbed his laptop, bringing it over to Ning.

"Here is the three-dimensional structure of a resonance protein. Stretches of positively charged, negatively charged, and neutral amino acids are color coded red, blue, and yellow, respectively."

"OK," Ning said.

"And here," Adam continued, "is one of the theoretical structures of a protein that is encoded by one of the viruses Silloway gave me, courtesy of Dr. Williams."

He pressed a button and another color-coded structure took to the screen. Although, the shapes were far from perfectly complementary, Ning easily saw that the vaccine protein seemed to 'wrap around' the resonance protein, as if the two proteins were three dimensional puzzle pieces trying to fit together.

There was also an 'inverse homology' to their amino acid sequences near points of close contact between the two structures. There were oppositely charged amino acid stretches, regions where three or four red (positively charged) amino acids were directly across from the corresponding number of blue (negatively charged) amino acids.

"Those positively and negatively charged regions are going to interact, and, I'm guessing, there will be a complex folding interaction that takes place—and that may be how the viral vaccine protein is able to stabilize the resonance protein and prevent its decay. Of course, this is just a theoretical model. It's no proof that the viral vaccine even works."

Adam's eyes turned to Ning, as if he expected her to answer the lingering question.

"I have some good news," Ning began, "some perplexing news, and some news that is damn near terrifying."

Adam gulped.

"How about I hear it in that order."

"The encouraging news is that I believe the vaccine that Silloway gave you works. I injected the vaccine into Rhesus monkeys, and they were subsequently protected from Salison's pathogen. They survived coming in contact with other infected monkeys and tissues containing a ton of Salison's Hantavirus and *Y. Pestis*.

The monkeys I injected with the vaccine were also protected from Salison's engineered sound train as well. So this vaccine is, thus far, the best weapon we have against Salison's plague."

"So it works. That's great." Adam said.

Ning continued, "The perplexing news is that there was another monkey in the cage that I injected with the vaccine that was also exposed to the pathogen (another internal control). The thing is, the monkey that had been in close physical contact with the vaccinated monkey, but not vaccinated himself, was also protected against the plague."

"What?" Adam said. "You're saying the vaccinated monkey's immunity was somehow transferred to the unvaccinated monkey?"

"I know it sounds crazy." Ning said. "But I'm starting to think that's the case.. I can't yet explain it though. I've got more experiments to run."

Ning shook her head, puzzled, as Adam inquired, "Why would Salison create such an efficient vaccine? If he was trying to attack the whole of the world?"

"I don't know. Maybe it wasn't Salison who created the vaccine. But, in either case, the preliminary studies are showing that the vaccine works, incredibly well."

Adam was pondering,

"It doesn't make sense. But I may have an idea on how it was possible to create such a vaccine."

"Yes?" Ning asked.

"Well," Adam began, "one of the viruses I found suspended in the solution, has regions of DNA that are homologous to DNA sequences that are found in the Hantavirus. The 'Hantavirus' I found in the vaccine is not the same as the normal version of the virus found in nature though. Nor did it match the version that Salison used to create his pathogen. It looked to have the pathogenic sequences deleted and vast sequences added, some of which—curiously enough—code for protein that could potentially bind to and interact with resonance proteins."

"So, just as Salison used the Hantavirus, for its property of remaining active and 'alive' in the open air, to transmit the pathogen, he was also using the Hantavirus, in his vaccine, so as to create a contagious cure?"

"Yes," Adam said. "In theory, it could work. We already know how efficient his pathogen is."

"We need to produce as much of the viral vaccine as possible." Ning said.

"Agreed." Adam replied. "But I'm still eight hours away from harvesting the first batch of virus particles. What about the 'other' news." Adam asked, timidly.

Ning continued, with a different air to her voice.

"The CDC has multiple models that they use to predict how efficiently an outbreak of a pathogen will spread and how many people will ultimately be killed or infected. And I've seen the projections. Taking into account the speed of Salison's disease, how fast it kills and how easily it can be transmitted, if the signal that Ben heard is broadcast on Orion, there will be no stopping it; it will spread like wildfire in dry, summer field—it could be a global killer."

Adam simply nodded his head, in light of this terrible fact—he had already anticipated this.

"The detective said he was trying to shut down Orion?" he asked.

"Yes," Ning replied. "But that is easier said than done. No one at Orion wants to believe an inactive pathogen could be infecting the whole world's population and that this dormant pathogen could be activated by sound alone. They believe that the pathogen is transmitted like all other viruses or bacterium, through contact with other infected tissues or individuals. I can't say I blame them though. There is no precedent for something like this."

"Ya," Adam said, "until now. With your new data, we can prove that sound alone can be used to activate the pathogen."

Ning nodded.

"That's what I'm thinking, but it's going to be hard to persuade them of that. We need more data. Brennan appealed to a judge to shut down Orion, but Orion's lawyers are doing their best to make us sound like fools. They don't want to interrupt service to their forty million customers."

Ning shook her head.

"It's an uphill battle. I have a lot of work to do. I just thought we should touch base. I'm going to continue to work with the vaccine and try to find out the proximity and timing constraints that govern the transmission of immunity from one individual to another. So, I'll be around." As she turned to leave, she finished with, "Good luck."

"I'll let you know how things are going." Adam replied.

Ning smiled as she left.

Adam, now alone, ran a hand through his short, dark hair that was wet with perspiration.

Earlier in the day, Adam had examined the waveform of the sound byte that Salison used to trigger the virus, the one that Ben had been exposed to. On looking at the sound byte, Adam had come to the realization that it was he who had provided Salison with the key to creating his perfect plague. The waveform of the sound that Salison used to trigger his plague had the same 'backbone' of the song that Adam sent Salison, upon his request, three days ago.

Salison and Silloway had used him.

Salison had made minor changes to the song, but the fact remained that Adam had supplied Salison with the vital piece of the puzzle necessary for creating the ultimate weapon.

Adam could not help but feel guilty. The feeling had been churning in his stomach, like a tightness in his core. He figured the knots would begin to unwind as he put his energy into fighting the thing that he, and Salison, had created.

As he picked up his micropipette and got back to work, he tried to push the thoughts of his involvement in Salison's dastardly plan from his mind. Adam began to relax, as he pipetted small, equal volumes of cherry-colored liquid into 14-well plates.

Adam would have loved to listen to his internet radio, as he often did as he worked; but with Silloway out there, he sure as hell wasn't going to risk it.

So, Adam worked, in silence—he now knew that his actions, his processes of thought, his efficiency, and his drive, could shape the future. If Silloway was ever able to unleash her father's flood, the vaccine she gave him could be mankind's only hope to survive and flourish (provided Adam was able to reproduce it soon enough and in large enough quantities).

Adam pipetted on, knowing it was going to be a long night.

***

Six miles away, Detective David Brennan stood at a second-story window, overlooking the street beneath the Gloucester Police Station. He ended a phone call with a press of a button.

"Motherfuckers!" he said.

He had just gotten off the phone with higher ups at Orion Communications. They were still refusing to shut down the station, despite the growing death toll. Brennan was trying to get a court order, but the Judge was not listening to Brennan. No judges, no lawyers, or anyone in law enforcement had heard of resonance proteins—the small molecules that could change their shape in response to sound.

Brennan had sent the judge a recently published review article that highlighted the properties of resonance proteins, which showed data demonstrating that truly, certain proteins could be activated by sound alone. The judge had come to understand resonance proteins—or so he said—but still was not convinced that sound alone could activate a dormant virus.

Brennan hoped Adam and Ning would be able to come up with irrefutable evidence.

Officer Middler walked in and shook his head, knowing the reason for Brennan's distress.

"We have to find another way to shut it down," he said.

"Banks?" Brennan asked.

Middler and Brennan, without the sanction of the rest of the PD, had kept Christopher Banks in protective custody. The young, nervous man was not under arrest; but Brennan knew that the kid could be useful.

He told Banks that he could work to make amends for hacking Orion Communications for Salison, if he were to work on a second hack that could be used to shut down Orion Communications, if there ever was a hint of a pirate signal on the network.

"Still nothing," Middler replied. "The kid's working on it though. I don't think he slept."

"And what about the leads from Riley—the bunker at Sinsway's property and Moorea's cottage?"

"Adam was telling the truth about their being a hidden passageway underneath the shed at Salison's property. Our locksmith was able to get us underneath the shed, into a lit, hidden passageway that led to a thick, metal door. As of yet, she hasn't been able to get through the door though, claiming the locking mechanism is complex and secure."

Middler continued, as he took a seat in the thin wooden chair opposite the desk Brennan had claimed.

"I brought someone out to perform ground radar of the area. There are two structures buried out there. One of them is a fairly large room, presumably the 'study' and storage area that Riley described. There's also a second, much larger space behind that room that looks to contain multiple, distinct compartments."

"Behind?", Brennan asked.

"Ya, there's the study and a thick wall, composed of a metal alloy that we can't identify, separating the study from a second, much larger, bunker. So, two separate, subterranean structures. One of them much larger than the other, yet connected."

Brennan took in the dark of the surrounding night, as he looked out the window, and ran a hand through the stubble on his face.

"And what of this Jonas Moorea's property?"

Just as Middler began to answer, Brennan's phone vibrated.

"Give me a second," he said to Middler, as he looked at his phone, and answered.

Brennan talked on the phone for about a minute before he said, "You've got to be kidding me."

Brennan went to his computer and opened his internet browser.

After a few clicks of his mouse, he spoke, "I'll be damned."

For a few moments, he stared at his computer screen.

"Do you know where he is now?" Brennan asked, as he spoke into his phone.

He paused, listening.

"I bet I can guess. What's Interpol doing about this? Or the local authorities?"

Another pause, more listening.

"Goddamnit, Julian. I don't care about any of that, you've seen the news. We think that bastard is the one who set this all up. That man may be a murderer. And you know the pathogen was most likely engineered, right?"

……

"I don't care what the news is saying. I'm here!"

…..

"Yes, of course we have proof."

…..

"Well, that I don't know."

Brennan sounded annoyed.

"Yes, I'll get it. But believe me when I tell you—you need to find and apprehend that man. He is extremely dangerous."

Brennan shook his head, frustrated.

"I'll get back to you, soon. He hung up the phone.

Still shaking his head, he said, "You're going to want to see this."

Middler made his way behind Brennan's desk to view his glowing computer.

"My God." Middler said with a laugh.

On Brennan's computer screen was a still image of a tall, bronze-skin man, who looked to be speaking to a uniformed agent in an airport.

It was Salison Sinsway.

"The son of a bitch is back from the dead." Brennan said. "He used a fake passport to get into Switzerland. This was taken at the airport in Geneva. One of the employees, a physics buff, recognized him as he was leaving and went back to look at the tapes."

"How is he still alive?" Middler inquired.

"I have no idea. But I bet I know where he's headed."

Middler thought for only a moment before he spoke, "You think he's headed to the particle collider? But why?"

"I don't know, but Salison gravitates towards great minds; or they gravitate towards him. And that place is a hotbed of geniuses. I bet, at some point, he'll be there or damn near there."

"We don't have jurisdiction in Europe," Middler said.

Brennan nodded, turning to the young cadet.

"When was the last time you took a vacation?"

51

Day 5

The island of Cyprus lies like a tear drop of land, that fell into the Mediterranean Sea. Three miles inland, over rocky uneven terrain, and bouts of olive, carob, and lemon trees, was the quadrant of space whose coordinates were sown into the pale Ottoman's mathematical map. Here worked the mathematician Judith Arai and the archeologist, Charles Klein. They sat in an eight-foot pit dug out from the Cypriot soil, on a remote plateau in Northern Cyprus—the pair were covered in perspiration, plant matter, dirt, and clay, with their breaths heavy in their chests—both bathed by the soft yellow glow of excavation lights, set up above.

They had followed Saatçi's map, from the small village of Denizli, to the countryside, to a place where the night air resonated with scents stemming from fruit blossoms abound.

Klein was taking a drink from his canteen with his back up against a slanted wall of dirt, his eyes on the object that he and Judith freed from the earth.

"Your name will be known now." He said, "For finding something like this." He laughed, shaking his head,

"How old do you think it is?" Judith asked—she was rubbing her hands and forearms, leaning against the earthen wall of the pit. There were small abrasions on her palms—her tank top saturated with sweat,

"Well," Klein said, "My guess is we are sitting in the courtyard of an ancient palace. I saw stress fractures in the large stones that make up the ruins of the outer wall. This region of Cyprus was rocked by major earthquakes in 332 and 342 A.D. So I'd guess it's at least that old, which means we could be sitting in the palace of a Roman governor, under the charge of Licinius I or Constantine II."

Klein scratched at his beard for a moment as his blue eyes churned in the overhead lights,

"It could be much older though." he said,

There was reverence in his gaze, as he took in the thing before him—a towering iron pillar, cobalt in color, and smooth to the touch, rising up towards the stars with its tip terminating in smooth circular grooves that bulged out subtly from the main body of the column.

"The depth at which this was buried," Klein continued, "and the patina on the region that was exposed to the open air, makes me think the site could be hundreds of years older than when the earthquake struck—it could have been built before the birth of Christ."

He let his voice trail off.

"Which would make this the oldest standing iron pillar in the world…"

Judith had her wide eyes trained on the ancient pillar—it was beautiful to behold, with stars shining down on it.

"So it's older than Saatçi…"

"Oh ya." Klein answered with a grin. He was not sure if Judith was asking or stating the curious fact, but he went on, "I would say by at least a thousand years. Which makes the mystery of who that frozen man was, ever more intriguing."

Klein looked to have regained some energy, "The information must be here.", he said, as he set down his canteen. He was referring to the values of the variables that Judith needed to solve the mathematical equations in the Ottoman's cloth.

The column, thus far, had been devoid of characters, completely smooth to the touch.

Judith leaned her head back against the dirt wall she sat along. She looked far less motivated than Klein; she was jet-lagged and the pair had been digging for half the earth's turn about its axis. The young woman closed her eyes.

Klein was soon chipping away at the crust covering the pillar, with a small hand pick, frequently using his hands to pull off patches of wet, compressed soil. In half an hour, as Judith lay with her eyes closed against the sloping wall of the pit, Klein had most of the newly excavated portion of the iron pillar exposed and cleaned.

He wiped the metal with a cloth and leaned in close to touch the pillar,

"There's something here.." He said, softly.

Judith stirred and the speed of Klein's movements increased subtly.

There were characters carved into the surface of the pillar. Judith opened her eyes and focused on the towering column—there, she saw a beautiful flowing script. Her attention peaked, as she rolled over, onto her hands and knees, and crawled a few feet towards Klein. She kept silent, as her heart rate elevated.

Judith sat down next to Klein. Time seemed to drag on and on as she watched him delicately clean out the crevices of the characters that were carved into the iron pillar, with small metal tools, a brush, and his own hands. In a dozen minutes, Klein relaxed his arms and took a few tranquil breaths, his eyes on the passages he had just uncovered. For some time, he took in the text; with his hands upon the iron.

Then, he laughed and turned his eyes to the sky, before looking at Judith.

"This molded metal is much older than I thought." He said, with a laugh.

Charles Klein then read aloud, as floral aromas swam abound around him, with Judith Arai, and a cascade of brilliant stars above, looking on as he did.

"This pillar stands,

to honor Stasanor of Soli,

Satrap of Bactria and Sogdiana,

Officer of Alexander,

Son of Phillip and the Greeks.

A patron of higher thought

and a builder of machines."

***

AN EVOLUTION OF MINDS

Three hundred and thirty-three years Before the Common Era, a man who may have been the world's greatest military commander, Alexander the Great, was fresh off two major victories against the Persian Empire. Alexander and his Macedonian forces had defeated the Persian Army at the muddy banks of the Granicus River (where Alexander, spattered with blood and sweat, had led a cavalry charge himself, through the Persian lines, and killed several high-ranking Persian nobles with his own sword), and at the River Pinarus, at the battle of Issus (where Alexander, despite being outnumbered by hundreds of thousands of men, crushed the Persian forces, forcing King Darius III to flee into exile).

It was the beginning of the end of the Persian Empire.

Onward, towards his conquest of Asia, Alexander—at twenty-two years of age—turned his sights to the coastal base of Tyre, the only Persian port remaining that did not capitulate to Alexander. Tyre was strategically located on a small island a kilometer offshore from the Mediterranean coast. It was not going to be easy to capture. Its city was walled up to its island cliffs; and Alexander, at this time, had no navy to speak of.

On the march to Tyre, Alexander sent emissaries to the naval leaders of his recently captured Persian states and to the Satrap (or governor) of the city Soli, in Cyprus, in order to summon a Navy capable of taking Tyre.

When the Satrap of Soli, Stasanor, met with Alexander, he pledged his allegiance, and 120 Cypriot warships, to the Macedonian King. He also promised to lead the fleet himself against Tyre and was made to be an officer in the Macedonian Army.

Stasanor came to learn that Alexander was a curious, worldly, knowledge-seeking man, and eventually shared with Alexander a most compelling story. A story, which would shape Alexander's future—it was about a mysterious people that Stasanor was searching for—a lost civilization so to speak, that had origins from before a time when the whole of the world was covered in ice. Stasanor said that these people belonged to a secret thread of world history, that was somehow connected to the gods and royal priests of ancient Sumeria, the Israelite prophets and their Yahweh, and also the gods depicted in the ancient Indian Vedas, the Mahabharata and the Ramayana. Stasanor had a theory—that the military-minded, flight capable gods depicted in these religious stories, whom all used multiple types of flying machines, were not really gods at all... And that the answer to who these technologically advanced 'gods' really were, somehow lie with the elusive people he was searching for.

Stasanor flamed a wonder in Alexander, of traveling further east into India, to the land of falling water, to where Stasanor believed there were remnants of this civilization, and perhaps even a way to connect with them… At the Siege of Tyre, Stasanor was in charge of building and maintaining Alexander's diving bell, an invention of Aristotle's. Alexander was using the bell to inspect underwater defenses, as he built a mole into the Mediterranean Sea to reach the island of Tyre. It was Stasanor, who would eventually suggest there were much more interesting things to search for beneath the sea, in such a device.

The violet-eyed Stasanor of Soli, told Alexander of his own origins as well, of his true home, which he described, at one time, as being a 'place of balance', lying across a great and vast sea.

52

In a private lab, just outside of Bologna, Italy, the accelerator physicist and engineer, Tonino Lutzo, was working late into the night. For the past eight months, Lutzo and his team had been building an intricate and complex device—the first of its kind—which they believed, would revolutionize particle physics.

Lutzo and his team of engineers, who specialized in magnet and radio physics, had taken on multiple jobs for the European Organization of Nuclear Physics (CERN), and had built a number of components that were now in use by the Large Hadron Collider. The Large Hadron Collider was a massive particle accelerator, that would accelerate miniscule particles, like protons, round and round the collider (to near light-speed) until the particles collided—creating, for fleeting instances, the most basic building-blocks of nature.

Lutzo's team built electromagnets (to keep particles in a narrow beam as they traveled round the supercollider), microwave generators (that made the waves on which the soon-to-be-smashed particles would ride), and cooling systems (that would remove the great heat generated by the magnets and other components of the collider). Nine months ago though, Lutzo was asked to build something quite a bit different—a director from CERN had come to him, with a proposal that, at the time, had seemed a bit more-than-ambitious.

The director asked Lutzo to build him a device capable of trapping exotic matter.

A few years ago, a team of physicists, working at the Relativistic Heavy Ion Collider in Upton, New York, had been the first to detect exotic matter—by smashing charged gold atoms together, creating negatively charged anti-matter.

Other types of exotic matter had since been *detected* at the Large Hadron Collider; but as of yet, there was no way to *trap* the newly generated particles.

Built within the ring of the LHC, is a massive seven-story particle detector, that takes snapshots of the collisions, in order to detect and identify newly generated particles. But there was currently no way to trap and collect the exotic particles generated. For one, the particles that were created in the collisions were very short-lived; some decayed within billionths of a second. And also, due to the strange charge of some of the particles generated, especially exotic matter, there was no easy way of trapping them using devices made from 'ordinary' matter.

The delegate from CERN though, claimed to have solved both of these problems. And he provided Lutzo with the blueprints for a device that he claimed could collect and stabilize exotic-matter particles, once they were created in the ring of the supercollider.

On looking at the blueprints, Lutzo was intrigued. The blueprints depicted a machine, about the size of a large microwave oven, that employed multiple trapping beams of laser light, and stabilizing harmonic radio frequencies, in order to collect and preserve exotic matter, once it was generated.

The trap itself was formed by one hollow 'tube" ' of laser light and two 'sheet' beams of laser light that would create a repulsive potential for the exotic particles. This was accompanied by both a magnetic field gradient (to cancel out the gravitational forces that could potentially interfere with the particles) and harmonic radio frequencies of sound (used to corral the particles together and keep them from decaying).

The blueprints caused Lutzo to recollect a theoretical exotic matter trap that was proposed a few years earlier by a group at Cambridge, but the CERN scientist had taken the idea to the next level.

It was eight months since Lutzo had first seen the blueprints for the trap; and now, the device was for the most part, finished.

Lutzo, a short, stocky man, with a friendly face that was enshrouded in a dark, chaotic beard, was now calibrating the lasers within the trap, testing their focus, their pulse frequency, and their power. As Lutzo tinkered with a voltmeter, he cursed, in Italian, and slapped the tabletop.

On a television screen near him was a European soccer match. A group of players in black and yellow garb were celebrating a scored goal that had been sunk in the ninety-third minute of the match. Lutzo sighed and swore again.

There was a sharp knock on the laboratory door that stole his attention and before Lutzo could approach the door, it swung slowly open.

An odd, giant specimen of a man, with dark-glowing skin and churning purple irises entered.

"*Buonasera*," the man said, in Italian.

"Salison? Can it be? I heard the most awful rumor." Lutzo spoke, in Italian, and held a look of disbelief as he got up from his workbench, "...that you were dead."

Salison outstretched his hands.

"I am alive."

Salison Sinsway took in the object that Lutzo had been working on.

"It is ready?" he asked.

"Yes," Lutzo said. "We have made it to your exact specifications. It will fit snugly into the heart of ATLAS. Much love, my friend. I thought we would be putting this thing to use without you."

"I thank you, Tonino. I will be taking the trap, if I may."

"Of course." Lutzo said, admiring the device he had built, looking as if he was not quite sure he could let it go, just yet. "When will you install it? When do you think you will be running the experiments?"

"Very soon."

Lutzo turned, for a moment, to look at his TV. He let off a string of curse words, in Italian, as stoppage time ended.

He turned back to Salison.

"I will get some alternate lasers for you and some different types of lattice magnets that you can use, depending on the particles you're going to smash. Some cleaner insertion magnets and well..." He looked around the lab. "...and a few other things you may be needing."

Lutzo made his way around his lab and placed a few items into an open cardboard box; some of them were wrapped in protective casing and handled quite delicately. He then set the box down and approached the exotic matter trap.

Lutzo gently placed the trap in a Styrofoam box with a plastic lining, and then closed the lid of the box, before using the vacuum air supply of his lab to remove the excess air from within the container, shrinking the plastic around the device.

"That should be about it. I suppose you know better than me; you designed the thing."

Salison stayed silent as Lutzo smiled and spoke, "Let me help you take this out."

In a matter of minutes, Salison and Tonino Lutzo placed the exotic matter trap, and a couple boxes of supplementary supplies, into the back of Salison's rental Land Rover. As Lutzo finished rearranging the boxes, Salison—out of view of the man—took a syringe from his pocket and filled it with .22 cubic centimeters of clear liquid from a small glass vial. Lutzo approached Salison, as Salison held the syringe behind his back.

In an instant, Lutzo slapped at his arm, as Salison freed himself of the syringe.

"These god damn mosquitos." Lutzo said, smiling and rubbing his arm.

Salison, for the first time, smiled back, and in a slower, more drawn-out form of Italian, spoke.

"Tonino, my friend, you are a bridge-builder—and your path will be blessed."

With that parting sentiment, Salison hopped in his Land Rover and took off driving north with his exotic matter trap, towards Switzerland, where, he prayed, one journey would end and another would begin.

53

At a speed that would have caused even a tenured hiker to break down, Jonas Moorea trekked through the rocky valley of Zanskar—towards the saman tree which bloomed out of season and the mysterious woman in white who had brought about the miracle.

Dr. Jonas Moorea had flown in a helicopter from a private airfield just outside of the north Indian city of Srinagar. After stopping once to refuel, the helicopter dropped him off in a clearing only a few hundred yards from the muddy Tsarap River about a mile away from the Phuktal Monastery.

After about a half-hour long trek along the rocky banks of the winding Tsarap River, Moorea, left the river behind and journeyed into the outskirts of the Himalayas.

Moorea was now nearing the coordinates Hassnain had given him—near the blooming saman tree.

Moorea had been singing softly in Aramaic as he traversed the land, practicing his syntax and his grammar. He had begun to learn the ancient language soon after having first met Hassnain those nine years ago in Srinagar.

On leaving Asia, Moorea knew that his search for the white-robed, Aramaic-speaking sect of the Essenes was not over.

During his journey through Zanskar, Moorea noticed several cliffs—some of them quite steep—which harbored dark openings—chiseled out of the rock. Moorea saw a handful of natural caves as well. Perhaps it would not be hard for someone, or even a group of people, to hide out here in the wilderness, and go undetected for centuries, or even millennia.

The isolation Moorea felt out here was near complete; since he awoke, he had only seen one other person, a woman, hours ago, collecting long, grassy reeds from near the river bank.

Moorea climbed up an uneven crest of rock and stopped at the top of it to check his GPS. He was over two and a half miles above sea level; yet, he was looking down on a small oasis, a 'bowl' in the mountain top, which had dimpled in—in the center of the saucer was a small, grassy plain.

In that plain of grasses, rising up from the soil, was the saman tree, still in bloom. Its branches twisting upward, away from its trunk— spreading out and weaving to and fro, before splitting into twigs that harbored rows of swaying, small leaves and flowers.

The wind picked up, and the clouds that whisked by in the thin air abound turned dark, having gathered mass from moisture. The clouds hung in the air, menacingly, as they began to bleed together. There was a growl of thunder as Moorea scaled the wall of the cliff, leading him down into the basin. The climb down was trying and it was another twenty-five minutes of scaling rock, before Moorea arrived in the clearing.

Small, cold, beads of rain began to fall from the sky, rippling into a small stream, as Moorea jumped over it.

Moorea approached the saman tree as the rain fell around him—he ran his hand along the rough bark of the tree and slowed to take it in. The saman had a peculiar feel to it, giving off a unique energy. It shined with a colorful aura. Moorea gently plucked one of its pink and magenta flowers for himself as he reveled in the tree touched by god.

There was no one here though, so Moorea kept moving, away from the tree in bloom. On the other side of the basin, at the base of the cliff, there was a reservoir of water that sprung from the rock and ran off towards the hill of the saman.

For the time being, the rain—that had been falling steadily— stopped. Moorea looked up, to the edge of the basin nearest him; here the land towered above him, higher than at the other side of the rim. Moorea saw, nestled near the peak of that steep shelf of land was a dark hole bored into the rock. He began climbing toward it, as the rain began to fall again—this time harder, as the wind picked up.

For thirty-seven minutes, Moorea fought against gravity, as he increased his elevation and approached the cliff-face cave. The rain came and went, until it stopped altogether and the dark clouds around him dissipated. The sun was low in the sky, as Moorea rolled his body onto the floor of the ledge of the cave. The air, growing colder, caused Moorea to shiver. He peered into the opening of rock. Sunlight illuminated the entrance, but darkness swallowed up the light, as the cave turned and stretched out into the heart of the mountain.

At this great height, Moorea drank water from his canteen and fashioned a strand of elastic cloth, attached to a small but powerful flashlight, around his forehead. Moorea then grabbed a second, handheld flashlight from his pack, before he swung his pack back over his shoulders.

Moorea blinked the Himalayan rain from out his hazel eyes, as he began into the narrow cave, which was no doubt natural—apparent by the small stalactites hanging from the ceiling.

After a hundred yards or so of traveling downwards through the tunnel, the cave widened to become a large chamber—which, incredibly, was lit by the sun. Blades of light cut through the darkness. Someone had carved out slants in the rock ceiling above, to allow for light to shine through. The narrow cuts in the rock must have been strategically located, for they let in enough light for Moorea to see around the cavern without his flashlight on.

The touch of human hands, in this natural cave, made Moorea sure: *This is the place,* he thought. *The woman in white is here.*

Moorea heard running water, trickling around the cave, and occasional *plunks,* that he assumed were from drops of water falling from the ceiling into pools of liquid below.

After a few minutes, the high ceiling began to come down, and Moorea approached another narrow tunnel. Here, the darkness again bloomed. Moorea saw two more tunnels further along the rocky wall, but he decided on taking the one nearest him.

After fifty or so yards, of traveling through a narrow, dark cave, Moorea began to see light ahead and was soon approaching what looked to be another large chamber—there must have been many more slants cut into the ceiling of mountain rock above, for from the ceiling, dozens of rays of light cut through the darkness, lighting the large hollow chamber that he approached, as if it were day.

Moorea took a step into the cavern. The air was damp, and there was soft soil on the ground beneath him. In a few yards, grass even. Plant life was all around him; ferns, shrubs, small trees, and flowers of red and blue.

Moorea turned off his flashlight. *The architect of this place must have been a master of their craft,* he thought, as he walked through the garden—a small lizard ran across the grass, only to disappear beneath the above-ground moss-covered roots of a large tree with a broad canopy overhead. Moorea was amazed that such an ecosystem could be maintained beneath the earth.

There was a small stream that ran through the garden with branches that traveled like a spider web around the cavern floor; its tributaries, no doubt, used to quench the garden's roots. Moorea knelt down and felt the water; it was ice cold. The stream must have been fed by melting snow and ice above—a constant flow of freshwater for the cavern oasis.

As Moorea walked through the garden, he heard a soft sweet song being hummed. He followed the sound; the melody was hypnotic and alluring—beckoning him forward. He gently pushed away a group of lush bushy fern stalks from amidst his path and, in a few paces, Moorea saw a woman, kneeling down, tending to a group of six-petaled, pink wildflowers.

She looked up as Moorea approached. The woman was the most beautiful thing Moorea had ever seen; not because of her dark, glowing, porcelain skin that camouflaged her age, nor because of her black hair falling seductively over her face, nor even because of the curves of her body that Moorea saw under her light robe—it was the depth of thought in the woman's eyes, that called to Moorea—he found himself lost in the woman's gaze. And she did not appear surprised in the least, to see him.

Curiously, the woman was not wearing white, as Moorea anticipated, but was robed in cloth as black as night.

The woman rose to her feet, without a word. She locked eyes with Moorea and seemed, for a time, to be taking him in. She reached out, gently, to touch his face, running smooth fingertips over the thin dark stubble that had begun to accumulate.

The woman's presence was powerful; Moorea felt her in his mind and in his heart.

She began speaking—a more fluid form of Aramaic than what Moorea was used to hearing in his lessons.

"I can see you are on the path, walking towards the light." She said,

Moorea noticed that the woman's grammar, and her syntax, was not as he would have expected. There was a rhythm to her words as well, which rang faster than he would have expected. It made translation tricky.

The woman in black, motioned to herself, "Adlai." She said, she beckoned Moorea as if she wanted him to follow. "Jonas." Moorea said, motioning towards himself. Adlai looked as though she already knew Moorea and needed not a name, as the two began walking through the massive underground cavern—an arboretum of flora, insects, and small animals. Moorea saw a pair of butterflies, doing a delicate dance around each other in midair, as Adlai continued,

She spoke a few lines of swiftly flowing Aramaic.

"If you are a righteous man…" she began, then Moorea could not follow what she said, he recognized a variant of a word that meant 'to give' words for water, calm, and of waves, and what could have been circular motion. Then, she used a word that could have been a plural form of the word for 'future'.

Adlai stopped by a small bushy tree that had clusters of white, four-petaled flowers—she appeared receptive, as if she were waiting for Moorea to speak his mind. Moorea did not fully understand her last words though, so began with his own thread,

"Is this your home?" he asked. Moorea knew his speech would no doubt sound odd and clunky to her.

"Here we are in the garden of knowledge." Adlai replied, 'This is why you have come."

Moorea understood those words well,

"The power." He said, "You possess it?"

Moorea's peripherals picked up movement in the overhead branches. There he saw a four-foot long, fairly large, tree snake, slithering in the branches just above his head. The iridescent indigo scales of the animal shined in a penumbra of a light ray, that fell from a narrow cut slant in the ceiling. Smooth tremors radiated through the snake's scales, as she slid and curled her body over the branches.

"The power is all around you." Adlai said. Moorea caught the scent of charcoal, as the pair walked through the garden, coming to a pool of water carved into the rock.

Adlai touched the pool, causing ripples to fan out from the point of contact. Again she used the words that Moorea was not familiar with, dealing with what he believed to be circular motion, and futures. He shook his head, not sure of what to say.

Moorea caught the woman's midnight eyes though, then peered into the pool. He was amazed by what he saw—there were dozens of different types of fish in the rock aquarium, some quite colorful (tropical-looking even). Moorea saw that there were a variety of different algae and plant life in the pool as well. Atop the rim of rock that surrounded the aquarium was a block of salt. Moorea, curious, dipped his finger into the water; it was warm. Moorea licked his finger; it was saltwater.

Adlai had a saltwater fish tank, complete with oxygenating plants, algae, and… Moorea peered over a shelf of rock that made up one of the sides of the pool. It traveled five or six feet down, then was cut away. There was a narrow space carved out from under the aquarium—that's where the charcoal smell was coming from. Moorea saw faint orange lights radiating from the embers that were burning beneath the pool, which was not only oxygenated and salinated, but heated as well.

Moorea smiled, as he took in the woman before him,

"The power?" He asked, "How did you come to possess it?"

The curiosity in Moorea had been steadily filling to an overflow, the woman stayed silent though, as the pair of them passed a small deciduous tree, with broad crimson leaves. Moorea went on,

"Are you one of the Essenes?—a descendent of Jesus Christ and John the Baptist?"

At this, Adlai stopped and ran her hand through a patch of reeds, that rose out of the shallows of a small pond, a frog leaped into the water, with a *plop*.

"We possess much knowledge." She said,

Moorea's attention was peaked at the 'we'. So she was a part of a group of other individuals…

"Who is we?" Moorea asked, "I wish to know of your history."

"Our order is ancient." Adlai replied, "We possess the gospels of Christ and those of the Essenes. But it is not their knowledge you seek—their gospels will not show you the path to the power you wish to possess."

"No?" Moorea asked.

The light of the setting sun, held a hue of pinkish purple, and caused the whole cavern to glow crimson-violet—Adlai's sepia skin was saturated by the color, as she leaned in close to Moorea's ear.

"You seek the wisdom of Didymos Judas." She said, softy.

Moorea was surprised to hear that name; Didymos Judas Thomas was one of Christ's disciples—a man whom some would argue was closer to Christ than any of his other disciples. It was written in the Gnostic texts, the *Gospel of Thomas* and the *Acts of Thomas*, that Didymos Judas helped spread the word of God around India, before the arrival of Christ, *after* his crucifixion, and also, that Christ even shared intimate and secret knowledge about his enlightenment with Didymos Judas, that no other disciple had heard (*Gospel of Thomas* saying 13).

Adlai led Moorea to a small, round, burning fire pit. Smoke and hot air therein, rose, into a long, dark tunnel above (presumably until it exited the mountain). Moorea saw, further along the cavern wall, a small opening, which was lit by firelight, looking to lead deeper into the earth.

Moorea turned to Adlai, "Will you share with me the secret of Didymos Judas? The secret that you shared with Salison?"

Adlai was dipping a wooden torch into a pool of water that was crafted into the surrounding stone. The water was murky—more so than in the other pool, but Moorea could see gliding bodies beneath the surface of the water—he dipped his finger into the liquid and brought it to his lips, testing its salinity.

"Tonight, pray on your future(s)," Adlai said, as she wrapped a cloth dripping with black liquid, around the wet wooden torch. She then lit the torch within the flames of the fire pit, as she continued, "And *we* will decide if you shall be graced with the knowledge you seek."

Adlai turned to the entrance of the yet unexplored cavern, as sparks flew around her. Moorea followed her as she led the way, flame in hand, deeper into the earth.

Hours later Adlai sat alone in a large chamber, that was lit by four hanging lanterns. She sat Indian style on a large circular carpet, surrounded by hundreds of smooth wooden bowls, each covered with a tight lid. The wooden containers were laid out in concentric circles around her, in an orderly fashion, spreading out until they reached the rock walls of the cavern.

Adlai held a polished glass lens above a large spider that was spread out on a wooden slab—the arachnid had been run through with a pointed coniferous needle, and split open by a sharp knife of obsidian.

Magnified in her curved glass, were small, yellow-green sacks, that lie below the fangs of the spider.

Adlai grabbed a thinner species of coniferous needle than the one used to pin the spider down, and focused on the small organs beneath her glass lens—but then something stole her attention. She stopped, and listened.

She set down the wooden plate, and her glass lens, and rose to her feet.

The airflow in her large chamber was oscillating ever in the slightest degree—Adlai's flames were swaying softly, and she could hear a gentle rising and falling whistling sound, in tandem with the movements that echoed throughout her chamber.

Adlai had a feeling that the source of the phenomenon was the cavern where she left Moorea.

Adlai was smiling, a curious spark in her eyes, as she walked out of her large chamber, leaving the firelight behind. She walked through the cave in darkness, towards Moorea's room. The frequency of the swaying airflow and the corresponding amplitude of the whistling wind that ran through the cave system intensified as she, in the darkness, came closer to Moorea's room.

As Adlai turned a corner, she saw firelight lapping up against the dark, rocky walls of the tunnel. When she was twenty strides from Moorea's room, the curious airflow and accompanying sounds died down swiftly and then stopped. The air still resonated with lingering movement though. Quietly, Adlai moved forward, until she was to Moorea's room. Jonas lay in the center of his fire-lit chamber. He was collapsed on the ground, atop a large, open cloth, breathing heavy—his skin covered with perspiration—a rose-hued liquid shined red as it slid over his body in the flickering light—the man's sweat was tinted with blood.

There was a look of cautious contentment, or satisfaction, on Adlai's face, as she turned, and left Moorea to his exhaustion, and his slumber.

Hours later, a sweet sensation caused Moorea to wake from his sleep; he tasted wildflowers and honey in the air as he heard the soft sound of footsteps. In the scarce firelight, Moorea saw Adlai coming near to him, her features dark and alluring.

Adlai did not speak as she drew nearer; there was a hint of curious wonder in her eyes though, as she knelt down, to lie next to Moorea, placing her head on his chest, closing her eyes.

Moorea sensed loneliness in the woman, as she simply listened to his heartbeat. It was not long though, before she and Moorea were fast asleep, their minds, breaths, and bodies in sync, drifting into the night.

Day 6

When Jonas Moorea awoke, he found himself alone, in darkness that was near complete. His fire still gently burned—its embers softly lighting the cavern. Moorea, with his canteen of water filled from one of the cave streams, freshened up, washing his face and mouth as he woke up in the dim light. He then grabbed his pack and began walking back to the underground garden, which he knew was around fifty meters away, through a twisting, single dark tunnel.

For some time, Moorea walked, with his eyes closed in meditation; this was familiar ground, and his mind had more important things to do, than process visual information that it did not need to navigate. Moorea's *memory* was lighting his way.

When Moorea arrived in the garden, it was illuminated by the morning sun. He heard Adlai humming a sweet song, as she toiled with her plants.

As Moorea approached, she rose to her feet, with dirt on her hands, again dressed in silk as black as night. Moorea began to speak, to inquire about the questions that were churning in him, regarding her nature and the origins of this incredible place; but instead, Adlai put a finger up to his lips.

"I am sorry," the woman said, in flowing Aramaic, looking deep into Moorea's eyes, "I wish we could have *known* each other; but you must go, if you are to have your chance."

"My chance?" Moorea asked.

Adlai's eyes recollected Salison.

A chance to stop him, Moorea thought.

Adlai reached into the pockets of her robe and handed Moorea a leather pouch. Moorea felt weight within the small sack, as if it were filled with a few small marbles that varied in their size and weight. Adlai leaned in close to Moorea and pulled herself to his chest; she brought her lips towards Moorea's ear and whispered three things to him, as the man's hazel eyes churned with revelation. Then, with Moorea's eyes still blossoming thought, Adlai embraced him—she took a deep breath as she did; her touch was electric, magnetic and full of feeling—Moorea had never experienced anything like it before. Adlai exhaled smoothly, and rose her gaze to Moorea's, stepping back,

"Go you now, to center of the circle." she said, "To the place where worlds collide."

Then, the air around her began to vibrate, as the leaves abound shook with an unseen force. Pulses of air fanned out from Adlai, as a humming, oscillating sound emanated from her.

Moorea stepped back, as light danced around the woman; he watched, as shards of a small coniferous tree behind Adlai appeared *through* her, as if the woman were a window, a mosaic whose pieces disappeared and reappeared, passing in and out of the visible spectrum in waves.

Then, with a rush of air, the woman was gone. Leaving Moorea catching his breath; underground and alone, holding in his hand, a small sack that may have held within, the means by which he would be able to fight the future—a future that Salison Sinsway, if unabated, planned on soon setting loose.

54

On the Mediterranean Island of Cyprus, the ever-searching archaeologist, Dr. Charles Klein, found himself in a dream-filled sleep, as the dawn began to break. All through the night, Charles Klein traveled through mazes and hidden passageways—he fell through trapdoors, found himself in secret gardens, and pressed onward through buried temples tucked away in dense jungles and crevices in time.

Even in his dreams, he searched, pining for the mysterious things to be found deeper underground or farther off in the distance. Klein awoke with his heart racing, covered in sweat, wondering where he was. Visions of his travels faded, as he focused on the here and now.

The sun had risen, and the hot Cypriot air batted gently at the blinds. On a separate bed next to him, the MIT mathematician, Judith Arai, was still asleep. Klein reached for his watch on the dresser, and as he did, groaned softly. His arms and back ached from the exertion of the previous day.

Klein's old Casio watch was flecked with dirt—the small, riveted, metal knobs, earth-encrusted. The face was clear enough though for him to see that it was 10:24 a.m. Cypriot Time, which meant it was 8:24 p.m. back in California.

Klein felt as if he could sleep for another few hours; but instead, he grabbed his laptop and popped it open, setting it on his bed, leaning over onto his side. The archeologist felt shoddy, using a search engine to find information, when thousands of years ago, one could travel for months, even years, across turbulent seas, sweltering jungles, and unforgiving deserts, risking life and limb, just to reach hubs of knowledge, such as Alexandria, Nineveh, or Constantinople; places, which at the time, were the only places *in the world* where certain forms of knowledge could be found.

He, nonetheless, scanned the libraries of thousands of universities at once, as he typed into the search bar: Stasanor of Soli.

Despite his attempt to find new information on the man, all Klein could find on the internet were things he already knew—Stasanor was a citizen of the Northern Cypriot town of Soli and a distinguished officer in Alexander the Great's Macedonian Army during Alexander's campaign into Asia.

Although it was generally believed that Stasanor joined Alexander's company around the time of the Siege of Tyre, when the Cypriot Navy helped Alexander capture the strategic costal base, the first time Stasanor was mentioned in military records was in 328 BCE, during Alexander's campaign in Bactria.

Alexander dispatched Stasanor to put down a rebellious uprising; and when Stasanor returned victorious, Alexander rewarded him the governorship (or satrapy) of lands in present day Afghanistan and Turkmenistan.

After Alexander's death, Stasanor's history became less clear. He was believed to have remained the Satrap of Bactria and Sogdiana in the Afghanistan/Turkmenistan region, until at least 316 BCE, when he disappears from record.

Taking into account the inscription on the recently excavated pillar, it did not take too great a stretch of the imagination to envision that Stasanor of Soli found his way back to Cyprus and built a villa on the top of a Cypriot plateau, with the Mediterranean Sea swaying off in the far distance.

A soft chime on Klein's computer let him know he had received an e-mail from one of his contacts. In a few clicks, he saw that it was from Karen, his ex-wife.

Klein's eyes scanned the e-mail. It seemed that Karen, by chance, had come across something incredible.

A few days earlier, Karen had sent an e-mail to a genetics expert, an old friend, to see if he could help her glean any information about Saatçi's origins. She had supplied the man, Dr. Jean Hebert, with the Ottoman's genotype and asked him to keep the information confidential. In the frozen mummy's blood, there were vast sequences of DNA that Karen had never seen before. That was until Hebert got back to her.

Hebert claimed that he had recently discovered a family, a father and daughter pair—the Sinsways—who exhibited rare genetic phenotypes and who shared many alien DNA sequences with Saatçi.

Hebert made it a point to say though, that there were differences in the genotypes—when comparing the Sinsways and Saatçi—and he likened it to comparing the genotypes of modern-day Eastern Asians to Europeans. There were genetic similarities between them, enough to tell that they are both modern-day humans; but it was also evident that they were from separate populations that harbored distinct genetic backgrounds.

So there was some sort of a connection between the Sinsways and Saatçi..

Their genomes were more similar to each other than they were to the rest of the human population. But their genomes were also, in a way, distinct from each other.

Apparently, Dr. Hebert did not know the origins of the Sinsways or Saatçi. He was still, at this time, just as puzzled as the team at Columbia, in regards to the origins of the Sinsways and Karen's mummy; but Hebert knew that Karen and her team had found something special.

Karen concluded the e-mail by saying that her ankle surgery had been rescheduled by three days and that Jeremy, her student, had begun to recover quite well from his injuries. Karen also inquired about Klein's progress.

As Klein composed his reply to Karen, the sound of Judith waking, interrupted his flow.

"Ahhhhhhhhhh." she groaned. Her body no doubt sore from the exertion of digging out the pillar.

Klein smiled.

There was nothing else from the young woman, until a few minutes later.

Klein clicked SEND on his laptop, as Judith yawned softly and swung her legs over the edge of the bed, facing Klein.

Perhaps it was the morning light dancing around the room, or the fact that the mathematician was without her large glasses; but Judith looked different—quite attractive despite just waking.

She wore running shorts and a white MIT T-shirt. Klein saw the curves of her body, the length of her legs, and the small, dark centers of her breasts through her shirt.

He averted his eyes, as she spoke again.

"Coffeeee. Need coffee."

Judith laughed, to herself, as she stood up and ran a hand through her dark hair. She sighed, and then smiled, catching Klein with her eyes.

"Good morning."

"Morning," Klein began. "I was just about to wake you. We should start getting ready. We have a full day of work ahead of us."

In ninety-six minutes, Klein and Judith were pulling over their Suzuki Jimny to the side of the road. Stasanor's plateau in the near distance. The two had opted to eat during the drive to conserve time; and Klein had filled the young woman in on his knowledge of Stasanor and the fact that there was a family out there, in today's population, who had genomes somewhat similar to Saatçi's.

The information regarding the genetics was curious news; Klein could not yet make sense of it. And it only made him more curious in regards to what was hidden out there, under the dirt and Cypriot soil.

As Klein gathered the equipment from out the Jimny, he had to wonder how these genetically diverse individuals were connected to Stasanor's pillar.

Klein figured that to answer that question, he was going to have to dig.

Late in the afternoon, with the sun falling towards the horizon, Judith and Klein found themselves in a twelve-foot pit with the towering, iron pillar above them.

The bottom fifth of the tower, recently excavated, was still encrusted with dirt and earth over millennia old.

The night before, Judith and Klein found only the inscription, which dedicated the pillar to Stasanor of Soli, but the pair had yet to find any characters on the pillar that could be used to give values to the unknown variables in the Ottoman's cloth—which would allow Judith to solve the encrypted equations.

Klein went for his finer tools, as Judith dropped her shovel and grabbed her water bottle. After she gulped down a bit of the liquid, she looked back to Klein.

"Can I do it?" she asked.

Klein smiled, with a hand to his beard.

"Let's do it together."

Klein sprayed the towering piece of iron with liquid, while Judith used small metal tools, and at times, her bare hands, to break away the dense soil that was caked onto the pillar.

Klein let Judith work for half an hour, before he spoke up.

"OK, that's good."

He rose to his knees, and pointed to a region, where there was a slight but noticeable change in the color of the pillar, where it transitioned from two shades of dark cobalt.

"This is where the original base of the pillar was. You can tell by the different degrees of oxidation in the two regions."

Klein looked upward, to the top of the pillar, to where the setting sun shined against the metal.

"Stasanor knew how to work metal, I'll give him that."

Judith continued with her excavation, and struck a dense slab of earth strongly with her small hammer and chisel, the large slab of compressed earth came cleanly off the iron pillar.

"Damn." Klein said, "You definitely have the hang of that."

Judith did not answer. She was grinning, there, on the pillar, below the ground level boundary, there were smooth curved lines etched into the pillar.

Klein too, saw the characters. He moved in closer to the pillar with a dirt-soaked soft cloth, and began to wipe the iron clean,

"Hey." Judith said, with a wanting look in her eyes,

Klein conceded, and moved back from the pillar, handing his cloth to Judith.

After thirty minutes of working the pillar, once the light of the sun had begun to take on a setting red hue, Judith wiped the iron clean.

Klein who was nearby, nodded his head,

"You've done it." he said. "That's it. That's the key."

55

As the sun went down on the East Coast, Detective David Brennan was getting off the phone with the governor of Massachusetts. She called Brennan personally, once the death toll had climbed over 300 people—it was officially at three hundred and forty-seven in Boston alone.

Salison's disease was spreading like black oil from a torn tanker into the sea. The governor wanted to know what, if anything, could be done to stop or slow down the disease. Brennan assured her that he, and the rest of the crime lab, were doing everything they could to combat the disease and also told the woman that a vaccine was in the process of being created.

By now, well over a dozen countries around the world harbored individuals that were infected with Salison's pathogen. The death toll (according to some reports) was around 900 killed and a few thousand more infected. The majority were in either Australia or in the United States (near Boston)—the two places where it was believed the pathogen was first activated.

Brennan was still not able to shut down Orion Communications; and Christopher Banks was still working on hacking their system in order to shut it down, with as of yet, no luck.

Brennan's phone vibrated in his pocket; it was a text message from Officer Middler.

"Just landed in Geneva. Heading to CERN. So excited!"

Brennan managed a small smile, while shaking his head. He had sent his young cadet to Switzerland, in order to not only find Salison Sinsway, but, more importantly, to find the mobile laptop and the transmitting pole that Christopher Banks created for Salison—the transmitting pole that would allow Salison access into Orion

Communications, and to subsequently activate his engineered, dormant, pathogen. If Middler was able to secure the transmitting pole, then the vast majority of the population would be protected from the pathogen-activating sound, and Brennan and his team could focus on containing the disease.

Brennan pondered his leads. He had learned that Jonas Moorea, the neuroscientist that worked with Salison and kidnapped Silloway, had left Boston and traveled to India, via London. The bastard had gotten out of the country just before he was labeled a person of interest (and would have then been held for questioning at the airport).

Brennan was not yet sure how Moorea fit into the equation. He was clearly working against Silloway (as he kidnapped her) and perhaps Salison (as he not only assaulted him at the hospital, but also matched the description of a man who dropped off information regarding Salison's pathogen to the police).

The jury was still out though on whether Jonas Moorea was friend or foe.

On returning from Roque Bluffs, Maine, Officer Middler not only brought Adam Riley with him, but Thomas Bishop as well. The young man had received quite a blow to the head, and it looked as if he had fired a shot (from an unregistered gun) at Adam Riley (although the kid had, luckily, only been hit by a ricochet).

It was a convenience that the police chopper that brought Middler and Bishop back to Massachusetts had landed on a hospital helipad. For once Thomas Bishop had disembarked, he passed out. Bishop was soon admitted to the hospital, and Brennan traveled there to see him.

Bishop was found to have extensive malignant peripheral nerve tumors, neurofibromatosis, and multiple Schwannomas as well; each of which were very serious cancers of the nervous system. Bishop, at best, had months to live.

Bishop's doctors had not allowed Brennan to get many words in with the young man; but Brennan was able to glean that Bishop, despite his weakened state, held quite a rage within himself and believed Salison Sinsway was the cause of his dire condition.

How though, Brennan was not able to find out. Bishop told the detective to "go to hell" and refused to say anything more on the matter.

Brennan was of course curious as to how Bishop had contracted multiple types of cancers of the nervous system, and how Salison could have been involved, but Brennan knew that the first priority was to secure any information that could be used to stop the spread of Salison's deadly pathogen, that was bounding around the globe unabated.

Towards this end, Brennan was still searching for Silloway Sinsway; but the woman had disappeared. She was last seen at Salison's property in Maine, before taking off in a cruising yacht from a boathouse on the property.

Brennan knew, with Salison's resources, she could be anywhere. The only inkling he had of where she could be was the massive chamber that was attached to Salison's bunker at his property in Green Harbor.

So far, neither the locksmith that did jobs for the station, nor any others, were able to figure out how to gain access to the underground complex; the structure was, thus far, impregnable, and its contents, a mystery.

There weren't many leads, but if there was hope, in this whole dire situation, it was with Adam Riley. The young man, along with Ning, had been working day and night to produce a vaccine for Salison's pathogen. And Brennan had heard that the results, thus far, were promising.

Ning had told him that Adam would soon have enough of what she called a 'viral vaccine' to vaccinate two to three thousand people, depending on how fruitful the production of the virus was.

Brennan was just about to call Ning for an update, when an officer walked up to Brennan's desk, which, at this new station, was surrounded by a few others.

"Detective Brennan?" the woman asked.

"Yes?" Brennan replied.

"This came for you, today," she said, as she handed Brennan an envelope.

Brennan's interest rose, as the female officer walked away.

The letter was addressed to Brennan from Silloway Sinsway.

Brennan carefully examined the letter, up against the light. The paper used to make the envelope was unremarkable. The letter had been addressed from Boston, from Silloway's residence. And there appeared to be an object within the envelope; a small, spherical ball, along with a single piece of paper, which looked to have writing on it.

Brennan thought, for a moment, then grabbed his pocketknife from his belt and flipped it open. He slit open the envelope and dropped the object that was inside onto his palm—it was a blue marble. But it was like no marble Brennan had ever seen. There was something in its center, a small, black sphere—that was covered by a cerulean storm that drifted into the marble's interior.

Brennan held the curious thing in his hand, as he fished out the small piece of paper inside the envelope. It was folded in half, smelling of lilacs. Brennan unfolded the paper—on it, there was a single line, written in English. Brennan recognized the writing as gospel, but could not remember what passage. His olive eyes churned, as they revealed his inner thoughts pertaining to the message, as he wondered what the words could mean:

'Seek and you will find; knock and the door will be opened to you.'

56

After Doctor Jonas Moorea had his fateful encounter with Adlai, the beautiful, electric, disappearing disciple, the neuroscientist walked alone through the garden cave and back up the narrow underground passage that led to the cliff-face entrance.

He carefully climbed around the rim of the mountain that held the hill of the saman tree in its bowl, and then hiked back to the Phuktal Monastery. There, he was picked up again, by helicopter, and had the pilot bring him to the nearby city of Bhuntar.

From Bhuntar, it was a six and a half hour journey to Mumbai, via airplane. During his journey, Moorea had a hard time prying his thoughts away from Adlai; her enigmatic nature, her gospel, and her powerful presence had intrigued him. She was like nothing Moorea had ever seen or heard before, and he was not going to be able to forget her.

Dressed all in black, Jonas took a seat in his terminal at the airport in Mumbai, waiting for his flight out of India. He leaned back and closed his eyes, trying to calm his mind; readying himself, for what he knew would be a trying encounter with Salison Sinsway.

A chime from his phone broke his train of thought, and Moorea soon realized an e-mail from his lab had arrived, one that he had been waiting for.

His lab had finally sequenced Salison's blood and spinal fluid. They ran a myriad of tests on Salison's tissues in order to determine what, if any, pharmacological agents were present in the man's body. Moorea told his lab to perform the tests, after he obtained samples of Salison's blood and spinal fluid while the man was sedated at New Life.

AN EVOLUTION OF MINDS

The results were astonishing and they gave credence to a theory about Salison and Adlai, that Moorea had been pondering (see Appendix 1). There were dozens of naturally occurring drugs that target the nervous system found in Salison's blood and spinal fluid; drugs from spiders, lizards, snails, snakes, scorpions, and even marine worms. There were also dozens of plant-derived drugs in Salison's system as well.

Moorea's lab indicated that the concentrations detected for many of the substances were less than what was generally believed to be needed to generate a biological response in the body. Despite that, Moorea was confident that these were the hidden ingredients that Salison had been using to heighten his enlightenment; Moorea figured that these were also the drugs that were included in the pouch that Adlai had given him, grown within and taken from, her Garden of Knowledge.

Moorea knew that all the agents listed in the email could potentially be deadly; but he also knew that the difference between poison and medicine was the dose.

The report also mentioned there were dozens of other pharmacological agents found in Salison's body, that the lab was able to identify...

Moorea knew there were billions of neurons in the brain—neurons that govern our senses, our sight, our perception, our cognitive abilities, as well as our balance, our speed, and our movement. He knew that there were thousands of types of neurons, and that they were not uniform in their morphology, gene expression, or cellular characteristics; but instead displayed striking differences. Accordingly, some neurons were more (or less) affected by certain drugs that target the nervous system.

Moorea figured that the cocktail of drugs that was introduced into Salison's system had functioned to slightly tweak the properties of specific groups of neurons that were more readily affected by the individual drugs used in the potion; and that the groups of neurons targeted, played major roles in generating our concept of time and space and thus our perception of the outside world. Moorea guessed that other neurons targeted were responsible for both physical and mental speed, and our fine and coarse motor movements as well.

By altering the properties of perhaps billions of neurons, and trillions of connections between them, Adlai's potion could alter a multitude of neuronal circuits, in both the central and peripheral nervous system, in order to ultimately, generate a higher level of thought and being. Anyone who had taken amphetamines and found themselves with a heightened focus, or adrenaline and found themselves with a heightened energy and altered perception of the passage of time, had experienced such effects, to a very small degree.

The effect on Salison's system must have been exponentially different and his results much more astounding though, due to, among other things, the sheer amount of pharmacological agents that were being used, and the other methods that Salison was using to heighten his enlightenment.

Adlai though, had warned of the dangers of using such a potion (or shortcut to enlightenment), saying that, if one were not ready, for the power of heightened sense and movement, their signaling systems would pay the price—this sentiment caused Moorea to recall Salison's violent seizures, that he suffered nearly a week ago in Boston, leading to his hospitalization. Moorea figured that Salison had tried to manipulate too much of space and time with his mind and body, which had thrown his nervous system into a state of chaos and hyper-excitability.

Although Adlai had not told Moorea, she knew that it was Didymos Judas Thomas's use of this elixir that caused his rift with both Christ and the Essenes (*Act of Thomas, Gospel of Thomas, Gospel of Awakening*), which would ultimately send Thomas down a separate path, towards a *different* form of enlightenment. One more engineered, than obtained through genetic potential and strenuous spiritual training.

The wheels of Moorea's mind turned, as he pondered the possibilities.

As he did, a young Indian man rolled up to him in a silver wheelchair. He appeared to be in his early twenties, and was good-looking, with a strong upper body. The young man carried a hockey stick and a duffle bag across his lap. Moorea saw that beneath his bag, the young man's legs were severely atrophied. He had seen such cases before, of cerebral palsy. Most likely caused by the death of neurons which govern both thought and movement in the brain and body—neurons that died before the young man was even born. There was a clear spasticity in one of the young man's arms as well; pulling his elbow towards his body.

This person had never walked his entire life, never felt the wind pick up around him into a gust as he gained speed in a sprint, nor had he ever seen the sun set from a great height, exhausted, after a day's hike up a mountain's trail.

The Indian man smiled at Moorea and said hello, in English. Moorea smiled back.

"Are you on vacation?" the young man asked.

"Something like that. What about you?"

"I was visiting my parents, for my birthday. I'm Andrew."

Moorea smiled, "I'm Jonas. Is that your gift?"

Moorea motioned to the hockey stick Andrew carried, positioned under his bag.

Andrew grinned, "Yup. I play sled hockey, we have a tournament next week. Have you ever played hockey?"

Moorea shook his head, "Never, but I respect the speed, agility and focus one needs to play the sport. And you guys sure like fighting."

Andrew laughed, richly.

"No, no, I wouldn't fight. You're from America?"

For the better part of an hour, young Andrew talked Moorea's ear off. It amused Moorea. Andrew had a spark to him that was, in Moorea's state, refreshing.

For some time, Moorea and Andrew got acquainted, but it was not long before the boarding call rang out for Moorea's flight to Geneva, Switzerland.

The young man, who introduced himself as Andrew Vogt, was catching another flight, to London, before heading back to Ohio.

Moorea looked the young man in his dark, brown eyes.

"I am a doctor," Moorea said, "who specializes in your sort of ailment. May I try something?"

With curiosity in his friendly eyes, Andrew said, "Yes."

Moorea knelt down near the base of Andrew's wheelchair and began humming a soft sweet tune. He closed his eyes, and placed one hand on Andrew's thin left thigh, and the other on the back of Andrew's neck.

Moorea's fingers slightly resonated, as they touched Andrew's bare skin. In his mind's eye, Moorea saw frail tissues and sick neurons, whose receiving and sending poles were damaged and distorted, having decayed decades ago.

Moorea focused on the cells, the surrounding blood vessels, and the extracellular spaces between them, as he hummed. In Andrew's cerebellum, at the base of his brain, healthy neurons, which allowed him some rudimentary movement over the years, reverted back to their most primitive state—a state whereby they could turn into any type of cell in the body—becoming stem cells.

Then, the stem cells divided, over and over, creating multitudes of healthy cells, that soon after dividing, began to differentiate into specialized cerebellar neurons that aid in the generation of movement.

In a similar fashion, neurons were being born in Andrew's cortex; where motor fibers arise that control the movement of our arms and legs. After dividing, these neurons began sprouting thin processes—axons and dendrites, to send and receive information. A bundle of growing, reaching, twisting, and at times, retracting, axons began to form—setting out on a journey to Andrew's midbrain and spinal cord, where they read molecules that had been secreted from surrounding cells, like guideposts—the malleable arms of the axons, following a trail of guidance particles, like a map, down Andrew's spinal cord, until they reached his anterior horn.

Neurons were also being born in Andrew's spinal cord; they too began sending out projections, towards Andrew's muscles and to the tips of each of his toes.

Moorea prayed, humming all the while.

Neurons in Andrew's body were being reverted back into primeval cells, like they were in embryonic development; then, they were turning into mature neurons—being reborn, *healthy,* able to wire up as they should have, before young Andrew was born.

In Andrew's body then, trillions of connections began to form, between billions of separate neurons—old and new neurons wired-up together, allowing for the transmission of electrical and chemical signals between them. It were as if a vast highway was being lain throughout Andrew's nervous system, allowing for the transmission of neuronal information from the top of Andrew's body to the bottom, as it had never been done before.

"I can feel something." Andrew said—there was a hint of awe and wonder in is voice, as a realization began to bloom in him.

Moorea tended to the young man's limbs, spinal cord, muscle fibers, nervous tissue and bone density, for a few more minutes, as Andrew's eyes began to wet.

Then, Moorea rose. For a brief instant, he looked to be physically drained—yet he regained his composure quickly, and smiled at Andrew, kissing him on the forehead,

"You need not believe in me," Moorea whispered in Andrew's ear, as he knelt down. "But for God's sake, believe in yourself!"

With those words, Dr. Jonas Moorea, dressed all black, as dark as the encompassing night, fastened his shoulder bag around his back and jogged up to his gate, not looking back.

Behind him, Andrew Vogt, now had within himself a true *belief*. With tears falling from his eyes, he unraveled his right arm and stretched it out; then, with new touch and new feelings, he rubbed his legs, and, for the first time in his life—on his own—began rising from his chair.

57

Day 7

As the hot sun rose in Cyprus, the land took on a healthy glow; rays of light fought through softly swaying silk blinds along the windows and shined in Judith Arai's dark eyes, as she slowly awoke.

Normally, if the mathematician were to rise this early, she would roll over and do her best to get back to sleep. But not today. She knew that there would be no calming her mind enough for her to fall back asleep, not when there was such a problem before her that was so begging for a solution—a solution that would point her in the direction of something that could quite literally be, out of this world.

Judith had listened to her mentor, Dr. Timothy Levine, rave on and on about the device that was found with the frozen Ottoman—a device that was clearly built using superior technology and may have even utilized unknown laws of physics.

Levine had spoken of Saatçi's timepiece, as if it held within, the technology to shape the future.

Judith had to wonder if the answers to the questions regarding Saatçi's mysterious origins, and his physics-defying timepiece, lie at the end of the map that he had been found with. There was a curiosity burning in her, in regards to the man's origins, his possessions, and the mysterious, ancient object that could be hidden at the end of his map.

Judith rolled her legs over the side of her bed and yawned, running a hand through her dark hair. The young woman's mind felt fresh; her thoughts were clear. And she felt it in her bones—she would be gleaning the solutions to the encrypted equations on this very day.

She had made significant progress the night before and was now ready to take the next step. Even in her sleep, she saw numbers, like puzzle pieces that she rotated, turned, and twisted about in her mind, so that she could roll them into their proper concave cavities, as gravity guided their gait, along a vast chessboard of pits and pockets within the earth.

With her dreams falling away from her, Judith rose and made her way to the minibar, grabbing a bottled water.

The archaeologist, Dr. Charles Klein, was still asleep in the bed next to her.

Judith thought it would be nice to surprise him, to solve the equations and find the location of their next excursion, before he awoke.

After a light breakfast and a quick shower, Judith resumed her spot at her desk—with a mound of mathematics before her. She had a yellow notebook that was brimming with equations and her laptop open, with her display screen showing the mathematics that were depicted in the Ottoman's stolen cloth.

Judith worked, in silence, as the Cypriot sun rose steadily in the sky, elevating the heat of the land. The young woman's mind churned with mathematics, for nearly two and a half hours, before Klein awoke. She did not even notice him, as he rolled over onto his side and opened his laptop computer.

Fifteen or so minutes after Klein awoke, Judith set down her pencil and leaned back in her chair. She held a page of mathematics before her. With her finger, she traced scripts of mathematics down the length of the page; slowly, while her dark eyes took in each line. She checked her work three times, before she smiled and turned to Klein.

"This is it." she said, enthusiastically.

Klein smiled.

"I knew you would figure it out. How did you come about it?"

Judith spoke, with a hint of pride in her voice, glad Klein took interest not only in the solution but the journey to find it.

"Initially, the cloth contained six unknown variables." she began. "Three of those variables were carved into Stasanor's pillar, and to solve for the remaining three, we'll call them x, y, and z, I plugged each of the three known values into an algorithm that was provided in the cloth. You know what an algorithm is, right?"

"It's ah, set of directions, or rules to be followed, right?"

"Yes, that's right." Judith answered. "The algorithm in the cloth was complex. It may be one of the most advanced algorithms for the time period. So, I followed the set of rules given in the algorithm and transformed the x, y, and z values into longitude, latitude, and elevation—the same language that was used in the first part of the cloth dealing with spherical geometry."

"So you know the coordinates? You know where we're headed next?"

"Well," Judith answered, "I do have cells in my brain that help me navigate, kind of like a GPS; but I don't have all the coordinates on the planet memorized." She smiled. "But I can tell you, it's relatively close to here. Can I borrow your computer?"

Klein had been reclining in his bed, with his back against a pillow that was propped up against the headboard. He sat up and brought Judith his computer; she was sitting at her desk, next to the balcony. The morning light poured over her, and Klein, again, could not help but feel a hint of attraction towards the brilliant young woman, as she took the computer from him and set it on pages of mathematics.

With a few clicks of the mouse and quick movements of her nimble fingers on the keyboard, Judith brought up a map of Cyprus.

"With this resolution, I'd say we're to head fifty-some miles to the south, to a region on the coast, surrounding a Cypriot bay called Episkopi."

Judith thought for a moment, and then went for her pack that sat up against the wall. From her pack, she grabbed the GPS that she had been using to navigate. It was much more accurate than the simple longitude/latitude system she had generated from the original cloth.

Judith typed the coordinates that she gleaned into the small handheld device.

"…and according to the GPS," she said, "the exact coordinates are just off the coast, near a cliff face, out in the Mediterranean Sea, below sea level."

"Sounds like there might be a dive involved." Klein said, "Do you have any experience with diving?"

He approached Judith and motioned as if he wanted to take the GPS from her.

Judith smiled as she handed Klein the GPS.

"Oh ya," she said. "I can dive."

Klein did not look too convinced, as he took the GPS and began to check the coordinates himself.

Neither Klein nor Judith were aware that during their first trip to Stasanor's plateau, someone had snuck into their room and placed a small transmitting microphone within it.

This was the same person who had stolen the Ottoman's ancient cloth; but having examined it, realized that its weaver was no fool—the cloth had been encrypted. The man who had stolen the cloth did not know how to decipher the mathematics within it. But he knew that the archaeologist, and the young mathematician, would soon be able to.

So that man, a traveler, a soldier from afar, had followed the pair to Cyprus, where he lie in wait, until he heard the right words spoken.

As Judith and Klein talked back and forth at each other, trying to determine their next move, there was a loud *crack*! that emanated throughout the room.

The hotel room door had been broken off its hinges, and in its place stood a tall, pale-skin man, with blond hair, an uneven gait and sunken, cold, blue eyes, like ice. He held a gun.

Klein and Judith were both, for the moment, stunned; then, Klein cursed softly, looking over to his dresser drawer wherein lie the Taser he bought a few days ago. It was well out of reach.

The intruder aimed the gun at Klein and said, in an odd, forceful accent, "Let me receive." while motioning to the GPS that Klein held.

Klein's blood boiled. He was guessing that this ugly bastard was the man who assaulted his ex-wife and her stuttering student and had then stolen the original cloth. Although Klein would have loved to 'dance' with this guy, now he had to play it cool, for not only his, but Judith's sake.

Klein put up his left hand, in a nonthreatening, peaceful manner as he spoke, "Sure, here it is."

Judith moved closer to Klein, as she clasped the bottom of his shirt with her small hands; she was breathing fast.

With an underhanded throw, stepping in front of Judith, Klein tossed the intruder the GPS. The man caught the device with his right hand, as he held his gun in his left, still pointing it at Klein.

"Much thanks." the man said, "And now you no follow." he finished, as he pulled the trigger.

Judith felt Klein shutter slightly, as a projectile traveled into his body. Klein stood, for a moment, and then hit the floor as Judith screamed. Then, the gun-wielding man turned and took off in a jog, towards the exit.

The pale pit-eyed shooter ran out of the hotel; as he did, he felt a sharp pain in his back. He quickly lost his balance, dropped the GPS that he held, and fell onto his knees. Once on the ground, he sat up, and turned towards the direction of the blow he received, all while trying to reach the spot on his back with his hands, where his pain stemmed. He felt disoriented and lost his focus.

As his vision blurred, he saw a slender, violet-eyed young woman approaching him. There was a look of fury on her face, as she fastened the tranquilizer gun she had used to shoot him behind her back and picked up speed.

She looked him in the eyes, as she kicked him hard in the chest.

The pit-eyed shooter fell onto the hot pavement.

Silloway Sinsway grabbed the man's gun from his holster and took the safety off, pressing the barrel to the man's chest.

"I know what you are, you son of a bitch. Now you are never going home."

With those parting words, Silloway pulled the trigger, putting a bullet through the man's heart. She then grabbed the GPS from off the sidewalk and took off in a sprint, away from that small, homey hotel in Northern Cyprus.

58

In the small village of Meyrin, Switzerland, the perfect circle of a yellow sun was coming up over the countryside, shining down over fields of golden wheat and clusters of fir and chestnut trees—causing them to cast long, bushy shadows over the land. The Italian particle physicist and director of CERN, Fabiola Gionatti, made breakfast in her small cottage, as she reviewed an article that was being written by her and her colleagues, regarding the nature of the cosmos.

Fabiola, a classically trained pianist, and a lover of harmony and physics, had chosen her residence strategically. For one hundred and twenty-five meters beneath Fabiola's feet was a large tunnel. Within it, was housed the most massive and complex machine ever conceived and built by man—the Large Hadron Collider—a giant subterranean ring with a circumference of twenty-seven kilometers that was used to smash charged particles together in order to recreate the conditions that occurred just after the Big Bang—the explosion that gave birth to the universe.

By smashing charged particles together, Fabiola, and an army of scientists, were able to produce, and then identify, the most elementary building blocks of nature.

Fabiola adored the notion, of that when she slept, deep below her, miniscule particles were being accelerated to near light speed, round and round the collider, before they were smashed together with incredible velocity, creating—for fractions of a second—the most basic and mysterious components of matter.

Beneath her, worlds were being born.

In her kitchen, Fabiola scanned her article, while pondering the related, groundbreaking experiment that she and her team were performing this very day.

All of a sudden, Fabiola felt a rush of air. She was pulled left, then right, gliding quickly back and forth on her wooden floor in her wool socks. Nearly immediately after her movements, there was a sharp slam of a door, as Fabiola tried to steady herself against her countertop, lest she fall on the floor, as her hips traced a quick ellipse in the air.

The woman's front door had just been opened and closed in a mere fraction of a second, causing waves of air pressure to bounce around her house—Fabiola had been pulled into a small vacuum, then spun back out, as someone entered her abode.

Fabiola then heard a sound that she will never remember. She experienced an innumerable cascade of notes in an instant. Fabiola felt ripples in the air, as they shook her house, spiraling about the room in rounds and rounds of golden ratios. It was as if someone had composed an entire sonata, using all of a piano's eighty-eight keys—thrice over—and played it during a single heartbeat.

The hairs on the back of Fabiola's neck stood on end. She felt connected to something, but she did not know what. The sounds rang her like a bell and vibrated her body.

She caught her breath, and, with curiosity guiding her gait, walked into her study, where her grand piano faced the window and the snow-peaked Jura Mountains in the distance.

In her study, standing to meet her, with his violet eyes catching the morning sun, was Salison Sinsway.

The room still resonated with his echoing sonata.

Fabiola's eyes reflected blossoming thought; questions burned in her. She stayed silent though, as Salison, for a few moments, seemed to take her in, as a calm breath was drawn in and expelled from her.

"I am enjoying your singing." Salison said.

His violet eyes softly saccaded about the woman's body.

Fabiola was still resonating with Salison's sonata, as she replied, "But I am not singing, Salison."

Salison, his body tall and strong, with a calm emanating from him, narrowed his focus.

"If it's all just vibrating strings, my dear, then you're singing even when you're not singing. And I am basking in the sounds."

Fabiola shook her head, trying to make sense of the spectacle before her.

"Tell me." she said.

"Yes," Salison said. "It is high time."

Fabiola had known Salison for thirty years, and in that time, she had become increasingly aware: *That there was something very different about the man.*

It was not only his appearance—his towering form, his violet eyes, and his strange flowing accent, there was also his genius and the fact that, in all the time Fabiola had known Salison, the man had not aged a day. If anything, as of late, he looked *younger* than before the time they met, at a conference, on the shores of the Black Sea, all those years ago.

Fabiola had come to recognize that Salison was too smart; his wild theories had been dead-on, too many times; his insight was uncanny, and he often came up with machines that, at first glance, were decades, ahead of their time (such as the exotic matter trap that was currently installed within a seven-story particle detector, within the path of the supercollider beneath their feet).

Fabiola had not planned on running the exotic matter experiments so soon, but Salison had pleaded with her to postpone the scheduled collisions, which were designed to search for the Higgs Boson—the theorized GOD particle that holds all matter together—and to instead, use the supercollider to generate and collect exotic matter, using Salison's exotic matter trap that he would allow CERN to use, *only* if they were to perform the experiments in the next few days.

So Fabiola, much to the initial dismay of hundreds of physicists, agreed to recalibrate the collider to perform the exotic matter experiments instead of the ones searching for the Higgs Boson. Capturing exotic matter would be a huge accomplishment, and she could not pass up the opportunity.

Salison had already drawn up the experiments and had the individual physicist teams briefed on the changes in experimental protocol.

Fabiola had a condition of her own though. If she were to perform the experiments Salison desired, Salison had to be honest with her and divulge to her his true origins.

As Salison spoke to Fabiola in her study, with particles traveling at near light-speed beneath their feet, a picture of Salison began to emerge that defied Fabiola's interminable logic, yet made a strange sort of sense.

Salison said that he was from across a great sea. Not a sea of water, or a sea of land, but a sea of foam.

Many physicists believed, although Fabiola was not yet convinced herself, that our universe was just one of many universes; that our universe, all we can see and perceive, for light-years in every direction, was just one bubble in a vast sea-foam of other universes that make up the multiverse.

Salison said that he was from a separate bubble of the multiverse, and that his original home was a jungle continent, where he worked as a particle physicist, at a subterranean circular superstructure—an even more powerful supercollider than the Large Hadron Collider, with the diameter of thirty-three kilometers, which required the efforts of nearly 15,000 scientists and half-a-century to build.

Salison had joined his team of jungle-dwelling particle physicists long after others had used the supercollider, just as Fabiola and her team had (to create and study elementary building blocks of nature).

For thirty years, Salison's supercollider had been used for a new purpose. Having believed that all species of fundamental particles had been identified, Salison and his team began using the collider to smash charged particles together, in order to create miniscule tears in the fabric of space-time.

There was a large number of physicists, Salison included, who believed that the small tears in space-time, that were created by the supercollider, could manifest into wormholes, which, in theory, could connect separate bubbles of the so called 'multiverse'.

Since the generation of the first space-time tears born of the supercollider, Salison and his team had been working to generate a wormhole from the tears, in order to bridge the gap between separate universes.

Incredibly, the conception of the supercollider was not sparked by Salison's civilization; the mathematics, physics, machining, engineering and blueprints required to build the collider had been exquisitely described in texts that were found in a massive subterranean complex— a time capsule—that was discovered deep underground, beneath a lost city, nearly six hundred years earlier.

AN EVOLUTION OF MINDS

The famous explorer, F. Sorlerla, had discovered the lost city in the center of a deep, dark, dense jungle continent—Salison's continent. The story surrounding the discovery of the so-called 'Temple of the Spinning Wheel' had often been mythologized; but it was known, Sorlerla spent 132 years excavating the massive underground complex, finding it contained fantastic machines, a vast stock hold of art, plant and animal specimens, fossils, and an extensive archive of books, written in thousands of different languages.

When the capsule was found, the most educated of Salison's ancestors were astronomers, miners, and metal workers. Once the time capsule was uncovered though, the brightest of them donated much of their time to the study of the capsule's contents and the mysterious source of power that lit its interior.

The linguists, those that knew all of the dozen or so continental languages, worked fervently to translate what was believed to be the *master text*—a book written on an unknown material that contained several short passages translated into around 6,000 languages.

It was believed that once the *master text* was translated, it would be possible to decipher the main language that was universally used throughout the capsule, in manuals that accompanied every machine, and in texts that accompanied every plant and animal specimen and work of art.

It took decades to translate the *master text*. Once the translators had done it though, there was a great explosion of knowledge. A society obsessed with the stars and the movement of the planets, now had the means and mathematics to build telescopes, electron microscopes, and to travel outside of the earth's atmosphere.

From that point on, Salison's civilization experienced frequent exponential leaps in technology. Even though it was believed that only half of the massive underground time capsule was intact when it was found, and that the rest of it had been destroyed, perhaps by earthquakes, continental drift, or the movements of massive glaciers over the land.

At any rate, by the time Salison was born, modern-day science had already caught up with, and eclipsed, the technology of those who had built the great time capsule.

Salison Sinsway's civilization was one that was reverse-engineered and only now, after setting up shop on the shoulders of giants, did his society's scientists begin to ponder the next step—the one they would be the first to take.

One of those 'next steps' for Salison's civilization, was using the supercollider for more than just identifying subatomic particles, and using it instead to create wormholes between space-time tears. Salison and his team would smash charged particles together, at near light-speed, in order to create tears in space-time, and were subsequently using advanced sub-electron microscopy to view regions of space-time beyond the tears.

They were actually able to *view* separate universes.

With advanced medical knowledge as well, Salison's civilization had also generated detectors that could pick up on thought itself. Neuroscientists of his time had discovered a force of nature, like heat from a candle, that was emitted from all life forms that harbored the cellular machinery to generate consciousness. Surprisingly, they detected these waves of consciousness, to some degree, not only in humans but in all living things, plants and animals alike. And thanks to the brilliant insights of one of Salison's contemporaries, the device used for scanning for and studying thought was redesigned, so that it could be focused into the scopes that were used to peer through the tears between separate universes.

There was a group of thousands of jungle-dwelling scientists that used the supercollider to open up tears in space-time, and then scan for conscious thought (as it was that both light and the medium of thought could travel through the gap).

After years of searching, a team of researchers believed they had found a small, blue planet that orbited a white sun, that may have harbored life—and the power of thought that came with it.

Extra-dimensional viewers they were called, and they could not have operated without Salison and his team, who were in charge of running the supercollider and smashing protons together, to create the wormholes (or tears in space-time).

Concurrently, Salison's twin brother, Stasanor, was working on a separate project.

Stasanor Sinsway had been a part of a team that built a massive underground complex, that was used to house and connect thousands of supercomputers. Vast portions of the cubed complex were cooled to the coldest temperatures in the universe via liquid hydrogen chambers, to allow the supercomputers to operate on the quantum level and to compute at an unbelievable speed, allowing for the near instantaneous transfer of information between more separate points than there were stars in the universe.

These supercomputers were used by Stasanor, and his team, to unravel the mysteries of teleportation.

Fabiola almost could not believe her ears. Separate universes, wormholes in space-time, a medium of thought, and teleportation. She knew that there were correlates of each of these things in her 'modern' world though.

She could think of a dozen experiments, offhand, that hinted that there could be multiple universes (that were governed by distinct rules, which may, or may not, allow for the formation of planets, stars, and ultimately life within them).

The properties of particles in the Standard Model of particle physics seemed also, at times, to adhere to the multiverse model of the universe as well. Fabiola also knew that black holes were postulated to be the tips of wormholes, and that even Albert Einstein postulated on the possibility of their being *bridges* between separate regions of space-time.

There were also researchers, neuroscientists, Fabiola had read about, that picked up signals of thought *outside* of the brain, measured as changes in voltage across the scalp. These voltage potentials were generated by groups of neurons firing in sync within tissues of the brain.

There were even multiple groups of researchers who were able to utilize quantum teleportation, in order to teleport particles from one location to another. For instance, in 2003, nearby scientists at the University of Geneva were able to teleport photons a distance of 1.2 miles through a fiber-optic cable; and in 2004, a team teleported an entire Beryllium atom, instantaneously, from one position, to another.

Fabiola knew, however, that modern science was far from being able to teleport any living thing, or even a large molecule, like sugar. The key thing holding us back was the sheer amount of information involved.

Even with the best communication channels available, transferring all the information in a human body and brain between two points would be impossible, or would take the age of the universe.

Salison had mentioned thousands of connected supercomputers though. *That might do the trick.* Fabiola's imagination flared, as Salison continued, his story.

According to Salison, his twin brother Stasanor, and his team, had created a machine that could teleport living things, even primates, for distances as long as they were able to detect, which had been hundreds of miles.

It was Salison who had first thought of the idea of traveling through the breach, through the wormholes that were created by his supercollider—to teleport to a separate universe, using his brother's technology.

There was a major problem though. As it was, only light—electromagnetic radiation—radio waves, and the medium of thought (which in truth, was believed to be made up of particles, similar to light) were able to travel though the wormholes.

The wormholes were like strings connecting two cups. You could send signals through the connecting wires, but you could not transport matter through the line; for that you would need a tunnel, rather than a line of string. So Salison theorized a way to open the wormhole up to such an extent, as to allow for more than just electromagnetic radiation to travel through.

Building on the work of others, Salison had come up with the answer: exotic matter. If exotic matter were injected into the wormhole, it would cause the wormhole's rapid expansion and would create a traversable pathway, that would, theoretically, persist for seconds, even minutes—this due to exotic matter's strange charge and repulsive potential.

So Salison built an exotic matter trap, and after allocating supercollider time to the generation and capture of exotic matter particles (using a protocol that was extensively described decades earlier), Salison had joined forces with his brother and designed a protocol whereby Stasanor's teleporter was used to teleport exotic matter into the center of an artificially generated tear in space-time (that was the tip of a wormhole); then, immediately after, once the wormhole had expanded, solid objects would be teleported into the wormhole as well.

After a couple of pilot experiments, Salison and Stasanor believed that they were indeed able to transport solid, carbon-based objects, like large melons, and even small living animals, like mice, into wormholes, and, ultimately, to the small blue planet that was found on the other side of the void.

For months, Salison and Stasanor performed many experiments that worked to characterize the properties that governed interdimensional teleportation; having done so, they stumbled on a number of curious properties of teleportation.

Stasanor had noticed that living things, like mice, when transported into the wormhole could still be detected, for some time, *within* the wormhole, before they disappeared into it. Stasanor had postulated that due to the enormous amount of information that was being transferred from one place to another, the teleportation of living things was not instantaneous.

There was a time-lag that developed, due to the amount of time it took to break down the enormous amount of information that was contained in a living organism, before that organism could be transported to a separate location. An object or animal that was being sent had to first be scanned and then broken down into a stream of information—which took a massive amount of computing power and thus time.

The team had also attempted to retrieve the objects that were sent into the wormhole, bringing them back to their universe; however, they soon realized that only inanimate objects could be retrieved. Living animals, however, could not be teleported back into their universe.

Neither Stasanor nor Salison could make sense of it; the teleporter provided the pair with information that mice and other animals, once teleported, had made it to the alternate universe, and, subsequently, after the retrieval attempt and second teleportation event, had even left the small blue planet on the other side of the void; but where they had gone once they left that small blue planet, was a mystery, as they were not coming back to Salison's universe.

Then, one night, Stasanor made an amazing discovery. He had planned to send a cat to the alternate universe, and then, to subsequently try and retrieve it.

Before the experiment began however, when Stasanor had gone to fetch the animal, he had found it drenched with water. Stasanor was perplexed, but he had an incredible hunch. So he had sent, instead of the cat, a rotating camera and an empty cup through the wormhole.

Once the camera was sent, it was set to take photos and, as it was not living material, it was subsequently teleported back to Stasanor's lab. The images that the camera had captured were of a violent downpour. And Stasanor's cup was filled to the brim, with, what analysis later confirmed was pure rainwater.

So living things *had* been coming back to Salison's universe, once having been teleported to the alternate universe; but, incredibly, they had been returning *before* they were sent out in the first place.

Stasanor could not quite explain it, yet he believed the phenomenon could have arisen from the dilation of space-time in or near the wormhole itself. He postulated that as living things were teleported back into his universe, the original copy of the object—the one to be later teleported—would be annihilated, once the teleported object came back before it was sent, leaving only one copy—not two—in Stasanor's universe. This was why Stasanor had not picked up on the incredible phenomenon earlier.

Stasanor was even able to create a remote link to the supercomputers from the teleporter, so that when the teleporter was located in the alternate universe it would still be able to connect with the massive complex of supercomputers in Salison's world, which meant that it was possible to teleport objects to different locations *within* the alternate universe.

Running more experiments, Stasanor came to realize that animals transported to the alternate universe and subsequently back, would usually return five to ten minutes before they were sent, with the more complex life forms arriving further back in time than the simpler ones.

For instance, cats came back, at maximum, a dozen minutes before they were sent; while mice came back just a few minutes before they were sent. Stasanor nor Salison could, yet, completely understand the nature of the phenomenon or why it only applied to living things.

Before they could find the answer, however, Salison's and Stasanor's work on the transfer of biological material to alternate universes through wormholes born of the supercollider began to slow, due to the current political climate. A rival power, from across a great ocean to the east, had been, for the past few hundred years, sending parties of warships across the ocean, with what spies had confirmed were intentions to take over Stasanor and Salison's land and to kill and enslave their people.

After traveling across the ocean, spies from Salison's community painted a picture whereby the land-lusted empire from across the sea had been sending armies into surrounding territories, killing and castrating people by the hundreds of thousands, to force their will, religion, and brutal oppression upon them.

Salison likened the empire across the ocean, in his world, to the German Nazis of WWII—they were brutal, and led by a man with misguided beliefs (that his was a master race and that all others must bow before him). This man had generated a great and evil force that had been exterminating people by the millions to *cleanse* the land of the inferior species. This tall, pale-white skinned, icy-eyed race was a blight on the planet, a scourge that could not be quenched with an ocean of blood.

In the time capsule that was found by Salison's civilization, there were no weapons—no swords, firearms, siege engines, nor nuclear devices—only records of life, artwork, and sciences that the previous planet-dwellers had generated; technologies and medical knowledge that would aid a curious people in the understanding of their own minds, bodies, planet, and place in the cosmos.

Although Salison's people were skilled in martial arts and the use of steel weapons, they had long ago come to a consensus not to use the superior technology they had been gifted with, nor their ensuing original breakthroughs, to create objects that could take life. This decision was made for many reasons, one of which was the consequences of such high-tech weapons falling into the hands of an empire such as the one across the sea.

So, with sharpened, forged, blades of steel, were Salison's armies equipped, as they had been for thousands of years. With these weapons, thus far, they had been able to stave off occupation from the evil overseas. There were rumors though, that the troops across the ocean were mobilizing a grand army that numbered over a million.

One fateful night, with the hot, sticky jungle air almost suffocating (above ground), Salison found himself working late, doing calculations that could aid in the production of longer-lasting, more stable wormholes. As Salison sat in his study, a loud wailing noise began to fill the air. It was the war sirens. Salison's village of scientists and scholars was under attack.

Salison quickly learned, from coworkers, that a fleet of ships had been found anchored just offshore, near the southern region of the continent, and that a few battalions—troops numbering in the hundreds, after weeks of cutting their way northward through the dense, dark, jungle, were now beginning to infiltrate the village.

Salison figured the encroaching troops had intelligence reports regarding the nature of the science that was being conducted in the village. Surely they would make for teleporter. If they got their hands on it, they could transport the whole of their army to anywhere on the planet, including Salison's continent, and forgo, the perilous journey across the ocean. An ocean, that, for the most part, had protected the village and hundreds of surrounding villages from the empire for hundreds of years.

Salison would just-as-soon destroy the machine than let it fall into the hands of the invaders, who would destroy Salison's land and enslave, or kill, everyone—men, women, and children, alike—if they somehow found the means to do so.

On an off-road bicycle, Salison pedaled furiously over dirt-laden jungle trails, towards his brother Stasanor, who he knew was working late at his lab.

It took Salison six minutes and thirty-six seconds to reach his brother's lab. As he neared a large mound of earth that roofed the lab beneath it, he saw, through the trees, a dozen or so men—soldiers from across the sea—approaching the front of the lab. Salison headed towards the back entrance. He did not have much time.

Salison jumped off his bike, while it was still moving, and rushed into the teleportation lab, just as two soldiers who had broken away from the main group were coming in through the front door. Through a pair of windowed corridors, the men saw Salison enter, and they ran in his direction.

Salison was soon in his brother's lab. Stasanor was working with semi-spherical headphones on, oblivious to the attack and the approaching peril. Salison slapped his brother's headphones off his head. His slow, drawn out language was spoken unusually fast.

"We have not much time. *They* are coming."

What to do?

Salison knew that if the empire from across the sea were to capture them and the teleporter, their civilization and perhaps the whole continent, would be conquered (meaning Salison's friends, family, coworkers, and daughter, would be enslaved or killed).

So Salison did the only thing that he could think of. Furiously, he adjusted knobs and dials on the circular control panel that surrounded the circular teleporting platform, deaf to the wail of the sirens cutting through the air and to his own brother's inquires.

Salison restructured the spatial area of the region to be teleported, from a few square feet above the teleporting platform in the center of the room, to the whole room itself.

Salison planned on teleporting the entire lab, including himself and his brother, out of harm's way. He knew, if he were to teleport anywhere on his planet, the soldiers would still be able to capture the second teleporter that was located a few miles away. It was an early prototype, but still worked perfectly and would be able to transport all the soldiers that were waiting across the sea.

Salison needed not only to get away from the encroaching soldiers and to get the teleporter away from them, he also needed *time*. And Salison had an idea. With the press of a button, the engines of the teleporter came alive, and an electric hum began to resonate around the room. Then, a brilliant, spinning, translucent bubble, was born of a bead that lie at the exact center of the teleporter. The clear bubble soon began to expand, as it spun light about its surface. The surface of the bubble slightly oscillated, looking to get smaller, before it would resume its expansion, these movements in tandem with the subtle rising and falling of the hum of the engines. Soon the translucent bubble began to engulf the entire room, with Salison and his twin brother *within* the clear sphere.

Salison turned to his brother as light danced along the swirling surface of the bubble that surrounded them,

"We are taking a trip. It is the only way.", he said.

It was then Salison noticed it—there was only enough exotic matter in his trap to accommodate one journey through the wormhole. The realization reflected in Salison's violet eyes, as the two soldiers broke down the door of the lab, and, with bloodied swords in hand, came at Salison and his twin brother, breaking through the spherical, translucent, bubble, as it rhythmically pulsed—having now engulfed the whole room and the four men within in it. Red lights then fanned out from two curved planks that rose up above the teleporter; the red lights darted quickly around—scanning the whole of the room, and all those within it. In just over two seconds, the lights completed their scan, and were drawn back up into the planks that surrounded the teleporter.

Then, with a great flash of not light, but dark, the bubble collapsed, and the lab, and the four individuals that had been within, disappeared from their universe, leaving only an empty sphere of space where they had been.

***

Salison's voice portrayed a deep emotion that Fabiola had never before witnessed in the man, as he recounted how he had never seen his brother again. And that the pale blue sphere that they had been studying from their alternate universe, had been Earth.

Salison said that due to the time it took for their complex of supercomputers to break them down and transmit them through the wormhole, each of the individuals within the teleporter arrived on Earth at different points in time.

Salison had drastically underestimated the time gap between arrivals, and now figured that each of them had arrived on Earth hundreds of years apart, at the very least. He had a good idea that his twin brother Stasanor had arrived first, around the year 400 BC.

Stasanor must have known, then, that if Salison were to ever get back home and if their people were to be saved from the evil across the sea, he would have to find a way to preserve the teleporter until his brother Salison arrived on Earth, which so happened, would not be for another 2,200 years.

If anyone was ingenious enough to preserve and hide away the teleporter for hundreds, even thousands of years, it was Stasanor.

Stasanor also knew though, that through time, both of the attacking soldiers would be teleported to earth as well, with the mission of finding the teleporter, either to destroy it, or to bring it back to their universe and their army.

Stasanor knew he would need to encrypt the teleporter's location so that the soldiers, who obviously knew about it and would be searching for it, could not gain possession of it.

Salison believed that his twin brother had, indeed, not only been able to hide the teleporter, but also pass down the encrypted knowledge of its hidden location, in a carbon fiber cloth (a cloth that was taken from within the teleporter, unraveled, and then re-sewn, with a new purpose).

After seeing an article in the Smithsonian magazine, depicting his brother's long-lost, sown cloth—which was meant to be passed down to Salison—in the hands of one of the dead and mummified soldiers who had been after it, Salison immediately shifted his focus to finding the cloth, which he knew was a map—to the teleporter. Perhaps there was still hope to get back to his home and save his friends, his family, his daughter, and his civilization, from the invading enemy.

Salison knew that if he were able to generate enough exotic matter to open the wormhole, and was then able to teleport back to his universe, he would arrive *before* he left in the first place. This gift of time could be enough to change his people's fate and perhaps the world's as well.

So Salison sent his daughter, Silloway, to retrieve the cloth that Stasanor had weaved for him, while he worked to generate and trap enough exotic matter that, once injected into the wormhole, would allow for his passage through it.

Salison had divulged much to Fabiola, as he promised, but had left out a couple of, what one may call, relevant facts about his home world.

One fact, was that his tribe of jungle dwellers, turned scientists, respected and revered all forms of life; thus, they went through great lengths to protect the land they lived on and to preserve the grand diversity of life that was found in their jungles and rivers.

They only killed animals for food and used as much of the fallen prey as they could, not wasting a thing. If a species dwindled low in numbers, hunting or killing of that animal was prohibited, under pain of death.

Salison's society strived to keep their own population under control as well. For instance, no more than two children were allowed in any family, and all those who wished to bear children, had to first apply, to have the *would-be* father's mandatory vasectomy reversed, for a brief period of time, during which a couple would try to conceive a child. Permission was rarely granted.

But that was not all. With an average lifespan of around three hundred years, Salison's society had to do more to keep the population low.

Every full moon, all would gather at the center of their civilization, in a large circular coliseum that was carved from stone and covered in moss and vines as it rose up from the jungle floor.

In the stone coliseum, a most intense sport was played, similar to European soccer, that involved teams of sixteen players, using their feet, hips, heads and hands, to place a soccer ball-sized sphere through one of a half a dozen circular goals that rose up to different heights above the ground.

Each full moon, teams were chosen at random, from Salison's village and surrounding territories—eight men and eight women—who would engage in the sport. What made Salison's society's sport different than any of ours today, was that after the match, the whole of the losing team was ritualistically sacrificed—killed in the center of the coliseum.

Salison had learned that this practice of human sacrifice was similar to those found in extinct cultures in South and Central America.

But the sport, however barbaric, not only kept the population's numbers under control, but also made it every person's priority to stay active, fit, and in shape.

None in Salison's population were obese or even slightly overweight. Not only that, but all had a respect—or fear—of the sport, that, in the end, instilled in each of them a deeper appreciation for life and of balance, that could not be gleaned any other way.

On inhabiting the pale blue sphere in the universe apart from his own, Salison had become sickened by some of the behaviors exhibited by his new planet's societies. Not only their utter disregard for plant and animal life, but also their vast ignorance and recklessness when it came to their own growing population.

Although the numbers of the planet's human population was spiraling dangerously out of control, many families were having up to a dozen children, sometimes more. Salison thought it was despicable and unacceptable. Had he the time, and his own army, he would have ordered billions of castrations, to save the earth from this disease of man, like the pharaohs of ancient Egypt who castrated hundreds of thousands of conquered men, upon their defeat, ensuring no new generations were spawned—stopping bloodlines in their tracks.

Salison knew that before he left this new world, one way or another, he would have to bring the planet that had clearly lost its way, back, to balance.

Another curious aspect of his world that Salison did not mention to Fabiola, was that the empire across the ocean was rumored to have a select few soldiers that, through either strenuous physical and mental training, or an advanced medical procedure, or perhaps a combination thereof, were able to become somewhat superhuman.

There were reports, brought back from spies across the sea from Salison's civilization, of entire towns being crippled by what could have been, a single soldier, a single man that was able to move faster than any normal individual; who was able to disappear, like a ghost, leaving in his wake dozens, hundreds, even thousands of dead bodies.

Survivors only saw flashes of light and color, as their friends and families were cut down.

Salison's civilization, as of yet, had no way of combating these so-called *super soldiers*. Salison had not full-heartedly believed the stories, until the night of the attack on his village. For as he pedaled furiously through the dark jungle, on a well-packed dirt trail, towards Stasanor's lab, he had seen, through the trees, the second teleportation lab—the one that was built first. In a small clearing, just in front of a mound of earth that housed the lab beneath, there was a group of men, resistance fighters from Salison's village; the men were yelling—sounding confused and scared—as they attempted to fight, looking disorganized.

Salison saw the men being cut down by an unseen foe; their limbs falling away from their bodies, violently. The demise of the soldiers was accompanied by flashes of color—red, silver, and pale skin glowing in the moonlight—the shape of not one, but many men, bleeding together at times, surrounded by soft yellow fluorescent fauna illuminating the massacre.

Fabiola listened to Salison tell his tale of his home world and his incredible journey across space and time, to reach Earth. She had dozens of questions for Salison, once he had finished.

But the man told her that he had to get back to the Large Hadron Collider, more specifically to ATLAS (a hub that was built into the supercollider, that housed a giant seven-story, circular, particle detector, and as of late, an exotic matter trap, that was set up inside the heart of it).

The Large Hadron Collider had been running collisions all through the night, generating and trapping exotic matter. Salison figured that by this time, he may have already trapped enough exotic matter to facilitate his travel back home, so that he may finally attempt to save his first born, and his people; provided Silloway was able to secure him his vessel—the teleporter.

Before Salison left Fabiola's cottage, he plugged in a custom-designed hard drive to her landline. As he turned it on, a small red light began to blink, indicating that the modem was ready to transmit. Also plugged into the modem was Salison's laptop that held a painstakingly designed sound byte and a computer program that had now run to completion. The program would allow its user to hack into Orion Communications and subsequently release what would be the greatest plague ever to befall the men and women of Earth. The laptop, and the modem, sat on Fabiola's desk, merely waiting, desperately, for an incoming signal to set them off.

59

At 11:00 p.m. the previous night, young officer Patrick Middler arrived in Geneva, Switzerland. He flew out of LaGuardia Airport, in Queens, New York—since all of the flights into and out of Boston had been delayed, indefinitely, due to Salison's spreading plague (that was generating an incredible death toll which was spiraling out of control).

The scary thing was, it could all get much, much worse, if Salison were to unleash his pirate signal over the airwaves.

If Middler could find Salison, or Christopher Banks' hard drive, perhaps he could prevent the signal from being sounded.

Before Middler left for Europe, Brennan gave him a small handheld device that looked almost like an old Nintendo Gameboy that Middler played when we was a bit younger. Brennan said that Banks created it. The young computer scientist had not yet been able to hack Orion Communications new security protocols, to shut it down, but he was able to create a device that could find Salison's specially designed hard-drive; although there were some caveats.

Banks told Brennan, who later told Middler, that he had taken a radio receiver and tuned it to the radio frequency that was used to connect the two wireless transmitters with the main transmitting pole (Salison's stationary hard drive).

If either of the wireless transmitters were on, as well as the stationary hard drive, there would be a radio-link between them; and the device Banks made would be able to detect the radio waves that linked the two devices together.

Unfortunately, the radio signal, that linked the wireless transmitters to the receiving pole, was relatively weak. The wireless transmitters would only work to trigger the transmitting pole, if they were within forty or so miles away from it; and this was the distance that Middler would have to be within, if he wanted to detect the signal.

On the monitor screen of the radio-wave detector that Banks made, there was a circle, and outside of it, a row of parallel bars, ranging from short to tall, ascending, in order. If the device were to pick up the radio signal, there would be a colored dot on the screen within the circle, indicating the direction of the transmitting pole.

The ascending bars would then begin to light up, as one came closer to the transmitting pole. If the small bars were lit up, it would indicate a weak signal; the large ones would indicate a stronger one. There would also be a beeping sound that would increase in its frequency the closer that the receiver got to the transmitting pole. The device was, no doubt, rudimentary; but right now, it was their best chance at finding Salison and Christopher Banks's hard drive (provided the hard drive and one of the transmitters was turned on).

With turbulent weather over the Atlantic, it had taken Officer Middler ten hours to get to Geneva. On landing, Middler rented a car and set course for a small Inn, located in the Swiss countryside.

Middler stopped at the Inn, dropped off his luggage, briefly hit on the young blonde receptionist—no doubt, the daughter of the Innkeeper— and then, although he was tired and jet-lagged, jumped back in his rental and headed for CERN.

He figured that the physicists would still be up—despite the late hour—analyzing data, running experiments, or doing whatever else geniuses do. He knew it would be worth talking to them, to learn if they knew anything in regards to one of their directors, Dr. Salison Sinsway.

On arriving in Switzerland, Middler turned on Banks' tracking device; but as of yet, the signal linking the transmitting pole with the wireless transmitters had yet to be detected.

Middler was soon to CERN, and came to realize that security was far from lax. So Middler appealed to the security guards with the truth; he said that he was a detective from Boston, investigating a man that could be linked to the outbreak of the deadly pathogen, which was now killing thousands of people, all over the world.

On showing the head of security his police badge and reminding him of the dire circumstances in Boston and a dozen other cities (which was now world news), Middler was given a guest pass and a security escort, which allowed him limited access to some of the research facilities.

AN EVOLUTION OF MINDS

Through computer labs and lecture halls Middler walked, with his security escort; he found many scientists that were still up and working away. It did not take him long to pick up on the fact that the general mood of the place was gloomy; and it was no wonder as to why—everyone here thought that the great physicist, Salison Sinsway, was dead. The physicists all thought he had died in Boston five days ago. They spoke of the man with reverence and were confused when Middler asked if anyone had seen him or his daughter, Silloway, or even Jonas Moorea—which he provided a headshot of.

Although some of them recognized Silloway, none of them knew her location; and everyone Middler talked to, seemed to think Salison was dead. A few people even lamented the fact that Salison would not be able to win the Nobel Prize, since the prize was not given out posthumously.

Middler, with his escort, drove around in an ivory golf cart, with the night air swirling around him. The two drove, in near darkness, to multiple hubs of the Large Hadron Collider within the path of the great circle.

Within the Large Hadron Collider were separate detectors that were specifically designed for certain types of collisions, and detecting certain types of particles. Most of the particle detector control rooms donned skeleton crews, while some of them were completely empty. Middler had no leads, nor had he met anyone that believed Salison was alive. It was 1:22 a.m.

The last hub of the LHC that Middler went to was ATLAS. ATLAS was a 7,000 ton particle detector that lie in an underground cavern, 130 meters below ground—the particle detector was a marvel of engineering; it stood, circular, and shining, like a giant seven-story Swiss watch.

Once at ALTAS, it did not take officer Middler long to notice the mood was a bit more upbeat. There were dozens of scientists, even camera crews, in the nearly full control room (although Middler, himself, was not allowed to enter the control room). Middler learned that the ATLAS crew was, on this very day, performing collisions that were designed to generate and *trap* exotic matter—something that had never been done before.

There were plenty of people to talk to in the corridors surrounding the control room and soon Middler was speaking to a young blonde-haired woman, an experimental physicist, who worked on the ATLAS project. She became quite interested, when she found out that Middler was looking for Salison, or his daughter.

"You think Salison is alive?" she asked, with a curious smile.

"Yes. To be honest, we're not sure how he was able to pass for dead and then come back; but his body is unaccounted for, and we have a reliable witness that saw him alive, two days ago at the Geneva Airport. Why, do you know something?" Middler asked.

The woman had a pondering nature about her when she spoke, "Well, three days ago, everyone working at ATLAS received an e-mail that stated we were to, at the spur of the moment, switch experiments. We had been planning on getting at the Higgs; but all of a sudden, we're to restructure our experiments, so that we can *trap* exotic matter.

Fabiola sent out the e-mail, but she had been pushing the Higgs experiment for months. It didn't make any sense."

Middler read about CERN, and he knew that Fabiola Gionatti was the director of the ATLAS experiment.

"You think Salison was behind the switch in experiments?" he asked.

The woman shrugged.

"Smells like him. And there's also the dark matter trap that Fabiola pulled out of thin air."

A vibrating noise emanated from the woman's purse. She fished out her cell phone, answered it, spoke a few words in French, and then hung up.

"Sorry, I gotta go. My ride's here. Good luck."

Middler bade the woman farewell, and then asked around awhile longer. All the scientists here were perplexed in regards to questions about Salison. Middler felt like he was bringing them down, causing them to recollect a memory that was souring the joy of the current atmosphere. And apparently, Middler had just missed Fabiola, who had retired to her cottage for the night, not fifteen minutes prior.

Middler, with the cool night abound, had the security guard drive him back to the parking lot. He then thanked the man, and called Brennan. It was 2:21 a.m. in Geneva, and 8:21 p.m. in Massachusetts.

Brennan answered, gruffly, and was filled in on the situation; he looked up Fabiola's address for Middler and was quickly off the phone—telling Middler that he would call him in the morning.

On the drive back to the Inn, Middler swung by Fabiola Gionatti's house. From the driveway, it looked as though all the lights were off. Middler hopped out of his car and walked around the house. His shoes, socks, and bottoms of his slacks were soon wet from the countryside dew that shined in the moonlight.

There was not a hint of light, within the windows of Fabiola's cottage, save for the stars and waxing near half-moon reflecting in the glass. Middler figured he would try to catch Fabiola at CERN come morning, or he would come back to talk to her the following day. He had a feeling she may know where Salison was.

Middler drove back to the Inn and was soon in his room. He threw his badge, wallet, keys, and cell phone onto his dresser; and then stripped and fell into bed.

The young officer was soon passed out; his brain was quick to embrace those electrical rhythms that govern sleep, consolidation of memories, and travel through vivid dreams.

Middler awoke with a start with the sensation that he was falling. He smiled, not used to feeling the pull of gravity so strong beneath him. It was now the morning of the present day—he had breakfast in the living room of the Inn which was served by the cute, Swedish woman, who Middler was now sure (from her *'papas'*) was the daughter of the Innkeeper.

As Middler ate, he conversed with the woman, who spoke English quite well and seemed glad to be practicing it. She shot Middler a smile, as he left.

Middler, with the autumn air energizing him, jogged to his rental car and hopped in, heading to CERN.

When Middler arrived at CERN, he had no idea that Fabiola was not yet there, and that she was a few miles away, speaking to Salison about his origins.

Middler parked in the guest lot and walked up to one of the security stations; the same one he had seen the night before. Unfortunately, there was a new security guard working the booth.

Middler spoke to the man, a Frenchman, trying to persuade him to allow Middler access to CERN and ATLAS. The security guard was not as sympathetic as the one the night before. He suggested that Middler sign up for a tour.

Just as the Frenchman spoke the words, a beeping began emanating from Middler's shoulder pack—it took Middler a couple of seconds to realize what it was.

It was Christopher Banks' radio tracker.

The device was detecting the radio signal that functioned to link Salison's wireless triggering devices to the transmitting pole that had the power to unleash hell on earth. Now, Banks' transmitting pole and triggers were active; and from the relatively high frequency sound of the beeps, Middler guessed the transmitting pole was close.

Middler quickly undid his pack, grabbed Banks' tracking device out of it, and examined the display screen. He then took off in a sprint, towards his car, knowing that he may only have seconds, minutes, but hopefully more, before Salison would activate his signal and release his pathogen unto the world.

Four hours before Middler began to hear the signal from Christopher Banks' tracking device, and three thousand six hundred and sixty-eight miles away, across the Atlantic Ocean, Detective David Brennan was fast asleep. That was, until his cell phone lit up and began vibrating on the top of his bedside dresser. Brennan slowly awoke and clicked on his bedside lamp. He tried to gather himself as he checked the time; running a hand over the stubble on his face. It was just after one a.m.

Brennan grabbed his phone.

"Yes?" Brennan answered, gruffly.

'Hey, Mr. Brennan. It's me, Christopher. Christopher Banks."

"How goes it?" Brennan asked.

Banks sighed.

"I still can't make the hack into Orion, but I was able to hack the program I made for Salison."

Brennan sat up in bed, gaining a bit of energy.

"So you can shut it down?" he asked.

Banks hesitated.

"No, not yet. I'm working on it, but I was able to glean the status of the hack, to tell how far my program needed to run in order to give Salison access to Orion."

"And?"

"Well, according to my data, the program I made for Salison already ran to completion. It finished running two days ago."

"So Salison has been able to unleash his signal for the past two days and hasn't?"

"Ya..."

Brennan softly rubbed his temple, speaking more to himself than to Banks:

"Well then, what the hell is he waiting for?"

60

Judith Arai, the brilliant mathematician turned amateur archaeologist, sat in a small pool of blood on the floor of her hotel room, with the hot Cypriot air abound, as she held Charles Klein's head. Her hands and lap were covered in blood.

It had only been two minutes since Dr. Klein was shot in the chest; he was still conscious and had broken out into a cold sweat. Klein's breaths were staggered and seemed to be heavy for him to pull into his body—there was no doubt as to why; there were air bubbles and blood coming from out the bullet wound, which Judith was trying to cover with her hands—Klein had been shot in the lung.

"Just like… Alexander…",

Klein managed to say, with short, drawn out breaths. During their dig, Klein told Judith a story about a man he revered—Alexander the Great, and how during the siege of a Mallian city, the king had been shot with an arrow through the lung, as he led a charge over the city's walls. Alexander's wound was so severe, it bubbled blood, yet he fought on, till he lost consciousness..

Judith managed a smile, with tears in her eyes, as she held Klein, putting her hand over his wound, trying to keep pressure on it.

"We'll have to sail you down the river Hydraotis. Just hang on."

After about another minute of Judith holding Klein, trying to keep pressure on the wound, an older French man—a tourist, no doubt—came to curiously peer through the broken down doorway. When he saw the situation inside, he rushed in.

The man moved with purpose. He took off his own shirt, bunched it up, removed Judith's hand, and put the cloth over Klein's wound. He told Judith to keep pressure on it, as he ran back out of the room.

Judith heard sirens approaching, in the distance, and soon the man was back into the room.

"Get some blankets, will you?" he said, as he quickly used a knife to cut away Klein's blood-soaked T-shirt.

He then removed his own bloodied, bunched up shirt from the wound—he wiped the bullet hole clean with gauze before applying an amber liquid to the tear of flesh, he then wiped it dry again, for just a moment, as it bubbled blood.

The man covered the cleaned wound with gauze pads and then gently raised Klein's body (as Klein groaned) so that a bandage could be wrapped around the gauze.

"Have you called the paramedic?" the man asked, as he finished wrapping Klein's wound.

Judith nodded, she had used the hotel phone to call the police, soon after Klein was injured. Sure enough, after a few minutes of Klein breathing shallow and growing colder, two paramedics entered the room—they rushed in and took up the space around Klein. They checked his dressing, looked as if they approved, and then quickly loaded the middle-aged archaeologist onto a stretcher. To Judith's dismay, the paramedics told her that she could not ride with Klein in the ambulance, saying she would have to wait for the police.

As Klein was carried away, to the exit, with an oxygen mask around his mouth, he managed to squeeze Judith's hand.

Judith was glad he was still conscious and had enough strength in his limbs to do so. Now, the young woman felt as if she were in shock. With blood on her clothes, she thanked the man who helped and then stuck around,

"Are you a doctor?" she asked.

"I'm an accountant." the man replied, "who knows where they keep the first-aid kit."

Judith shook her head, as the man smiled, sympathetically.

"Your friend will be alright. I can tell he has a strong heart. I'm going to get cleaned up."

He headed to the bathroom.

Judith approached the balcony, looking out onto the entrance of the hotel. She saw Klein being loaded into the ambulance before it left, while another ambulance sat parked in the drive— its sirens were still on— lights turning silently.

People were crowded around something; there looked to be a body that Judith could not quite see entirely, which lie on the pavement.

Judith, with a spark of motivation, quickly changed out of her bloody clothes, grabbed her pack, the Taser from the drawer, the keys for the Jimny, then headed to the door.

Judith managed to slip out of the hotel, just as the police arrived. She saw, on the pavement, the dead body of the man who had shot Klein. Judith was glad he was dead. And she wondered who it was that shot him.

A part of Judith wanted to go to the hospital, to check up on and be with Klein; but she knew that time could be running out—someone was clearly after what was hidden at the end of Saatçi's map; and Judith did not want all of her and Klein's hard work to be for not.

She wanted to know the nature of the mysterious thing that was hidden at the end of the map. Klein wanted to know as well. And Judith knew that all she could do for him now was finish what they started together. Judith guessed that if she talked to the police, it could be hours, maybe even the whole day, before she would get done being questioned. And by then, whoever had the GPS, would have already had ample time to find and spirit away whatever was hidden out there, in the rock and sand of Cyprus.

Once in the Jimny, Judith pulled out onto a dusty Cypriot street and began heading dead south. It was about an hour and a half's drive to Episkopi Bay and the small village of Alektora—there, somewhere offshore, about thirty meters underwater, the map ended. Judith had a feeling, a hope, that in that place, something lay hidden, something that could have been there since the time of Alexander the Great.

As Judith drove, there were olive, carob, and almond trees splayed out in rows upon the land, and the Troodos Mountains falling away in the distance. The woman drove as fast as she could when there were no other cars on the road, and was to Episkopi Bay in sixty-eight minutes.

Her first stop was to a local dive shop. The coordinates that she had gleaned from Saatçi's map indicated that she was heading to a spot of open water, just offshore, about thirty meters beneath the surface of the Mediterranean Sea.

The deepest Judith had ever dove was around forty meters, just off the coast of Panama, where she had visited the wreckage of a 1733 Spanish Galleon ship, the Herrera, whose cannons sat half-buried in the sand, alongside shattered planks of the bow.

Judith, with a fraction of the money her boss had given her, bought a wetsuit, flippers, a snorkel, tanks of oxygen, a respirator, and, since a Taser would not work underwater, a simple, reloadable elastic-powered spear gun.

Unfortunately, there was no easy way to get to the spot in the ocean where she needed to be. It was just offshore from a group of the tallest cliffs that surrounded Episkopi Bay—Judith was going to have to charter a ride to take her miles along the coastline (the distance depending on where she could find a suitable marina where she could charter a boat).

In minutes, Judith was at the tourist pavilion on Aphrodite Beach, looking out over the azure Mediterranean, swaying in the midday sun. A large Cypriot man, with a shining bronze chest and a little-too-tight speedo, was there to meet her. Judith was glad he spoke (a much accented) English.

The Greek man told Judith that there was a small fisherman's pier a few miles away, further along the coast, where she could perhaps charter a ride, or even, with the right amount of money, purchase a small fishing boat.

Judith jumped in her Jimny and headed northeast, along the coast. There were only a few roads, and finding her way around was quite easy. She knew it would be different out on the water though, so she purchased another GPS in town—a cheaper version than the one that was stolen from her in Denizli. It was a convenience that she had memorized the coordinates to the end of the Ottoman's map, only a few moments after she had generated them.

In a few minutes, after riding with the hot Cypriot wind on her face, Judith pulled up to a small cove dotted with fishing boats bobbing in the bay. A wooden pier jutted out from the shore, until it branched into a 'T', spreading out over the water.

There was no driveway or parking lot near the beach; the road merely traveled straight by the small cove, as if the fishermen there were all local. There were no cars to be seen either, save for one—and from the looks of it, it was another rental.

Judith pulled over to the side of the road, parked, and jumped out. She went to examine the other car; it was an older, red, Volkswagen sedan. *(Perhaps the car belonged to the shooter in Denizli? The coordinates would have led them here too...).* There was a bag on the backseat; but other than that, the car was empty.

Judith pulled on the door handles, but the doors were all locked. There was a nearby rock (actually a few of them) that Judith thought she could use to smash in a window of the vehicle, in hopes of getting inside and learning something useful about its driver.

But Judith decided against it. Some of the fishermen, near the shore, had already noticed her. She figured smashing in a car window while they were watching, may dissuade them from supplying her with a boat.

Judith took off in a light jog, towards the men. Behind them, she saw small fishing boats; wooden and weathered, some with oars, others with gasoline engines. The boats swaying in the harbor, roped to the weathered planks of the dock.

Soon, Judith was near the men. They had rough beards, curious eyes, and tattered clothes, as they watched her approach.

"Hello," she said. "I am hoping one of you speaks English."

Judith, despite being a prodigy, only knew three languages: mathematics, English, and Japanese.

The three men looked at each other and then back at Judith.

"No English, *ormorfi*," one of the men said, in his Greek tongue.

Judith had the feeling she had just been given a compliment. She smiled, but shook her head.

"One of your boats," she said, pointing to the harbor.

She took out a roll of bills that she had prepared beforehand—a thousand Euros.

"I need one of your boats."

The men looked at each other and smiled.

Yes, you understand this, don't you? Judith thought.

In few minutes, after some minor bartering, Judith purchased a simple fishing boat for nine hundred euros. The men then helped Judith bring her diving gear over to a small, wooden, gasoline-powered boat swaying at one end of the 'T' of the dock. One of the men took a nearly-empty gas container from off Judith's boat and filled it to the top, from one of the tanks of a neighboring vessel. He then set the canister of fuel in the back compartment of her small boat, near the engine. There was then a more somber look to the man's face, as he pointed out to the sea, saying something in Greek.

Judith shook her head.

"I'm sorry, I don't understand."

The man said the words again. It sounded more like a question, as he circled his finger in the air, around the bay.

Judith got the message; the man sounded concerned. She smiled.

"I'll be fine, I can take care of myself. I'm not going far."

She spoke the words as if the aged man could understand her. And maybe with her eyes, her tone, and her body language, he could.

The man seemed to be satisfied. He then helped Judith start the engine, and showed her the basic movements used to steer and work the motor. Then, he said something else, in Greek, as he grabbed Judith's shoulder gently. He caught her eyes and smiled, before hopping out of the boat and untying her line from the pier.

The men waved as Judith took off—as she began navigating by her Global Positioning System, along the coast; her boat bouncing rhythmically in the shallow Mediterranean waves as she traveled away from the small harbor.

Back on the shore, the men celebrated as if they had won the lottery. That was the second cheap fishing boat they had sold to a cash-toting young woman today.

Who could believe it?

Just over three miles journey from the small fishing harbor was Judith's destination. The coast jutted upward into tall rocky cliffs, with waves of the sea biting at the base of the towering rock.

After fifteen minutes of traveling along the coast, Judith came up on her destination. Ahead, she saw another small fishing boat, gasoline-powered as well, anchored twenty yards or so away from the sheer coastline.

"Here we go…" Judith whispered, as she approached.

Whoever it was that murdered that bastard back at the hotel and stole her GPS was now here. Their boat swayed in the sea, anchored by a steel chain that ran below the surface of the waves.

If there was truly something down there—Judith would find it. And Judith figured that she had the element of surprise going for her. After the attack at the hotel, she reasoned that the shooter would not be expecting her.

Judith let off the throttle, allowing her vessel to drift in the sea for a few moments, before she silently let down the heavy metal anchor over the side of the boat—peering beneath the surface of the water as she let go of the steel chain, watching it sink into the sea. She traced the anchor and its chain links, as they sank, about fifteen meters or so beneath the surface, before she lost sight of it. The visibility of the water was optimal, and this spot seemed fairly calm, which meant that the diving conditions were most likely pretty good.

Soon, Judith was changing out of her clothes into her diving gear.

When she was all suited up, she mentally went through her diving checklist. She made sure that her buoyancy compensator was inflated and that the inflator/deflator buttons were working properly. She checked that her diving weights were unobstructed and could be easily released. Then, she checked her air and her regulators, before inspecting the visibility of her mask.

After situating herself on the edge of the boat and grabbing her spear gun, she took the plunge, falling into the clear Mediterranean waves below.

Once in the water, using her buoyancy compensator, Judith began a controlled descent, sinking deeper into the sea, in between brief moments where she achieved neutral buoyancy and hovered at a constant depth.

Judith saw a myriad of different types of fish around her; most of them were quite small. A school of silver fish with black stripes moved in unison to avoid her, as a group of what looked to be large goldfish with patches of black around their eyes swam past.

As Judith sank, she saw more fish, some with long snouts, some with fanning fins, or colorful stripes, swimming past. Soon Judith was approaching the sandy floor of the sea. There were patches of coral and different types of fish to meet her, which looked to be bottom-feeding and camouflaged, swimming slowly around, oblivious to the young woman.

Judith did a three-sixty, to get her bearings. To the south, there was water as far as she could see. Towards the coast though, there was a massive assembly of sedimentary and metamorphic rock that made up the base of the cliff. The current here, was fairly weak. Judith began swimming to the base of the cliff and up ahead, she saw an opening of rock in the underwater cliff face.

There was an underwater cave at the base of the cliff, that someone must have found, long, long ago. Aside from the fish, a few rays, and a pink sea anemone slowly moving along the floor of the sea, Judith was alone. She guessed the owner of the boat above had traveled into the underwater cliff cave.

So Judith too, swam towards the opening in the rock. She fastened her spear gun to her belt, while she unhooked her handheld diving light and clicked it on. A good deal of the sunlight from the surface had already been swallowed up by the sea, before Judith had even reached this depth.

She swam forward, entering the cave, her body swaying back and forth, as the sea pushed and pulled against the coast. She swam against the sea's soft oscillations and made it into the cave, which was wide and dark, with a low ceiling.

Judith swam for some time, in a near straight line, under the island of Cyprus, until she saw ahead of her, the cave coming to an end. A few yards before it ended, the ceiling began to rise.

So, the only way to go is up.

Judith checked her depth and began expanding her buoyancy compensator. Her ascent was slow, and she frequently stopped and used her flashlight to peer upwards, making sure there were no obstacles above her.

The space she was in seemed to slant, as it rose. Judith, slowly followed the slant upwards, in darkness that was only cut through by her handheld flashlight. Four yards from where she believed the surface of the water was, Judith stopped for three minutes, to reduce the risk of decompression sickness.

Then, she swam up another few yards. There, just a few feet from the surface of the water, Judith thought she saw a faint glimmer of light about the surface. Sure enough, when she clicked off her flashlight, she was not left in darkness. There were waves of light dancing on the water above her, where the sea met the open air.

With her flashlight off, Judith inflated the rest of her buoyancy compensator, then silently rose up in the water until her head broke the surface. Judith removed her respirator from her mouth, and took off her SCUBA mask.

She was now in a large, underground, dimly-lit cavern. From her vantage point, Judith saw a few small stalactites hanging from the ceiling; the rock of the land rose up from her for a few dozen feet, before it cut away to where Judith assumed it leveled off.

Judith climbed out of the water, silently and slowly, so that the only sounds abound were the water swaying against the pit of liquid she was in. Soon, her diving suit and SCUBA gear were off. Judith was now donning a crimson bikini. Her toned body was tense as she shivered lightly; the Mediterranean Sea dissipating off her, as her skin cooled.

Judith changed sitting down, and now, sure to not let her head over the crest of land that hid her from the rest of the cave's interior, she moved up along the incline, on her hands and knees.

In one hand, she carried her spear gun, along the ground, as she carefully moved forward trying to be as quiet as she could. Soon, she was to a higher elevation, where she saw the rest of the large cavern.

What she saw, she could not believe.

About thirty yards in front of her, behind a powerful, portable lantern, that was set up and glowing bright, was an enormous, cylindrical, glass bottle, lying on its side. The glass had a dark blue tint; it was thick, cloudy, and looked incredibly aged; and the bottle was segmented, with regions that looked to be fused together—as was apparent by subtle grooves worked into the glass.

The blue glass bottle looked to be at least ten feet tall and fifteen feet long. It was a spectacle to behold, made, no doubt, by a master craftsman. Judith, in the soft light of the cave, saw what she believed were shadows dancing *inside* the bottle. Looking around her, Judith saw that there was another set of SCUBA gear and divers equipment, lying nearby, on the ground.

They're inside the bottle, Judith thought.

The glass of the massive bottle was too thick and cloudy to see through; but there was, at one end of the vessel, an opening that perhaps had been *corked* for the last two thousand three-hundred-some years.

Judith walked silently to the mouth of the bottle, hearing noises coming from within. The opening was circular, looked smooth to the touch, and was so large that someone could easily climb their way through it. Judith, brimming with more curiosity than had ever filled her before, peered through the opening of the bottle.

Inside, she saw a tall, slender, young woman, standing on what appeared to be some sort of machine, a perfect half-sphere, balancing upright on the curved glass of the bottle below. Within the center of the half-sphere was a circular waist-high platform. From its center, a thin, somewhat pointed piece of what appeared to be metal, stuck up into space, culminating in a small round bead that appeared as if it could be located at the exact center of the device.

Around the circular platform, in the middle of the machine and its central *seed* was what could have been a control panel, again circular, wrapping around the circular platform. The young woman appeared to be focused on modifying the controls.

There were also two curved strips of material that jutted up from either side of the semi-sphere, rising as if they were following the surface of the invisible top half of the sphere—until they rounded off, near to where the top of the sphere would be.

Judith looked with awe on the device, pondering its nature.

So this is what Stasanor had gone through great lengths to hide and protect—some sort of machine encased within a brilliant, giant, blue glass bottle.

To get a better view, Judith cautiously climbed up into the glass mouth of the bottle. For a split moment, it appeared as if the woman inside the semi-sphere looked in her direction. Judith knelt down quickly.

"I can see you," a voice rang out, coming from the woman that was still working the control panel that encircled the center of the sphere.

The tall, slender woman sounded as if she were more concerned with her task at hand than with the intruder in the cavern.

"I have to say," the woman continued, with her eyes still on the controls, "I'm surprised that you made it this far."

Judith was not sure what do to.

Does this woman have a weapon? Is she dangerous?

Judith popped her head into the bottle opening again, glancing the woman, as she spoke.

"Me?" she asked. "You wouldn't be here if it weren't for me. Charles and I dug that pillar out of the ground, and I solved the mathematics and generated the coordinates. I have more of a right to be here than you."

The woman seemed preoccupied with the dials and knobs before her.

Then she spoke, "You are right. I would not be here if it weren't for you. But you don't even know what this machine is—whereas I'm gathering it for one of the men who built it. And I have to say, I'm sorry about your friend. Charles, is it?"

Judith spoke to the woman from over the lip of the bottle.

"What is this place? What is that machine?"

Still not taking her eyes from the circular control panel in front of her, the woman, Silloway Sinsway, spoke,

"It is a ship in a bottle my dear, and I'm about to set sail."

Judith's curious dark eyes peered at the mysterious object within the blue glass.

"It's a spaceship?" she asked.

Silloway stayed silent, in response to Judith's question. She finally took her eyes from the controls though, before running a hand through her dark hair,

"Do you want some free advice?" Silloway asked. "Get your friend, get back to that plateau in Soli, and stay there, until there is silence for a hundred miles in every direction."

"I don't understand." Judith said, "What is this thing, really? Who built it, and how?"

"Have you heard of the multiverse theory?" Silloway asked.

Judith contemplated, "You're not serious."

For a moment then, Judith caught Silloway's violet eyes; there was nothing but truth in them.

"So you are from a parallel world?" Judith asked.

Silloway was raising a lever on the control panel, meticulously,

"I am not from there, but my father is.", she said, "and his world is not parallel to ours, any more than bubbles in an endless frothy sea are parallel to each other."

Judith's eyes showed revelation, as Silloway returned to the controls. Judith recalled the conversation she had with Klein on the way to Stasanor's pillar, a day before.

"You're one of the Sinsways?" she asked.

At this, Silloway looked surprised, raising her eyes to the woman.

"Yes, that's right.", she said.

"How does this machine get you to the…the…ah, other multiverse world?" Judith asked.

"It's a teleporter." Silloway replied.

"Jesus." Judith whispered, *Her mentor, Timothy Levine, was right*, "So your father, he's from another planet?"

"Well," Silloway answered, "not exactly."

Then, without another word from Silloway, the machine she stood upon, the semi-sphere balancing on end, hummed and vibrated as if it were returning to life.

In truth, the machine had never been dead; it had gone into a deep SLEEP MODE for over two thousand years, using only a small amount of power that was constantly replenished by a matrix of spinning spheres within, that all harbored tiny *sails*, so that they could collide with neutrinos (that were constantly traveling through all of us), providing a constant source of energy to the machine and allowing it to deplete itself completely of power, at which time it could begin re-charging itself.

"If I were you, I would stand back," Silloway said, as she took a glass bottle (actually, a glass bottle within a glass bottle) from out her pocket, with directions wrapped around it, and gently tossed it along the blue glass floor, sliding it away from her, towards Judith.

By this time, the hum of the engines had grown louder; the sounds of the spherical machine rose and fell, harmonically. Judith did indeed step back, straight back, and as she did, she saw Silloway and the events unfolding inside the giant glass container, through the bottle's mouth, at eye level.

With the hum of the engines switching between louder and softer intensities, Judith bore witness to a brilliant and rare phenomenon. From the exact center of the semi-sphere, from the shiny, spherical *seed* elevated above the circular teleporting platform below, a thin, translucent bubble was born.

The clear bubble expanded, growing, with slight, small, rhythmic oscillations, sometimes shrinking a bit smaller before resuming its expansion. As it grew, the bubble bent light and caused images of the blue, age-tinted glass surrounding it to ripple in waves and swirl about its surface.

Soon the bubble encompassed the circular teleporting platform in the center of the machine, and it kept growing. The hum of the machine's engines seemed to be in sync with the rhythmic movements of the ever-expanding bubble.

Silloway took in the phenomenon, as the translucent sphere moved *through* her.

Judith watched, in amazement, as the bubble, in its expansion, passed through Silloway's chest and head, before it encompassed her entire body.

The whirr of the engines was now a soft roar, as the bubble, still spinning blue light about its surface, continued to grow. Soon, a perfectly spherical bubble encompassed the whole teleporter (and not a micron more). Then, the bubble stopped growing and, instead, pulsed gently while still in tandem with the oscillating sounds of the engine.

Then, from the two curved planks that rose up from the semi-sphere, towards its northern pole, came out brilliant red lights. The lights danced around Silloway, studying her, scanning her, running up and down her body countless times. In only a few seconds, the red lights had performed their task, and were drawn back up into the smooth, curved scanners. Then, with a blinding flash of not light, but dark, the great oscillating bubble collapsed, and disappeared into that space beyond, along with Silloway and the spherical teleporter, leaving behind, an empty blue glass bottle, deep beneath the Cypriot soil.

In the Swiss countryside, there was a broad field of yellow forsythia flowers that were basking in the sun as if this day could be their last. Within that spot of land, lay the exact center of the great circle that is the Large Hadron Collider (which lie deep below the ground). It was here that Salison indicated Silloway should make the jump, from Episkopi Bay.

With a blinding flash of white light, and a decrescendo-ing electric purr of the engines, Silloway Sinsway, and the semi-spherical teleporter she traveled in, appeared in that yellow field of forsythia flowers within the Swiss countryside.

The young woman had to catch her breath. She was now, technically, a different person than she had been in Cyprus, having been taken apart down to the quantum level and then reassembled, in a process that had taken, in our time, an hour and fifty-five minutes (time in which, a physicist or philosopher could argue about the state of Silloway's existence—was she alive or dead in that time?).

There to meet her though, when Silloway arrived in that field of forsythia flowers, was her father, Salison Sinsway, with the sun shining off him as it sat high in the sky. Under his arm, he held his particle trap. Within it, a small amount of exotic matter that could be used to expand the wormhole that connected his bubble of the multiverse to ours, and once paired with the teleporter, would allow his passage back home.

61

As the hot Swiss sun shined down on the land, Officer Patrick Middler raced his sedan down a narrow, nearly empty, country road, with Christopher Banks' tracking device in hand, giving off a fairly high frequency beeping sound. Middler tried not to veer of the road, as he glanced down to follow a blinking dot on the monitor screen.

Salison's transmitting pole was close, due southeast.

Middler had a good idea where it could be. He had been to Fabiola's house the night before, and knew that he was only about a mile away from her cottage, which, he figured, was located along a direct line of sight, towards the coordinates indicated by Christopher Banks's tracking device.

As Middler drove on an empty stretch of country road, with golden fields of wheat to either side of him, he grew closer and closer to Fabiola's cottage. When he was about a mile away, with the woman's property nearly in sight, Middler was struck by an optical phenomenon, to the west. Middler saw a great flash of light from out the countryside, as if a small white sun had been sparked hot, for just a fleeting moment, before it disappeared. And in it its place, was...was some sort of vehicle, a machine, a half-sphere, sitting in a field of yellow forsythia flowers. On it was a woman, and nearby, a tall, bronze-skin man.

Middler, with his eyes off to the periphery, lost his way on the road, and accidentally drove onto the shoulder, clipping a mailbox belonging to a cottage that lay along a brick driveway behind him.

The man in the field was Salison, and the woman must have been Silloway.

What the hell were they doing out there in that field of flowers? And what on earth was that balancing, gleaming, hemisphere?

Middler pulled over to the side of the road. He was fairly sure that from this distance, neither Salison nor Silloway (if it were her) could see him. Middler, for a split second, pondered his options. He was about halfway between Salison and Fabiola's cottage—each were about a mile away from him.

Should he go after Salison, or shut down the transmitting pole?

There was no road to Salison, just fields of wildflowers, wheat, and tall grasses—that rose and fell softly as the land gently sloped downward. Middler wasn't sure if his sedan would be able to handle the off-road terrain, but he could certainly try.

Middler did not have his firearm though, only an aluminum baseball bat that he picked up near Geneva, now sitting in his backseat. He wondered how easy it would be to take down a seven-foot tall, muscular man who could dodge tranquilizer darts and cheat death.

And if he were to approach Salison, perhaps the man would activate his handheld wireless transmitter before Middler could even reach him, and set loose his pathogen-activating signal. Middler already knew that the device was ready to transmit, since he was picking up the signal that linked the transmitting pole to the wireless receiver.

The safer bet was to try and disable the transmitting pole at Fabiola's cottage.

From what Middler understood, if he were to turn off—or, better yet, destroy—the transmitting pole that Banks created for Salison, there would be no way to broadcast Salison's pirate signal and unleash his pathogen (a pathogen, that currently, was only being held at bay by resonance proteins). Salison could press his wireless transmitter all day, and nothing would happen, not without his transmitting pole being intact.

Middler made up his mind and put his sedan back in gear; he was headed to Fabiola's place, to destroy the transmitting pole, before Salison even knew anyone was on to him.

Middler saw that Silloway had jumped down from the machine. And Salison, now with a device that could have been a microwave (although Middler very much doubted this was the case), agilely hopped up onto the circular platform within the semi-sphere.

As Middler accelerated his sedan back onto the road, he saw, just over a ridge of grass, further away than Salison, a black SUV, traveling at a great speed, come crashing over a ridge near Salison, plowing down grasses and reeds alike, heading straight for the center of the supercollider, straight for Salison and the machine.

"Shit," Middler said, as he put the pedal to the floor—accelerating quickly towards Fabiola's cottage and the transmitting pole that lay in wait, within.

Jonas Moorea's hazel eyes focused on his target, as he barreled over the land, driving a 5,000-some pound vehicle towards Salison, the man who, now having the means to generate his passage home, was about to unleash death upon the whole of the world, to bring her back to balance.

Moorea had come to learn that within the sack that was given to him by Adlai, were three soft spheres—medicinal pills that contained the ingredients to heightened enlightenment. Within the spheres were dozens of pharmacological agents derived from plants and animals alike (that lived within Adlai's Garden of Knowledge), which, once taken, would cause Moorea's nervous system to function *differently*.

Each sphere needed to be taken at a precise time, counting down to the region of space and time when, and where, one desired the maximum effect of time dilation.

Moorea had taken one of the bitter-tasting, chocolate-coated pills, just as the helicopter picked him up from the Phuktal Monastery, en route to the Bhuntar Airport. He had taken the next pill, (bitter still, yet with a hint of honey) on an airplane, just before he touched down in Geneva. The third pill had a tougher exterior. Moorea rolled it around now, in his mouth, not yet cracking its surface.

At seventy-seven miles per hour, Moorea drove at Salison and the semi-sphere he occupied.

Salison was kneeling down, working on installing a box-like object into a column that rose up from the center of the semi-sphere. An outside observer may have seen Salison's body, but his fingers and arms moved in blindingly fast waves, as he hooked up his exotic matter trap into a device that would eventually shoot the exotic matter into the *seed* sphere of the teleporter (the small sphere that lie at the exact center of the machine was where the eventual entrance to the wormhole would form).

Salison rose and now would have appeared, to anyone other than Moorea, to be in multiple places at once, engaged with different knobs and dials all around a circular control panel that surrounded the central sphere.

Salison's saccading eyes jetted back and forth, ever so much faster than anyone else's could, as he acquired and decoded data far quicker than any 'normal' individual. If Salison would have cared to turn and train his violet eyes on Moorea, who approached in his Mercedes truck, he would have seen the vehicle traveling slowly towards him.

For Moorea, too, time was dilated. He watched as Silloway, reacting to Moorea racing towards the teleporter in an SUV, slowly backed up and caught her ankle on a stone behind herself. She fell through the air, backwards, as Moorea grew closer and closer to Salison.

Moorea aimed his truck in such a way, that it would clip the vessel that Salison stood in. Perhaps that would disable it. Whatever the device was, it was surely important to Salison, and this might put the bastard at a disadvantage.

With Moorea's truck only a foot away, Salison—who had, until that moment, been flying around the controls—stepped down off the teleporter, off the opposite side that Moorea planned to clip, and spun his body around in a pirouette, before his hand grabbed the rim of the semi-sphere, and he spun it up into the air.

The teleporter rose and revolved round and round, over Moorea's truck, Moorea—as he traveled at over eighty miles per hour—crushed the third sphere that Adlai had given him between his teeth. He then opened the driver's side door and stepped out of the vehicle.

As he did, he grabbed the door handle and pulled with all his force, accelerating himself in the opposite direction of the speeding truck. The kinetic energies of Moorea moving forward, due to his careening truck, and backward, due to his thrust, fought against each other as he traveled through the air, slowly falling to the earth, away from Salison.

With the teleporter still rising above him, due to his toss, Salison steadied himself and focused on Moorea. Salison took a stride forward but slightly to the right, then forward but slightly to the left as the tail end of Moorea's truck past.

Salison then took another stride, forward and to the right, gaining energy as he grabbed ahold of Moorea's truck (as it was nearly stationary) and propelled himself forward.

Moorea, off to his left, fell away from Salison. Finishing his strategic route, with gained energy in his steps, Salison swept up to Moorea, set his feet and prepared to deliver a blow before the neuroscientist hit the ground. Salison's fingers were pointed, his palm upturned.

Moorea was, for the moment, nearly helpless, a victim of Newton's first law; he was an object in motion, and would remain in motion, until he came in contact with something that could alter his course. Until then, he was in free-fall, with no significant forces to oppose his movement.

Salison's fingers fanned out, as they gained speed and approached Moorea's solar plexus, near the center of his chest.

Moorea did not have many options—he grabbed ahold of Salison's fingers, as they traveled towards him. Moorea pulled sharply on them, to change his momentum. Using Salison's solid limb as leverage, Moorea pulled himself towards Salison, over the man's head.

Salison made a counter move, and accelerated his right hand, upwards, to Moorea's ribs.

Silloway, still falling backwards, saw the semi-sphere of the teleporter, rotating and rising into the air, over the approaching black truck. She had just seen her father inside the teleporter, drifting in and out of her vision, as he appeared to be in multiple places at once, but never at *exactly* the same time.

Then, her father disappeared altogether, reappearing for a moment, to toss the teleporter up into the air, spinning as he did. For an instant he was gone again, while the black SUV sped past her. For a split second, Silloway saw Jonas Moorea hovering in space, then he was falling backwards. There was a zigzag of flashing color that approached Jonas as he fell; Silloway assumed it was her father, in motion.

Moorea spun, slowly, in space-time: under the teleporter and above Salison, as he countered Salison's upward thrust, pushing away Salison's hand and shoulder with great acceleration. Moorea continued his path towards the ground; although now his trajectory was altered, having shoved Salison away.

Moorea spun around in the air, still in free-fall, as Salison gathered himself, and came again at Moorea. By this time, the teleporter, above, had reached its crest and had begun its trip back to the earth, gripped by gravity.

Salison came at Moorea like lightning; Moorea was helpless as he fell towards the ground. Salison cusped his left palm, pointed his fingers, and accelerated his hand towards Moorea's floating ribs.

Just as Salison would have made contact, with what would have been a devastating blow, the tip of Moorea's toe touched the ground. He transferred a great deal of energy and acceleration to that one toe, and twisted his body, swiveling around, throwing himself out of the way—narrowly dodging Salison's blow.

Salison, for a moment, now seemed to lose a bit of his intensity, as he caught the teleporter on its fall, and gently glided it to the ground, side-stepping, to accommodate the landing of the machine.

At this time Silloway also touched the ground, after her trip over the rock, falling roughly onto her bottom. She sat there and watched her father, as he spoke to Moorea, who picked himself up off the ground.

Moorea's black SUV ghost rode into the field beyond.

Salison spoke, slowly, to Moorea in English, preaching, in his yellow field of forsythia flowers.

"This track in time you wish to perturb is like a river that flows from this moment to that—and its course cannot be changed. You are merely a pebble amidst a swiftly flowing current my friend. I have seen this current in motion—and I must say, you may as well step aside. There is no fighting this future. And I do not wish to harm you."

"On whose authority do you do this, this terrible thing?" Moorea asked, rubbing his fingers together, still feeling the incredible power waiting at bay beneath the surface.

"I am acting on the behalf of all life, and abiding by laws that govern not only men, but all things that harbor the spark of consciousness." Salison said,

Moorea shook his head.

"There are good people here, Salison; not everyone deserves to die."

Salison held out his hands. He almost looked to be pleading with Moorea, as he spoke,

"There is no other way. You read the face of the sky and of the earth, but you have not recognized the one who is before you, and you do not know how to read this moment."

"Damn it, Salison, you are not a God!" Moorea shouted, as he came at Salison, with a great speed and focus.

The bitter taste of Adlai's cocktail was still on Moorea's tongue; and the power it wrought, still flowing through his mind and body. Salison imagined his counter-moves, as Moorea let balance and speed guide his gait, taking one…two…three strides towards Salison.

Moorea saw Salison sidestepping to his right, so he spun around, on the spot, swinging his arm towards Salison's throat as he moved.

Salison stepped back to dodge the blow, then took another step back to gain energy, before stepping forward, planting his feet and extending both his arms (together as one) towards Moorea's chest.

Moorea was able to use his hands to block Salison's lightning-fast, powerful blow; but he caught quite an impact with his palms, propelling him backwards. Moorea was airborne, just inches off the ground, flying away from Salison. Before Moorea had time to hit the ground, Salison took a step back and propelled himself forward, in a sprint move that got him airborne, coming fast at Moorea.

Free-fall is not my friend, Moorea thought.

He was going to have to find a way to keep his feet on the ground.

Salison landed just in front of Moorea, while Moorea was still airborne, and began throwing blows with both his left and right hands.

Moorea, falling backwards, was able to counter each of Salison's moves, towards his throat, side, chest, and head. Moorea landed on the ground and pushed Salison off him, gathered himself.

Before Salison even made the move, Moorea felt it in his mind—Salison had a wireless transmitting device in his pocket and was about to reach for it, in hopes of pressing the TRANSMIT button, and setting loose his plague.

Moorea, with everything he had, sprinted towards Salison. Before Salison got his hand into his pocket, he had to contort his body, to counter multiple fluid moves from Moorea, as the man tried to deliver a damaging blow—with punches, kicks, his elbows, knees, and swift brief leaps into the air.

Salison moved back, defensively, with his hands and arms flashing light, countering Moorea's every move.

Silloway, sitting only a few yards away, stared in direction of the men. She saw them exchange words, while circling each other; but then lost sight of them, as they moved at each other with incredible speed. There were streaks of color and light in the air, that she knew reflected the men, who were moving too fast for her to see.

There was chaos in that small field of forsythia flowers; Petals, stems, and flowers were exploding on impact, from the men's lightning-fast movements. There was a thin cloud of yellow and green plant matter in the air, and Silloway frequently saw puffs of plants, bursting in the sun, as they were obliterated on contact. It were as if the two fighting men were calculated hurricanes in that small field, leaving a wake of floral destruction in their paths.

Silloway not only saw flashes of color, coming at her, sometimes in waves; she also heard rhythmic pulses of sound, that seemed to rise and fall with frequencies correlated with the speed of the colors that spun around her.

Moorea and Salison fought on.

Salison underestimated Moorea's power. Whenever he got the slightest break from Moorea's blows, he reached for the wireless transmitter in his pocket. Every time he did though, Moorea would be there to block his arm and deliver, what would be a crushing blow, were it not properly defended.

After a combination of thirteen moves, strung together like a flowing melody, Moorea finally landed a blow to Salison's chest and knocked the man backwards with a great force.

Taking a page out of Salison's book, Moorea propelled himself forward, towards Salison, as the bronze-skin man was in free-fall. Moorea came at Salison with a rage, his body oscillating left…right, left…right, right… left, right…left, with kicks, knees and bounding jumps.

Salison countered every blow, before landing on the ground. Now the man was sweating and he seemed, for a second, to relax.

Moorea too, took a breath, inhaling and exhaling, as the air around him moved in tangent with his body's rhythm.

Salison stood immobile, for a few moments, looking to be sizing Moorea up, with his violet eyes trained in Moorea's direction.

"You don't look so sure of yourself, Salison." Moorea said.

Salison waited a moment, then, Moorea picked up on something; it was a feeling that Salison had, a soft saccade of his eyes, off to a region behind Moorea.

Moorea turned behind himself. Silloway was standing upright. She had unmasked a pistol from her waist (the firearm that she obtained from the shooter in Cyprus). She had fired three quick shots towards Moorea.

Moorea's mind and body were focused. Time, for him again, dissipated. He saw the projectiles, traveling at a moderate speed towards him. The bullets approached from one direction—Moorea turned to the other. Behind him, Salison was again going for his wireless transmitter.

Moorea, moving faster than sound, accelerated towards Salison, as a sonic boom radiated through the air. With forsythia flowers exploding on the ground below, Moorea hit Salison with a devastating blow to the left side of his body, breaking ribs, no doubt, and rearranging—for an instant—Salison's insides.

This time, before Salison could be knocked away, Moorea grabbed him, and landed another blow to Salison's jaw, with his elbow—quickly twisting his upper body, hands raised over his head, after catching Salison's shoulders.

Salison looked to be seeing stars.

Moorea moved to deliver another blow, but Salison twisted his body away. The physicist fell onto his knees, spinning around, knocking Moorea down as he did a three hundred and sixty degree rotation.

Moorea and Salison then, were both on their knees, upon the ground.

Salison, the bigger man, lunged at Moorea and wrapped his arms around his body.

Within Salison's grasp, Moorea could not move, he was now on the ground, facing Silloway, who was standing twenty or so yards away, still pointing the gun in his direction. The three projectiles that she fired were traveling towards him; the nearest one was only a few feet from his face, and coming in fast.

Officer Middler raced to Fabiola Gionatti's cottage. The woman's small house came into view over a crest of land. Middler saw Fabiola's brick driveway, and there, upon it, was Fabiola—she was loading two duffle bags into the trunk of her Fiat. Middler was still about half-a-mile away from the property.

Fabiola closed the trunk of her car and hopped in. She quickly drove backwards, skidding out onto the road. Then she switched gears and accelerated towards Middler.

Middler checked his handheld radio-frequency detector. According to it, the signal from the transmitting pole was still immobile and most likely in the same place it had been when Middler first picked up the signal. Middler's eyes caught Fabiola's, as she passed him on the road, speeding in the opposite direction.

Middler knew, if nothing else, it could be a diversion; so he kept to his route, closer now than ever to Salison's transmitting pole.

Almost got you, you son of a bitch, Middler thought, as he accelerated his rental car over Fabiola's healthy lawn, forgoing the brick driveway, as he approached Fabiola's house, and the transmitting pole that was set up within.

***

Three bullets traveled towards Jonas Moorea, as he knelt down on the ground, back in that field of dismantled forsythia flowers. Moorea tried, with all his might, to move—backwards, left, or right—but Salison, was now an immovable object—his grip steady and strong, as he held Moorea in place. The bullets in the air moved ever closer to Moorea, with a trail of ripples behind them, as they collided with green and yellow plant matter in the air. Moorea watched the collisions of the bullets with the organic mist in the air, as if they were small fireworks, all the while trying to fight Salison off.

The nearest projectile, which had been fired first, was just about eye level to Moorea and was traveling closer and closer to his temple.

Before it made contact, Moorea twisted his body free of Salison's grip, set his feet, and lunged himself—and Salison—backwards, away from the approaching bullets.

Both Moorea and Salison landed on their backs. Moorea quickly spun Salison off him; and then picked himself up off the ground.

With the three projectiles Silloway fired still traveling in the air, Salison and Moorea moved at each other with incredible speed, their martial arts training apparent in their movements and counter movements.

Moorea seemed to have the upper hand, landing two quick blows to Salison's kidney and ribs. Radiating energy, Moorea kicked Salison onto the ground. As Moorea moved towards Salison, with hopes of incapacitating him, he had an odd sensation, feeling almost as if something was wrong.

Time, although dilated, had been passing smoothly for Moorea; now there was a *jerk* in Moorea's perception of time—an interruption in its fluid flow. Moore felt his limbs tense up.

Salison, on the ground, knew what was happening and in a flash was on his feet.

Then, Moorea, began seizing, violently. He had been warned by Adlai that the closer he came to stopping time completely, the more his nervous system would be at risk of hyperexcitability. Moorea had attempted to move too fast, to control and contort too much of space-time; now, his brain and body were paying the price, just as Salison's had seven days ago.

Salison had been holding back. He knew what would happen if he were to get too close to the border; he had, on multiple occasions, been there and back. But he also knew that he could not afford to slow time down too much, lest he get too close to losing control, and end up seizing.

Moorea's teeth chattered, as he bit down hard. His body resonated and oscillated, with a great rhythm that tore apart the waves of air and light around him.

Salison held Moorea strongly, as he shook, and turned him to face the bullets that were still flying at them both, at a great velocity. Salison held Moorea, as the man's eyelids batted quickly, his hazel eyes, reflecting, for brief moments, the bright, hot, sun above.

The first bullet Silloway fired lurched forward quickly. Just before it hit Moorea in the temple, Salison spun Moorea around like a baton and placed Moorea's right wrist in the bullet's path.

Moorea's sensory neurons were experiencing vast waves of epileptic activity; so the man did not register the spinning bullet traveling through his body.

Nor did Moorea feel the second bullet, as Salison again spun him around, allowing the second bullet to travel through Moorea's left wrist.

The last bullet Silloway fired flew through the air, Moorea, for a few microseconds, became aware of himself, within his unique cloud of space and time, feeling Salison's hands upon him.

Salison had him gripped too hard though; the man could not be budged, and this time, Moorea felt the bullet, as it traveled through his left foot—Salison was making sure that if Moorea were to come out of his mental and physical rut, he would be totally incapacitated. His mind then, might be able to manipulate time, but his body would never be able to follow suit and move through the altered time-frame.

And with these injuries, Moorea would live.

Salison, still holding Moorea with an eternal embrace, rearranged Moorea's body in his space-time, repositioning him so that the third bullet could travel through Moorea's body again, now through his left foot.

Moorea, once again, lost his senses to a seizure.

Salison had done his damage—neutralizing the one great threat to him, the one person that could have stopped him on the planet. Salison exhaled, as two bullets whistled off behind him. The third bullet was still caught in someone's altered time frame.

After the third bullet traveled through Moorea's foot, his seizing subsided. Moorea had clarity of thought and his altered time frame back. There was a great pain though, radiating through his feet and his hands, and he was in free-fall, since Salison had let him go, horizontally, in the air.

Moorea, with his fingertips, grabbed onto the third bullet as it traveled under him, using it to gain leverage, pulling himself downwards, to the ground, while straightening out. The pain in Moorea's feet and hands was intense. There had been much damage done; but, for the brief moment, Moorea maintained his footing, having slowed down the third bullet by only a small amount.

Moorea reached over to Salison's shoulder, as the man moved away, off towards the teleporter. Moorea grabbed Salison's shoulder, and using the bullet as leverage, spun around, throwing Salison behind himself, as he let go of the bullet, with Salison now spinning off ahead of it.

Three shots then rang out, from that defeated, yellow-green field of forsythia flowers. Moorea, damage done to his limbs, fell to the ground, as Salison spun to a stop.

Salison was breathing heavily as the Swiss air teamed with stem, leaf, and flower particles. Within Salison, there was now a deep resonating pain. He reached down to his side. He could already feel the path of the bullet within him.

Silloway's third shot had entered Salison's abdomen and traveled between the gaps of his floating ribs; the bullet punctured the man's diaphragm and pierced his right kidney. As this happened, Salison had been spinning in space-time; the bullet changed course in his body, blowing through his liver, coming to a stop within him, near the base of his large, hepatic portal vein.

Salison dropped to his knees, as Silloway ran towards him.

Moorea, lying on crushed flowers and dry earth, tried to control his pain, his body, and his mind, while fighting off the aura of what he knew could be his next seizure.

Silloway helped Salison up. Once the man stood, holding his side, he took his steps on his own, to the teleporter, taking out the wireless transmitter from his pocket.

***

AN EVOLUTION OF MINDS

Officer Middler heard three gunshots, off in the distance, as he skid to a stop in Fabiola's front yard, his sedan streaking tire tracks of dirt across her lawn. He popped open the door of his car, with the high frequency beeping sound of Christopher Banks' radio-tracking device emanating from his hand. He pocketed the device as he ran up to Fabiola's front door, kicking it in before even checking the lock.

Back in the field of dismantled forsythia flowers, Salison painfully held his side. He knew he could not generate enough energy to heal himself, when he was injured to such a great extent, as he was. But Salison did know a place that had the technology to treat such a wound, with ease.

Salison spoke to his daughter, as he approached the teleporter, holding his side.

"Both my world and yours are in your debt, Silloway."

Salison kissed her on the forehead.

"If ever you feel the need, you know how to find me; but it will be a one-way journey. I will never forget you."

Salison hopped up onto the teleporter, still holding his side, as Silloway stepped back.

Once on the teleporter, Salison threw Silloway the wireless transmitter.

On the ground nearby, Moorea writhed.

"Salison!" he yelled.

Salison tweaked the controls of the teleporter, slowly now, within Silloway's sight, as he spoke back at Moorea.

"My flood will cleanse your planet, Jonas!" Salison yelled, as a rhythmic hum began to emanate from the balancing semi-sphere.

A bubble was then born, from the central *seed* sphere within the heart of the machine; it began expanding, as it gently waxed and waned, its movements in tandem with the hum of the engines.

"These people can be saved!" Moorea yelled, over the growing sounds of the engines.

"Yes," Salison said. "I am saving them!"

Moorea was fast losing blood; and he knew, if he were to pass out here, alone, in the countryside, he would die. He clung to consciousness, as he lay on his side, trapping his hands between his thighs, trying to stop the bleeding, all the while taking in the phenomenon before him—of Salison and his teleporter.

The intensity was out of Moorea's voice, as he spoke, with his face in the dirt, "Salison…don't…"

The engines of the machine roared, as the spinning, sunlight-reflecting bubble came to encompass the entire sphere of the teleporter. Salison was so tall, that he had to kneel down on one knee, so that the whole of the bubble encompassed him. Red, scanning lights then fanned out from the curved planks that extended over the semi-sphere; the red lights flooded over Salison, as he pressed a button on the circular control panel. At that moment, the exotic matter that he had generated and trapped, was injected into the wormhole—a wormhole that for over two thousand years (our time) had been as a string, not a tunnel. The bridge between our universe and Salison's then expanded into a traversable tunnel, due to the repulsive nature of the exotic matter that had been shot within. Salison looked over to his daughter; she held the wireless transmitter in her hand.

As Silloway locked eyes with her father, for what could have been the last time, she pressed the TRANSMIT button.

A signal could then be heard, throughout the world, as it was broadcast on every continent.

It was a sweet sound, like a whistling, a chirping, which rose and fell, harmonically.

Some who heard it, described it as a bird's song. They said it was beautiful.

As Judith Arai, in Cyprus and in silence, injected Charles Klein with the antivirus, as Klein dreamt of Stasanor's plateau (a place he would surely return, to discover more secrets hidden in the dirt and sand), as Adam Riley distributed his vaccine—which would go on to save hundreds of lives—and as Adlai, now wearing white, fed her garden fish, the sweet song played on.

Moorea watched, as Salison, covered in scanning red lights, looked over at him, and spoke through the translucent bubble.

"I am the bringer of balance, in my world, and yours!" Salison said.

Then, with a bright flash of dark, the bubble that encompassed him and the spherical teleporter, collapsed, as Salison was broken down to the quantum level, into a stream of information, and sent through the wormhole, back to his own world—which, in truth, was our world, hundreds of millennia into the future; a place where men and women had learned to live in balance with the land and forces of nature that they had come to intimately understand.

Salison was heading back home, to a future that he, himself, created, to a place he had one more war to wage.

Epilogue

Three hours before Salison's pathogen-activating signal sounded, Detective David Brennan awoke in his bed, alone. The dark night subsumed the land and poured through his second-story studio window.

It had come to him in the night; the answer to the riddle that Silloway had posed him:

'Seek and you will find; knock and the door will be opened to you.'

Brennan threw on his clothes, grabbed his keys, and bounded down the steep stairs in front on his brick apartment complex. Early morning fog blanketed the land. Brennan saw his breaths, as clouds of mist, as he drew in and expelled them. It did not take him long to jog to, and jump in his Camry.

In the center console of his car was the cloudy, blue marble that Silloway had sent him. Brennan planned on passing it off to a Cambridge researcher come daylight, so that the man could take X-ray, infra-red, and high magnification images of the marble, as well as study its magnetic signatures, and God knows what else, in order to determine the nature of the blue marble and the smaller, black sphere inside of it. Brennan pocketed the cerulean stone, which sat within a plastic bag, and sped off, towards Green Harbor.

In just over an hour, Brennan was driving down the earthen road that led to Salison's cottage. He passed the spot where he headed off into the woods, five days ago, to find Salison's elaborate greenhouse. He now figured, rightfully so, that it was Salison who he was following that day.

Brennan recollected his hike and his fall over the cliff face to the coarse earth below, as he parked in Salison's driveway and jumped out of his car. Now, he was heading in the opposite direction of the cliff and the greenhouse; he was on his way to the lake and the small shack that lay about a mile's hike behind Salison's estate.

Brennan grabbed a strong flashlight from his backseat, as the sun had yet to rise and night still blanketed the land. He approached the beginning of the trail that led to the lake behind the house.

Brennan jogged over a smooth dirt trail that cut through the woods.

The sun rose during Brennan's run, and the mist over the land began to dissipate, as it clung to the limbs of trees and scattered grasses that blanketed the earth.

The forest thinned out, and Salison's lake came into view, just as the morning sun began rippling across it.

Brennan's breaths were heavy in his chest, as he slowed his pace and walked past the rickety dock that jutted out onto the placid, swaying lake. He approached the old shack (the façade) that hid beneath it a secret stairway, a study, and a massive, mysterious, and up until now, impregnable, underground complex.

Brennan pushed open the flimsy door of the shed and walked inside, setting his flashlight on one of the wooden shelves, as the morning light streamed into the small structure. The hidden stairway was already open. The locksmith had gained entry to the stairs and the hallway it led to, but not the study that Adam Riley had described, nor the complex beyond.

The detective bounded down the stairs and came to the narrow hallway that led to a locked, shining, metal doorway a few dozen yards or so away. Brennan cursed himself for not thinking of it sooner.

Silloway's clue now seemed obvious, yet Brennan still felt, for a moment, unsure of his hunch—that the blue marble Silloway sent him was the key to Salison's structure.

Brennan took out the plastic bag that held the cloudy blue marble and dropped the smooth stone onto his palm. He felt the small weight of the thing, as he rolled it around in his hand and approached the locked door.

As Detective Brennan walked forward, the thick metal door before him began sliding open. Brennan smiled, and his curiosity piqued. He held Silloway's blue marble in his hand, as he walked into the study, viewing the planked wooden ceiling above, blood-red sofas, and a cluttered desk, at the end of the room.

Brennan's eyes scanned the space as he walked through it, coming to the bend of the 'L', where Salison's desk sat. On turning to his left, Brennan saw ahead of him a wooden door, riveted and nearly see-through. He approached it and swung it open. It looked to be a storage area. There were duffle bags, bottled water, blankets, and canned food.

Brennan scanned the shelves and moved on. It was then he saw a curious thing—a smooth, intricately carved, wooden arch built into the wall. Under the arch was a cloudy, glass-like material, looking smooth to the touch.

As Brennan walked towards the archway, it slowly began to slide open, the glass-like material being drawn into the ceiling.

Salison's massive underground complex held three separate locked compartments. Brennan had just been granted access to the first of the three.

Lights clicked on in front of Brennan as he walked under the archway into Salison's secret bunker. Brennan noticed that the 'glass' door that was being pulled into the ceiling, was not a thin panel of material, but a large rectangular block that covered the length of the tunnel—he had to wonder, if he would ever have gotten through the thick, dense, slab of unknown material without Silloway's cerulean stone.

In three quick strides, Brennan was through the tunnel of the entrance, and had a full view of the hidden room.

The space was wide, circular, and spread out about forty yards to either side of him. There were rows of dark wooden shelves along the walls that held, what looked to be, thousands of books and a myriad of artifacts. There were dark wooden tables around the room as well, with several objects on each of them, many covered in a clear, glass, semi-spherical casing. It was a library all right, with the feel of a museum as well.

On the table closest to Brennan, there were numerous objects, one of them looked to be a mechanical device. It reminded Brennan of a machine he read about in *Discover* magazine—the Antikythera Mechanism, an ancient analog computer that was built by Greek scientists around 100 years before the birth of Christ. It was used to predict astronomical positions and eclipses. The one on Salison's table looked in much better condition though, but was clearly ancient, with rust and patina apparent upon it. Next to the mechanical device, was an early metal compass. Next to that, a Chinese Abacus—an ancient computing device, made out of wood, containing rows of beads, for performing mathematical computations.

Brennan saw a Medieval broadsheet on another table—a single piece of aged parchment that looked to depict an aerial battle, with spheres and pillars fighting in the sky, and the sun, with a yellow painted face, looking on in the heavens. It was an original flier that had been sent out in Germany, around four hundred years prior, depicting a mysterious aerial battle that hundreds had witnessed over the city of Nuremberg on April 14, 1561.

Brennan walked to a desk covered in aged journal articles, dealing with quantum theory, astrophysics, and advanced mathematics.

On this desk was a picture.

Brennan was aware that there were nearly no pictures of Salison Sinsway—the famous physicist. There were none of the man—that Brennan was aware of—before the late eighties. Brennan picked up the picture from the desk. It was a black-and-white photograph of Salison, standing tall, with a shorter, light-skinned man, donning a suit and tie. The two appeared to be engaged in conversation, near a row of trees that traveled off into the distance behind them. Both the front and back of the photo were visible in its glass case.

Brennan removed the photo from its stand and examined the back of it. There was an annotation:

'Always grateful for your insights, you smug bastard'– Jon Von Newmann, 1933

"Jesus." Brennan whispered.

As Brennan approached another desk, he heard a soft beeping begin to ring out from the room.

Brennan searched for the source of the sound. In just over a second, the sound localization system within his brainstem, directed him to one of the dozen or so tables within the room—one which held an aged, wooden box that looked to be slowly leaking a white, gaseous mist; leaning on the box was a thin envelope, and next to that a small timer—still ringing. Brennan opened the top of the wooden box. Inside, there was a cloud of white mist that Brennan had to swipe away with his hand, so that he could see what was beneath it. As the white gas dissipated, Brennan saw a medium-sized glass container within, with an orange top screwed onto it. Within the glass container was about a half-liter of clear liquid. Beneath the bottle was bedding with dry ice that had nearly all but dissipated away.

The bottle was cold to the touch, as Brennan picked it up and held it in his hands. He turned his attention to the envelope that leaned against the box. Before he opened the letter though, he checked the timer, which was still beeping.

To Brennan's surprise, the timer was counting down. There were thirteen seconds left… Brennan slowly stepped back, as he set the timer down, his mind playing out scenarios. He quickly grabbed the envelope from the desk, the bottle in his other hand, and ran towards the exit.

He passed tables of cultural, historical, and scientific artifacts from all over the world, as he quickly approached the entryway. Sure enough, just as he came to it, the thick, rectangular, glass-like structure above began to come down as the doorway closed.

The pillar of glass was lowering quickly. Brennan had to duck down, as he leapt forward, through the wooden archway, just as the block of material came down with a loud 'thud'. Brennan was back in Salison's study, apparently with a 'gift' from Salison in his hands. The bottle contained five hundred milliliters of the viral vaccine that Salison created—which could be used, not only to protect a single individual from Salison's pathogen, but also anyone that person came in close physical contact with.

Between Adam's batch of antivirus and Salison's (could they be distributed in time), there was enough for upwards of five thousand people to be made immune from the devastating pathogen that was soon to be unleashed.

Salison had done work to ensure that the genetic diversity of the human species would be preserved.

Brennan did not know what was in the bottle as he held it in his hands, sitting on the floor in Salison's study, against the cold, smooth, glass-like panel under the wooden arch.

He opened the envelope, which had been leaning against the box.

Perhaps the contents of the bottle was listed in the letter?

Written down on the piece of paper within the envelope was a passage that Jonas Moorea would have recognized, as it was from the Gospel of Thomas (these were words that Jesus Christ once spoke). There was one simple passage, written in a flowing English script, shedding light on Salison's intentions:

'I have cast fire upon the world, and see, I am guarding it until it blazes.'

Brennan stood up. With the bottle and letter in hand, he began jogging back to the stairwell, back to the morning sun above, and the dawn—a dawn that, for billions of people, would be the last peaceful one they ever experienced.

Weeks after the pathogen-activating signal had sounded, once the world had been bathed in sickness, and millions had died, with Salison's pathogen still spreading, Fabiola Gionatti found herself walking along the dock that extended out over the softly swaying lake that lay within Salison's property.

Once Fabiola left her cottage, for the last time, on the day the signal had sounded, she drove from Switzerland into Italy; then to France, where she arranged passage on one of her uncle's cargo ships, heading to the East Coast of the United States.

During the two week-long journey, the crew had learned that the whole of the world had been ignited with the most deadly pathogen that had ever been transmitted from one person to another; and that the pathogen was spreading like the sound of a firecracker through a dark, silent, night, as hundreds of millions of people perished.

With the sickness spreading throughout the land and on the ship as well, the port of Newark, New Jersey (the ship's destination) had been closed, indefinitely.

On arriving to the East Coast, Fabiola, and a few who had survived the pathogen, lowered a lifeboat from the frigate, and headed to the New Jersey coast.

On land, the stench of death was ever in the air. Morgues and cemeteries had long overflown, and there were now piles of decaying dead bodies, slowly writhing in the heat, piled in the thousands in random locations, such as parking lots, fields and baseball diamonds, while others were laying lonely under trees and in open spots of land.

Salison had done his work well, resetting mankind's clock.

Fabiola, who had been made immune to the pathogen by Salison, found a vehicle easily, since all the nearby dealerships, garages, and factories had been abandoned. Fabiola procured her vehicle from an empty lot of a food processing plant, near the shore; and as per Salison's instructions, then began heading to his property, in Green Harbor.

It was a five hour drive to Salison's land in Massachusetts, where Salison told her was a portal for her to escape the saturating sickness—a portal that would allow her to travel to a new world...

Salison's civilization had not only been able to generate tears in space time, machines that could teleport individuals across the cosmos, and receivers that could pick up the medium of thought, they had also perfected a compound that was found in forest tree frogs; a secreted cryoprotectant, that allowed the small amphibians to freeze up to two thirds of their body at once (to stop their heart beating and lungs pumping air, for weeks, even months at a time), allowing the animals to go into a suspended animated state of hibernation.

During the winter months, the frogs could freeze their bodies solid, by first dehydrating and then rearranging their organs, while using a secreted natural cryoprotectant (similar to antifreeze), to lower the internal freezing temperatures of certain vital tissues (as the liquid surrounding their organs was concurrently pooled and turned to ice).

Scientists, a part of Salison's loose conglomerate of villages, had isolated the amphibious antifreeze and tweaked its structure, so that it could be utilized in mammals and for a much longer period of time. They had then built cryogenic freezing tubes, that made it possible to freeze human beings, for, at least, decades at a time.

These cryogenic freezing tubes, built by Salison's community, ran using the neutrino-collision based power source, and could thus function, as long as the tube remained intact (which, when taking into account the materials used to construct them, was near indefinitely).

Salison began constructing three cryogenic tubes, to store living material, as soon as he arrived on Earth in 1888 (from his home world, which was earth, six hundred thousand years in the future). He initially fashioned nearly all the components for the cryogenic tubes himself, from metal ores or other raw materials, until technology advanced enough for the tubes to be completed.

Possessing a curious, ever-thinking mind, Salison, in his home world, made himself intimately aware of the science behind the cryogenic freezing process and the naturally derived, chemically altered solution that was used to protect the body (and mind) during cryogenic hibernation.

It had taken him over a hundred years to do it, but Salison had built three cryogenic freezing chambers—creating a way for a select few to follow him into the future.

Salison would have frozen himself, to transport himself back home, but the unfreezing process was complex and, if not performed properly, would result in the cryoprotected never returning to their natural form; they would die. There needed to be someone waiting on the other side (so to speak), to aid in the intricate thawing and reanimation processes. Unfortunately, it was not as simple as setting a timer and jumping out of the cryogenic chamber when it rang. Bodily tissues and whole organs had to be reconstituted and rearranged.

In truth, Fabiola had learned of the frogs, of the species *Rana Sylvatica* (that must have been the ancestors of the frogs that Salison's civilization used to generate the mammalian 'antifreeze'), featured in a nature documentary years prior. The woman had learned then, that the Arctic frogs were on the brink of extinction.

Fabiola realized that if Salison would not have come back to the past and wiped out nearly all of the human race, *Rana Sylvatica* would have most certainly gone extinct, and Salison's future civilization would have never been able to isolate the anti-freeze-like compound from the frogs' bodies to eventually make the cryogenic freezing of humans possible, in the 'first' place.

She knew the whole of the planet, and all species of plants and animals, were in Salison's debt; but that did not stop her from hating the man—the man that she once loved. Many of her friends and family, in Italy and all over Europe, had been killed by Salison's pathogen; and they had not approached their demise peacefully.

As Fabiola walked on the dock jutting out over Salison's property, she took from her pocket, a small, rectangular container. She popped the black container open with a click and looked on the object before her. Within the container, in a foam mold, was a smooth, flesh-colored thimble. The bowl of the thimble was round, to accommodate the shape of her slender fingertip, and on the point of the thimble was a sharp, small tip that was fashioned (along with the thimble) from an ageless, advanced polymer of plastic. The pointed, plastic tip was hollow.

If Salison ever found her, and awoke her (as he said he would, once he secured his land from an outside threat), Fabiola planned on making him pay for his trespasses.

Fabiola's brother was a chemist, in Novara, Italy, and worked for the Italian National Institute for Environmental Protection and Research (ISPRA). One of the many compounds that her brother had access to was radioactive waste; dozens of studies were conducted by ISPRA on the properties and toxicity of radioactive products of decay, such as a radioactive material that Fabiola was particularly interested in—Plutonium-239, an isotope of Plutonium that emits alpha radiation. Plutonium-239 is not harmful if you come in contact with it outside of your body, but if internalized, will travel throughout your tissues, through your blood, and into your bones and internal organs.

There were documented cases of workers at nuclear weapons facilities that died within just days after brief accidental exposure to Plutonium-239, via an incredibly fast-acting cancer of the bone, lung, or liver. And not only was Plutonium-239 fatal if introduced into the body (in miniscule amounts), its radioactive products of decay were 'stable' and lethal for hundreds of thousands of years.

Fabiola filled the tip of her thimble with a half gram of radioactive decay from Plutonium-239, enough to kill someone a thousand times over, if they were ever impaled with the point of her flesh-colored camouflaged thimble.

As the edge of the red hot circle of the sun came to hit the tops of the forest trees in the distance, Fabiola trained her eyes on the horizon and pocketed the deadly radioactive waste containing thimble. She walked upon the rickety wooden planks of the aged dock, back to the shore.

Once to the grassy land, she took from her pocket a small, cloudy, red sphere that had a smaller black sphere nestled within it. This, Salison told her, was the key—an object that would grant her access to the second chamber of his massive underground complex—to the area that housed the cryogenic chambers.

Before Fabiola made her way into the rickety old shack, which hid the entrance to Salison's complex beneath it, she turned and took in the glowing pastels of the setting sun, splayed out about the horizon in the distance. She took a few breaths of the fresh evening air, and then entered the small wooden structure. The next time Fabiola saw a sunset, it would be on this same brilliant blue sphere, hurtling through space around a white-hot sun, but it would be hundreds of thousands of years into the future, where she would need only one touch to make Salison Sinsway pay for his sins.

***

Months after Fabiola settled in for her long sleep, Dr. Jonas Moorea, with scars apparent on his wrists and feet, where bullets had traveled through his body, stepped into the sun from out the shadow of a dark, dry, deep cave in France. There he faced a vast field of tall green grasses and reeds—the expanse of land dotted with wildflowers. Moorea began to jog, away from the mouth of the cave, through the field and the desolate countryside of Crozet.

Inside the rocky cave that Moorea left behind (which Moorea called home for nearly eight months), Silloway had nursed him back to health and worked with him until he had full use of his hands and feet. The woman took Moorea straight from the field of yellow forsythia flowers, to the secluded cave, after his bout with Salison. With Silloway's help, Moorea healed well from the wounds he sustained.

Moorea was quite surprised, when he regained consciousness in a cool, fire-lit cavern, to see that the very woman who had shot him was now tending his wounds.

Silloway, in her quiet nature, had not apologized for her actions; she said what she did was the *only* way to bring the world back to balance, to preserve the genetic diversity of all plant and animal species, and to save the planet from its greatest threat.

Jonas felt it in his soul; that there had been a great loss of human life.

Silloway had explained to him the nature of Salison's plague and the role of resonance proteins; it was a brilliant and sinister plan, to infect the whole of the world without its knowing, and then to activate the plague, all at once (in everyone), exponentially increasing the amount of people that would be infected, compared to if the pathogen spread via human-to-human contact (like nearly every other known pathogen).

Moorea had questioned Silloway at length on her motives and her lack of guilt for what she had done; but the woman had stayed steadfast in her resolve.

She helped Moorea regain his strength and movement, and said little on the great death that she helped unleash, only saying, quizzically, that the left hand must have truly not known what the right was doing.

One morning, when Moorea was nearly completely healed, he awoke to find Silloway gone.

The woman had spoken about returning to South America, to convene with her mother's people, an uncontacted, isolated, Brazilian tribe, the Vale de Javari; a mysterious jungle-dwelling people that lived in the dense wilderness of Brazil, near the muddy Javari River.

Silloway, as she rolled around a small violet marble in her slender hand, said that she had more business to attend to; but that she would pray for Moorea and wished him well on his future journeys.

Once Moorea left the cave, he felt one hundred percent, perhaps even more, for he still felt Salison's enlightenment project coursing through his veins. Moorea obtained a vehicle from outside a quiet farmhouse, feeling, knowing, that there was only death inside—just as there was all over the countryside.

CERN had been deserted, and as Moorea drove through the countryside, he was struck with the overwhelming sensation of silence, coming from every direction.

For five days, Moorea drove on empty roads, from Geneva through Western Europe, Turkey, Iran, Afghanistan, and Pakistan until he finally arrived in Northern India.

The death upon the land that Moorea saw during his journey, brought about by Salison's plague, was unbelievable. Moorea felt as if he were driving through passages of the *Book of Revelation* or *Dante's Inferno*; the scene was apocalyptic—a fiery hell had been unleashed on the land.

The scene was more placid in Raru, where a few friendly, yet curious, leather-skinned villagers had spotted Moorea.

They looked healthy, as they tended to their land and livestock.

Moorea came in contact with about half a dozen people, in small spread-out homes that dotted the uneven landscape, near the base of the Himalayas, as he hiked from Raru to Chatang, Chatang to Purne, and then on from Purne to the Phuktal Monastery.

Moorea had no way of knowing that the scholar Eric Hassnain, was still alive and that Salison, on delivering the blow to Moorea at New Life, had afterwards injected Moorea with the antivirus, meaning that both Hassnain and the young Indian man that Moorea met at the airport in Mumbai (and their families) had both been protected from the pathogen, as they had come intimately close (in proximity), to Moorea.

Moorea climbed down into the mountain's bowl that held the oasis of the saman tree. Once reaching the bottom of the sheer cliff, Moorea narrowed his focus, and began jogging on the grassy mound. He passed beneath the saman tree. It's limbs were now free of flowers as they twisted up towards the heavens. Moorea's gaze drifted to the cliff face opposite his entrance, there, up high, on a narrow ledge, was the entrance to Adlai's cave system.

Moorea thought of the woman; her power, her spirit, her electric touch, and her ever-churning dark eyes, as he climbed up the mountain's bowl, to the pinnacle of land above.

With sweat on his body, Moorea pulled himself onto the Himalayan ledge that held the entrance to Adlai's cave system.

AN EVOLUTION OF MINDS

As Moorea walked into the cave, he had to smile; for within, he heard a sweet humming, and a pulsing, rhythmic sound, that echoed from the deep, dark cave, as it tunneled through the earth.

Jonas Moorea took a step into the cave, with air moving in rippling waves about him, knowing that now, with the world at peace, he had finally found his home.

K.R. JENSEN

AN EVOLUTION OF MINDS

Appendix 1:

E-mail from Moorea Lab to Jonas Moorea indicating the pharmacological agents found in Salison's blood and spinal fluid, along with their source and mechanism of action:

Spider:

Drug	Species	Common name	Target/ Mechanism of Action
ω-agotoxins	*Agalenopsis aperta*	Desert Grass Spider	Blocks VGCCs
ω-grammo-toxin	*Grammostola spatulata*	Tarantula	Blocks VGCCs
Pro-TX-II	*Thrixopelma pruniens*	Green Velvet Tarantula	(?)
SNX-325	*Segestria florentina*	Tube Web Spider	N-type CC
SNX-482	*Hysterocrates gigas*	African Tarantula	R-type CCs
ω-filistatoxin	*Filista hibernalis*	Southern House Spider	antagonist of VGCCs
PRTx3-7	*Phoneutria reidy*	Wandering Spider	VGCC
PhTx3	*Phoneutria nigriventer*	Aggressive-armed spider	L-type CCs

Sea Snail:

Small peptide (1)	*Conus magnus*	Snail	VGCC
Small peptide (2)	*Conus victoriae*	Snail	VGCC
Small peptide (3)	*Conus asprella*	Snail	(?)
Small peptide (4)	*Conus calibonus*	Snail	(?)
ω-conotoxin	*Conus geographus*	Snail	VGCC

VGCC = Voltage gated calcium channel

Marine Worm:

Glycerotoxin	*Glycera convulata*	Marine worm	VGCC(?)

Snakes:

Calcicludine	*Dendroaspis (?)*	green mamba	VGCC
Calciseptine	*Dendroaspis polylepis*	black mamba	VGCC

Scorpion:

Kurtoxin	*Parabuthus transvaalicus*	South African, black	Na-channels
Kurtoxin			(?)
Kurtoxin			(?)

Lizard:

Kallikreins (4)	*Heloderma alverezi*	Beaded Lizard	Hemo-toxin (?)

Plant:

Cynarin   *Cynara scolymus*   Artichoke

Drug	Species	Common name	Target/ Mechanism of Action
Anisodamine	*Anisodus tanguticus*	Flowering Herb	Anticholinergic
Betulinic Acid	*Betula Alba*	White Birch Tree	Anticancerous
Digitoxin	*Digitalis purpurea*	Flowering Perrenial	Decrease ATP
L-Dopa	*Mucuna pruriens*	Velvet Bean (legume)	Neurotransmitter precursor
NGDA	*Larrea tridentata*	Creosote bush	Antioxidant
Papavarine	*Papaver somniferum*	Opium Poppy	μ-opioid receptor agonist
Vasicine	*Vinca minor*	Common Periwinkle	Cerebral Stimulant

Acknowledgements

I thank Holger Kersten for his enlightening book, 'Jesus Lived in India'. His research, and his journeys, greatly helped me shape one of my characters. I also thank the well-read Nicholas McKeehan for his critiques of the early manuscript.

Made in United States
North Haven, CT
11 September 2023

41434869R00203